SUMMER LIES BLEEDING

Nuala Casey graduated from Durham University in 2001 and moved to London to pursue a career as a singer-songwriter. However, her experiences living in Soho, where she chronicled the comings and goings of the people around her, took her life in a different direction. She went on to work as a copy-writer and was awarded an MA in Creative Writing. London and the voices of the city continue to provide inspiration for her writing.

Web: www.nualacasey.com

Twitter: @NualaMaeveCasey

Facebook: Nuala Casey Writer

SUMMER LIES BLEEDING

Nuala Casey

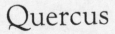

Quercus

First published in Great Britain in 2014 by

Quercus Editions Ltd.
55 Baker Street
7th Floor, South Block
London W1U 8EW

PB ISBN 978 1 78206 350 6
EBOOK ISBN 978 1 78206 351 3

10 9 8 7 6 5 4 3 2 1

Printed and bound in Great Britain by Clays Ltd, St Ives plc

Typeset by Ellipsis Digital Limited, Glasgow

For my son, Luke

'We shall find peace.
We shall see the sky
sparkling with diamonds'

Anton Chekhov

PROLOGUE

March, 2013

It feels good to be back by the water, despite the solemnity of the day. She has seen plenty of lakes in her time, but there is something about this one that makes her want to stay, linger for a few moments while the rest of the guests scatter across the deep expanse of parkland, like tiny specks of light bouncing off the spindly branches of the horse chestnut trees.

As she sits she thinks of the lakes of her childhood, the clear, crisp waters of past summers; those fertile depths brimming with salmon and wild trout that had cleansed more than just her body. John the Baptist had cleansed the faithful in one, and those stories of baptism and rebirth that she had loved so much as a child are particularly appropriate today. As she closes her eyes and feels the cool water slip through her fingers it seems there is still a chance, despite her past, that she can be reborn; can start again.

Beyond the lake, across the dense blanket of trees flows the mighty Thames, the river of dreams and heartbreak; reflecting the city's image like a distorted mirror. Who knows what violence it has witnessed over the ages, what secrets it carries in the depths of its black waters?

She watches as a familiar figure makes its way across the grass. Rising to her feet, she waves her hand and feels a surge of energy go through her – like an electrical current flowing from the lake into her veins. She has been released; she is free from the pain of her past and the tyranny of memory. In Celtic mythology a lake had saved the legendary Fiann MacCumhaill from the jaws of a wild boar by appearing out of nowhere and swallowing up the savage beast. And now, released from her own demon, she can breathe. Seb was right; the lake *was* a saviour, guarding against evil and despair; a place where lost souls could come and find their way. As the first drops of rain start to fall, bouncing off the glassy surface and sending little spurts of diamond light spluttering into the air, she knows that, this time, she will not have to run for cover. She is safe.

MONDAY, 27 AUGUST 2012

1

Paula said she would take the train to London. Stella would go in the car. It would do them good to travel down separately, she said; give them space to think.

'I'll miss you,' says Paula, as she hurriedly kisses Stella's cheek and throws her pale blue travel bags into the boot of the taxi. 'But enjoy the drive, and don't spend the whole journey worrying. I know what you're like. Oh, and I've put the plants in the boot. I've padded out the crates but they're delicate little creatures, so no sharp turns okay?'

Her eyes twinkle in the pale afternoon sun as she climbs into the passenger seat. 'Don't look so serious, Stella,' she says, as she clicks the seatbelt into place. 'It's all going to be fine. It's just a few questions this time, and I'm the one who will have to do the icky bit, but then . . . then this could be it. This could be the start of our family.'

Those eyes again. So bright with hope Stella can barely look at them. It feels like they are boring into her, like a searchlight, exposing her, making her vulnerable and naked, standing there on the street.

'I'd better get back inside,' says Stella, the words coming out rather more brusquely than she intended. 'I've got a long drive ahead . . .'

Paula looks up at her with an expression Stella recognises immediately. It is a look she has become accustomed to over the years, though it is so subtle that an outsider would never even notice. It is uncertainty mixed with fear; fear of Stella's unpredictability, of the part of her that will always be an enigma, a strange, exotic creature who will never be tamed no matter how many retreats she is sent on, or cups of camomile tea she is forced to drink. Paula's eyes, just moments ago so full of hope and longing, stare unblinkingly out of the open window, silently pleading with Stella, willing her not to back out of this.

'Come on, angel,' says Stella, gently stroking Paula's arm. 'You're right. It's all going to be fine.'

She can tell Paula is not convinced by this show of chirpiness; her face looks small and creased as she winds up the window and mouths her goodbye.

As the taxi begins to pull away, Stella turns to go back inside, angry with herself for leaving it like that, for making Paula feel bad, but as she walks up the path, an excited voice, almost childlike, small and distant as though carried on the breeze, calls out thinly above the noise of the street.

'I love you, Stella,' it cries. 'I love you.'

And Stella feels it. She feels it so deeply, she can barely breathe.

The solitary man making his way down the aisle draws little attention from the smattering of passengers on the 13:30 to King's Cross.

Short brown hair, average height, a chunky body in loose-fitting black jeans and a baggy, hooded sweatshirt, his expression is tense, but his red eyes could be those of any man in his late-thirties. He could be a sleep-deprived new father or be battling the after-effects of a heavy night's drinking with the boys. He is as ordinary as the blank, beige interior of the train as he shuffles through the carriage, his eyes darting from left to right, looking for his seat.

Early afternoon had seemed a good time to travel; empty carriages, silence, space to think. This one, Coach D, the 'quiet coach', looks like a good place to spend the next three hours. He will need the silence to order his thoughts, to plan his itinerary, to make sure everything is followed through to the letter.

'Yes,' thinks Mark Davis, as he slides into 54A – a forward-facing, window seat – placing his light-coloured rucksack next to him and a long, black canvas bag carefully onto the luggage rack above his head, 'This will be the perfect place.'

His phone rings in his pocket. He takes it out and sees 'Mam' flashing on the screen. He switches it off and puts it back into his pocket. There is nothing more to say now. The talking is over.

He reaches across to his rucksack and pulls out a slim, silver iPod. Placing the headphones in his ears, he scrolls through the playlist, looking for the right piece of music to carry him along; to keep him motivated. He pauses at Track 10 on his list of favourites: the song his father used to play over and over when he was a kid.

'Look after your Mam and Zoe,' his dad had said, as he lay hooked up to tubes, dying of cancer at just thirty-eight. 'You'll have to be the man of the house now. You'll have to be my eyes and ears. You won't let me down, will you son?' He was only nine when his dad died, but he had taken his responsibility seriously. 'Don't trust anyone,' his dad had always said, so he didn't.

His father had been a soldier but in the end it was cancer that claimed him – the unseen enemy. His had not been a glorious death on the front line, or the battle field. It had been slow and painful and drawn out, and Mark had sat by his bed and watched as the big strong man faded into nothing.

He leans back into his seat as the slow, haunting opening bars of Lorraine Ellison's 'Stay With Me Baby' seep into his ears like a lullaby.

He closes his eyes as the train pulls out of Darlington Station and heads south. His sister's face is there. It is as clear and vivid as one of the last times he'd seen her, standing in their mother's tiny white living room with a fake Burberry suitcase in her hands. Off to London with nothing but her dreams and a few flimsy dresses, what sort of protection was that? She mouths the words of the song to him then throws back her head and laughs; her big, wide smile as warm and dazzling as the sun.

She had died alone, he tells himself. She had died all alone, with no one to help her; no one to hold her hand. He had let her down; let his dad down.

He opens his eyes and clenches his fists, the deep red ink of the George Cross tattoo turning pink as the skin stretches across his knuckles.

He reaches into his back pocket and pulls out a newspaper cutting. A handsome blond man smiles out of the page. He sits in an art gallery surrounded by his collection of work: large oil paintings of women; of roses and sunsets; athletes and newspaper sellers; paintings that, according to the article, sell for thousands of pounds. In the interview, he gushes about his expensive flat overlooking Battersea Park, his cute six-year-old daughter and his beautiful wife.

It is a gift, the interview, and when Mark saw it as he sat in a barber's in Middlesbrough he couldn't believe his luck. The bastard had handed it to him on a plate. Names, locations, times and dates – it was all there. The man's wife was launching a restaurant in Soho and there was going to be a grand press night on 29 August; every detail of it was there in the newspaper article. After all this time, Mark had found his war and it would be fought on the streets of Soho. Cheers, he mutters, staring at the face in the picture.

He switches the iPod to its highest volume and sits up straight. The song rises to its crescendo like a serrated knife cutting into his consciousness. If he is to carry out this plan, he will have to be focused, he will have to be cold. He will have to become a warrior.

Stella closes the door behind her and breathes in the tranquility of the empty house. Walking through the dark panelled hallway towards the kitchen, she luxuriates in the silence; the only noise, her shoes clicking on the stone floor and the whispery echo of her breath.

It doesn't seem right, this silence. For the five years they have lived here, from the moment they hauled their belongings through the door and said 'this is where we are going to be,' this tiny, honey-coloured cottage has been filled with noise.

The crackle of Radio 4 as it pours out of Paula's ground floor workroom; the yapping of Pip, their Jack Russell, and the pitter-patter of his feet on the floor; the whistle of the kettle and the ping of the oven as it finishes cooking another of Paula's delicious lunchtime concoctions. Gentle noises, reassuring noises, the kind that couples and families the world over take for granted: the noises of home.

Stella stands in the kitchen, illuminated in an egg-yolk glow as the afternoon sun begins to wane. She looks out of the window and sees Paula's pride and joy: a meticulous recreation of an Andalucian herb garden. It feels odd looking at it now, knowing that Paula is not here, that she is hurtling back to a place Stella has only ever returned to in her dreams. She looks impotently at the rows of herbs and notes how strange they look, like a group of orphaned children lost without their mother.

To Stella, the herbs are just a tangled mass, wild and out of control. She has little affinity with gardening and would be at a loss to identify more than a handful of the myriad plants that occupy every last square inch of the small walled garden, let alone point out their healing properties as Paula can.

Nonetheless, herbs, once so alien to Stella, have now become an integral part of her daily life. If she has a headache, Paula will place sprigs of lavender under her pillow; if she is restless there will be a cup of camomile tea waiting for her in the kitchen. In the sticky heat of summer, there are sticks of cinnammon hanging from the beams in the kitchen to ward off wasps and flies; in the dark, damp days of January and February there are tinctures of echinacea to soothe their coughs and colds. For every ailment, every problem, there is a plant to soothe it.

The only herb-free area is her study, high up in the eaves of the house, away from all distractions. Just her books and notes, her soft, high-backed reading chair and the spiders webs that cluster outside her window; all the things that bring her peace and calm. The webs have become a kind of talisman for her since she was told by an old lady high in the mountains of Andalucia that the spider helps *tejedores de palabras* – weavers of words. On misty November days, when the dew and moisture cling to the webs like tiny diamonds, she remembers the lady, the mountains and those words and she thinks about southern Spain with its blistering heat, its hardy people, its white towns and villages spread out like the icing on a wedding cake; the place that gave her nourishment, that brought her back to life.

And now she is to return to the place that almost destroyed her.

She walks up the stairs to the bedroom and sees her packed suitcase sitting on the bed. As she zips it shut, she runs over in her mind all the reasons why she should not go, all the fears and tensions that bubble to the surface whenever the prospect of returning is raised. But did she ever really leave? The monstrous tentacles of London have kept her in their grasp these past few years, tantalising her in dreams and teasing her with strange memories in her waking hours. She can be standing waiting for the kettle to boil or folding towels when, whoosh, she is back at another point in time. It is always Soho and it is always some insignificant moment. Sitting on the Number 19 bus as it crawls up Piccadilly; waiting to cross the road outside the Trocadero; paying for a coffee in Bar Italia. It is as though her brain wants to sort and compute her time in London for a particular purpose; to make sense of it in the light of what happened; what is about to happen.

She lifts her suitcase off the bed and takes one last look out of the window. The pretty street lined with pastel-coloured houses, the great weeping willows and beyond that the grand Regency crescents with their creamy rose façades and elegant occupants; all so civilised and easy on the eye. It will still be the same when she gets back, she tells herself. Everything will be the same.

As she walks down the stairs, she feels an ache in the pit of her stomach, a sudden sense of loss. She is about to drive away from this secure fortress and set about creating a whole new future and all on the hope of a one-paragraph email. If only she could be sure that all will be fine; if only she could reassure herself like she had reassured Paula.

She picks up her keys from the table in the hall and opens the front door. It is mid-afternoon. The sun is dipping in the sky and she can smell the sherbet-sweet scent of honeysuckle as she walks down the path.

Opening the boot of her car, she sees the terracotta pots of Moroccan jasmine plants that Paula has placed there like babies swaddled against a pillow of soft blankets. There is a note on top of the first pot with the words HANDLE WITH CARE in large red letters. She can hear Paula's voice rise and fall beside her as she wedges her case cautiously by the side of the crates: 'Drive carefully, Stella, no sharp bends, no sudden brakes. These are precious cargo, you know.'

Taking a deep breath, she closes the boot and tells herself to stay focused on what lies ahead, what she has to do. Any doubt, any stumble, and she will walk back into the house and close the door. Then she will never find out how the story ends.

So she climbs into the driver's seat and starts the engine. Back to London, a place so foreign to her now, she will need to learn its language all over again.

'Can we go the park first, Daddy?'

Seb Bailey looks down into his daughter's huge brown eyes and for a moment time pauses. The madness of the restaurant launch, the enormous pile of work still to get through at the gallery, the press releases, the VIP invitations, they all fall away. There is just this moment, this magic time as summer takes its last gasp and all that is demanded of him is to hold his daughter's hand and be Daddy.

He looks at his watch as they walk down Prince of Wales Drive. It is just after three; still early really. Yasmine will be busy briefing the maître d'; Seb won't be able to get in to hang the pictures until at least six. And it's such a beautiful day – fragments of lazy sun peep through the afternoon sky, bathing the pavement in pinky-gold rays – it would be criminal not to have a walk in the park.

'Okay, Cosima,' he says, swinging her hand in the air. 'Let's cut through and see what's new. Maybe we'll see that heron again by the lake, he was a strange old fellow wasn't he?'

'He wasn't a heron, Daddy,' says Cosima, her happy face wrinkling into a frown. 'He was a cormorant. Cormorants are stragglier than herons. Mrs Daley says they're the laughing birds because of their heads.' She skips alongside him as they cross the road and approach the park gates. 'The feathers on their heads are shaped like a jester's hat, you see.'

'My mistake,' laughs Seb. 'You have to remember that I'm not as clever as you when it comes to wildlife spotting. You'll have to be patient with me.'

'You can borrow my bird book if you like,' says Cosima. 'That will tell you everything you want to know.'

Seb smiles at her serious little face as the vast sweep of Battersea Park opens up before them. 'Now, we can't be too long in here. Granny will be expecting us soon and I hear she's making your favourite for dinner.'

'Sausage and mash!' Cosima yells, almost falling over a black Labrador bounding towards them.

'No,' says Seb, trying to keep up with his daughter as she runs towards the glinting metal railings of the play park. 'Guess again.'

She stops and puts her fingers to her mouth, looking up to the sky as though finding the answer to the most difficult question in the world.

'Let me think . . .' she begins, a wisp of a smile appearing

16

at the corner of her mouth. 'It couldn't be, could it? Sunshine rice!' she shouts. She smiles at him, a wide gappy-toothed grin and Seb's heart hurts.

Still, six years after holding her in his arms as a tiny bundle in St Thomas's Hospital, he can't quite believe that this beautiful, clever little being is his own, his flesh and blood, his responsibility. The enormity of being a parent is like nothing he has ever faced before. Sometimes, at three in the morning, he lies awake worrying about what would happen to her if he and Yasmine were to die; then he starts to worry about all manner of things: nuclear war; global warming; food additives, the price of housing . . . And each worry introduces another, bigger worry, on and on until there is a pile of them all stacked up on top of each other like toxic building blocks hammering against his head, daring him to try to sleep through their din. The concerns that occupy his mind in the early hours of the morning would amaze and baffle his younger self.

But he would not change any of it.

He smiles at Cosima. 'You guessed it,' he says. 'Sunshine rice. Granny's speciality.'

But his words disappear into the air. Cosima has reached the children's playground and is busy scrambling up the deck of a giant pirate ship.

He walks over to a bench by the railings and sits to watch his daughter play. Within seconds she has climbed to the top of the ship's mast, her little legs wrapped around it like a monkey. She waves at Seb then makes a sharp descent down the pole like some miniature firewoman.

Seb smiles at his fearless daughter. There is something about her that will always be a mystery to him; her pioneering spirit, her thirst for adventure, her brown eyes – deep pools of darkness inherited from her North African grandfather. There is something of the wild horse about her, something primordial and raw and free-spirited; a sense that she will one day break away and travel the world, soak up every experience, every piece of knowledge, every spine-tingling view. Though physically more like her mother, there are suggestions of Seb all around her but, like jumbled reflections in a lake, you have to look closely to see the resemblance. She has his pale, blonde hair and the same long, lean body; she shares his attention to detail and his love of beautiful things. He is glad she is feisty though, glad that she hasn't inherited his melancholy. When he was Cosima's age, he was just about to start his first year of boarding school. A timid, skinny boy, he had no idea of the horrors that lay ahead at that bleak school on a deserted hilltop on the south-east coast.

He shrugs away the memory and looks around at the great park, the spot that has become something of a place of worship for him these past few years. It seems to understand his changing moods; falls in sync with them and, like an understanding friend, never imposes, never demands anything, just wraps its emerald green cloak around his shoulders and offers him hope and solace.

Seven years ago he had come here with Yasmine. They had sat down next to the pond in the Old English Garden, while deep orange October sunlight cast its glow on their faces. And there, in that idyllic spot, he had asked her to marry him. They had only known each other for six weeks, but he knew from the first moment he met her that she was the person he had always needed to be with. And when she said yes, it was as though everything around them nodded in agreement; the silver fish in the pond, the monkey puzzle tree with its knotty, elephant's trunk; all of the life of the park seemed to breathe a deep sigh of contentment as they stood up and walked home together.

Two months later, on the shortest day of the year, as the tropical plants stood shivering in their mummy-like shrouds and a thick frost clung to the trees like sugar, turning the lake to ice and the air to vapour; they had returned to the park and said their vows in the little Pump House by the lake. And life had begun there, in that moment.

It was odd to think that Battersea Park had once been his guilty secret, the place he had conducted a secret affair with a married woman. It is eight years now since she died, yet it seems a lifetime ago, it is though he played no part in all that heartache and turmoil. He remembers how they would meet every day at 1 p.m. by the Henry Moore sculpture. She always got there first and he would see her waiting for him as he approached, still and serene, like the unofficial fourth figure of the piece. She loved that sculpture and was always trying to imagine what they were looking at, the three figures all huddled together, their faces held up to the sky. Were they witnesses to a rare comet or a message from heaven? She would never know.

He had almost killed himself drinking in the months after her death, and there was a point at which he thought he would never be able to live again. It had been all he could do just to wake up each day, to put one foot in front of the other, to remember to breathe. In those dark early days of 2005, he could never have imagined that his return to Battersea Park, to life, would be so triumphant.

'Daddy! I'm hungry, can we go now?'

He looks up and sees his baby skipping towards him. He knows it could all have been over in a whisper, his life. He knows that Yasmine and Cosima are his gift from God, his second chance. He dare not take it for granted, this happiness and love.

'Come on then,' he says, standing up and taking hold of Cosima's hand. 'Let's go and find that sunshine rice.'

Kerstin Engel sits at her desk staring at her computer, immersed in the series of numbers and words that are scrolling down the screen like tiny black flies glistening in the sun. Just two more pages to go and this section of the report will be complete; then tonight she can give herself a break – no punishing repetitions, no stair climbing, no counting.

The 'desk' is a large communal table around which sit six men and four women: traders, analysts and hedge-fund managers all squirreling away in this small, airless office five floors above St James's Street, the London branch of German asset management company Sircher Capital LLP.

But Kerstin is unaware of the other people sitting around the desk. She has learned to block them out, to focus only on the task in hand; to avoid any unnecessary distractions, any futile talk. She is in her safe place: lost in beautiful numbers which give her a tingle of elation as they reconcile themselves into neat ordered groups. But this feeling of control is as thin and delicate as a thread. If it snaps she will have to start all over again, scramble around in the darkness and try to pick up the loose ends. Still, something about this day makes her feel she can do it, she can keep her head above the water.

'Come on, lovely lady, time to pay the piper!'

She feels a sharp jab on her shoulder, blinks at the numbers on the screen and feels the thread loosen.

She recognises the sing-song west-country accent of Cal Simpson, Sircher's Junior Analyst, her assistant and general pain in the arse. Inspired by the buzz that accompanied this year's Olympic Games, he completed a half marathon in Brighton last weekend. But instead of straight forward sponsorship, Cal had asked his colleagues to guess his finishing time. If they guessed correctly, they would win one hundred pounds. If not, they had to pay ten pounds. It was typical of Cal, who rather resembled a young springer spaniel in both looks and temperament, to turn a simple sponsorship request into a gamble.

Kerstin is aware of him standing behind her but she will not let herself give up on the figures. She is so close, and now this idiot is going to ruin it all. She had got through the ordeal of lunch so seamlessly that she thought this afternoon was going to be okay, she was going to be okay.

Kerstin, along with the others, orders her lunch each morning via email, then at twelve noon on the dot a motor-cycle courier arrives at reception with armloads of sushi and pizzas, salads and sandwiches from various outlets around St James's. At five past twelve Mandy, the loud receptionist with the bright pink lipstick, will burst into the office shouting everyone's orders like a barmaid in a noisy bierkeller. What follows is a ten-minute dissection, led by Cal, of 'what's everyone having for lunch?', 'You've got sushi today have you, Karen? Is it good?', 'Jim's got a salad! What's the matter with you mate, you not hungry?'. Kerstin spends those ten minutes hiding behind her computer screen. She lays out her sandwich (always the same sandwich: tuna, no mayonnaise, wholemeal bread) on the paper napkin and begins to eat, starting with the crust and working her way in. Then when she has finished she will eat her fruit salad: grapes first, then the apple slices, then the orange. Once lunch is consumed in the right way, she can get on. And today, after overcoming the tension of the lunchtime banter she had really managed to make some progress on the report. But now as Cal stands behind her clearing his throat, the thread begins to unravel; the numbers flicker across the screen like seeds scattered by the breeze and she can feel the familiar tension rise from the pit of her stomach. Her chest tightens and her head starts to throb.

'Er, it's ten squids, when you're ready, Kerstin.'

She turns and looks at Cal. He is standing with his arms folded across his chest defiantly. He raises his eyebrows at Kerstin and grins at her.

Kerstin tries to hide the contempt from her face as she looks at the young man. So arrogant, she thinks. Look at him grinning at me like that. She looks at the time on her computer screen. It is just nearing 4 p.m. It's okay, there is still time.

Sighing, she reaches down beside her chair and picks up her bag. It is a neat, grey leather bag with small pockets and compartments. Pockets and compartments are important to Kerstin. They make her feel secure. She opens the front pocket and takes out a small, grey leather purse.

'You were close, Kerstin,' says Cal, looking down at his iPhone. 'I've got all the estimates listed here, and according to this you said one minute fifty, just six minutes shy of my time. It was a PB too, I was well proud . . .'

23

But Kerstin does not hear what he is saying. She is staring in horror at her purse, at the rip in the leather, a deep slash that has appeared over the course of the morning. It was fine when she last saw it, she thinks, her hands shaking as she turns the purse over and checks the other side. She retraces the morning's routine in her head as Cal taps his foot impatiently. She had taken the purse out at Tesco on the King's Road where she bought a packet of mints. Then, after she had been served, she had put the purse back into her bag; in the left-hand pocket on the front. How could it have ripped?

Panic starts to build in her chest as she grips the purse in her hand. She cannot spend the rest of the day sitting at this desk knowing there's a damaged purse in her bag. She stares at the rip; the fabric of the purse is poking out beneath, little wisps of straw-coloured thread jutting out. It looks ugly, wrong. She must not have ugly, broken things about her. It's a sign, a test. She has to get things back in order. There must be order and perfection. She hears her father's voice in her head. She must sort this out or else everything will fall apart.

'Kerstin,' says Cal, impatiently. 'Whenever you're ready.'

Kerstin jumps at the sound of his voice and with shaking hands, she opens the purse, pulls out a crisp twenty-pound note and thrusts it at him.

'There,' she says, brusquely. 'Well done.'

'Thanks Kerstin,' he says, brightly. 'Now hold on a sec, I'll get you your change.' He puts his phone down on Kerstin's desk and pats his pockets.

Kerstin grabs her bag from under the desk, shoves the ugly purse into the right-hand pocket – she will not let the left-hand pocket be contaminated by it – then pushes past Cal and heads for the door.

'Kerstin, where you going?' shouts Cal, holding out a ten-pound note towards her. 'I've got your money.'

But Kerstin doesn't hear him. She is running down the stairs, counting as she goes. She must not let herself stop counting until she has replaced the purse. As soon as she has the new one, the perfect new purse, then she can stop; then everything will be all right.

3

There is a slight jolt as the train slows down. Mark opens his
eyes and looks out of the window blearily, trying to focus on
the new vista that has opened up since he fell asleep at Don-
caster.

The train trundles through deserted little stations, the
names of which all appear to begin with 'H', then it slowly
moves out into open countryside, picking up its pace for the
final leg of the journey.

It's grim this place, Mark thinks, as he looks out at field
after field; so tidy and neat and groomed; so claustrophobic.
The landscape makes him think of those boxy gardens at the
back of suburban semi-detached houses; the ones that are
lined with shrubs and plants in faux-stone pots from B&Q, the
ones whose owners spend their weekends mowing the lawn
and trimming the hedges into uniform slabs of neat fuzz.

The fields rise into hilly mounds and Mark sees, amid the
curves of the land, little dots of primary colours, like pinheads

on a noticeboard. As the train gets closer he sees that the little dots are groups of sixty-something men and women dressed in red and blue sweaters, long shorts and sun-visors. They stand brandishing their golf clubs like medieval spears.

It's softer than the north, thinks Mark, as the train leaves the golfers behind and heads back into flatter territory. It's lighter: the earth, the grass, the sky. There is something intangible about it, something diluted and fragile, like it could all just dissolve in your hands. The north is different, it's as hard as metal. The north wears its industry like armour, like a soldier always ready to defend himself. His dad used to say that the north-east of England was like the shoulder of the country, carrying its burdens like Atlas carried the world.

It is seven years now since he and his mother travelled to London to identify the body of his sister. On the way down, they had made polite conversation, eaten sandwiches, taken phone calls from the police, from his aunts, from Zoe's friends; the journey had gone quickly. At King's Cross they had been met by Detective Inspector Christine Worsley, the woman in charge of the investigation. She had spoken kindly to them, offered her sincerest condolences, promised them that whoever had done this would be brought to justice. Zoe had been found with no belongings; no wallet, no phone, nothing to identify her by. If it hadn't been for her mother phoning the police after a week of no contact then Zoe would have probably ended up as yet another anonymous dead girl, another secret swallowed up by the dark, labyrinthine streets of Soho.

Mark and his mother were taken to Charing Cross Police Station where they were led deep into the bowels of the building to the morgue. It was freezing down there; he will never forget the cold. It was like the icy breath of the dead blowing down his neck, like every one of the poor, unfortunate souls who had ended up in that bleak, netherworld was suddenly released, swirling about the room like will-o'-the-wisps as he and his mother stood there waiting by a blanket-covered mound. When the detective pulled back the covers, his mother had screamed; it was a raw, gut-wrenching sound that seemed to come from the depths of her soul. 'Oh, my beautiful girl, my beautiful girl, what have they done to you?'

Mark had watched as his mother took his dead sister's face in her hands and stroked it, the way she had when they were both young, when they were poorly or upset. She rubbed and rubbed it as though she could somehow bring her back to life. Then she had started talking to her as though they were sitting round the table having a chat: 'Your hair looks nice, pet,' she had whispered. 'It suits you short. You always had lovely hair even when you were a little girl . . .' Then she had crumbled, the tears came and she sobbed and wailed, tore at her own hair as the detective covered the body. But Mark had remained silent. He had noticed other things that his mother hadn't or perhaps she had and was blocking them out. He had seen the red lines around her neck; the purple marks on her shoulders. His father had looked at peace when he died; serene and still, but Zoe was different. The expression on her face was horrific, an anguished, restless grimace.

The journey home had been unbearable. The train crew, noticing the state his mother was in, had upgraded them to a first-class carriage and the two of them had sat there like ghosts, sipping complimentary tea, his mother breaking down into staccato fits of tears which no amount of reassuring words could ever stem.

When they arrested a forty-seven-year-old crack addict, Martin Harris, for Zoe's murder, Mark and his mother had attended the trial. They had sat through hours of evidence, listened to witness accounts including the poor man who found her body, a street cleaner who had been left so traumatised he had become a virtual recluse, unable to leave his house. Then Sebastian Bailey had taken the stand. He had been the last person to see Zoe alive. He told the court how he had sat with Zoe on a bench in Soho Square for several hours before she was murdered. He said he had met her when she came in to the modelling agency he worked for. She had put together a portfolio of photographs and was looking to be taken on by Becky Woods, the chief model booker. Bailey told how Zoe had organised an appointment with Becky that morning but Becky had forgotten and Zoe had been left in the waiting room all day.

Bit by bit, Bailey had pieced together not just the last day but the last few months of Zoe's life. He told them about the landlady who had tricked her into going to a party that night, telling her it was a fancy celebrity event when really it was a crackhead wanting a prostitute. Zoe had been in the house of the man who would go on to murder her, she had drunk his wine and when she guessed his intentions, she had fled, taking a wad of money from her landlady's hands as she went. As each detail was recounted, his mother had put her head in her hands unable to imagine such a sordid series of events for her lovely, sensible daughter who had left for London so excited and hopeful.

When the guilty verdict was returned, his mother had bowed her head and made the sign of the cross. For her, it was closure, she could get on with the grieving process, slowly rebuild her shattered life. But Mark had been unsettled by Sebastian Bailey. There was smugness in his eyes as he gave his evidence; a chilling composure that didn't seem right.

As the years have gone by Mark has watched his marriage break down, has heard his six-year-old daughter tell him she doesn't want anything to do with him and suffered the indignity of losing his job and having to move back in with his nervous wreck of a mother. And through it all, he has followed Bailey; he has Googled his name, Googled his wife's name too, once he found out what it was. He has seen this man grow more and more successful while he himself has gone further and further into the abyss. All the anger he felt in that morgue; all the rage and confusion sitting in the court listening to the harrowing details of his sister's murder has directed itself into this man. If, for one moment, Bailey can feel the heartache that Mark has felt these last few years, the fear and sorrow that has reduced his family to dust and left his mother a hollow shell, then he can draw a line under it all. Only when Bailey has been punished will Mark find peace.

The train slows down as they enter a more urban patch. Mark reads the name 'Welwyn Garden City' as they pass through another deserted station. There's nothing garden-like about this place, he thinks, as they pass row upon row of grey, decaying buildings, and where are all the people? Even from inside the train, he can feel it; that familiar tightening in his throat. He has convinced himself that the air gets thinner on the approach into London. He starts to cough. Jesus, he hates this place. He always gets like this when he travels south, the breath seems to drain out of him and as they pass the Emirates stadium, home of Arsenal FC, the giant collage of hyper-real footballers bears down upon him like a cage and he starts to wheeze. It's like being sucked into a deep river's current, spinning and whirling into its vortex with no oxygen, no hope of release. He takes his asthma inhaler out of his pocket, shakes it and takes a deep breath of salbutamol. He knew he would need it. He feels his lungs gently expand, feels the muscles in his airways relaxing. He breathes slowly, in and out, in and out and the wheezing subsides.

They slow down and come to a standstill just outside the station, waiting for the train in front to make a move. Every passenger seems to take an expectant breath as they prepare to enter the city, the dark, dirty city where people disappear, shrink themselves into nothing until all that remains are their voices, disembodied voices like the train announcer telling them to keep their belongings with them, voices that cling to the bricks and mortar, that echo in the tunnels and hidden places, that hide in the shadows waiting for someone to come and listen; to hear their stories; their secrets.

Mark stands up and takes his ticket out of his back pocket as the train starts to crawl towards the station. Outside spindly trees line the track, poisoned black by the belching grime of the trains. They curl towards the window, holding out their emaciated branches like beggars calling for alms.

There is no nature here, thinks Mark, nothing can grow, nothing can live. He coughs again, this time bringing up a thick substance that he tries to swallow but it lodges in his throat and fills his mouth with a sharp, metallic taste. Growing up, he had always preferred the countryside to the town. Zoe had been an urban girl and she would wince when their granddad suggested a nice walk in the hills. But Mark had lived for those outings as a kid and when they reached the summit of Roseberry Topping, that peculiar curved peak that the locals referred to as the 'Teesside Matterhorn' he could feel his lungs open up. He could think, he could breathe and for days afterwards he wouldn't need his inhaler. They used to joke about it, his mates, they used to say he was like those ramblers with the red socks and kagouls trekking out to the hills every weekend. He brushed aside their comments though because he knew it was more important than just having a stroll among pretty scenery; the hills were his oxygen supply, they were the tap he could drink from to clear his head and open his airways. He needed them to live.

When the train finally stops, he lifts the large, long canvas bag from the luggage rack; feels its weight in his hands, the reassuring bulk of what lies hidden in there then he shuffles with the rest of the passengers towards the exit doors. Darkness descends on the narrow corridor as the train passes through its final tunnel, then with a whoosh, shards of bright white artificial light swim in front of his eyes, making him blink. The little button on the door turns from yellow to green; someone in front of him presses it, the door slides open and they step out into the noise and glare of King's Cross Station.

He looks at his watch. Half past four. And so it begins . . .

Stella sits on a plastic chair cradling a polystyrene cup of tepid, watery coffee. Taking a sip, she looks out of the floor-length window of the motorway services café that hovers precariously above the fast lane of the M4.

Thick wedges of inky-blue sky tussle with the last of the light-tinged clouds as, down below, little red lights on the motorway race sheep in a nearby field.

It is 4.30 p. m. In an hour or so she will be in London where Paula is waiting in their hotel room. She has already received four texts from her, updating each stage of her train journey and enquiring in a not too tactless way if 'the plants are okay'. Stella has not replied to any of the texts. Why does Paula insist on doing that; on filling their time apart with constant updates and reminders and messages?

She takes another sip of coffee. It tastes disgusting but it feels good to be alone; truly alone. Away from the house, away from the street with the chatty neighbours and their unnaturally happy smiles, away from Paula's endless stream of herb-talk; the phone calls to and from suppliers; the Skype calls to her brother and his children who only live a mile away; the opaque verbal mush that drowns out Stella's thoughts, stifles her concentration so that she has to take refuge in her attic room like some Victorian hysteric.

She likes the stillness of her own company; likes those moments when hers is the only voice she can hear in her head. She never thought of herself as a solitary person before. In her twenties she had lived in a noisy studio flat in the middle of Soho where every second was filled with noise: the saxophone playing of her jazz musician boyfriend; the banging and crashing of bottles being delivered to the neighbouring restaurants and bars; the shouts and yells of partygoers outside the window. Yet because the noise was so constant, so extreme, it became a sort of white noise, so loud that she stopped hearing it. She had managed to place herself at the heart of the storm where she found her silence; her equilibrium. Still, back then there wasn't much about herself that she wanted to listen to anyway. She had spent those years in the grip of an eating disorder and Soho was the perfect place to hide it.

Sometimes, she dreams she is lost inside Soho; the streets melting into each other like molten lava, enveloping her; sucking her deep down into their depths. Other times, she dreams of Ade, the man whose heart she broke; she sees the flat they shared, the mess, the CDs scattered across the floor. And then she wakes up in her sumptuous brass bed in her pretty bedroom with its oak floorboards, embroidered rugs and tasteful sage green walls; Georgian elegance, not a hint of anything tacky or vulgar, but the ghosts of Soho, the musty smell of the flat, the warmth of Ade's body in the bed, stay with her throughout the day, lodged inside her head like an unspoken word.

She reaches down beside the seat and takes out a book from her handbag: Virginia Woolf's *The Years*, the subject of her PhD thesis. It is filled with tiny post-it notes with scribbles of ideas written in Stella's scrawly handwriting. This is part of the reason why she asked Paula to travel down separately. She needs time to prepare, away from Paula's chatter. Yet still the feeling of guilt won't leave her; the weight of this deceit hangs heavily as she opens the book.

But as she begins to read she feels herself slow down, feels a warm surge of contentment rise from the pit of her stomach; she is back on familiar terrain:

'. . . a rattle of cart-wheel; then a chorus of voices singing – country people going home. This is England, Eleanor thought to herself . . .'

Stella closes her eyes, allowing the words to whisper into her consciousness; to unravel themselves inside her head like coils of twisted, golden silk. She sees tall, sensible Eleanor sitting out on a terrace at twilight, with bats circling above her head. She sees the Pargiter family rising and falling through the decades like swimmers battling the waves. She takes a deep breath, opens her eyes and looks out of the window.

'You can do this, Stella,' she whispers. 'You're better now.'

It is getting dark, prematurely so for this time of year, she thinks. Yet, late August always does this, tricks you into thinking that it is autumn already, wraps a deep cloak of purple around the closing days of summer as if preparing itself for cold and decay.

Stella closes her book and as she places it into her bag she feels her phone vibrate in the inside pocket: probably Paula checking on the herbs. She takes the phone and as she sees the name, her cheeks redden.

All set for Wednesday. How does 2 p.m. sound? Dylan.

Stella takes another sip of coffee, still holding the phone in her hand; the open message blinking its unanswered question at her like a warning light.

Paula will be at the Chelsea Physic Garden on Wednesday; she will be lost in her own world among the herbs. Stella had told her she was going to spend the day at the London Library working on the final chapter of her thesis. Phones have to be switched off in the library; as far as Paula is concerned Stella will have stepped out of time for a couple of hours. She won't suspect a thing.

Yet still this guilt; this feeling that she is betraying her love, that she is being selfish; following her own interests instead of the collective plans that Paula has meticulously set out for them.

The phone's screen has gone dark, taking the message and all its connotations away into the ether. She will answer it later; when she gets to the hotel. But for now she is happy to stay here; floating in between two worlds, neither in Exeter nor London, but simply inhabiting this moment.

'This is England.' The line from *The Years* rattles round her head. She is disconnected from it all: from Exeter, from London, from England. They say it is Midsummer Eve when the veil between worlds is at its thinnest, but for Stella it is this time of year – the last days of summer, the melancholy drift towards September, to the harvests and clean, empty exercise books – that seems to allow her a glimpse into the next world. The weather changes sometime around now, and then stays in a sort of greyish no-man's land, trapped between one season and the next. Stella always feels raw in this period, exposed, like she is walking barefoot along a slippery log. Underneath, the water is dark, deep and unknowable and she feels like any moment she could fall in; so she waits, her foot dangling over the edge of the log, unable to let go.

She winces as she drains her cup of coffee which is now ice-cold and grainy. She can't put it off any longer; her moment of solitude is coming to an end. Contentment is so fleeting she thinks, as she puts *The Years* back into her handbag, it can be shattered in a heartbeat, like a fragile piece of glass.

As she walks out of the café towards the escalator, she feels her phone vibrate again and her throat closes up as she rummages in her bag. Taking the phone in her hand she watches as the familiar name flashes on and off. She will not answer it. She will allow herself one more hour of solitude before her head is filled again with all things 'Paula'.

She descends the escalator and steps through the automatic doors into the warm air. She looks up at the sky. It's a perfect late-afternoon light, and the thin sliver of a crescent moon is just visible above the trees that surround the car park. Everything will be okay, she tells herself, repeating Paula's mantra, and as she walks over towards her car, she almost believes that it will.

4

Kerstin stands at the traffic lights on Piccadilly and waits for the green man to appear, waits to remove the dark stain of the damaged purse from her bag.

As she stands she counts. She has been counting since she fled Cal and the office; she counted as she ran down the stairs, as she hurried through reception, out of the revolving doors and onto St James's Street. 'Six hundred and fifty-three,' she mutters to herself as the lights change and she rushes into the busy road, towards Bond Street and redemption.

The pavement beneath her feet sparkles like a thousand diamonds have been compressed into the granite. All the money of the city, all the bonuses and trust funds; all the savings and bribes, all the invisible credit, pours into this place like a hundred rivers running into the sea. It's what keeps the windows gleaming, the flags flying, the goods shining like the specks on the pavement. This is London's great pleasure-dome; an adult fairy-land where magic and illusion are attainable – at a price.

But Kerstin doesn't see the diamonds on the street, she doesn't look up to swoon at the flags and the handbags and the silk scarves fluttering in the windows like exotic birds. She cannot be distracted by any of it. She must keep counting until she gets to her golden number, the number of truth and light, then everything will be all right. When she gets to eleven hundred and nine – her birthday, the eleventh day of the ninth month, order and perfection, order and perfection – when she gets to that number then she will stop.

Nine hundred and twenty.

The intensity of the counting makes her feel dizzy as she strides down Bond Street, staring straight ahead. Orange spots dance in front of her eyes manically, like the prelude to a bout of travel sickness. But she must keep counting.

Nine hundred and fifty-two.

She weaves in and out of rambling window-shoppers like a sleek car navigating its way into the fast lane of the motorway. She must keep going for if she slows down, if she slackens her pace, she will be crushed.

Nine hundred and eighty-four.

Thoughts roll around inside her head like tiny ball-bearings. The ripped purse; the report; Dominic Stratton's last terse email. One thousand and six. It's all punishment, she tells herself, well deserved punishment for her shoddiness; her lack of control. One thousand and twenty-three. When she lets things slip, when she loses her faith in numbers, it all falls apart.

Boom!

A loud bang reverberates through the street. She jumps with the shock and the counting pauses; the number one thousand and twenty-four balances precariously on the tip of her tongue like a word she can't quite place. There's a second bang – a hard, heavy thud, a sonic boom it seems like to Kerstin's frazzled senses and she turns to see a man walking away from the back of a truck, his arms laden with boxes. It's fine, she tells herself, it was just a door slamming. But the noise has stalled her, it has taken her thoughts away from counting and led her back eight years; to the explosion outside the pizza shop in Cologne that fine June day in 2004.

She was a student, twenty-two, happy and hungover, making her way home from an all-night party. It happened so quickly, she could count it in the steps she took; one, two, three across the street then suddenly an apocalyptic smash and behind her, carnage and blood, nails embedded in flesh and the grisly smell of burning body, like bacon sizzling in a pan, and that man's face; the one that returns to her night after night. He had greeted her like a friend, just moments before it happened, smiling as he raised a cigarette to his mouth. One, two, three, and it could have been her lying there mangled and bloodied, eyes raised to the sky, asking why.

She gathers herself and scoops up the numbers like a mother calling for her children. One thousand and twenty-five. The delivery man deposits his boxes, the noise dissolves into the sharp, late afternoon air and Kerstin walks on, her heart thudding against her chest. One thousand and twenty-seven.

She wants to shout the numbers out loud; release them from the confines of her head; spill them out onto the pavement like loose change. A blonde, middle-aged woman in a floor-length camel coat and large, black sunglasses smiles at her as she passes. But the woman is smiling at the illusion: the smart, attractive young woman in an expensive, black trouser suit and neat, shoulder-length hair the colour of milky tea, walking along Bond Street in search of a purse. That is what the woman sees. Kerstin wants to scream at her, wants to show her the contents of her harried brain. If she could, she would throw the numbers at her, thrust them into her arms like an unwanted parcel. Then she would be free, she could walk happily through Mayfair, breathe in the late summer air and discover what it feels like to be normal.

One thousand and forty.

She strides along the street, on and on, leaving behind the Edwardian splendour of Old Bond Street and crossing onto the fashionable minimalist strip of New Bond Street with its black-and-white awnings and immaculately polished shop windows that bat the rays of the sun away like unwelcome customers.

One thousand and fifty-three.

Once, numbers had been her weapons; she could control them, distort them; manipulate them into things of beauty. 'Mathematics,' her father had told her, 'is the elixir of life.

Once you crack its code, you hold the secrets of the universe inside your head. Numbers are the only things you can trust in this life, Kerstin; they will keep you sane.'

One thousand and ninety-five.

Something brushes against her face and she looks up. One thousand, one hundred and three. It has just begun to rain, though the sky above New Bond Street is still blue and the sun is shining. This is a light, almost invisible rain. It isn't settling anywhere and when it comes into contact with the pavement it seems to leave no mark, just disappears into the granite like a secret teardrop.

One thousand, one hundred and nine. Kerstin stops walking and nods her head once, twice, three times. This is her signal that the counting is done, the glorious number has been reached. Now, all she needs to do is replace the purse and everything will be fine, nothing bad will happen to her. The numbers have saved her, like her father told her they would.

She looks at the place she has stopped outside. It is a double-fronted glass building; plain with no elaborate awnings. The glass windows are bare but the door, shaped like a rectangular lego piece, is painted gold. Kerstin steps towards the window. There is a row of pink handbag-shaped tissue paper parcels pressed against the glass and behind them a little pyramid of leather purses of all shapes and colours: red, purple, green and grey. Grey! It is the perfect replacement, thinks Kerstin, the perfect shade. She can buy it, dispose of the ripped one and it will be like nothing ever happened. As she pushes the gold door open, the maroon flag above it flutters with the back draft. A gold woodcut drawing of a tree looms above the name which is displayed in simple gold, block lettering: MULBERRY.

The first thing she sees as she enters the shop is a large circular gold cage standing in the middle of the room surrounded by mannequins in hot pants, patterned shift dresses and leather jackets, all holding a Mulberry bag. It looks like the cages used by cruel circus ringmasters to keep lions in, to taunt them with scraps of meat in exchange for performing tricks.

The shop, though rectangular in structure, gives the impression of curvature. Every surface is elongated, from the curvy display cabinets to the crescent moon shelves and they all seem to bend inward so that as Kerstin walks through it feels as though she is being led deeper and deeper into the centre of a great, complex puzzle.

She makes her way towards the back of the shop where she can see a long, oval, glass-topped counter. There is a sales assistant standing behind it, staring into space. Her expression is similar to the soldiers that stand guard outside Buckingham Palace, only instead of a busby she has a helmet of glossy, chestnut-coloured hair framing her immaculately made-up face.

She tilts her head slightly as Kerstin approaches, but otherwise her pose remains rigid and unmoving. When Kerstin reaches the counter, the woman opens her mouth, preparing to begin the long scripted dialogue that will start with 'Can I help you?' and end with a sale, but before she has the chance Kerstin speaks.

'I need a purse,' she demands, her German accent sounding more pronounced than usual, as it always does when she has been counting.

The sales assistant seems taken aback by this bluntness and the familiar, over-rehearsed lines desert her.

'A purse?' she replies. There is a sharp South African lilt to her voice and it seems as if she is trying to match Kerstin's terseness.

Kerstin is fiddling with the zip on her bag, trying to dislodge the ripped purse from the front pocket without having to make too much contact with it. She doesn't look up as she answers.

'Yes, a purse. I would like the grey one over there in the window. Could you get it for me? I'm afraid I'm in a bit of a hurry.'

The woman raises an eyebrow and languidly moves around to the front of the counter. She is very tall – five feet eleven at least – and her height is exacerbated by the vertiginous heels she is wearing. She brushes her hand through her hair and as she does so a trio of thin gold bracelets ripple down her arm like snakes.

'The grey one,' she repeats, looking into the middle distance as though trying to solve a difficult algebra equation.

'Yes,' says Kerstin, who has now managed to extricate the

damaged purse from the bag. She holds it between finger and thumb like a dirty rag 'It's in the window next to the pink handbags, I mean the tissue-paper handbags.'

'Ohhh,' says the woman, clasping her hands together as though in prayer. 'You mean the Continental wallets. Grey? That will be Parisian Dove.'

Kerstin nods her head, assuming that this is the one. After all, doves are grey sometimes aren't they? 'Yes,' she says. 'The Parisian Dove. I would like the Parisian Dove.'

'Of course,' says the woman, slowly. She smiles weakly at Kerstin then disappears into the curved maze of the shop-floor.

Kerstin taps her fingers on the glass counter as she waits. Then she stops herself. Tapping always makes her want to count and she mustn't count in here, otherwise she will never get out. Instead she looks at the pretty display cabinet next to the counter. It is filled with tiny leather key-rings and credit card holders. Kerstin smiles to herself. This will be the perfect purse, she tells herself. She likes this shop. She likes the bare wood and glass and gold, the simple decadence of it. It reminds her of the shops her mother used to frequent in Cologne. There was something so ordered and elegant about those places where all of the products were displayed discreetly on beautiful, square white tables; not like the department stores in London with their garish, fluorescent lights and messy piles of clothes loaded onto flimsy shelves. Those places unsettle her, the untidiness makes her feel unclean; makes her want to count and never stop. The memory of shopping in Cologne takes her back twenty-five years, a little girl following her beautiful mother as she picks up various scarves, blouses and perfumes. She remembers thinking that those airy palaces of light and wood were what money must look like.

'Is this the one?' She looks up and the image of Cologne breaks up like a shattered mirror. The woman has returned with the purse; a long, stippled leather wedge with a small, gold plaque in the centre.

'Yes,' replies Kerstin. 'That's the one.' The woman nods and takes the purse round to the other side of the counter.

Kerstin looks at her watch: 5 p.m. Her mouth goes dry. How is it so late? She must get back to the office; she must get on with the report. She pulls her credit card out of the ripped purse with the edges of her fingers, and puts it down on the counter.

The woman is carefully laying a sheet of silvery embossed tissue paper out in front of her.

'No, no,' says Kerstin. 'I don't want it wrapped thank you. I'll take it as it is.'

'You don't want it wrapped?' The woman looks appalled.

'No, I don't,' says Kerstin. 'If you could just put my card through now please. I'm in a great rush.'

The woman pauses, her hand lies flat on the tissue paper, as though not sure what to do next. This just doesn't happen in Mulberry. Customers always want their purchases wrapping in beautiful tissue paper and they always want to walk out holding the iconic carrier bag.

After a moment she moves the tissue paper aside and picks up the purse. Looking at the price tag, she types in a series of numbers on the till.

'That will be £275, please,' she says not looking up.

Kerstin pushes the credit card across the counter. The woman takes it and is about to slot it into the card machine when she stops.

'Would you like to be added to our mailing list?' she says, her voice deadpan as she reclaims her rehearsed lines. 'It just takes a couple of minutes to fill in your contact details and then we can let you know the latest news.'

Kerstin is becoming increasingly agitated. It feels like the tainted purse and the time ticking on her watch are burning into her skin like acid as she stands waiting.

'No, thank you, I would not. I just want to buy this purse,' she says in a loud, firm voice.

'Right,' says the woman, with equal firmness and she places the credit card into the slot. 'If you could just type in your pin number.' She holds the machine towards Kerstin.

Kerstin looks at the buttons on the machine and for a moment she thinks she can see the sweat from the woman's fingers glistening on the numbers. She cannot touch it; she cannot taint herself any further.

'Would you mind putting it down on the counter?' she asks

the woman. The assistant frowns and makes a clicking noise with her tongue as she puts the machine down.

'Thank you,' says Kerstin, as she pulls the sleeve of her silk blouse over her index finger and gently taps in the pin number.

The assistant shakes her head and picks up the machine. After a long pause, the machine whirrs and the assistant rips out the sales docket, removes the card from the slot then smiles weakly at Kerstin.

'That's all gone through.'

She hands the card back to Kerstin, who receives it with her sleeve still stretched safely over her hand. Then, grabbing the new purse, she rips off the price tag. The woman looks at her with a horrified expression, but Kerstin doesn't notice. She takes the old purse and starts to empty its contents onto the gleaming counter: her ID card for work; her debit card; her Sainsbury's loyalty card; four twenty-pound notes. Then she unzips the middle section and pours a pile of loose change out.

'What are you doing?' asks the woman.

'I need to get rid of this purse,' says Kerstin as she slots the cards and notes into their new home. 'Would you mind putting it in your bin?' She puts the damaged purse onto the counter. The woman looks at it in horror, like she is being handed a dead fish.

'Put it in the bin?' she says, her expression one of utter bewilderment.

Yes,' says Kerstin, as she scoops up the coins and drops them into her new purse. 'It's ripped.'

'Oh,' says the girl, taking it from the counter. 'But this is a Prada wallet.' Her eyes light up as she touches the golden lettering. 'Are you sure you want to get rid of it. It's not a huge rip.'

'Yes, I'm sure,' says Kerstin, tucking the new purse safely into the left hand pocket of her bag. 'Thank you.'

She walks away, leaving the woman holding the Prada purse like it's an abandoned child. As she steps out onto New Bond Street she takes a deep breath. The purse and the counting must surely have rectified it all. If she keeps calm, she can still get the report finished by Wednesday and redeem herself. Her mind falls silent as she walks back to St James's Street.

Seb smiles to himself as he walks across Albert Bridge, Cosima's voice still ringing in his ears: 'Bye, Daddy. Don't work too late!'

He has safely deposited her with Yasmine's mother, Maggie, in her tiny, cluttered maisonette on Battersea Bridge Road; the flat his wife grew up in. It is difficult to imagine a family of four sharing such a cramped space for so many years. Even now, with her children grown up and left and her husband dead, Maggie fills every last square inch of the space, though so tiny herself. Yet, the happiness and loving disorder that permeate that flat is hard to resist; there is always something delicious being cooked in the kitchen and Magic FM is a constant in the background, creating a kind of easy-listening aural soup that you have to swim through as you walk in the front door. When Seb left Cosima she was dancing around the kitchen to 'Build Me Up Buttercup' while her grandmother chopped the onions for the sunshine rice, her feet tapping on the linoleum floor, her bottom wiggling in time to the beat.

It is a world away from the immaculate Dorset country house where he used to visit his own grandmother as a child. Visits there were sporadic and pained. When he was a toddler, his grandmother would only let him into the house if his parents kept him strapped into the pushchair or held tightly on their knees. Heaven forbid he should scrape the polished floor with his toys or smear chocolate on the William Morris patterned sofa. On the rare occasions when he was allowed to play on the floor, he would feel anxious and wary, looking up for approval from his parents who would be sitting miserably around his grandmother's oak dining table, politely drinking tepid tea and nibbling tasteless, expensive cakes. He remembers his grandmother's beady eyes watching him intently; waiting to pounce the moment his little hand came too close to an ornament or vase.

His family is a sore subject between him and Yasmine. Coming from a loud, carefree family where anything and everything is freely discussed, his wife finds it hard to understand the lack of communication that blights Seb's family. He has never discussed anything personal with his parents;

he doesn't know how he would even begin. The idea of hiding feelings, of burying hurt and pain had been so ingrained in him as a child that he had thought it normal. It was only when he met Yasmine that he realised it was not a sign of weakness to feel depressed, to have bad times, to be vulnerable.

Yasmine has gone some way towards opening up communication with Seb's parents; in fact she gets on with her father-in-law splendidly. He likes her pragmatism and boyish sense of humour; while she understands his military bluster and eye-watering bluntness. Yet his father cannot look Seb in the eye; he has never understood his artistic second child who cried at the beginning of each school term and was more at home in the art studio than on the rugby field. Even now if they find themselves alone in a room for more than a few minutes, a heavy awkward silence descends; the sound of two people who are utterly bewildered by one another. It saddens Seb, it always has, but that is the way it is, and anyway, it is the only blot on his otherwise blemish-free world.

It is a beautiful afternoon; the sun is still hanging onto its last moments and sharp silver light streaks across the windows of the seventeenth-century terraces on Cheyne Walk as Seb crosses the Embankment and heads towards Oakley Street.

As he walks, he plans his evening: if he can get three of the pictures up tonight then there will be time, in between meetings tomorrow, to finish off the big painting – his surprise gift for Yasmine. She has put her heart and soul into launching this restaurant and she deserves to be a success. When they first met, she was working as a sous chef in a little French restaurant in Waterloo. Their dates were spent walking along the South Bank in the early hours looking at the twinkly blue lights in the trees and the alien glow of the London Eye as it hovered above the river like a giant space ship. Her hours were crazy – 9 a.m. to 2 a.m. most days – but she was a hard worker and passionate about food. She was always trying out new ideas, new combinations of flavours; testing out her creations on Seb. She had even enticed him, a committed vegetarian, to eat meat with her sumptuous, slow-cooked Moroccan lamb dishes. She was never going to settle for being a sous chef, though, and soon she was ready to take on the next challenge, becoming Head Chef of a fusion brasserie on Lavender Hill.

But it was North African cooking, the food of her ancestors, where her passions lay and as Seb's painting career started to take off with the help of three sell-out London shows and a wealthy collector investing in some of his back catalogue, the idea began to form that maybe they could open up their own restaurant. When Seb's best friend and business partner, Henry Walker, came on board, they knew that it was going to become a reality. Henry doesn't believe in failure and whatever he invests in receives the full force of his enthusiasm and ambition. After building a successful model agency, an art gallery and a string of fitness studios, a London restaurant was next on his wish-list. But not any old restaurant, no that would never do for Henry; he was going to take them right to the gastronomic heart of London: Soho.

Seb had smirked when Henry showed him the proposed site – a vacant building right next door to Seb's old drinking haunt, The Dog and Duck pub on Frith Street. For a moment, he had hesitated. What if being back in Soho resurrected old demons; what if the temptation to slip back into his binge drinking proved too great? But then he had looked at how far he had come – his family, his successful business, his sobriety. It would take more than a little strip of street to tear all that away from him. And Yasmine had fallen in love with it on the spot, so he had given Henry the go-ahead and here they are, eight months later, ready to launch Soho's newest restaurant: The Rose Garden.

As he crosses the busy King's Road, he sees a number 19 bus in the distance. Happiness surges through him as he walks towards the bus stop. There is something so complete about this day; all is as it should be. He feels sharp, clear, completely connected to everything around him: the gleaming red fire engines lined up outside Chelsea Fire Station; the sparkling fairy lights twinkling in the window of Heals, even the angry-faced newspaper seller outside the bank – they all have their place, their roles to perform, just like him. Yes, he thinks, today is a positive day.

He smiles as the bus comes closer; its destination displayed in thick, white letters: PICCADILLY. He climbs aboard, scans his

Oyster Card and takes his seat by the window. As he stretches his legs out in front of him, rain, that has been threatening all afternoon, starts to fall; a gentle rain, smearing the windows and giving the world outside a vague, dreamlike quality. The doors close and the bus pulls away towards Sloane Street. The rain starts to come down quite heavily and as they stop at the lights a procession of tight-faced women clutching large carrier bags from Harrods, Prada and Harvey Nichols run across the road, umbrella-less and exposed, their perfectly blow-dried hair wilting in the downpour. Seb smirks, thinking of his grandmother's perfect drawing room; her hawkish eyes. Rain is the great leveller, he thinks, it makes sopping wet rags of us all.

5

'Damn,' exclaims Stella as she squints to see the road ahead. She hit a patch of heavy rain just outside London and now, as she navigates Earl's Court Road, her vision a blur of watery car headlights, she hears her phone beep.

'Not now, Paula,' she shouts to the empty car. She hadn't expected this; she had imagined her return to London would be epic, she would sweep into the city like a prodigal child and the great buildings, the statues and monuments would bend towards her in a kind of embrace. But real life is different; real life is sitting in traffic watching windscreen wipers sweep in front of your eyes; listening to the toneless voice of the Sat Nav as it directs you towards a multi-storey car park. Real life is wet and insipid; the golden sunrises, the blazing colours and rhapsodic sounds only exist in the imagined world, the place Stella finds when she writes.

She swings the car into a vacant space, turns off the engine and closes her eyes. So now it begins. All the build-up, all the expectation and this is where it starts, in a grey car park in Earl's Court. She picks up her phone and smiles. She is ready now, ready to hear Paula's voice, to take her place at her lover's side. The solitude is over and she is happy that it is. She types in the security password that until a few weeks ago had been unnecessary and as she presses the call button, she feels a little stirring deep in the pit of her stomach. Paula is there in the hotel room; she imagines her lying naked on the bed, her black, bobbed hair framing her green pixie eyes, half-closed with desire; her beautiful lithe body stretched out, waiting for Stella to come and take her. It has been weeks since they last made love and now Stella feels that absence and wants to make up for it, she wants to drink in every last drop of Paula, to love her until they are both spent.

She holds the phone to her ear and after a couple of rings a terse voice answers: 'Stella, where the hell are you? I've been calling and calling.'

'Oh, hello to you as well.' Stella's erotic thoughts dissolve into the chill evening air as real life returns with a thud.

'Don't be sarcastic, Stella,' says Paula. 'I was worried sick. I thought you'd changed your mind or worse, had an accident. Really, it doesn't take much to send me a quick text to say you're okay . . .'

Stella holds the phone away from her. Paula always gets shrill when she is agitated. When the voice falls silent, Stella puts the phone back to her ear. 'Are you finished? Because I'm sitting in a damp car, after driving for two-and-a-half hours in pelting rain and if it's all right with you I would like to come and join you, have a glass of wine and relax. This is supposed to be a break you know, Paula. We are allowed to enjoy ourselves once in a while.'

Paula sighs down the phone and it crackles like white noise into Stella's ear. It is the sigh Stella has become accustomed to, the one that says that Paula is disappointed but is swallowing her anger lest it causes an argument. There has been a lot of that lately; the two of them avoiding confrontations, sighing deeply and heading to their respective rooms at opposite ends of the house. 'Right,' says Paula. 'Well, I'm in the apartment – it's lovely by the way, good choice. I can't believe I've never been here before. The bed's a bit weird, it's on a kind of plinth, but it's a really big space and pretty too. They've put some lovely peach roses on the table and the fridge is full of goodies.'

Stella smiles. That sounds like the old Paula, all excited about food and flowers. Stella had booked the garret above The Troubadour – the little fifties coffee house on Old Brompton Road – a few months ago, when they got their appointment at the fertility clinic. It was one of her favourite places in London; a little piece of Parisian bohemian heaven tucked away in a quiet corner of Earl's Court and she had been so excited to bring Paula along to see it; to show her the pretty coloured glass bottles in the window that always made her think of an ancient, London apothecary

'I'm so glad you like it,' she says to Paula. 'I can't wait to see you. I'm just going to get a ticket for the car then I'll be with you. I love you.'

She goes to press the end call button on her phone, then hears Paula say something on the other end.

'What was that, angel?' she says softly.

'I said, don't forget the plants,' says Paula, the tenseness creeping back into her voice.

A damp feeling of anti-climax spreads across Stella's chest.

'No, I won't forget the plants,' she says, as she clicks the phone off and puts it into her bag.

Mark stands holding onto a metal rail as the packed Piccadilly line train hurtles towards Russell Square. He left King's Cross later than planned after eating a cheese-and-tomato baguette and a plate of spiced potato wedges under the great golf-ball dome of the newly refurbished station. He didn't recognise the place as he came through the ticket barriers and turned left, expecting to see the usual dirt-encrusted gloomy pubs and half-hearted burger bars. It was so slick and shiny, like some futuristic airport lounge, and, for a moment, Mark imagined he was heading off on holiday; that this trip was about plea-sure rather than anger and pain. As he headed towards the Underground, curiosity got the better of him and he decided to get something to eat. Hunger is bad for concentration and he wanted to have all his wits about him once he got to Soho.

The next station is Holborn. Change here for the Central line.

The voice fizzles through the carriage like static electricity. As the doors open and release a smattering of passengers, Mark spots a vacant seat towards the middle and lifting his rucksack off his back he flops down as the doors start to close. A rotten smell wafts under his nostrils and he looks around the carriage trying to locate the source of the stench. His eyes rest upon the woman sitting opposite him. She is in her late-fifties, dressed in batik print scarves and a long, brown woollen skirt. Her black hair is threaded with grey and she wears no make-up on her thin, sallow-cheeked face. She is reading a copy of the *Evening Standard* and on her knee rests a plastic tub containing a hard-boiled egg which she is taking bites out of in between reading. The egg smells putrid and stale, rather like the air in the carriage.

He stares at the woman. She looks like a teacher he once had at school – Mrs Rogers, that was her name, miserable old bitch – who took him for English and History and made his life a misery for five years because he didn't understand the meaning behind books like *Lord of the Flies*. She would make snipey comments as she handed his homework back to him: 'Well, Mark, what can I say? Your essays are a masterclass in completely missing the point!' Dried-up old cow. He wonders what became of her; she's probably sitting in some nursing home dribbling into her tea. He shudders. The thought of Mrs Rogers and the smell of the woman's egg makes him feel nauseous. He shakes his head and looks around the carriage. There is a young man standing by the door wearing low-slung skinny jeans and a skin-tight leather jacket, giving his arse a good old scratch as he scrolls through his phone with the other hand; in the seat next to him, an old man in a blazer and slacks is hacking up phlegm while opposite, the woman bites into her egg with a slapping, slurping noise. People really are repellent, thinks Mark. They are just a mass of stinking, putrid waste.

The next station is Piccadilly Circus. Change here for the Bakerloo line.

Mark stands up as the train slowly pulls into the station. As he waits by the door, his eyes meet those of the woman with the egg. He stares at her and suddenly he is back twenty years looking into the eyes of his nemesis. The woman in front of him is chewing the last mouthful of egg and she looks vulnerable, pathetic somehow, but her eyes bore into Mark as though she is reading his thoughts, as though she knows what he is going to do and is making her judgement. As the doors open with a screech, he looks again at her but she has returned to her newspaper. He steps down onto the platform and as he hoists his rucksack onto his back and picks up his black bag, the train starts to pull off. He looks up and sees the woman staring at him again; there is something about her expression that fills him with rage and he contorts his face and mouths the words 'fuck off' at her departing form. He tries to shake it off, the strange encounter, but her face is still in his head as he turns the corner and heads up the escalators and the noise and bustle of Piccadilly Circus.

The rain has stopped and the air smells of soil and grit as Stella turns the corner into Old Brompton Road. A small figure slowly walks towards her; its hand waving like a pearly white globe against the darkening sky.

Paula. She has changed out of the jeans and jumper she was wearing earlier and put on the pretty green silk tea dress that Stella bought her last Christmas.

A deep feeling of desire washes over Stella as she approaches. In the distance she can see the mottled lights of the Troubadour; can hear the clinking of glasses and the light chatter of people gathered outside for drinks.

She has missed this: the sounds of London in the early evening. It's like the first sip of wine; the prelude to something wonderful. Other cities, other towns, don't sound like this. In St Leonards, the genteel enclave of Exeter where Paula and Stella live, early evening is heralded with the clattering of shutters going down over shop windows, a collective sigh that the working day is done; in Vejer de la Frontera, the little white town in Southern Spain where Stella and Paula spent the first eighteen months of their relationship, early evening sounded like midday anywhere else: the shouts of street vendors and stall holders, children's laughter and the ring of the cash register in brightly lit shops; while in the small Yorkshire village where she had grown up, early evening was a pure white blanket of silence, broken intermittently by the swish of curtains being drawn, the growl of a wheelie bin being dragged down a driveway and the collective switching on of television sets.

She had forgotten this feeling; had, over time, attributed the buzz to Soho, but it is the same all over the city. London at this time of day truly is the best place on earth to be. She could have this again; just like that she could come back . . .

'Hello, you,' she says, dreamily, as Paula draws closer. 'You look beautiful.'

Paula smiles then gives a little shiver. 'Well, I thought I would make an effort just for you,' she giggles. 'Although I should have put my jacket on, it's getting quite cold now.'

Stella leans forward and kisses her on the mouth. Paula, as always, smells of orange blossom. It is a fragrance she concocted herself as a teenager and is now such a part of her that if one day she decided to wear another perfume something fundamental, something distinctly 'Paula' would be lost for ever.

'Have you got the plants?' Paula asks as she gently releases herself from the embrace.

'Oh, they'll be okay in the car for tonight, won't they?' says Stella, not wanting to walk all the way back to the car park now she is within spitting distance of a comfortable chair and a large glass of wine.

'No, they can't be left in the car,' says Paula. 'I won't rest tonight if they're not within sight. I did ask you to bring them. Do you know how much those plants are worth? If the car was stolen, I would be in deep trouble. Yasmine Bailey is expecting them tomorrow for her launch on Wednesday, plus she's already paid for them.'

Stella sighs. There is always something. 'Look,' she says, placing her hand on Paula's shoulder. 'I'll just put these bags into the room then I'll go and get the plants, okay?'

Paula looks pensive, like she is imagining all the potentially catastrophic things that could possibly happen to her plants: a drug-fuelled joy ride across Earls Court; a smash and grab in Mayfair.

'Give me the keys and I'll go and get them,' she says, holding out her hand.

'Oh, Paula, for goodness sake,' says Stella. 'I'm talking a matter of minutes. I wish you would relax. They'll be fine. It's a secure car park.'

'It would just put my mind at rest if I go and get them,' says Paula, softly. 'Then I can enjoy our evening. You go and freshen up, it's been a long drive. Go on and I'll follow you up.'

'Okay,' says Stella. 'If you're sure.' She retrieves the keys from her coat pocket and hands them to Paula. 'It's just round the corner, first left. The car's on the ground-floor level, right by the entrance.'

Paula takes the keys and nods. 'Oh, you'll need this as well.'

She opens her handbag and pulls out a large, Alice in Wonderland-style key with a big square wooden key ring attached.

'Wow,' says Stella, taking the key. 'It must be a big door.'

They both laugh, then Paula leans towards Stella and strokes her cheek. 'I can't wait to be with you these next few days,' she says, tenderly. 'It's been so long since we've had a proper break. I love you so much, you know that don't you?'

Stella nods her head and smiles.

'It feels good to be back,' she says, looking beyond Paula, into the darkening night sky.

Paula flinches; it's a miniscule gesture but Stella notices; it's Paula's worst fear: that London will reclaim Stella, will drag her so far back into its folds that Paula won't be able to hold on to her; that she will lose her control.

'Now go on and get the plants, you little worrit,' says Stella with a giggle. 'I'll see you in the bar.'

Stella stands and watches as Paula disappears into the darkness, then she turns and walks briskly towards the Troubadour.

6

How could I have been so stupid? thinks Kerstin, as she sits at her desk furiously speed typing data she knows so well she could recite it verbatim.

When she got back to the office after buying the purse, she had clicked open the document containing the Delta report and found that the whole section she had completed that morning was gone.

'I pressed "save", I know I did,' she had cried, as she desperately scrolled down the page. Cal had overheard and was there in seconds, standing by her elbow, offering help, pressing her keyboard. Please get off, she had willed him. By touching her computer, by tainting the space around her, he was just making things worse, much worse.

'Nah,' he had said, after five minutes of clicking various help settings on the computer. 'It's gone. You can't have saved it, you plonker. Still, you ran out of here in such a mad rush, I'm surprised you remembered your own head.' He had then offered to stay behind to help her, but that was the last thing she wanted and she had fobbed him off saying he would be a better help if he got started on the Gonshalff Report the next day, which would give her a head start. And now, at last, she is alone in the silent gloom of the office.

She presses 'save' after each paragraph just to be sure and after the fifteenth 'save', leans back in her chair, her eyes sore from staring at the screen. It is then that she notices the picture on the wall opposite.

Last week there had been a photograph in that space – a grainy print of a firework igniting; sparks of light flickering from its mouth. It was a menacing picture, not helped by the fact that the firework in extreme close-up rather resembled a gun. Now the picture has been removed and replaced with an Impressionist-style painting of a man sitting in a boat on a lake of lily pads.

Kerstin does not understand this sudden vogue for 'office art'; the idea that employers can somehow control the moods of their workers through the images they display on the walls. Sircher Capital signed up to the scheme at the beginning of the year and now each month a new piece of original artwork appears on the walls, seemingly by magic. The fact that a man called Colin Andrews from the Essex-based Art Works company comes to the office after hours and discreetly hangs a new piece is less intriguing than the thought of the pictures just appearing. But Kerstin finds the ever-changing view disconcerting and rather than speeding up her productivity it saps her, makes her feel tense and uncertain.

She looks at the picture; it is a pastiche, a badly executed piece of nothingness; ugly, like everything else in this place. The office, with its pine table and beige rugs is dry and anaemic; like a body drained of its blood. The flowers on the windowsill look artificial, even though they are delivered twice a week from a florist in Mayfair. Their colours – pale lemon and lilac – are insipid and drab and they melt into the beige walls and window blinds like spilt tea on a dirty carpet. The leaves are compressed against the clear glass vase, dead and motionless like they are stuck in formaldehyde. The air they breathe is static, the oxygen being sucked up into the lungs of the traders as they shout out the minute-by-minute fluctuations of the stock market. The flowers should not be here, she thinks. They should be in a beautiful garden with moist soil to drink and fresh air to keep them alive.

Kerstin stands up and walks over to the flowers. Instinctively she bends her head to smell them but there is nothing, no fragrant flower smell just a dusty half-scent like cardboard or used money. Maybe that is it, she thinks. Maybe that is what happens inside these four walls; all that is natural and alive becomes tainted with the very thing that is being cultivated in this hothouse; maybe the only thing that can survive here is money.

The apartment building in Cologne, where she grew up,

had been designed to bring in the light. She remembers an abundance of pale wood and glass, the scent of fresh flowers and plants, alive and green and thriving. At this thought, she steps away from the flowers and returns to her desk and the report accumulating on her computer screen.

Delta, a Cologne-based construction company with a €10 billion portfolio are slowly changing the landscape of Kerstin's home-city. Known for their elaborate high-rise constructions; concave behemoths of coloured glass where young, wealthy professionals can buy pod-sized one and two bed apartments for the same price as a detached house with land, the Delta brothers caused controversy a couple of years ago when one of their proposed developments, a helter-skelter shaped apartment block known as 'The Snake', had threatened to block out a substantial part of Cologne's most famous building, the historic cathedral whose mighty spires can be viewed from almost any point in the city. After huge opposition from various heritage bodies, the brothers had to modify their plans and the view of the great cathedral remained intact. Kerstin's mother, Eva, a leading art historian and the daughter of Klaus Engel one of the team of stonemasons and wood carvers who rebuilt the cathedral after the Second World War when the city had been reduced to a pile of rubble, had been one of the loudest detractors.

As a child, Kerstin had often visited the cathedral; its bulk gave her a great sense of reassurance, it was impossible to get lost in the city while that sleeping giant watched over you from every point. Her mother would take her to midnight mass on Christmas Eve and they would pray by the shrine of the Magi whose relics were housed in there. As they walked home through the icy streets, Kersten would listen to stories of her grandfather, Klaus; how one night while working alone in the crypt of the cathedral, he had been distracted by a faint knocking sound coming from the entrance, as though someone had entered the cathedral and closed the heavy wooden door behind them.

He had put down his tools and walked out onto the altar, shading his eyes with his hand to get a closer look. As he stood there, he felt an overwhelming sense of peace and warmth. Though it was the dead of night, a glorious light filled the room, seemed to stream through the stained-glass windows; while underneath his feet, a muffled noise rose slowly. It was unlike any sound he had heard before: sublime choral voices singing in Latin how death is not the end; how life endures in glorious colours beyond the final resting place. He had put his hand to his chest as he stood, cloaked in this sublime feeling of protection. Then, as suddenly as they had started, the voices stopped, the light dimmed and he felt something brush against his face, as delicate as a breath. In the darkness, he could just make out the figure of a woman walking down the aisle towards the door; the folds of her blue dress billowing slightly as if blown by a breeze. Then he heard the door close, as he had heard it open just moments before. And he had returned to the crypt, taken up his tools and worked until morning when the other stonemasons arrived. But he never told them of his experience; he kept it hidden in the depths of his heart until he lay dying, a happy, contented man of eighty-one, when he took his only daughter's hand and told her of the night he had been visited by an angel.

Her mother has always been a mystery to Kerstin; an artistic bohemian spirit who believes in horoscopes and muses and angels. Her relationship with Kerstin's father, a professor of Physics at the University of Cologne, had been brief and tempestuous. He was thirty years her senior and far too set in his ways to embrace the world of babies and nappies and nursery rhymes. But the relationship had created a scientifically-minded child who went to bed reading mathematics textbooks rather than stories; who abhorred the chaos of her mother's cluttered life; who preferred numbers to words; theories to intuition. But though Eva would never truly understand her, Kerstin's grandfather seemed to see something in his intense little grandchild. When she was a toddler she would sit for hours placing her building blocks into neat piles of even numbers. In the months before he died, her grandfather would watch her with a smile, then he would pat her head, turn to Eva and tell her that it was good that the child searched for order in this chaotic world; hadn't he done the same when he helped rebuild the cathedral; turned that pile of rubble into a place of worship once more?

Kerstin looks at her watch. It is almost 7:30 p.m. Just a couple more pages and she will have made up the ground she lost earlier. It will be her name on the top of the report, her writing, her insights. She has worked hard on this report, with more diligence than she would afford others. How could she not, with something as close to home as Delta? But where she should be feeling pangs of guilt – for her mother's tireless conservation efforts, the legacy of her grandfather – she feels strangely indifferent, as though this report is a piece of abstract art, a paper trail that will dissolve once it hits the air. They will be proud of me, she thinks, her parents, proud of their diligent daughter with her gift for moulding words and numbers into coherent statements of intent, calls to arms for wealthy investors with deep pockets. Yes, they will be proud, she concludes. Her mind is calm as she works; three months of research now ready to be reconciled into order and coherence. She will not let herself get distracted by dark thoughts because that will only lead to the counting, and for now the only numbers she needs are the ones on the screen in front of her. With her grandfather's words ringing in her ears, she returns to the report.

Seb stands in the empty restaurant looking at the picture that he has spent the last ten minutes hanging on the wall. He puts his head to one side and squints.

'Hmm, I'm still not sure,' he says to Yasmine, who is sitting at the table opposite, busily writing menu plans for Wednesday night.

She looks up from her work and sees the picture. It's a line drawing of a fig tree bursting with fruit; one of her favourites from the twenty pieces chosen as part of a community arts project run by Seb's gallery, Asphodel.

'I think it looks great,' she says, enthusiastically. Yet, she can tell just by looking at her husband's pensive expression that he will spend the next ten minutes or so moving the picture a millimetre this way, a millimetre the other way, before returning it to its original position. It's like he distrusts things falling into place too easily; he always has to look at something from all angles before making a decision.

As he adjusts the picture, she shakes her head and smiles then returns to her carefully crafted menu. At the top of the page she has written 'Iced Tea Shots' to be served on the roof garden and a little ripple of excitement flutters through her body as she remembers the smell of that incredible jasmine.

'I got a call from Paula Wilson this afternoon,' she says, not looking up from the page.

'Who's Paula Wilson?' asks Seb, as he takes the picture down from the wall for the third time.

'She's the herb supplier I told you about,' says Yasmine. 'The one I met at the Bath Food Festival. She grows these amazing jasmine plants – Andalucian jasmine. It has the most incredible scent. I brought loads back with me, you remember; I made that iced tea and you said it was the best iced tea you had tasted outside of Morocco.'

'Oh yeah,' says Seb, only half-listening. The drawing is starting to annoy him. It just doesn't look right. There is something twee about it, something banal and over-simplistic but Yasmine had insisted on it as soon as she saw it among the pile of entries that had poured into the gallery. She said it reminded her of the fig tree that had grown in her grandfather's back yard in Tangier; said it represented abundance, fertility and nourishment. So Seb has no choice now but to keep trying to find a spot for it.

'She's dropping off a potted pair tomorrow,' says Yasmine. She puts her pen down and sits watching Seb fumble about with the picture. 'I told her I was happy to pay for them to be delivered but she insisted, said she's going to be in London and would like to come and see the restaurant and meet us. That was nice wasn't it? I'll invite her to the launch if she's still here on Wednesday.'

'Hmm,' says Seb. He is standing back, looking at the picture, which he has hung back in its original place.

'Honestly, babe, it looks great there,' says Yasmine. 'You mustn't over-fuss. If you analyse something so intently it's bound to look wrong. That's what you're doing now. Trust me, it looks fine where it is.'

Seb shrugs his shoulders, walks over to where Yasmine is sitting and flops down into the chair opposite her.

'I know I over-complicate things, Yas, but I just want it all to look perfect.' He reaches across the table and strokes her cheek, 'I'm so proud of you,' he says, gently.

Yasmine smiles and holds his hand against her face. 'Say that again when Wednesday's over and nothing's gone wrong,' she says, kissing his hand. 'I just keep thinking there's some huge detail I've overlooked, something really obvious that I'll only remember at 6 p.m. on Wednesday night when it'll be too late. I'm having nightmares every night about it – last night I dreamed the kitchen blew up, the night before that I dreamed that we had no oven . . .'

'That's natural,' says Seb. 'This is a huge undertaking; it was the same with me when I set up the gallery. Do you remember, I used to get up at four every morning to write lists?'

Yasmine nods her head and smiles. 'Yeah, and I was no help: six-months pregnant and full of hormonal rage.'

Seb laughs. 'We got through that though, didn't we? And we'll get through this. Everything is in order, and it's a trial run really. But even so, we've got fantastic staff, a fantastic menu, an amazing location and the world's best chef.'

Yasmine rolls her eyes at him teasingly. 'Yeah, who needs Ferin Adrià,' she laughs, leaning back in her seat.

It is the most relaxed she has looked for weeks and Seb thinks how he would like to press the pause button just for a moment, stop the momentum, the juggernaut that is this project, and stop and breathe, just the two of them.

'. . . and here's Henry with the guest list,' says Yasmine, with more than a hint of cynicism in her voice.

'Guest list? I don't know about any guest list!'

They look up and see Henry Walker, the supposedly 'silent' partner of the restaurant venture, walking towards them with his usual air of largeness. Despite being short and rather portly, his voice, his manner, his whole demeanour makes him seem much bigger. As he approaches the table like a giant, a mythical warrior king come to pay a visit to his minions, he slaps his large hand onto Yasmine's shoulder and laughs.

'I'm just kidding you, darling. Everything's under control.' He wedges himself into the chair next to Seb. 'Charles Campion's coming, *Time Out*, *Observer Food Monthly* – I think they're sending Jay Rayner, I like him, he's a good bloke – oh and bloody *Adrian Gill*. What else? Oh yeah we've got a great band – Becky's new bloke found them believe it or not – real, authentic North African vibe, I've got the CD back at the office, I'll bring it tomorrow and let you hear it, they've just signed to Universal. Oh, and Lauren, our new PR, has compiled the very best VIP list: the elite of London will be ripping open their invitations as we speak.' He rubs his hands together and grins broadly at Yasmine, waiting on her response.

'Lauren?' she says, her eyes serious, all of a sudden. 'Lauren, from Honey Vision? Oh God, Henry, she'll have invited all her mates and I told you I don't want any glamour models or reality TV stars. They just turn up to get their photo in the paper. I want foodies, people who are going to really get what we're doing here.'

'Don't worry, darling,' says Henry, his smile fading. 'I gave Lauren your list of people and those invites have been sent out too. There's no harm in a few high-profile celebs, the more publicity we can get the better . . .'

Seb has drifted away from the conversation. He is looking round at the deep crimson walls, the gold lanterns and thick church candles. Against this background, the drawing just looks odd, out of place; it is bothering him but he doesn't raise it with Yasmine. He will just have to concede on this one.

Otherwise the room is really shaping up: clusters of tables of all shapes and sizes are dotted about; the long ones line both sides of the room and are accompanied by church pews scattered with sumptuous gold, red and green velvet cushions. The smaller tables are situated about the middle of the room and all are draped in embroidered tablecloths in shades of green, turquoise and red. Yasmine had been adamant that the restaurant would reflect her memories of visiting her grandparent's house in Tangier: there had to be lots of colour, lots of textures and a feeling of informality with just a hint of decadence; lovers would want to come here for a first date amid the soft candlelight but families would feel just as comfortable coming to share a platter of mezze at lunchtime. Yasmine had made several trips to Tangier over the last few months coming back with bags full of fabrics and pots and dishes. Cosima has helped too: giving up her afternoons to sit with Yasmine and put little rose plants into the tiny terracotta pots that will serve as the table centrepieces.

'It looks wonderful,' says Seb, turning back to Yasmine and Henry. 'It really does.'

Henry's phone beeps and he sits up straight and grins. 'That'll be Poppy,' he says, his eyes twinkling.

'Poppy?' says Yasmine. 'What happened to Lydia?'

'Didn't work out,' says Henry, elusively, as he reads the message on his phone. 'Ah, super, she's here, she's outside.' He stands up and straightens his jacket. 'We're having supper at Scotts; I said I'd be here. She's dying to meet you both. Half a sec . . .' He rushes towards the door.

'Great,' mutters Yasmine, rolling her eyes. Seb shrugs. He knows Henry all too well. The idea of a long-term relationship is anathema to him; his attention span is short and he has no patience with needy women or women who want to commit. Still, his girlfriends all come out of the same mould: Skinny, posh and not too bright.

'Oh, wow, this place looks awesome!'

They look up to see a tall, red-haired woman dressed in a black leather pencil skirt and low-cut purple silk blouse. She is standing underneath the arched ceiling near the front desk, a large black handbag hanging from her wrist.

Yasmine gets up from her seat wearily and brushes a hand through her short, dark hair. Seb looks up at her as she stands. She is exquisite. He knows she's tired, he knows that she feels rather self-conscious in her jeans, T-shirt and trainers next to another one of Henry's leggy models, but to Seb she is timeless; her beauty exists outside of fashion and faddishness. He would like to draw her tonight, in this light, with her hair all messy and tousled, then he would like to make love to her slowly and deeply, do all the things that she loves . . . He stops himself, feeling the blood rush to his groin. The last thing he needs is to greet this Poppy woman with a hard on.

'Guys,' says Henry, guiding the woman towards the table with his hand placed on the small of her back, 'this is Poppy Lawton-Fields.'

'It's so good to meet you,' says Poppy. Her smile is wide and fixed. She reminds Seb of a gelding and she is very young, twenty-five at the most. Next to her, Henry suddenly looks old, frumpy even, in his navy blazer and crisp blue jeans.

'So you're off to Scotts?' says Yasmine, cutting into the rather awkward silence that is hanging heavily in the air. 'Make sure you try the oysters, they're amazing.'

'Oooh, I love oysters,' says Poppy. She looks at Henry rather pleadingly, like a child waiting to be taken out for a treat. 'Although, I'd better not have too many, I've put on so much weight lately.' She pats her stomach and giggles.

'You're joking, Pops,' says Henry hugging her towards him. 'I've seen more fat on a chip, and anyway oysters are hardly calorific. I'm going to order you a nice, juicy steak, fatten you up a bit.'

'Oh, you are so naughty,' shrieks Poppy. She taps a long, pale pink fingernail on the edge of Henry's nose in admonishment.

Seb tries not to meet Yasmine's eye. If he does, they will both lose it; best to save the laughs for later.

'Would it be okay to have a look at the garden?' asks Poppy, her eyes wide and excited. 'Henry said it's utterly divine.'

'Of course,' says Yasmine, nudging Seb. 'Follow me.'

They walk in a procession up the wooden stairs; past the first floor dining room and up another flight of steps to the second floor bar; a mirror-image of the other two floors, but with more of an after-hours club vibe; the kind of space where people drop in for a quick drink, then get so relaxed they end up staying for dinner. Tucked away in the far corner is a discreet set of French windows, almost obscured by a thin strip of cream lace. Yasmine tries the handle – the doors are unlocked – and they step out into Arcadia.

Poppy gasps. 'Oh, my God, this is amazing.'

Yasmine's touch is everywhere, thinks Seb, as he follows them out. The lanterns, the colours – her favourite combination of red and gold – the hexagonal pattern on the tables, the green glass bottles that, come Wednesday evening, will be filled with sweet peas and eucalyptus; it is Yasmine's meticulous re-creation of the hidden corner, the magical garden they encountered on their honeymoon in Marrakesh. They had stumbled on it, like all life-changing moments, by taking a wrong turn, both tired and short-tempered in the heat of the noon-day sun. Yasmine had walked ahead of him and he heard her gasp as she turned the corner. 'Come on Seb, you have to see this.' They spent the rest of the afternoon sitting on deep green velvet cushions sipping mint tea in the shade of a fig tree, while flecks of sunlight trickled through tiny holes in the hand-shaped leaves and wondered how such a sumptuous, bountiful place could exist just moments away from the crowded dusty heart of the marketplace. It was here that the seed was planted in Yasmine's mind; Seb had watched her as they sat there, her eyes bright with excitement and longing, drinking in every last detail of the enchanted world that had opened up in front of them. When they returned to their hotel that evening, she had laid out her plans for a restaurant cast in the mould of the garden; it might take years, she said, but she would recreate that corner one day, and allow others to feel the way she and Seb had felt for those idle few hours.

The four of them stand motionless looking out over the railings at the darkening red sky.

'My God, you can see the whole of London from here,' shrieks Poppy, as she leans over the railing. 'Who needs Primrose Hill?'

'Careful, Pops,' says Henry, holding her arm and guiding her gently away from the edge. 'It's a long way down if you lose your balance.'

Seb shudders. The air has grown colder and the skin on his bare arms prickles in the breeze.

'Come on then,' says Henry, looking at his watch. 'I've got the table booked for 8:30. We might just have time for a cheeky cocktail first.'

'Sounds good,' says Poppy, linking her arm into his. 'Guys, it was so nice to meet you both,' she says, turning to Yasmine and Seb. 'I am ridiculously excited about the launch, it's going to be awesome. I've told all my girlfriends about it. We have *so* needed a new supper venue in town. Oh, I meant to tell you Henry, my oldest, oldest friend Ollie just started working for Decadence. He's going to mention you to Freddie Montague.' As she says this name, her eyes widen and she looks at each of them in turn, waiting for a response.

Henry chuckles. 'We've already got Decadence on board, darling. Seb and I were at school with Freddie; I was best man at his wedding.'

'Wow,' says Poppy, looking up at Henry in awe. She turns to Yasmine and places her hand firmly on her arm as if about to impart the secrets of the universe. 'That is amazing; you've got the elite of the elite of concierge services recommending you. That's your clientele sorted.' She clicks her fingers, a little too close to Yasmine's face for comfort.

Yasmine smiles but Seb can tell that her teeth are well and truly gritted.

'Well it was good to meet you, Poppy,' she says, ushering

Seb inside. Poppy and Henry follow them back down the stairs.

As they open the front door, the noise of Soho hits them like a sharp gust of wind. Seb stands behind Yasmine, his hands resting on her shoulders, as they wave goodbye to the departing figures – short, stocky Henry and his tall, leggy date – disappearing up the street. The rain has left little silky strands of water on the road and the lights of The Dog and Duck next door are reflected in them like opalescent pools. The air is still and warm.

'The calm before the storm,' says Yasmine, as they stand on the threshold looking out onto the busy street. Soho is open for business: the restaurants are full, people are spilling out onto the street over at The Carlyle on Bateman Street, huddling together as they smoke cigarettes. It's funny how the landscape stays the same while the clientele evolve, thinks Seb; those smokers over there look so young; or is it just him growing old? Yet some things don't change and though restaurants can open and close within the space of a few months, a few endure, the chosen ones that survive through the decades, as though in possession of some sort of magic, some Soho gold dust that protects them from the fluctuations of the city. Maybe, just maybe, The Rose Garden can be one of those places.

They are about to go back inside when a young couple cross the street and come towards them. They stand with their arms linked, looking in at the darkened windows. Seb reckons they are on their second, maybe third date; they still have that look of wonder in their eyes, a certain disbelief at being together. It's the period in a relationship before meals on the sofa, before fighting over dirty socks left on the bedroom floor and crying silent tears as you curl up to sleep back to back. These are the days of longing looks over candlelit tables; of being curious about every tiny detail of the other person's story; this is sex with the lights on and talking until dawn.

'Are you open?' asks the young man, tentatively.

'Not yet, but we have our press launch on Wednesday night,' says Yasmine, smiling. 'Why don't you both come along? There'll be champagne and delicious mezze, live music. It's going to be a great night.' She rifles in her pocket and pulls out a creased invitation.

Seb looks at his wife as she hands it to the young man. She looks radiant, her eyes sparkling with excitement. If he were religious he would say a silent prayer right now, ask God to make this restaurant a success. Not for the money or the acclaim but just so that Yasmine will always be as happy as she is now.

'Sounds good,' says the young man. He shows the invitation to his companion and she nods enthusiastically.

'Excellent,' he says, his voice firmer than before, perhaps attempting to sound more mature, more controlled. 'We'll come along.'

They say goodbye and Yasmine heads back inside. As Seb closes the door he sees the young couple walk across the road, holding hands. As they reach the other side they stop and share a long, lingering kiss. Something inside Seb chills; it's like he is looking at two ghosts; holograms from his past, from a time and an age he will never know again. 'Freedom,' a voice inside his head whispers and then again: 'freedom.' He feels a warm pair of hands slide around his waist and he turns to see Yasmine. She has her coat on and her large satchel is strapped across her front. He smiles. She's still the same person he met seven years ago; life has weathered them, certainly, but it's made them stronger. He still has his freedom; it's just a different kind.

'Come on then,' he says, taking her hand in his. 'Let's go and find Cosima.'

Yasmine locks up and they walk hand in hand down Frith Street. A beautiful, straw-coloured moon lights their way and bathes the street in its glow. As they walk, Seb shivers. 'Are you okay?' asks Yasmine, rubbing his arm with her free hand. 'I'm fine,' he whispers, though his heart suddenly feels heavy.

Enough, he thinks, as he holds his wife closer and quickens his pace; there is no space for ghosts tonight; the dead must rest in peace now. Yet the cold stays with him as they cross Shaftesbury Avenue; it is there as they enter Leicester Square tube station and descend into the depths of the city, and as he sits on the half-empty Northern Line train, listening to Yasmine talk, he feels as though his body has turned to ice. He needs to be with his little girl; he needs to get home and tuck her safely into bed. He counts down the stations in a trance – Leicester Square, Charing Cross, Embankment – until the doors open and they tumble out into the gloom of Waterloo underground.

7

Mark shifts his weight from one foot to the other; he feels like he is drowning in a sea of lime green as he stands looking at the bowed ginger head of a young man named Stuart; a man who is here to help, to assist Mark in any request he may have; anything, it seems, but give him the key to his room.

He feels charged, dizzy with adrenalin after seeing them in the flesh. It was dark but their two bodies were illuminated in the light of the restaurant; they had glowed in the darkness like a burning pyre, unaware that he was watching them from the doorway of Hazlitt's Hotel. He will be closer on Wednesday, hidden away in a room overlooking the restaurant; he will be the invisible enemy, the unseen silent man, waiting for his moment, the glorious moment when he can charge across the neon-lit wasteland and claim his prize.

But that will all come later; the posh hotel, the suit, the charade. His budget will only stretch to one night in the hotel, so he has had to take what he can, and here it is, a backpacker's hostel tucked away in a little street behind Piccadilly. The fact that the door of the hostel almost blends into the brick work, reassures him, makes him think that here is true privacy, here is a place so discreet he can slip in and out over the next two days like a ghost; a non-person.

'I'm sorry but I've got you down here as a shared dorm,' says Stuart, looking up from his computer. He bites his bottom lip as he imparts the news, as though trying to distance himself from the mistake.

'Ah, bollocks to that,' says Mark, slapping his hands down onto the lime green plastic counter. 'Look, mate, when I booked online, I specifically requested a single room.'

Stuart, who suddenly looks ruffled, types something into the computer. 'I am very sorry, Mr Davis, I think there must have been some glitch there, but not to worry, we'll see what we've got.' He sucks his lips together as he scrutinises the information on the screen. 'We're in luck. There's a single room free on the first floor, but I'm afraid it's a little bit more expensive than the shared one you booked.'

'How much more expensive?' asks Mark, preparing for the worst.

'An extra ten pounds, I'm afraid, says Stuart.

Mark is getting weary of Stuart's condescending tone and right now he would pay a thousand pounds if he had to, just to be able to check into his room. He takes his wallet out of his pocket, slides a ten pound note out and hands it to Stuart.

'Here's ten pounds. Now can you check me in?'

'Into the single room?' asks Stuart, taking the money.

'Yes,' sighs Mark. 'Into the single room.'

Stuart types something into his computer while Mark stands clutching his bags close to his side. Without looking up, Stuart informs him that there are sheets, pillows and a quilt in the room but towels are extra.

'How much extra?' asks Mark, digging out his wallet again.

'Twelve pounds,' trills Stuart. 'For a hand towel and bath sheet.'

'Twelve quid for a couple of towels,' says Mark. 'It never said that on the website when I . . . oh never mind, here.' He pushes another ten pound note and a couple of coins across the counter.'

'You can collect them from the laundry room on the lower ground floor,' says Stuart, ringing the money into his cash register. 'We have free WiFi in the building as well as computers in the refectory on the first floor. You can also purchase a wide range of tea, coffee, confectionary and snacks from the vending machines there.'

Mark nods his head. He has no intention of stepping foot in the refectory; all he wants is for Stuart to hand over the entry card which he is holding tantalisingly aloft in his hand.

'We have a travel service on site, based on the second floor. If you want to book the next stage of your trip or need any travel advice, that's the place to go.' He thrusts a pile of leaflets across the counter, advertising working holidays in Brazil and gap-year trips to New Zealand with bunches of tanned twenty-somethings clad in shorts and vests grinning out. Mark pushes them back towards Stuart.

'If it's clubbing you're after, then we can help,' says Stuart, his voice brightly persistent. 'We arrange nightly trips to some of the best clubs in Central London. Everyone gathers in the refectory at nine and then . . .'

'No thanks, mate,' says Mark, his voice coming out louder than he intended. 'I just want a room. No travel plans, no clubbing, just a room.'

Mark had not gone to university but he imagines that this hell must be pretty close to what it is must be like. All this smiling and hugging; having to pretend you're happy and having an amazing time, all the time; refectories and communal living; dormitories and never ever being left alone . . .

Mark coughs. The reception area is small and compact and he can feel his lungs begin to tighten. He reaches into his pocket and takes out his asthma inhaler. While Stuart looks on with a wide-eyed expression of concern, he sucks a deep breathful into his lungs.

'Pharmacies,' says Stuart, with a tinge of glee in his voice. The man seems to get high on offering advice.

'If you need a pharmacy during the course of your stay, we have one of the biggest right on our doorstep: Boots on Piccadilly. You'll find a wide range of medicines, first aid . . .'

'I think I just need to have a lie down if that's okay mate,' interrupts Mark, his voice thin and raspy. 'It's been a long journey, yeah.'

'Sure,' says Stuart, nodding. He hands Mark the entry card. 'It's room 42, on the first floor. If you need anything there is a fully staffed reception desk down here, twenty-four hours a day. There's also a security button in your room, next to the door, above the light switch; if you have an emergency, or fall ill during your stay and you can't leave the room, then press the button and someone will come and help you.'

Mark nods and takes the card from Stuart's outstretched hand.

'Cheers, mate,' he says as he picks up his bags and goes to head for the stairs.

'Oh, and don't forget to collect your towels from the laundry on the lower ground floor,' calls Stuart. 'You'll need this.' He holds a pink card in his hand. 'It's your receipt, to show that you've paid for them.'

'Thanks,' says Mark, taking it, 'but I think I'll go and put my bags down first.' He stuffs the receipt into his pocket.

'It's up to you,' says Stuart. 'Enjoy your stay and if there's anything . . .'

He is interrupted by a group of young Japanese backpackers approaching the desk.

'Konbanwa!' he shrieks, his eyes brightening.

The group look far more likely to be interested in the travel centre, the refectory and clubbing, thinks Mark. As he closes the door of the stairwell behind him, he hears Stuart commence his spiel: 'Welcome to the hostel. My name is Stuart and I'm on hand to help you with any enquiries you may have over the course of your stay . . .'

His voice disappears into the green walls as Mark begins to climb the stairs. His lungs feel heavy as he goes; each step feels like ten. The air smells of stale laundry and tomato soup; it's a familiar smell, though Mark can't quite place it. School maybe, or the hospital ward where his father died? The first floor is signalled by a large number 1 painted in white at the top of the stairs. Mark opens the glass door on the landing and steps out into a long, narrow corridor.

The walls here are painted a bluish white. It's just like the hospital, he thinks; the long, seemingly never-ending corridor that smelled of bleach and tinned puddings and death. The floor is covered in thin maroon coloured carpet and Mark can feel his tired feet clod heavily on it as he walks along trying to find room 42.

Posters line the walls: most of them adverts for gap-year travels, larger versions of the leaflets Stuart had tried to off-load onto him earlier; others are the usual university bedroom fodder that students from Birmingham to Beijing will be familiar with: Bob Marley smoking a giant spliff; Audrey Hepburn gazing into the window of Tiffany's; Kurt Cobain smashing a guitar; all interspersed with those hackneyed quotes that nobody over the age of twenty-five ever uses: 'Dance like no one is watching . . .', 'Life is not measured by the number of breaths we take but the moments that take our breath away. . .', 'I hope I die before I get old. . .'.

Mark shakes his head as he walks through the blurry tunnel of messaging. 'Load of bollocks.'

His head is throbbing but he is getting closer. 34, 36, 38, 40. Number 42 at last, and as he puts the card into the slot, he imagines himself lying down on a large, warm bed, dissolving into nothingness. After three attempts the door finally opens with a click and he walks into the room that will be his home for the next two days.

It is grim. The garish colours of downstairs are not in evidence here. The room is white and bare but for a flimsy camp bed wedged against the far wall. There is a waste-paper basket by the door and a clothes rail opposite the bed. The small window is made of frosted glass and is framed by a pair of lank brown curtains that look like they have been cobbled together from potato sacks. A solitary, un-shaded light bulb hangs from the ceiling, casting a sickly green glow onto the room.

'Fuck it,' Mark sighs. He is not here to have a holiday and the grimness of the room is rather appropriate; it will remind him why he is here; remind him of Zoe's final hours. He needs to have that fresh in his mind if he is to stay strong; stay focused.

He closes the door, takes his trainers off and puts the two bags down onto the floor. Then he flops onto the bed and lies looking at the ceiling. The bedsprings dig into his back, but that is good, he thinks, the discomfort will keep him alert. Despite the bed, he feels his eyelids grow heavy but before sleep can claim him, he reaches onto the floor and pulls the black bag onto the bed. He lies down, curled around the bag, holding it and its secret close to his body as he falls into a heavy sleep.

'God, I love this place,' says Stella as she settles into her seat and looks around at the warm cranberry walls and black wooden beams of the Troubadour. 'It's wonderful to be back, it really is. It must be nine or ten years ago that I sang here. You know Bob Dylan's played here, in the club downstairs, and Joni Mitchell and Jimi Hendrix.'

Paula's eyes look glazed as she sits reading the menu.

'Sorry,' says Stella. 'I guess you've heard all this before.'

'You've mentioned it a few times, yes,' replies Paula, not looking up from the menu.

Stella sighs. They have reached that point; the place where all couples get to eventually; when you know everything there is to know about the other person. There are no new stories to tell because they have all been told.

As they sit in silence, both of them pretending to be engrossed in the menu, a young man approaches the table; a notebook poised in his hand.

'Are you ready to order, ladies?'

'Yes, I think we are,' says Paula, nodding at Stella in confirmation. 'May I have the pan-fried haddock with a side order of new potatoes, please?'

The young man jots it down then turns to Stella.

'And for you?'

'I'll have the Caesar Salad, please,' says Stella, in a quiet voice.

Paula raises her eyebrow. 'A salad? Is that all you're having? You should have something a bit more substantial after that long drive.'

Stella winces as she picks up the wine list from the wooden rack in front of her. 'A salad will be fine,' she mutters.

'Drinks?' says the young man, a hint of impatience in his voice. The restaurant is filling up quite rapidly.

'May I have a sparkling mineral water, please,' says Paula, handing the menu back.

'Sure,' he says, taking the menu and slotting it under his arm.

'Hmm,' says Stella, scrolling her finger down the wine list. 'I will have a large glass of Sauvignon Blanc, please.'

The young man nods his head, scribbles the order onto his notepad then with a flourish, whisks Stella's menu from her outstretched hand.

'Thanks ladies,' he says. 'I'll be back in a sec with your drinks.'

Stella looks over the table at Paula. She is gazing around the room; her eyes look tired.

'Are you okay?' asks Stella, taking her hand.

'I'm absolutely fine,' says Paula, sharply. 'It's you I'm worried about. You should have more than just a salad.'

'Oh, Paula, please,' says Stella, removing her hand. 'Can we just have a nice evening, can we just relax? I wish you wouldn't do this.'

'Do what?' asks Paula.

'Tell me what I should and shouldn't eat, especially in front of people; like just then with that guy, you made me look like a silly child.'

'I worry, that's all,' says Paula, her voice softening. 'When you're tense, you don't eat properly. I know what you're like. You forget, I was with you throughout your recovery process, I know the warning signs.'

'No, I don't forget,' snaps Stella. 'How can I when you remind me all the time? Yes, I had an eating disorder but I am fine now, you know I'm fine. How do you think I am ever going to be able to move on if you constantly bring it up? It's almost as if you want me to be ill.'

Paula shakes her head. 'Oh, don't be silly, darling. I love you and I just don't want you getting stressed. It's a big thing we're doing, a massive undertaking. I mean, my God, we're going to create a child. But we're in this together, you know that don't you?'

'One sparkling water.'

The light, breezy voice of the waiter drifts across the table like a life-raft sent across the ocean to rescue the floundering conversation.

He places the glass and a bottle of water in front of Paula. Then he lifts a large glass of wine off the tray and places it next to Stella. 'And one Sauvignon Blanc.'

'Thank you,' they both reply in unison.

'No worries,' chirps the waiter as he disappears into the darkness of the restaurant.

'Cheers,' says Stella, raising her glass. 'Here's to us.'

'And the baby,' says Paula.

'Yes,' says Stella, as their glasses clink together and she tries not to meet Paula's eyes. 'And the baby.'

8

Kerstin pauses at the edge of the pavement and pulls the keys to her flat out of her coat pocket – another of her rituals. She must hold them for the duration of this, the last part of her journey home.

She turns left off the King's Road and onto Old Church Street clutching them tightly in her hands as she walks. She strides purposefully up the street, making sure not to step on any cracks or drain covers for if she does she will have to go back to the top of the street and start again. But she manages to avoid them and a feeling of deep calm flutters across her chest as she walks past the upmarket charity shop where millionaire Chelsea housewives deposit their cashmere sweaters and silk scarves, past The Pig's Ear pub where dressed-down bankers squish uncomfortably onto shabby-chic leather sofas and pretend to be lads. The road darkens as she walks across a narrow, dimly lit side street, ominously named Justice Walk, where the old courthouse that once held prisoners bound for the colonies and is now a multi-million pound super-pad, peeks nervously out of the shadows as though hiding its murky history in the half-light.

This little corner of Chelsea that weaves its way down to the Embankment where the statue of Sir Thomas More sits in contemplation outside the church that gave the street its name, has been home to Kerstin for three years now, yet still she feels like a stranger.

She stops outside a thin, rather bland modern building: the apartment block where she rents a tiny one bedroom flat on the top floor for more money per month than she would pay for a three bedroom house in Cologne. But it suits her to live here; it is private, quiet and clean and, most of the time, she can carry out her routines and rituals without disturbance.

She walks up the path tentatively, wondering whether the communal hallway will be empty. As she approaches the glass outer door with its two neat potted bay trees she sees the light is on in the hall and hopes that Clarissa, the elderly, upper-class lady who lives in the ground-floor flat, is not on another of her nightly rounds. An interruption from Clarissa can wipe a good thirty minutes from Kerstin's evening and set her and her rituals back hours.

Kerstin looks through the glass. Clarissa's door is shut; there is no one about. Kerstin smiles with relief but there is still a strip of hallway to pass before she can get to the stairs and freedom. She turns the key in the lock cautiously and pushes the door open, closing it behind her gently so it doesn't slam. Clarissa listens out for any comings and goings and at the slightest noise, she will materialise in the corridor asking questions; telling stories about her mother, Sybil, who was a suffragette with a beautiful soprano voice: 'She sang at Wigmore Hall in the twenties you know . . . she even made a record . . . and Dame Ethel Smyth said she had a voice like a nightingale.'; about her brother Lawrence who fled to LA to join a commune in 1972 and was never seen again: 'I think he may have been queer you know and didn't want to tell us but it wouldn't have bothered me a jot. Mummy had tons of female lovers, one did back then because Edwardian men were so damned uptight and prudish. They wouldn't know a female orgasm if it leaped up and bit them on the bottom . . .' The stories go on and on, seaguing into another and another like a vast map of interconnected tributaries, taking in cul-de-sacs and sweeping avenues, motorways and dead ends like an out-of-control car. Clarissa is Kerstin's daily challenge; the obstacle she must overcome as she leaves for work in the morning and returns at night; like the troll under the bridge but with a sunnier demeanour.

Kerstin tiptoes across the hall to the foot of the stairs. She can hear a faint noise coming from behind Clarissa's door: chamber music playing on a vinyl record then a high-pitched, mournful voice singing: 'If you were the only boy in the world and I was the only girl!' She's listening to her mother singing, thinks Kerstin. She pictures the old lady draped in fuchsia pink silk reclined on her antique chaise longue with a glass of scotch in her hand, thinking about suffragettes and missing brothers and the glory of the English upper-classes.

As Kerstin climbs the stairs, she feels the tension ease from her shoulders. She is always polite to Clarissa but she wishes she didn't have to deal with the constant threat of disturbance. Yet she pities the old lady; after all, there must be some reason why she grasps hold of people the way she does and off-loads her stories in an incessant stream of consciousness. She talks rapidly, without drawing breath, like she has just been rescued from solitary confinement and must tell her rescuer everything, all at once.

One evening, after a particularly trying day at work, Kerstin had returned home and started to scrub the flat from top to bottom, furiously trying to atone with bottles of bleach and wire wool for whatever mistake she had made that day. She scrubbed so hard, the skin on her hands started to crack and blisters formed on the tips of her fingers, but she didn't care, she had to keep going or everything would fall apart. She was kneeling in the middle of the floor, squirting Flash Multi-Surface Cleaner onto the tiles when there was a knock at the door and there stood Clarissa armed with a bottle of Tanqueray Gin and a thick, white book.

'Some photos of Mummy and her friends in the WSPU, thought you might like to see,' she trilled.

Kerstin had almost pushed the old lady out of the door, telling her she was very sorry but now wasn't a good time. Clarissa had looked at her quizzically, possibly noting Kerstin's red face and breathlessness; then she had smiled. 'Oh, you've got a gentleman caller,' she shrieked, clapping her hands together. 'Well done, darling. Oh, I do miss all that. I'm afraid my days of making love and dancing naked are over. All I have left are my memories.' She had tapped her forehead and winked at Kerstin as she turned to go. 'Tatty bye, dear,' she had trilled as she walked away. 'And don't forget to take precautions, there are so many nasty diseases nowadays.'

The phantom boyfriend had provided Kerstin with a good few months of excuses as to why she needed privacy. As she passed Clarissa in the hallway each morning, the old lady would smile knowingly at her and ask after her 'gentleman friend'. 'You shall have to come and have tea with me one Sunday afternoon,' she would say. But Kerstin always found an excuse: the boyfriend was away on a business trip; he worked weekends; he had been hospitalised with acute appendicitis. It certainly stopped Clarissa from making any more night time visits to the second floor, though sometimes Kerstin would hear faint footsteps on the landing outside the flat.

Then, six months ago Clarissa had fallen in the street on her way to the post office and broken her ankle. Now reliant on a walking stick, the stairs are strictly out of bounds though she still manages to wedge herself into the desperately narrow lift to go down to the communal laundry room in the base-ment. Kerstin wonders if Clarissa should be living on her own; surely she needs extra care now, a nursing home with plenty of people to tell her stories to. But no, Clarissa told her, she would leave Old Church Street in a box and not a moment before, so she remains in her flat ruling the ground floor like some elderly gate-keeper, resplendent in her silk headscarf and jewelled Moroccan Slippers.

Kerstin crosses the first-floor landing, past Flat 2, now empty after being bought a year ago by a Russian businessman for his socialite daughter who decided it was too small. Clarissa is furious that it hasn't been put up for sale yet but Kerstin likes the fact that the first floor is unoccupied – it makes her feel safe.

At last, she reaches the second floor. She is tired and hungry but she must get everything in order, check that everything is in its right place, before she can even think of preparing dinner. She closes her eyes and counts to seven before putting the key in the lock. Then, opening her eyes, she slowly unlocks the door, satisfied that the first of her many nightly rituals has been observed successfully.

The door opens into a small white living room and as Kerstin flicks a switch on the wall the grey marble surfaces of the thin strip of kitchen that runs along the right hand side of the room sparkle under the bright spotlights. The whole flat is illuminated by 100-watt bulbs. Kerstin cannot bear half-light, for she has learned that monstrous things hide in shadows ready to jump out and take her by surprise. She hangs her handbag on a silver hook on the back of the door then steps gingerly across the pale wood floor.

Now for the inspection.

She opens each of the kitchen cupboards in turn, counting then recounting the packets and tins that are lined up in neat rows like soldiers on a parade ground. There are exactly twenty tins in the cupboard; ten on the top shelf, ten on the bottom. Kerstin knows this because she never cooks; these tins are remnants from another time, a time when she would open a messy tin of tomatoes and throw them carelessly into a pan, and stir and splash juice on the hob before eating it sloppily out of a bowl, and leaving the dirty dishes until the next morning. Now the only foods she allows herself are clean ones; things that won't make a mess, won't upset the order of the kitchen: baked potatoes, steamed vegetables and ready-cooked chicken breasts, eaten with disposable plastic cutlery.

On she goes, opening the fridge then the oven and the grill. All clean, all immaculate and unchanged since this morning. She crosses the living room with its white two-seater sofa and pale wooden coffee table; nothing under the sofa cushions – good. Next she goes into the bathroom, checking the linen cupboard twice, behind the shower screen, even the toilet. Nothing.

As she stands at the door of her bedroom, she closes her eyes and again counts to seven, muttering to herself in German: *'ein, zwei, drei . . .'* She opens her eyes and steps into the room. The curtains are open and a beautiful moon pours its silver light onto the white bed. Kerstin flicks the light on and the moon is obliterated in the harsh glare. She darts across the room and draws the curtains before pulling back the bedclothes and checking under the bed. All is as it should be. Just the chest of drawers to go.

She approaches the white drawers reverentially, as though approaching an altar, which it is to some extent. Sitting atop the drawers is a small wooden sculpture of the Virgin Mary, given to Kerstin as a baby by her grandfather. A set of ruby-red rosary beads are draped around the sculpture's neck and after Kerstin has checked each drawer she stands and runs her fingers gently over the smooth, round beads, offering up a silent prayer of thanks that she has been spared anything horrible happening despite the two 'incidents'.

She goes over to the small white desk in front of the window and picks up a thin brown notebook. Opening it up, she reads back through the last few entries:

Friday 24 Aug: Statue turned the wrong way. Toilet seat up when I left it down. Discovered during check at 8 p.m.

Wednesday 22 Aug: Memory stick lost in office –sometime between 11 a.m. and 3 p.m.

Friday 17 Aug: Books on shelf in wrong order; specifically checked before leaving this morning.

Monday 13 Aug: Shampoo missing from bathroom cabinet. Discovered during check 8 p.m.

Ordinary misplaced objects; things that other people would never notice, but Kerstin notices and that is why she began to write them down, to reassure herself that she wasn't completely losing her mind. At first she thought it might be Clarissa, letting herself into the flat while Kerstin was at work and having a snoop, but with a broken ankle she hasn't been able to get up the stairs in months. And what kind of burglar would break in and rearrange books and shampoo? No, it's a test, Kerstin is convinced of this. She knows who is doing this; what is doing this, she should say, and why, and she must keep one step ahead of it at all costs.

She takes a pen and writes in today's entry, makes today's mishaps real.

Monday 27 Aug: Purse ripped. Discovered: 3:56 p.m. Report not saved. Discovered: 5:10 p.m.

She puts the notebook and pen back onto the desk, in the very centre, then walks across the bedroom and out into the living room. Two large pictures hang on opposite sides of the room, dominating the bare white space. One is a print of Whistler's 'Nocturne in Grey and Silver', a sixteenth birthday present from her mother. It reminds Kerstin of the walk across Cologne from the home she shared with her mother to her progressive school on the other side of the Hohenzollern Bridge. She likes bridges; she admires their symmetry, their practicality and endurance. In another life she would have liked to have been an engineer.

If the Whistler is a meditative print, a reminder of happy times, then the other picture is a warning of what might happen if Kerstin lets go, if she stops her checking and counting. She had seen the original painting of Bruegel's 'The Triumph of Death' in the Museo del Prado seven years ago. She had been in Madrid with her boyfriend Matthew. It was the beginning of their relationship, they were living together in a beautiful flat in Bloomsbury, she had just started working for Sircher Capital, Matthew was a hedge-fund manager at Goldman Sachs. Life was wonderful. Weekends were spent on mini-breaks to Venice, Paris and Madrid, or wandering around Borough Market eating and laughing, or curled up in bed, making love.

Yet though she had been happy that day in the gallery, Kerstin had been mesmerised by the painting and its chaos: black, burning skies, bodies scattered all around, armies of skeletons running rampage, cutting people down with scythes. She had been accustomed to all kinds of art growing up with an art-historian mother but none had moved her as much as this one. The painting stayed with her as they left the museum, as they strolled through the city to find a restaurant to eat in and as they curled up to sleep later that evening. It was like an icy chill, a glimpse into pure evil, the darkest heart of humanity.

A few months after that trip, she had woken up on a drizzly July morning and headed to King's Cross tube station to catch her usual Piccadilly line train to Green Park. She had arrived a few minutes after a quarter to nine just as a packed train was closing its doors and pulling out of the station. She had cursed to herself as she stood on the platform watching the train disappear into the tunnel; cursed the train for leaving without her; for making her late. And then the darkness came; pure black nothingness. Like the bomb in Cologne, death had come for her again and she had escaped it by seconds.

In the weeks that followed she spent every waking moment reading about 7/7 in newspapers, online forums, television documentaries; gobbling up every bit of information she could lay her hands on in an attempt to find a pattern, a reason out of the chaos of that morning. She wrote down the numbers of the carriages of the stricken tube train, the time the bomb exploded, the date. She asked her father to send her a copy of his PhD thesis in which he had analysed the number and frequency of bombs that were dropped on Cologne on one night in 1942, the infamous 1000 bomber raid by the Allies on the city during the Second World War. He had identified a pattern within the frequency, an average number that seemed to defy the random scatter-like release of bombs during a raid. They appeared to fall in clusters, away from the targeted areas, as though making the decisions themselves where to fall. He took this pattern and formulated it into a law that could be applied to other seemingly random events – avalanches, earthquakes, wars and uprisings.

His PhD had gathered dust in the library at the University of Cologne until a group of young physicists working in a Californian laboratory in the eighties published a thesis outlining the idea of Complexity Theory and Power Laws. Her father had been called upon to address illustrious scientific bodies around the world, taking his findings from the Cologne air raids and expanding on them, relating them to current research. Surely Kerstin could find a similar pattern behind the 2004 bombing and 7/7. But she was a statistician and a conservative one at that, she believed in order and predictability, numbers were the blanket she wrapped around herself, to shield her from the dangers all around her. She did not have her father's scientific mind or the boldness to strike out and question what she had been taught. Instead she began to use numbers in her day-to-day life to keep death at bay, as a way of outwitting it. She couldn't stop thinking of the intense heat, the dust, the fumes, the rats down in that tunnel; it was like 'The Triumph of Death' made real and when she saw a print of the Bruegel painting in a little shop on the Charing Cross Road, she knew she had to have it, to hang on her wall as a constant reminder of the day death almost claimed her.

As the years passed, Matthew grew more and more intolerant of Kerstin's obsessive behaviour – which also included a complete refusal to use the tube, the bus or fly in an aeroplane, citing the fact that the planes struck the twin towers in New York on her nineteenth birthday, how could all these cataclysmic events not be connected to her? – and in 2009, he had told her it was over and she had nodded her head. Inside she was screaming, begging him to stay but her compulsion for order was stronger than her need for Matthew. They had moved out of the Bloomsbury flat, and on a freezing February morning while her ex-lover boarded a plane taking him to a new life and a new job in the US, she had carried her few possessions up to the little, anonymous flat at the dark end of Old Church Street where she has stayed ever since, living a life as silent and spartan as a contemplative nun.

She turns on the gleaming, stainless steel oven and places a small potato into a glass dish. She knows she is trapped, a prisoner of London as well as her obsession. Refusing to use the tube or buses means she has a four-and-a-half mile round trip on foot each working day. She is constantly exhausted and it is beginning to show in her work. She is finding it more and more difficult to finish reports on time. Factoring in her daily rituals, work has become an inconvenient obstacle. Dominic Stratton has made his disappointment clear in recent weeks, which is why the Delta report is so important. She cannot afford to lose this job, and there are plenty around her desperate to take her place. Cal Simpson would eat off his own hand to do so. But she can do it, she will be able to get it delivered on time as long as everything remains just so, no ripped purses, no mess, no disorder. She puts the potato in the oven and sets the timer for thirty minutes. Just enough time to get some cleaning done.

Seb sits by the window looking out onto the shadowy mass of trees that constitute Battersea Park at night. Though the room is in darkness, his face is illuminated by the streetlight outside and the soft white glow of the moon which hangs above the park like a great twinkling eye.

He can hear Cosima snoring gently in her little bed on the other side of the room. He hears the muffled sound of the television in the living room along the corridor and Yasmine making tea in the kitchen, but the clanking of cups and the BBC news, normally a comforting sound at this time of night, makes him anxious. The feeling that had gripped him as they walked through Soho and made their way home has returned.

He hadn't felt it when they arrived at Maggie's to pick Cosima up, but then it is hard to feel anything but sunny in Maggie's eccentric world. Cosima had greeted them at the door with a little dance that she had picked up from a TV programme, then as they walked home along Battersea Bridge Road, she had talked non-stop about what she had eaten for dinner, about the photo album Maggie had shown her of Yasmine's father when he was a young boy in Tangier – 'he looked just like Mummy' – and the playdate she has tomorrow at Gracie Marshall's house in Wandsworth – 'and she's got guinea pigs . . . can we get a guinea pig, Daddy?'

By the time they got home, they were all exhausted and Cosima had gone straight to her bedroom and flopped onto the bed while Yasmine wriggled her into a clean pair of pyjamas. Seb had spent ten minutes in his study, answering emails then he had come and sat by Cosima's bed to read her a bedtime story. This was normally the highlight of his day, sitting making up stories with funny voices and elaborate characters while his little girl shrieked with laughter. Tonight though, he wasn't in the right frame of mind to make up a story so he had reached over to the little bookshelf by the bed and taken out a thin volume that Cosima had borrowed from the library. Underneath the protective plastic sleeve there was a picture of a little boy and a dinosaur and Seb had squirmed at the crudeness of the illustration as he often does with children's books. As a child he had loved the dark, squiggly drawings of Arthur Rackham, they seemed to have so much more magic and bite than the generic, flabby drawings in modern children's books.

He had started to read but his voice must have been as uninspired as the story because Cosima was sound asleep by page two. Seb had closed the book and placed a kiss on his little girl's forehead but as he tucked her in and switched off her bedside lamp – a paper lantern showing the map of the world – he was struck by an indescribable sense of doom and horror, a force drawing him back into the room.

One day she will grow up and I won't be able to protect her.

The words roll round his head as he sits in the chair, it's a comfortable chair and Cosima likes having it in her room because it is the chair Yasmine used to sit in to feed her when she was a baby.

He looks out onto the street; a young woman walks past carrying a pizza box and a bottle of wine. She looks tentative as she hurries along, casting furtive glances over her shoulder. It makes him think of that song by The Cure: the one where the woman is being followed down a dark street. As she disappears from view, he wills her to keep walking fast; to get home safely. An inky blue cloud moves across the moon and the park looks like a deep, black hole sucking all the light out of the street. Beyond the park flows the river; the dirty, brown serpent that has dragged so many souls into its depths. It's an uncompromising city, thinks Seb, a cruel, wretched place.

It had been a night very much like this one; warm and still, with a moon that was almost full. London had just won the bid to host the 2012 Olympics, not that he had cared back then. He had drunk himself silly in a bar and ended up sitting on a bench in Soho Square Gardens where he had amused himself with apparitions and voices. He was convinced that his dead girlfriend had come back, he could hear her voice, feel her breath on his face as he sat there alone on the bench, falling into a drunken stupor. Then he had woken up to see another girl standing above him: Zoe. The girl from the office where he was working at the time – a glamour model agency of all things, dreamed up by Henry in his quest for world domination.

She had wanted to be a model; had arranged an appointment with Becky Woods, the chief model booker but Becky had forgotten and left Zoe sitting in the waiting room all day. And after such a crap day and the horrendous evening she went on to have – it all came out in court, how Zoe's landlady had set her up, tricked her into going to a party full of crack-heads and prostitutes and Zoe had fled with the landlady's ill-gotten cash – after all that, she still took it upon herself to see if Seb was okay when she saw him flat out on the bench. She thought he had collapsed so she pulled herself over the railings of the little garden square just to check, to make sure he was safe.

Seb shivers, though the room is not cold. He looks over at Cosima. Her chest rises and falls peacefully. Life, he whispers. This is all it comes down to: breathing in, breathing out, feeling safe . . .

He had not returned Zoe's concern. After unloading his tales of woe onto her as she sat beside him on a freezing bench for almost three hours he had left her standing alone in the street. What had she said again? 'I'll be fine. I'll go and find a McDonalds to sit in.' He had been so impatient to get back to the office to finish his painting of Sophie that he had effectively sent her off to meet her murderer. What was he thinking letting her go off into the night like that? She had been due to catch a train back home to Middlesbrough the next morning. He should have told her to get in a taxi to King's Cross where it would be light and full of people; he should have waited with her while they hailed one. She wasn't streetwise despite her bravado, she was like a lost child wandering away from her parent.

In court he had tried to keep it together. He had been called as a witness, the last person to talk to her. It all sounded so dodgy, their evening together – a drunk man sitting with a young woman in a locked deserted square for three hours in the middle of the night. She was young and attractive, she had been wearing a skimpy dress, surely something must have happened? He told them how he had seen her as he was leaving the office that night; she had looked like a little girl playing dress ups in her high heels and short dress. He had told her that Becky had gone, told her to try again tomorrow but she had burst into tears and handed him a set of photographs. 'Can you give these to Becky,' she had pleaded and because he had been in a rush to get to the pub, he had relented but he had put the photos in his bag as Becky's office was closed. He could feel the eyes of the jury bore into him, though he was not the defendant; somehow his cross examination made the whole evening sound seedy, as though he were in the same league as the sleazy landlady and the crack-head who had paid for Zoe to come to the party then murdered her. Despite his sharp Paul Smith suit and his confident public school-honed voice, he had felt vulnerable, a fraud.

As he had walked to the witness stand he had seen Zoe's

mother. She looked like a tiny bird, a lost, half-person, floating between worlds. Her face was grey and creased with deep lines, the result of day after day of incessant weeping. She held a set of rosary beads in her hands and when the details of her daughter's death were read out to the court along with the grisly post mortem photographs, she had wrapped the beads around her fingers so tightly it looked like they might snap.

The details of Zoe's murder were horrific. She had been stabbed fifteen times in the chest, puncturing her lung and sending her into cardiac arrest. After watching her slowly bleed to death, Martin Harris had taken her lifeless body and raped her before discarding her underneath a pile of bin bags at the back of Hanway Street.

When the Guilty verdict was returned, Seb had looked over at Zoe's mother. Her head was bowed and she seemed to be praying, her lips moving noiselessly as she stared at the floor. It was then that Seb caught the eye of the man sitting next to her, a thick-set, tough-looking man in his late twenties – Zoe's brother, Mark. His eyes were dry and he stared at Seb with such hatred, such menace that Seb had quickly looked away, but he could feel the cold, blue eyes upon him as he stood up and crossed the court room to the exit, as he opened the door and emerged into the stark, strip-lit corridor. When he finally got outside, into the noisy fug of Ludgate Hill, he had taken a deep breath and tried to rid himself of the horror of what he had just heard; the image in his head of Zoe bleeding to death while that psycho brutalised her, and the look in her brother's eyes. In those few moments when he had fallen under Mark's gaze it felt like he had been ripped open and examined; it felt like all his faults, all his weaknesses had been exposed, like it was him and not Martin Harris who had murdered Zoe.

'Are you okay?'

He jumps at the sound of Yasmine's voice in the dark, silent room. She is standing behind him. He turns and smiles at her comforting form. She is dressed for bed in a pair of his old stripy pyjamas and a grey ribbed vest. Her face looks tired and she suppresses a yawn as she stands there with her arms folded across her chest. He pulls her towards him and rests his head against her stomach. He wants to lose himself in the softness of her skin, burrow deep down into her warm body, breathe in all her strength, all her goodness.

'I'm fine,' he says, lifting his head. 'I was just thinking.'

Yasmine looks at him as though she doesn't fully believe him yet is too tired to dig deeper. She pulls the curtains and everything collapses into darkness. The room looks like a deserted theatre stage, the colourful, happy pink-and-purple decor dissolves leaving just a set of props: a bed, a chair, a table, a chest of drawers.

'Come on,' says Yasmine. 'We've got an early start tomorrow.'

Seb stands up and stretches. 'I'll be right with you,' he says, yawning. 'Just need to brush my teeth.'

He follows Yasmine out of the room but instead of going to

the bathroom, he walks along the corridor to the front door. It is a big wooden door, thick and sturdy. He turns the latch; it is locked. He looks at the metal chain hanging limply by the side of the latch. They rarely use it; being on the first floor they have always felt pretty secure but tonight he needs more reassurance. He holds the chain between his fingers like Zoe's mother and her rosary beads. It looks so thin; how can something so feeble protect him and his family from the monsters out there; the Martin Harrises who stalk the city's streets, who kill and rape and destroy lives. If Seb had a padlock he would use it now; he would put it on the door and double lock it but all he has is this chain, this delicate string of loops. As he slides it across the latch, he hopes it is enough.

9

Stella sits on the edge of the sumptuous king-size bed and slowly removes her shoes while Paula snuggles under the covers, propping herself up with a thick, fluffy pillow. She lays her green notebook on the bed in front of her and removes the lid of her pen in preparation.

Stella stands up and slips out of her dress. The warm air feels delicious on her bare skin and Paula looks so beautiful lying there in the half-light.

'Do we have to do this tonight?' Stella asks, pointing at the questionnaire that Paula is flicking through, the one that was sent from the fertility clinic almost a month ago. 'Why don't we fill it in tomorrow with fresh eyes; we can talk it over while we have breakfast.' She leans across the bed and goes to kiss Paula's mouth but Paula bows her head at the last minute and Stella's lips brush awkwardly across the top of Paula's forehead.

Paula looks up at her and raises her eyebrows. 'Stella, you've been putting this off ever since the forms arrived. I've asked you over and over this last month to sit down and fill it in and still, the night before the appointment, you're trying to put it off.'

'It's been a busy month,' says Stella, her libido draining from her like water down a plughole. It is strange, but lately Paula's voice has taken on a whiny tone. It grates on Stella, makes her think she is always on the verge of some deeply, unpleasant argument.

'Anyway,' says Paula, tapping the notebook with the tip of her pen. 'We have no choice but to do it tonight because there will be no time in the morning; I have to drop off the plants at nine and the appointment's at eleven.'

'Okay,' says Stella, pulling a cotton dressing gown round her half-naked body. 'Let's get started.' She climbs into the bed and rests her head on Paula's shoulders.

Paula turns and smiles. 'Thank you,' she says, gently.

Stella slides her hand under the covers and rests it on Paula's stomach, trying to imagine the alien concept of a baby growing inside that smooth, taut space.

'I love you,' she whispers, moving her hand slowly down to the top of Paula's pelvis.

'I love you, too,' says Paula, her voice rising with an inflection on the last word that Stella understands. It's a 'let's get on with this' tone of voice, a call to arms. Stella takes her hand away and sits up straight.

'Now,' says Paula, clearing her throat. 'There's a checklist here, a kind of wish list, I suppose, of what we are looking for in a donor. First attribute: ethnicity.'

There is a silence. Stella looks at Paula blankly. 'What do you think?'

'Well,' says Paula, briskly. 'I think the donor should be white, because we are. We want this baby to look like it's come from me and you.'

Stella nods her head. But the baby won't come from you and me, she thinks. It will come from Paula and some stranger, some random number on a test tube. Stella feels like she is standing on the edge of the room looking in, like a ghost. What will she be to the baby? Yes, her name will be on the birth certificate alongside Paula's but her blood will not run through its veins, there will be no familial features, no character quirks that she can say she contributed to.

'. . . yes, definitely green.' Paula is onto the next question already. She looks up at Stella, quizzically. 'Do you agree?'

'Sorry,' says Stella, blinking her tired eyes. The glass of wine at dinner turned into a bottle and now she is feeling a little drowsy. 'Er . . . you were saying, green?'

'Eye colour,' says Paula, sharply. 'I should think green if possible, don't you?'

Stella looks at Paula's bright face and smiles inside, remembering the first time she saw her: twenty-one years old with holes in her jeans and a mind as sharp as steel, she had sat down next to the shy sixteen-year-old Stella and mesmerised her with those beautiful, laughing green eyes. Stella strokes Paula's cheek, tenderly. Despite their bickering, despite all these years of living together, of knowing each other's bad habits and irritating quirks, Stella still gets an ache in the pit of her stomach when she looks into Paula's eyes. Yet it is a duller ache than it was at the beginning of their relationship; a melancholy one, perhaps mourning the zest and spark of those early years.

'Yes, let's put green eyes,' she says, gently. 'Although, with you for a mummy I think the baby has a good chance of having them anyway.'

Paula smiles and makes a little note on the paper in her spidery handwriting.

They breeze through the next three questions: Hair colour (dark); height (six feet); religion (any).

'Okay,' says Paula. 'Next one: occupation?'

'Artist,' says Stella.

'Why artist?' asks Paula, her eyes narrowing.

'It was the first thing that came into my head,' says Stella.

Paula's lips purse and she stares at the notebook, not speaking for what seems like an age.

'Well, we want someone creative, don't we?' says Stella, trying to keep her voice upbeat. 'Someone like us.'

'Yes,' says Paula, folding her arms across her chest. 'But you didn't say writer or horticulturalist, you specifically said artist.'

'A writer *is* an artist,' says Stella, sitting up. 'And what you do – well that's certainly art of a sort.'

'Hmm,' says Paula. 'Well actually I think we could do with a scientist then the baby might end up really contributing something to society – a cure for cancer or AIDs – or a mathematician, yes that might be good, we could have a financial whizz to help us in our old age.' She laughs a strange, snorty laugh but Stella remains straight-faced.

'I just think the donor should have some attributes in common with me,' she snaps. 'Otherwise, what the fuck am I doing here? Where exactly do I fit in with the plan?'

'Where do you fit in?' says Paula, her voice getting higher. 'You're my partner, you will be part of this baby's life for ever.'

'Yes, but what will I be to it?' says Stella. 'You're its mother, Mr Scientist's its father. What am I? The spare part?'

'Stella, you're being ridiculous,' shrieks Paula. 'We've discussed this at length for over a year and now, the night before we're due to set it all in motion, you're talking rubbish like this.'

'Rubbish?' yells Stella, leaping out of the bed. 'Is it rubbish to want to have a say, to have my opinion taken seriously rather than just be dismissed out of hand. To be told that being an artist doesn't contribute anything to society, so the work I do is of no consequence. Fuck it, Paula. Do you even like me?'

Paula sits in the bed, shaking her head. 'This is crazy, this is absolutely crazy. I knew this would happen, I knew it. This is the first time you've been back to London and already you're slipping back into the old Stella. It's too much for you, I can see that. You get yourself all hyped up and you've had a long journey on your own to stew things over in your head.' Her hands are shaking now. 'And then I read that article about that bloody artist and it's his wife who runs the restaurant – I didn't know that when I got the job – it's his wife who ordered the jasmine.' Her voice shakes and she starts to sob.

Stella sits down on the bed next to her, trying to take the anger out of her voice. 'What artist? What are you talking about, Paula?'

Paula leans across to the bedside table and picks up a copy of *Vogue*.

'Look at this,' she says. 'Page 103.' She hands the magazine to Stella.

Stella takes it and flicks through the pages, still unsure what this is all about. She opens it out as she reaches the back page and a face she has not seen for seven years beams out at her. Seb.

'Oh,' she whispers. She tries to speed-read the article, but her eyes are tired from the wine and she only registers a few words: 'Successful gallery . . . Yasmine . . . opening in Soho . . . The Rose Garden . . .' She is more interested in the photograph. He looks different. How old must he be now? Thirty-seven, thirty-eight? He was a bit older than her, she remembers. He looks well, perhaps a little rounder in the face but it suits him. His blond hair has grown longer but it's still curly and his face looks softer, less haunted than it did. As she looks at the picture a thousand memories flutter in and out of her mind: The Dog and Duck pub, the little studio flat on Frith Street where she spent five years of her life, Caleb the doorman from Ronnie Scott's with his cheeky smile . . . Ade, the sound of the saxophone streaming through the open window as she walked up the street . . . It seems like a century ago now, that time, that life.

She closes the magazine and hands it back to Paula. 'I don't see why you've got yourself so worked up over this,' she says, as Paula wipes her eyes with the corner of the quilt. 'I knew this guy a million years ago, he was a nice person, kind and gentle, and by the look of him he's done well for himself. But how has it got anything to do with us?'

'I don't know,' says Paula, slamming her hands down onto the bed. 'I guess I'm just feeling really vulnerable at the moment.' A tear falls down her face and she quickly swipes it with her hand. She looks up at Stella, her face red and swollen. 'I'm scared.'

'Scared of what?' asks Stella, putting her hand on Paula's shoulder.

'Of everything,' says Paula. 'God, look at me, what am I doing crying like this? It's just that I love you so much Stella, but there's a part of you I'll never really know, never fully understand. I don't feel it as much when we're in Exeter but even there you disappear into your own world – your books and your writing and I feel I daren't come near. It's as though there's this invisible border with you on one side and me on the other . . .'

She starts to cry again, great sobbing wails. Stella has never seen her like this before.

'Paula, please.'

'It's being back in London, that's what it is,' sniffs Paula. 'It's just making the wedge between us a thousand times bigger.'

'Paula,' says Stella, in a firm voice. 'Paula, listen to me. You have got to let this go, this feeling that you need to control me; that you have to fear me. When I met you, you were like the brightest light I had ever seen. You had no self-consciousness, no qualms, just a burning curiosity for everyone and everything. I'm your love, Paula, your best friend. You don't have to worry about me all the time, just be with me, love me, be my adventurous spirited girl again.' She rubs Paula's hand as she speaks. 'I know you rescued me when you took me to Andalucia. You found the clinic, you helped make me better, I know you did and I will never forget that but you have to trust me now, you have to let us move on, otherwise we can never be happy.'

Paula nods her head. She looks like a child, thinks Stella. What happened to the fearless girl she once knew?

'I'm sorry, Stella,' says Paula. 'It's just when you said "artist" . . . oh, I don't know, I've always been paranoid about that Seb guy, I always suspected you'd had a bit of a fling with him before we got together and then when I read about him and saw that it was his wife who had the restaurant, I just started thinking all manner of mad, crazy thoughts . . . like you were going to see him and fall for him and you'd run off and leave me.'

Stella takes her hand from Paula's and shakes her head, incredulously, trying to imagine this surreal series of events where she and Seb would make some theatrical escape through the streets of Soho.

'Paula, we're married, I love you. I would make love to you all day, every day if you let me. I don't want to run off with Seb, I don't want to run off with anyone. I just want to be with you, but I need to feel you believe in us, otherwise what is the point of all of this?'

'I know,' says Paula, quietly. 'I'm sorry.'

She looks up and Stella feels herself being drawn back in, back to those eyes, the warm, deep layers of their love. She moves the pen and papers from the bed and slips in, pulling Paula close to her, running her fingers along the outline of her lover's body. Paula lets out a moan but it sounds like a sob.

'It's okay, angel,' whispers Stella. 'You're a paranoid, crazy person, but I love you.'

Paula turns round and nuzzles her face into the crook of Stella's arm. She whispers something but Stella doesn't catch it.

'What's that?' she says, gently.

'I said, we can have an artist if you like,' says Paula, her head still buried in Stella's embrace.

When Mark opens his eyes he feels disorientated. He had been dreaming; they were strange, interwoven dreams that seemed to make no sense. A line of faceless figures stood in front of him, not speaking, not moving, yet imbued with a deep sense of urgency, as though they had something of great importance to tell him. Then, like a chalk drawing caught in a rainstorm, they slowly began to disappear, the blues and greens and reds of their clothes bleeding into each other until all that was left was a wet, blurry ball of grey. Out of this void stepped a man, a scruffy man, unshaven, with dirty, matted hair. He told Mark he would go and find him a map of London. Mark had tried to speak, to tell him that he did not need a map, but no words would come; it felt like his voice was stuck somewhere around his chest like an undigested piece of food. The man stepped back into the shadows, like an actor disappearing into the wings then returned moments later holding the map in his outstretched hands. Mark took it from him but as he touched the paper, it dissolved and fell through his hands like powdery snow. The man smiled; it was a horrific smile, evil and demonic. Then he took off his shirt to reveal an emaciated torso covered in a tiny, detailed map of the underground.

Mark shudders as he sits up in the hard bed, trying to shake off the deep sense of unease that the dream has left him with. He reaches for his phone which is lying on the floor by the side of the bed, and turns it on. The screen lights up and casts a greeny-grey glow onto the bed. It is almost midnight.

Pulling the blanket around him, he starts to scroll through the internet. He is wide awake now but his eyes sting as he types a familiar name into the search engine. It has been almost twenty-four hours since he last checked but he needs to know if anything has changed, if there have been any developments.

The search engine yields 1.9 million results for 'Seb Bailey'. Mark clicks on the top result: Seb's Twitter page. A thumbnail photograph of Seb sitting in a park with his wife and daughter comes up immediately and, as the page develops, a black and white landscape photograph of the words Asphodel Art provides a backdrop to the happy family shot.

Mark scrolls down the page to see if @asphodel1 has tweeted anything new. There are a couple of retweets – one about an arts project in Manchester looking for funding; the other a tweet from @therosegarden with a link to the opening night menu – but nothing directly from Seb since the last one on 21 August when he had posted a rather cryptic message:

From a puddle to a lake – almost finished x

Mark reads the tweet over and over, trying to make sense of it but it baffles him just as much tonight as it did when he first read it almost a week ago. He scrolls back up the page and clicks on @therosegarden. The page fills with deep pink roses set against a black background; a photograph of a tall, elegant Soho townhouse sits in the foreground. Unlike Seb's page, Yasmine's seems to be updated pretty regularly. Mark reads:

Two days to go until doors open! So excited! 1hr ago

Watching my o/h work his magic on the walls x4 hrs ago

She'd probably typed the last one just after he saw them. He wonders if they are there every day. Probably. There will be lots to prepare, getting everything ready for the press launch. He scrolls further down the page but the rest of the tweets are familiar, he must have read this page a hundred times at least.

He goes back to the search results. He is working on autopilot now; he could recite the information on the screen verbatim but still he has to check each day just in case some new piece of information comes up. It is not an obsession, he tells himself, it is reconnaissance, evidence gathering. This is what his father would have done before going into battle – find out as much about the enemy as possible, know their strengths, their weaknesses, their routines and habits. Know thy enemy.

Mark clicks on Seb's Wikipedia page. A fuzzy photograph of Seb in a black suit, holding a glass of champagne is displayed in the right-hand corner. Underneath is a brief biography:

Born: 18 February, 1975 (age 37), Garsington, Oxfordshire
Occupation: Artist
Spouse: Yasmine Bailey (nee Rachi)
Children: One daughter, Cosima
Then a link to his website:
www.asphodelart.co.uk

Though he knows the information by heart, Mark cannot help reading on:

Sebastian Bailey is an English painter and gallery owner . . .
Sebastian studied Fine Art at the Royal College, graduating in 1997 . . .

In 2005, he and his business partner Henry Walker launched the art gallery Asphodel in Battersea, South London . . . as well as exhibiting work by leading British and international artists, the gallery also supports new talent through its scholarship scheme . . .

Bailey has exhibited around the world and in 2006 he made the headlines when his oil on canvas painting entitled 'Rotherhithe' sold to a US dealer for a six-figure sum.

In late 2011, he was asked to produce a series of paintings as part of the 2012 Cultural Olympiad celebrating London life. These paintings were exhibited around London in the build-up to the 2012 Olympic Games; the most prominent being a three-metre high canvas, entitled 'Running Out of Time' which was displayed outside Leicester Square Tube Station.

Underneath this biography is a list of links. Mark scans his eyes across them then pauses at the bottom link – a new one. He reads the name: Sir Miles Alfred Bailey. Curiously, he clicks on the link and another Wikipedia page opens up.

Sir Miles Alfred Bailey CBE, QGM, KCB (Born 7th November, 1939, Edinburgh) is a retired British Army officer . . .

Mark sits up in bed, his eyes widening as he reads the words again. British Army Officer.

He tries to read the rest of the page but his head feels hot and clammy, the words float across his eyes without settling:

. . . educated at Bryanston School and Royal Military Academy, Sandhurst.

Military Career: Falklands War, Bosnian War, Kosovo . . .

Mark's heart thuds against his chest, an ice-cold shiver flutters through his body. The Falklands War. His father's war. He looks away from the screen and stares at the door, as if the answer lies somewhere out in the darkness of the room. He throws his phone onto the floor but the screen stays alight, illuminating the rest of Sir Miles Alfred Bailey's life: his two children Sebastian and Claire, his ex-wife Elizabeth Stanley, daughter of a South African landowner, now a resident of Knightsbridge, his new wife, Barbara Picard, a concert pianist with whom he lives in a grand country house in Somerset. But that information is lost to the scuffed, brown carpet; it is nothing compared to the words Mark now rolls around inside his head like a grenade.

A British Army Officer; the Falklands War. So Bailey had a father who had fought in that war, the war that had haunted Mark's childhood, turned his father mute, made him a pariah among the Thatcher-hating union men in the pub. Bailey had gone through that too, then, thinks Mark, experienced what he had: the tight feeling in the chest when his mam turned on the news; the roll calls, Goose Green . . . Bailey had gone through that too. A pinprick of recognition opens in Mark's consciousness letting in a miniscule shaft of light; a shared experience, a shared pain. But then Zoe's face appears before him and the light fades.

There is no greater pain than that, he thinks, no greater pain than what happened to Zoe. Fuck it, he spits. Bailey's father was an officer, a fucking Rupert. He was as far removed from Mark's father and his background as it is possible to be. He had heard his father talking about officers with his army mates – there had been a couple of half-decent ones, men his father had respected but Mark has made up his mind that Sir Miles Alfred Bailey was one of the bad ones. He can see the man in his head now, jowly red face, small cruel beady eyes, hawkish nose, an upper class tosser who lived on another planet from the men. Only by thinking like this will he have the strength to see it through.

'I wish you could hear me, Dad,' Mark whispers into the hot, cloggy air. 'I'm not going to let you down, like I did with Zoe. I'm going to rip that man's life apart, like ours was ripped apart. Can you hear me, Dad?'

Somewhere down the corridor a toilet flushes and he hears footsteps thudding past then the sound of a door slamming.

He turns over and pulls the thin quilt up to his neck. The news has rattled him, but he can do this, he really can. If he keeps focused, if he carries his father's war inside him these next few days, then he can take this to the end.

TUESDAY, 28 AUGUST

10

'Come on, Cosima, it's almost eight,' shouts Seb, trying to make his voice heard above the rumble of the boiling kettle and the shouting weather forecaster on BBC Breakfast News.

He sets the table: two glass tumblers, two earthenware cereal bowls, two spoons. It is just him and Cosima for breakfast this morning. Yasmine had already left for the restaurant when Seb's alarm went off at seven. He hadn't heard her get up, get dressed and leave, but then he never does; Yasmine has it down to a fine art now, creeping silently out of bed, tip-toeing along the passage, making sure the bathroom door is closed as she takes a shower. Seb's father, who stayed with them for a couple of days over Christmas, joked that Yasmine would have made a good SAS soldier, with her ability to enter and leave a building like a silent shadow.

Seb feels better this morning. The black mood that had settled on him last night seems to have dissipated. Nothing like a good night's sleep for a clear head, he thinks to himself as he ladles steaming porridge into the bowls. As he leans across the table, he becomes aware of a presence behind him. He turns to see Cosima in the doorway. She is wearing her lilac furry dressing gown and her long curly hair is tangled, the fringe matted to her forehead.

'Come on, sleepy,' he says, pouring fresh orange juice into the tumblers. 'We've got a busy day ahead and you're off to Gracie's house, remember? Just think, a full day looking after those guinea pigs of hers.'

Cosima makes a grunting noise as she shuffles into the room and plonks herself down onto the chair. Seb smiles to himself as he prepares the coffee; his daughter is certainly not a morning person, yet neither was he at that age. In the long summer holidays back from boarding school with its 6 a.m. wake-up calls and freezing cold showers, he would lie in bed until midday, buried under his quilt, away from the world, alone with his dreams.

He sits down at the table next to Cosima. She takes a large swig of orange juice then puts down her glass and wipes her mouth with the back of her hand. Seb watches her as she picks up her spoon and starts to eat the porridge. She is not a baby anymore, he thinks. She is becoming a person in her own right.

He remembers when she was about a year old he had been looking after her on his own one afternoon. She had just started to move onto more solid foods – sticks of carrot, slices of apple, bread rolls, cubes of cheese – and she was sitting in her high chair munching away merrily on a piece of apple when Seb's phone had rung. He had picked it up from the table on the other side of the room – he can't remember who it was now, someone from the office, maybe – and spoken for a few seconds when he heard the most awful noise, a rasping choking noise. He turned and saw his baby girl, her eyes bulging, her face red and contorted. He dropped the phone and ran towards her, desperately trying to unhook her from the straps of the highchair. Then he hauled her out, his mind utterly blank, panic enveloping his entire body. He did the first thing that came into his head – he shoved his fingers down her tiny little throat, something he would later discover was the worst thing possible to do. But his hands managed to get a hold of the scrap of apple that was blocking her airways and he pulled it out in one swipe. It was horrendous, Cosima started screaming, he was shaking and he clutched her to his chest and rocked her for what seemed like hours but was actually only a few minutes, because that was when Yasmine came home. The horror of those few seconds when he thought his little girl might choke to death prompted him to take a first-aid course. He had been so vulnerable, he had no idea what to do and that terrified him.

Now looking at her eating her porridge, a fine girl of six, he thinks how precarious every little stage is. Though he is less afraid of her choking now, there are new concerns, new dangers to look out for – talking to strangers being the biggest one as Cosima is such a chatty, outgoing child, trusting and open. And as she grows up there will be other dangers, ones that he won't be able to protect her from . . .

'Can we switch over to the cartoons?' Cosima's voice interrupts his thoughts. She is pointing her spoon at the small, flat-screen television that stands on the kitchen worktop, wedged between various open cookery books and a thick wooden chopping board. The bright red graphics of BBC Breakfast flash across the screen accompanied by sharp, tinny music. The cartoons would be a welcome respite from this, thinks Seb.

'All right,' says Seb, picking up the remote control. 'But just a couple, okay? We'll have to be getting ready in a bit.'

'Thanks, Daddy,' says Cosima, flashing her widest, gappy smile. She is starting to wake up now and her eyes dance as she follows the movement of the little cartoon mouse in a tutu and ballet slippers as it pirouettes across the screen.

Seb finishes his porridge and drains his cup of coffee then takes the dishes over to the sink. He picks up his iPad from the worktop and scrolls through his online calendar. Each day is filled with appointments, lunches, dinners, meetings, reminders and work schedules and today, 28 August, is no different. He glances down the page:

10 a.m.: Drop Cosima at Gracie's – Wandsworth Common

11 a.m.: Meeting Vita from Royal Opera House re: poss commission @Asphodel

1 p.m.: Lunch with Henry at Chelsea Arts Club

3–5 p.m.: Painting

5:30 p.m.: Collect Cosima

And there it is; almost every minute of the day accounted for, every spare moment filled. But it has to be this way, otherwise all would descend into chaos. He and Yasmine sit together every Sunday morning and compare their diaries, making sure there are no overlapping appointments. They made a decision early on that as far as possible, one of them should be with Cosima, and if that couldn't happen then Maggie would step in. Nannies and childminders were completely out of the question and anyway, Seb's hours are a lot more flexible than Yasmine's and he was happy to take on the primary carer role. Yet they still have difficult times. The restaurant launch has meant that Yasmine is often in Soho from early morning until last thing at night, and Seb has only just finished a big project for the Cultural Olympiad creating eight giant portraits of real Londoners that have been displayed around the city. From January to June, he was pretty much locked away in his studio at the back of the gallery, emerging late at night to eat a hurried dinner before falling into bed and waking up to do it all over again. That period was tough, he missed Cosima terribly, but thank goodness for Maggie stepping in as always, making everything okay.

But it will all be worth it, he tells himself as he closes the calendar. He and Yasmine are laying the foundations not just of their own future but Cosima's too, and there aren't many people who can say that they earn a living, a good living from doing the thing they love. The late nights and long hours are a small price to pay for the happiness Seb feels he is creating for his family.

'Come on then, tatty head,' he says, as the closing credits of *Angelina Ballerina* flicker across the screen. 'Time to get ready.'

'Oh, Daddy,' moans Cosima.

Seb is opening the blinds at the window. The sky is bright and clear and a hazy sun is filtering through the trees in the park. There are people walking their dogs, others are jogging, some are doing both.

'Right,' he says, clapping his hands as he turns from the window and looks at his daughter who is sitting at the table stirring the remnants of her porridge sulkily. 'I'm going to time you and if you're ready in ten minutes we can have take-away pizza tonight. Just don't tell Mum, okay?'

She looks up at him and raises her eyebrows. 'Ham and pineapple?'

'Ham and pineapple,' he agrees. 'And a tub of Cherry Choc ice-cream if you're ready in five.'

She jumps up from the table and disappears down the corridor, leaving Seb standing at the window. An old, lumpy dog stops outside, cocks his leg and pisses against the lamppost. 'Oh, yes,' thinks Seb. 'Another day in London town.'

Even before Kerstin opens the door she knows that something is wrong. She felt it as she crossed Green Park and stepped onto St James's Street just a few minutes ago; a strange sensation of change, of time altering, the silent inhalation of breath the world takes before one age gives way to another. It stays with her as she slowly climbs the stairs, as she steps onto the third floor landing and carefully types the numbers 6043 into the white plastic security panel.

It is such a strong feeling, that when she eventually opens the door and steps into the reception area of Sircher Capital it is like she already knows, has had a prior warning that things are not the same.

A rather cross-looking young woman, pale, with a doughy face and thin, bobbed, auburn hair, is sitting behind the reception desk, occupying the place that, yesterday, belonged to someone else. Like the art that mysteriously appears on the walls, someone had smuggled this girl into the office overnight, or so it seems to Kerstin. She hadn't particularly liked Susie, the last receptionist, had in fact found her loud and brash, an annoying presence, but a familiar one; part of the landscape of the office, like a desk or chair. The girl sitting here unnerves Kerstin with her newness, her strangeness, her out-of-place-ness. If she had known yesterday that there would be a new receptionist she could have prepared herself for the change. Doesn't Lindsay, the office manager, think it important to tell when the personnel changes or does everything have to be thrust on them, like the ever-changing artwork and Cal's choice of lunch, to keep them on their toes.

'Good morning,' says the receptionist, a thin, blank smile flickering across her impenetrable face, and Kerstin feels something die inside as she smiles politely and turns left into the office.

There is something unreal about the receptionist, about all the receptionists that come and go in this place; before Susie there was Christine, a bespectacled blonde from Northern Ireland; before her there was a black American girl called Hilary and before her someone else and someone else and someone else, a long line of them spreading back in time like holograms, fluid half-people, they seem like to Kerstin, propping up the beams of London without being seen, bit-players coming on and saying their lines – like this one's 'Good morning' – before disappearing into the shadows.

The issue of the receptionist bothers Kerstin as she sits down at her desk and turns on her computer; it bothers her as she opens up the unfinished report which now stands at twelve-and-a-half pages and tries to ignore Cal's loud post-mortem of his dinner last night. She tries to focus as she scrolls through her emails but it feels like her brain is stuck.

Familiar names flash in front of her as she mentally notes which need immediate attention, which can wait and which are pointless, and then she sees a name that she doesn't recognise: Honey Vision PR. Probably spam but she clicks on it anyway. The screen fills with black and then an outline of a tree emerges, followed by white fairy lights, spindly tables and chairs – a line drawing developing in front of her eyes like a photograph in a darkroom. Then the music starts, soft Moroccan voices and a hypnotic guitar, strumming the same vibrato note slow at first then faster and faster, the voices rising to a crescendo as the screen fills with rose petals falling down from the darkened 'sky' of the picture. As they settle they merge and form a set of words in pinks and reds and deep orange: Launch Party. The words then dissolve and the petals scatter and form a set of numbers: 29.08.12. The music grows louder and louder as the petals explode into the sky like fireworks then sprinkle across the screen as though tiny fireflies, dancing and twisting, jumbling and untangling themselves until, again, they reassemble and form a set of letters. The voices stop and the guitar strums one solitary note over and over while the words the petals have spelled grow bigger and bigger until they fill the screen, obliterating the tables and chairs and fairy lights. Kerstin feels like she has been hypnotised as she reads the name: THE ROSE GARDEN, then watches as it slowly fades and the screen grows dark.

'I see you got your invitation. It's cool isn't it?' Cal's voice snaps her out of the spell and she quickly closes the email.

'Yes, it's nice,' she says.

'Will you be going?' asks Cal, leaning back in his chair.

Kerstin shrugs, hoping that by not engaging Cal he will take the hint and leave her be.

'I bet you won't,' he says, rapping his fingers on the desk. 'You never come out; I mean I've worked here two years and not once have I seen you outside this office. We'd all love it if you came to at least one office night out.'

There is nothing Kerstin would like less, she thinks, but his use of the plural unsettles her. So they all talk about her when she is not there? When they are on their 'office nights out', they huddle together and pick her apart; probably egged on by Sharon Porter, the horse-faced PA to Dominic Stratton who has been watching her like a hawk for the past few months. Should she be worried?

Suddenly Cal leans over her desk and clicks the computer mouse.

'What are you doing?' She is horrified that he has touched her computer and she tries to rack her brain as to how many sets of counting she will have to complete to remove the taint of his sweaty hands from the mouse.

Cal grins at her as he walks across to the printer on the far side of the room.

She stares at the mouse in disbelief; how can she work today? How can she even begin to touch it now he has had his hands all over it?

'Here you go.'

She looks up and sees him holding out the printed invitation. She will not take it; all at once her whole world has become as filthy as a cess-pit; her carefully controlled work-space has been violated in the most horrendous way.

'Here you go,' he repeats, leaning across the desk and placing the invitation on top of her in-tray. Now you've no excuse not to come.'

'Let's see how we get on with these reports,' she replies, brusquely. 'Or we won't be going anywhere.'

Cal shakes his head playfully, then sits up and returns to his computer screen.

Kerstin slides her hand into her pocket and pulls out a packet of anti-bacterial wipes. Sliding one quietly out of the pack she rubs it across the mouse and counts to twenty and back. Satisfied that there is no trace of Cal left, she scrunches the wipe into a ball and tosses it into the waste-paper basket. Then, her heart pounding with anxiety, she clicks open a new document and begins to prepare a brief for Cal on the next report. But her head is full of Moroccan music as she types, the deep male voices and mosquito strumming of the guitar form a soundtrack to her fingers as they punch the numbers and letters on the keyboard, then settle onto the screen like a thousand petals forming and reforming until they make sense. She is so engrossed, so inside the music whirring about her head that when the phone rings, she thinks at first that it is part of the beat, a syncopated buzz, playing alongside the scratchy sounds in her head. Only when Cal nudges her and gestures to his ears does she notice the green lit screen of her mobile phone, another set of words appearing then disappearing like a dying light: *Mutter*.

She stops typing and picks up the phone, suddenly aware of where she is and of Cal's presence just centimetres away. She clicks the green square on the screen and hears her mother's agitated voice, telling her that her father has collapsed.

A thick fog fills the air, opaque and smoky like the room is on fire, as Kerstin listens to her mother telling her about the heart attack that struck as Kerstin's father was leaving the house yesterday morning, how a neighbour found him on the driveway spread out like a starfish and called an ambulance that took thirty minutes to arrive as it was delayed by a learner driver crashing into the back of it. And all that time he lay there, her father, her brilliant father, the man they called the human computer so precise and advanced was his brain, the brain that had spent thirty years engaged in theoretical physics, in Complexity Theory and chain reactions, in finding pre-determined patterns and sequences, finding answers to questions that other people did not know existed and trying to establish order from chaos; the brain that slowly shut down through lack of oxygen as he, Felix Morgen Bsc/Msc/PhD/ Emerit, lay sprawled on his driveway like a great, ungainly beached sea-creature.

There is too much for Kerstin to take in all at once. She needs to put the phone down, to silence her mother's stream of information, to let her own thoughts in.

'I will call you back in a moment, Mama,' she whispers, but as she goes to hang up she hears those words, dreaded words weighted with agony and impossibility.

'You must come, Kerstin. Jump on a plane and come now, before it is too late. You must come.'

She presses 'end call' and sits motionless. No tears come to her eyes, no compulsion to tell any of her colleagues what has just happened. Instead, she types out a hurried email to Karen, informing her of an urgent dental appointment. Then she switches off her computer, picks up her coat and bag and heads out of the door. Now she must focus, she must do the thing that will keep all of the bad things at bay; as she reaches the top of the stairs she begins to count.

11

It is hunger that eventually drives Mark out of the bedroom; a ravenous, gnawing hunger in the pit of his stomach. He had planned to have breakfast in some quiet café nearby, a big plate of bacon and eggs and a mug of strong tea to set him up for his day of reconnaissance. He was going to slip out of the room quietly, like a shadow, avoiding the huddles of backpackers in the refectory and grinning Stewart perched behind the reception desk ready to pounce. But this hunger is so powerful, he needs something instant to stem it. He rummages in his rucksack to see if there's a bag of crisps or some sweets he can eat to stave it but there's nothing but a packet of chewing gum.

He remembers the vending machines out on the corridor, the ones he passed last night. The hunger is making him light-headed, he hasn't got the strength to even think about taking a shower and getting dressed. He is still wearing the T-shirt and tracksuit bottoms he slept in last night. The day has not started as he had planned at all. He had set the alarm on his phone for 6 a.m. but then slept through it. If he'd got up then he could have gone across the corridor to the shower room without any fuss, without being hassled. Now, at nine forty-five, the hostel is alive, he can hear their voices outside, their high-pitched laughter, their heavy footsteps and the twang of someone attempting to play a guitar.

He looks in the mirror. His eyes look tired, heavy from over-sleep and a dark line of stubble has spread across his jaw. But as much as he would love to stay in this room, to crawl back into bed and sleep, hide away in this tiny cell, away from it all, he knows that he is here for a reason; he has to get on.

Taking his wallet from his bag, he picks up the plastic key-card and opens the door a fraction. He looks up and down the corridor; the noisy group that passed a moment ago have gone. He slips out, closes the door behind him and speed-walks down the corridor towards the vending machine.

The landing area is empty. Thank God, thinks Mark. He looks at the machine; everything seems to be £2 or more. Two pounds for a fucking Mars Bar, he mutters as he roots around in his wallet for some change. He counts out a pile of ten and five pences but they only come to £1.25. Sod it, he thinks as he unzips the inner compartment of his wallet but there are only ten- and twenty-pound notes in there and the machine clearly states in large black letters that notes are not accepted.

Mark suddenly fills dizzy with hunger and frustration and he slams his fist at the machine.

'You okay there?'

A female voice behind him; a low husky voice, American? Mark closes his eyes and sighs. Just what he doesn't need. All he wanted was a lousy bar of chocolate and now someone is here, and she will ask questions and offer to help when all he wants is to get the hell out.

He turns from the machine and sees a slight young woman sitting on the red sofa. Her hair is short and messy, a strange, dirty-blonde colour. She reminds him of the little stray Tabby cat his mother adopted when he was a kid. She has the same wide-eyed, slightly dazed expression, the same gaunt little body. She is sitting with her legs pulled up towards her chest and Mark can see the white lace of her knickers peeking out from her denim shorts.

'I'm fine,' he mutters. 'Er, don't suppose you can change a tenner?' He holds the note limply in his hand.

The girl stands up and starts to rummage in her pockets, pulling out sweet wrappers, travel cards, notes and a handful of coins.

She counts out the coins in her hand, lightly brushing her tongue along her bottom lip as she concentrates on the counting. 'Yep, I got a five-pound note and five pound coins,' she says, holding the handful of money towards Mark.

Mark nods his head and curls the corner of his mouth into

what should be a smile but which comes out as more of a sneer. 'Cheers,' he says, as he takes the money and hands the girl the ten-pound note.

'No worries,' she says. She is looking at him in that way; the way Mark remembers girls in the pub looking at him, before Lisa, before Zoe's death, back when he was a single young man without a care. The look unnerves him and he tries to block it out by returning to the vending machine, but his hands are shaking as he feeds the pound coins into the slot and waits for the chocolate bar to fall into the tray with a thud. He picks it up and sees the girl still standing there.

'I'm Liv,' she says, holding out her hand.

Mark's mouth goes dry, he feels the pulse in his head start to thump against his temples. It's the hunger, but it's also a sense of panic. He has to get back to his room, get dressed and get out of here. He has an itinerary to stick to, a list of places to visit, locations to reccy, a brain to get into gear; the last thing he needs is to be distracted, least of all by this girl with her slim, tanned legs and white lace knickers.

He ignores her outstretched hand and simply nods his head as he walks back to the corridor, back to the safety and ano-nymity of the room. As he closes the door behind him, he rips open the chocolate and stuffs it into his mouth, the sugar hitting his bloodstream in great instantaneous bursts.

He looks at the thin grey towel folded on the bed. He had collected it in the early hours of the morning, tip-toeing along to the laundry room like an intruder. Fuck it, he thinks. He can't face going back along the corridor to the shower room; can't risk another backpacker offering help and guidance and inane chit-chat. So he takes off his clothes, goes across to the small cracked sink and turns on the hot water tap. It shoots out in little intermittent sprays but it is warm and Mark splashes it onto his face, under his arms, his groin. Then after drying himself with the towel, he sprays a great stream of deodorant all over his body. It's not ideal but it will do and he can have a proper wash when he gets back tonight, he thinks, when it's quiet, when all those numpties have gone out clubbing or whatever it is they do.

He pulls his jeans and sweatshirt on and slips his feet into his trainers, then kneeling on the floor he drags the long black bag out from under the bed. This must stay with him at all times, he has to guard it with his life and he holds it to his body like a baby in a sling as he creeps along the corridor and makes his way out into the crisp Soho morning.

Stella looks at Paula as they stand on the steps outside the clinic on Harley Street. She looks thin and pensive, thinks Stella; scared, like a small child.

'Come on, we'll be late,' she says, grabbing Paula's arm and marching her up the steps.

Inside, the clinic is more or less what Stella had expected; a three-dimensional version of the website that Paula has pored over each evening for the last few months. The waiting room is painted a sickly pale peach colour, there are large posters on the walls of parents cradling chubby-cheeked babies, a glass vase filled with cerise and orange gerberas stands in the middle of the table, and the insipid hum of classical music floats through the chlorine-scented air.

They walk across the waiting room to the front desk where a nervy-looking receptionist is sitting.

She looks up at them, wide eyed, as they approach.

'Welcome to the clinic,' she says, the words rushing out of her like hot stones. 'Can I take your names?'

'Yes, it's Stella Blake and Paula Wilson,' says Stella, smiling as the girl shakily types their names into the computer.

'You're booked in to see Dr Wyatt is that right?'

'Yes,' replies Stella. 'For 11 a.m.'

The girl nods then picks up the phone.

'I'll just tell her you've arrived.' As she goes to dial in the extension number the phone rings and she quickly slams the receiver down, then picks it up again.

'Good Morning, The Vita Clinic, how can I help you . . . hello? . . . hello? . . . oh, damn they've gone.'

Her face reddens as she looks up at Paula and Stella.

'I'm really sorry. It's only my second day and I'm still getting used to the phone system.'

She replaces the receiver and tries again to buzz the consultant.

'Oh hi, it's Lara . . . erm I've got Paula Blake and Stella Wilson here to see you . . .' She puts the phone down and smiles nervously. 'If you want to take a seat, Dr Wyatt will be along in a minute.'

Paula looks irritated at the mistake with their names but Stella smiles reassuringly at the girl, remembering all too well the feeling of being new. She had worked as a receptionist herself once and can easily recall those first few days on the job; having to learn all the different extension numbers, the nuances of the switchboard, the entry system. All those details swishing around your head as you tried to remain composed and friendly as one person after another interrupted the flow and led you off in a completely different direction.

They take a seat by the window and Paula picks up a magazine. Stella watches her as she absent-mindedly flicks through the pages. Her face serious; her back curved forward, the pose she always adopts when she's nervous. Stella places her hand on Paula's arm; it's freezing. She rubs the prickly skin and Paula goes to speak but her words are swallowed by the high-pitched tones of the receptionist.

'If you want to go through, Dr Wyatt will see you now,' she says. 'It's the first door on the left.' She nods as though relieved that she has got through another task without stumbling.

Paula puts the magazine back into its rack and they hold hands as they walk towards the narrow corridor. It is lined with mirrors and Stella catches a glimpse of herself in the glass. Her dark hair falls in loose curls onto her shoulders; she is wearing black skinny jeans, a white silk top and her favourite navy blue blazer. She looks sophisticated, assured, safe.

Who are you? she thinks.

Thirty-four; not old but older, older than the receptionist, older than she was when she lived in this city. The ageing process is rather like diving down into another part of the ocean, not the deepest bit, but the next stage. Life is fluid, like this moment, the moment she is living through now, standing next to the woman she fell in love with as a teenager, holding her hand as they make their way into the unknown.

One day this will be a memory; like Soho is a memory and the eating disorder is a memory. Even tomorrow's meeting with Dylan O'Brien – such a loaded, potentially life-changing event – seems, at this moment, as though it has already happened, as though it has consigned itself to the long, unbroken line of memories that follow Stella now as she lifts her hand and knocks gently on a blank, wooden door.

She squeezes Paula's hand, reassured by the fleshy solidness of it. As Paula's fingers thread around hers she can feel herself departing; her 'real' self floating off into the air, waiting for the 'other' Stella, the duty-bound, serious married woman to do what she needs to do.

The door opens and they are greeted by Dr Wyatt, a tall, big boned woman with half-moon spectacles, who insists they call her Sarah.

'Do take a seat,' she says, gesturing to two comfy-looking armchairs that are wedged together in front of her desk.

It is all rather perfunctory and they sit there nodding and listening as Sarah explains the procedure to them, discusses their medical history and talks them through their options.

In her usual blunt manner, Paula explains that she will be the birth mother as Stella has '. . . a history of eating disorders and a still birth.'

Stella winces as Sarah smiles at her, a limp, pitying smile.

'Gosh, if you put it like that, I'm quite a catch aren't I?' Stella says it with a dry laugh, trying to lighten the situation, but neither Paula nor Sarah appear to see the funny side.

'So how long have you been planning this?' asks Sarah. Her body is curved across the desk and she reminds Stella of a Quentin Blake drawing; all big limbs and rollered hair.

'Well, we've talked about it for a while but began to think about it seriously at Christmas,' says Paula, nodding to Stella for affirmation.

Sarah starts to type something into her computer, making little noises of acknowledgement as she does so.

'And I've been getting into shape,' says Paula. 'No alcohol or processed foods and I've been drinking lots of red clover tea to help my fertility.'

'That's excellent,' says Sarah, smiling politely. 'You're doing the right thing in addressing your diet and it will certainly help if you reduce your alcohol intake.

Stella notices that the doctor avoids the subject of herbal medicine; she looks like the kind of no-nonsense woman for whom a tincture of red clover tea would be considered as about as much use to a woman's fertility as a voodoo doll.

'Now,' says Sarah, standing up. 'If you want to come with me I'll take you along the corridor for your ultrasound scan.'

Stella takes Paula's hand as they accompany Sarah out of the consulting room and back along the mirrored corridor. Paula looks up at her as they reach the door.

'You'll come in with me, won't you?'

'Of course,' says Stella, squeezing Paula's hand. 'I'll be right beside you.'

'It's a simple procedure,' Sarah assures them as she opens the door of the ultrasound room, where a young black nurse is pulling latex gloves over her hands. 'We just need to look at Paula's womb and ovaries. The scan will detect any cysts or polyps that may cause problems with fertility. I'll leave you with Joyce now.'

Stella stands back in the shadows of the darkened room as Joyce makes Paula comfortable on the examining table and covers her lower body in a blue paper sheet.

'You're not allergic to latex are you?' she asks.

Paula shakes her head and Stella sees in the glow of the lightened screen that Paula's hands are clenched into tight fists.

'This won't hurt at all,' says Joyce, her voice light and soft like she is addressing a child. 'But it might be a bit uncomfortable.' Paula gasps as Joyce inserts the probe inside her and the screen fills with the fuzzy, blue outline of Paula's empty womb.

And as Stella stands in the shadow of this glowing light, as she lives through this moment she can feel it waivering like the ripples on the surface of a pool, blurring, not settling into any particular shape or form. Only once she emerges will it solidify, become hard like rock and she will see it inside her head developing like a photograph in a darkroom but by then she will be inside the next watery tunnel, making new memories. She has no idea what any of this means but she knows that in a few moments, a few hours, she will.

12

Seb is just on time as he strides up Old Church Street towards the Chelsea Arts Club and lunch with Henry. The meeting with the Royal Opera House took longer than he expected but it was worth it: a dream of a commission, creating a series of paintings to promote next season's production of *Madame Butterfly*. Six full-length portraits of the leading opera singers – not bad for a morning's work.

As he approaches the long white clubhouse his phone beeps inside his pocket. He takes it out and reads the message, it's from Yasmine:

Some guy's just been outside asking for you. Wouldn't give his name. I told him he could catch you tmmrw. Call me when you finish lunch. Love you, xxx

He is trying to digest the message when the club door opens and a large, red-haired man greets him.

'Seb! How are you?'

It's Liam Kerr, one of the most successful portrait artists of his generation, famous in the nineties for his reportage-style paintings of Gulf War soldiers and civilians, he has always been one of Seb's heroes and now, through their similar painting styles and love of good food, a close friend and ally.

'I'm good, thanks Liam, really good,' says Seb, smiling warmly. 'Just here to meet a friend for lunch.'

'Business or pleasure?' asks Liam, holding the door while two women duck underneath his outstretched arm to enter the club.

'Bit of both,' says Seb. 'I've got a pretty manic week ahead: we've got the soft launch of the restaurant tomorrow.'

'The Rose Garden,' says Liam, his soft Scottish accent enunciating the name like poetry. 'We got our invitation in the post last week, thank you. Love the design, I wonder who was responsible for that.'

Seb smiles. 'I'm glad you like it. Yas is a tough taskmaster. I had to draw draft after draft of that invite before she was happy.'

'Well, Kate and I will be there,' says Liam, now holding the door open with his foot. 'And we shall starve ourselves all day in preparation.'

'Good stuff,' says Seb. 'Oh and feel free to bring the girls. Cosima will be there and she'd love to see Florence and Verity.'

'Okay, if you're sure,' says Liam. 'They're a pretty rowdy bunch en-masse, you know.'

'The more the merrier,' says Seb. 'And I think, in a way, it will help Yas relax, having the little ones about.'

'Then we shall come,' says Liam. 'Right, I'm off to meet my accountant; always the highlight of my month. See you tomorrow, my friend.'

'Bye, Liam,' says Seb, catching the door before it closes. He switches his phone to silent and tucks it into his pocket as he enters the dark, low ceilinged entrance hall. He has no idea who the strange guy at the restaurant is, but he can deal with it later.

The club is already starting to fill with people arriving for lunch and a great burst of laughter emanates from the bar to the left of the door, plates clatter in the kitchen and phones ring simultaneously in the tiny cramped office along the hall. Seb often pops in there to say hello to Emma, the frazzled office manager, to confirm a dinner booking or talk about his next exhibition. He still finds it hard to believe that four adults – Emma, her assistant Daisy, John, the operations manager, and Aubrey, the club secretary – can all cram into that tiny space, let alone sort out the intricacies of club business: taking dining room and bedroom bookings, organising events, paying suppliers, chasing membership subscriptions, as well as answering the phones that never seem to stop ringing. And they manage to do it all so graciously and still have time for a laugh and a chat with the members.

That's the beauty of the Chelsea Arts Club for Seb, it's like a gloriously eccentric home-from-home where priceless works of art hang on walls where the paint is peeling, where multi-millionaires sit wedged on threadbare chairs nibbling on Twiglets and sipping Bloody Marys. Still, multi-millionaires are relatively few and far between and for most of the artist members it's a case of feast or famine – one month they may be so skint they can't afford to eat, the next they might have a sell-out show and treat everyone to drinks all night. Any celebrities trying to wangle themselves membership without a genuine involvement in the arts are soon given short shrift by the formidable membership committee who can sniff out chancers like bloodhounds.

As Seb walks down the corridor past the office he can hear snippets of conversation overlapping each other. Emma is talking on the telephone: 'Yes, I know you need measurements but I'm trying to tell you that I can't give you them just now . . .' She is drowned out by Aubrey's sharp voice: 'Daisy, can you tell me WHY there is a cross through the loggia on this booking sheet . . . and can I say yet again, and I'm talking to everyone here, when you make a booking can you ALL initial it, otherwise we have no idea what we're doing,' . . . 'Oh, really, do we ever know what we're doing, darlings?' Emma's voice, now raised, intercepts Aubrey's: 'And the reason I can't do that is that we have no rulers in the office at the moment . . . what's that? . . . all I know is that we arrived this morning and there is not a ruler to be had, apparently the chef went quite mad last night, burst into the office and removed all the rulers. Now if you don't mind I shall have to call you back . . .'

Seb laughs to himself as he walks towards the dining room and hears Aubrey's voice call across the office: 'Daisy, I want you to go to the kitchen immediately and retrieve those rulers.'

As he walks past the staircase that leads up to the bedrooms, a plump ginger cat slinks round his legs. 'Hello, Bubble,' he says, bending down to stroke the cat's head 'Are you hungry too, eh?' He opens the door of the dining room and the cat runs in between his legs and makes a dart for freedom through the French Doors that lead out to the garden. The room is quite full. There are the usual familiar faces sitting round the large shared table in the middle near the kitchen while other members with guests sit at the tables for two, four and six that are dotted around the L-shaped room. The wooden floor creaks as Seb walks across to Marcy, the tiny maître d' who always reminds him of a figure from a Dutch painting with her long red hair, alabaster skin and black dress. She is busy totting something up at the till but as he approaches she turns and smiles warmly.

'Hi, Seb, your guest is here,' she says, handing him a printed menu. 'We've put you in the loggia today if that's okay,' she says, as she leads him towards the back of the room which opens out into the airy glass garden room.

'That's fine, Marcy,' says Seb, ducking his head as they walk under the low archway. 'It's so sunny, it'll be nice to sit in there today.'

As they walk through, he sees Henry sitting at the far table.

He always looks out of place here, confused and befuddled by it all. He has his hands folded on the table in front of him and looks rather like a schoolboy waiting for matron to arrive. Henry likes slick modern lines and chic formality; the chaos and shabby eccentricity of the club are just not to his taste. Mobile phones are not allowed in the dining room and as Henry's is permanently glued to his ear like an extra limb, he looks even more awkward sitting there twiddling his thumbs.

He looks up as Seb approaches and stands to greet him.

'Seb, one of these days you might just be on time.' He laughs as he pats Seb on the shoulder and sits back down.

Seb rolls his eyes and smiles at his friend. 'Wait till I tell you about the Opera House meeting.'

'What can I get you chaps to drink?' asks Marcy, standing back like a little ghost as Seb pulls out his chair and sits down.

'A couple of bottles of sparkling water would be great, thanks Marcy,' says Seb.

Marcy knows never to hand Seb the wine list, just as she knows the likes and dislikes, the phobias and foibles of almost every one of the members. Like the fact that Paul Redwood, the former-arts correspondent for the *New York Times* and now well into his nineties, will arrive at 1 p.m. on the dot each day, will be seated on the far right of the communal table and will order the rib eye with new potatoes and a glass of house red, alternating to the sea bass on Fridays with a glass of house white. He will bring his own newspapers with him, which he will read for the duration of the meal, then leave at 2 p.m. to go and take a nap in the living room of his small garden flat off the Fulham Road. That is his routine and Marcy would never dream of getting in the way of it. Seb smiles as Marcy removes the wine glasses discretely; he likes the fact that he can be a recovering alcoholic in a club renowned for its raucousness and carousing and he knows that if he can abstain from drink here, he can abstain anywhere.

'So what's this about the Opera House?' Henry leans across the table, his eyes bright with thoughts of new business, new money.

'It's a fantastic commission, H,' says Seb, lowering his voice slightly as two women are seated at the table opposite. 'They're putting on *Madame Butterfly* next year and they want six full-length oils, one for each of the principle singers, to be displayed inside the Opera House and to use on their posters and publicity material. And I want the bulk of this fee to go straight back into Asphodel for the scholarship funds.'

'That's very generous of you Seb,' says Henry, leaning back in his chair as Marcy arrives with the water and proceeds to pour it into their glasses. 'Are you sure you want to do that?'

Seb nods as he takes a sip of water. 'I'm positive,' he says, putting his glass down on the table. 'I've had an amazing few years, done more than I ever imagined I would do in a lifetime. Christ, Henry, look where I was seven years ago, I was on my knees, killing myself with drink. If I can help other young artists achieve what they want to do then I will die a happy man.'

'When you're a dapper man of ninety, living in luxury in the South of France with a twenty-one year old blonde nymphet,' laughs Henry.

Seb shakes his head and smiles. 'A dapper man of ninety with my beautiful Yasmine next to me. South of France, Battersea or bloody Grimsby, I don't care, all I need is her beside me.'

'Are you ready to order yet, chaps?' Marcy is suddenly there beside them.

'Oh yes please,' says Henry. 'This conversation is getting far too soppy for my liking. Can't bear sentimentality, particularly on an empty stomach.' He picks up the menu and scans the page. 'I'll have the Clam Chowder then the Duck Confit if I may?' He hands the menu to Marcy who tucks it under her arm.

'And for you, Seb?' She stands with the point of her sharpened pencil poised at the top of her notepad.

'I'll have the soup then the risotto, please.'

'Excellent,' says Marcy, removing Seb's menu with a flourish, and disappearing into the darkness of the inner room.

'Speaking of Yasmine,' says Henry, squinting a little as a bright shaft of sunlight pours into the room. 'I sensed a bit of tension last night, particularly over my choice of Lauren to oversee the guest list. You do trust me don't you, Seb? I mean, we'll need a good mix of guests; highbrow – yes, of course – but also a little smattering of celebs to get us in the papers, you know? Yasmine realises that doesn't she?'

Seb's mouth tightens. There is always a hint of sexism in Henry's attitude to Yasmine. Henry can't really fathom her, this strong successful woman with opinions of her own, who is beautiful but doesn't use her looks to get on.

'Yes, she gets the whole PR thing, Henry,' he says, trying to keep his voice light. 'Of course she does. She's a professional and she's been in this business since she was eighteen. Her only concern is that the launch will end up being high-jacked by some bimbo reality star wanting to get her face in the papers. You know this Henry, and you know what the Honey Vision girls are like, they'll take the whole place over. Even if you just invite a couple, they'll bring their mates. The Rose Garden is not that kind of restaurant; it's a warm, genuine, family-oriented place. You see I still like the idea of inviting critics and their families, their kids, to really reinforce the whole Mediterranean family feel.'

Henry pulls a face. 'I know you like that idea Seb and we've got a couple of, er, children coming but any more and it would descend into chaos, you'd have smashed glasses, screaming kids, utter bedlam ...'

Seb smiles. 'Children don't always cause chaos, H. I've seen more smashed glasses and bedlam caused by coked up celebrities than by little people. Anyway, let's just stick to the list Yas compiled yeah, save us all this hassle.'

Henry shifts uncomfortably in his seat. 'Well, unfortunately, Seb, Lauren's already sent out her invites. But she has assured me that it's not just the Honey Vision girls, she's also sent it round to her friends in the City – hedge-fund guys, bankers, traders, in other words big money, Seb. You can't turn that kind of custom away.'

Seb nods. Henry is right. It would be naïve of him to think otherwise.

'Okay Henry,' he says, as a waiter puts a bowl of steaming celeriac soup in front of him. 'I agree, but do make sure that Lauren has invited the people on Yas's list too. I know Liam Kerr has received his invitation so it looks like she's done it but if you could check with her and let me know that would be great. I don't want Yas to have anything to worry about tomorrow.'

'Leave it with me,' says Henry, as he places his napkin on his knee. He raises his spoon towards Seb in a mock toast. 'Here's to The Rose Garden, eh? It's going to be a triumph.'

'To The Rose Garden,' says Seb, raising his spoon. 'And my brilliant wife.'

Kerstin sits on her bed, turning the news over and over. Yesterday morning; it had happened yesterday morning. What did she forget yesterday, what important ritual did she fail to observe? Then she remembers the rip in her purse. It had appeared sometime in the morning yet she had not noticed it until well after lunch, almost four p.m. If she had seen it earlier she could have replaced it immediately; instead it had sat there in her bag, festering like an open wound, inviting bad things in, taunting death. If she had been alert, if she had not been so preoccupied with the report she could have rectified it, she could have saved her father's life.

She stands up from the bed and goes to the living room, counting to seven and back before crossing the threshold, warding off whatever darkness might have seeped into the flat while she has been sitting prone on the bed.

She looks at the green digitalised numbers on the oven door. Two p.m. Somewhere, in a hospital bed in Cologne, the city of her birth, the place she can never return to while this fear grips her heart, her father lies hooked up to wires and tubes, dying but being kept artificially alive for his daughter to come and say goodbye. But she is not there by his side as she should be, she is here in this barren flat in London, the city that is holding her hostage, the city that taunts her with bad things; with dirt and grime and contamination, leaving her with no option but to count, to throw numbers up against the threat and keep it at bay. She is trapped inside her head, trapped by the numbers that must never cease lest the whole thing comes tumbling down. She needs to release them; needs to fill her head with something else, something logical.

She walks across the room to where a narrow set of shelves stands wedged against the wall. She reaches up to the top shelf and takes down a thick, leather-bound book. The gap that its removal leaves on the shelf troubles her immediately and she starts to reassemble the other books in order of size. She does it once and it still doesn't look right so she repeats it over and over, until she is satisfied that there are no gaps, no stray pages sticking out and that all the spines are lined up neatly. Thankfully, during her full check of the flat a few minutes ago, she had found nothing amiss, everything was in its place.

Taking her father's thesis in her arms she walks across to the sofa, checking first that the cushions are lined up straight, that the seat is not dirty. One, two, three, she counts as she places the cushions into a neat line. Now, with everything in order she opens the book. The book is safe; the book is not contaminated, she gives herself permission to touch it as much as she likes.

She closes her eyes and smells the faint, dusty scent of the paper, feels the indentation of her father's name embossed on the front in thick gold lettering. This book was printed in 1954, almost thirty years before she was born; when the war was still fresh in people's minds and Cologne was putting itself back together after being ripped apart from above.

She opens her eyes and places the book on her lap, stroking the front of it as though it is a precious piece of silk, a luxury item to be lingered over and admired. As she opens the book, a small pale-blue envelope falls out onto the floor. She picks it up and sees her name written in her father's small, neat handwriting. He had sent her his PhD seven years ago when she was driving herself mad in the days and weeks following the 7/7 bombings; when she was still living with Matthew.

Matthew. His name sounds abstract, as cold and ancient as stone; "Matthew, Mark , Luke and John, bless the bed that I lie on,' – her mother's nightly prayer as she folded the linen sheets around Kerstin's body, kissed her forehead and turned out the light. Matthew: the biblical tax collector; Matthew, her modern-day banker; the man who shared her bed and her life and then disappeared from the face of the earth. Matthew: who only exists in her memory; if he ever existed at all.

She takes the letter out of the envelope and begins to read:

4a Leipziger Str

Weiden

50858

KÖLN

8th August, 2005

My Dear Kerstin,

I hope this letter finds you well. Your mother tells me that you are enjoying your new role at Sircher Capital and you are finding much of cultural interest in your newly adopted city. I am well, though age is playing its usual tricks and I wake each day with a new ache or pain to contend with. Still, I am finding much solace in my garden, watching the roses bloom as I sit out there with a coffee and a book.

I enclose with this letter a copy of my PhD which you requested on the telephone, and though I am flattered you want to read it, I was concerned by the fractiousness in your voice when we spoke and I only hope that reading my scribblings will not set your mind to more worry. I, along with most of the world, watched in horror the events that unfolded in London last month. My first, instinctive thought was for you and your safety, once that was established my mind turned to the events of sixty years ago in the city where I sit now writing this letter. I have never spoken to you about the event of which I will refer but I hope that in doing so I may offer you some comfort, human comfort of which you will not find in the accompanying thesis. All my life I have placed my faith in the laws of Physics, but my work, I can see now as an old man, was simply an act of escape, of running away from the fear and horror I witnessed as a boy. And though the theory I formulated went some way to explaining the pattern behind that night, I am still ignorant as to what it meant for me, my family and the hundreds of other families who were destroyed in the blink of an eye.

As you know, I grew up in Cologne with my parents Matthias and Gerta Morgen in a modest street, close to the cathedral. I lived in a small apartment with them and my two younger sisters, Julia and Hannelore. My parents met in 1927, they married in 1931 and a year later I was born, their only son. My father worked as a cobbler and my mother was a midwife of sorts, bringing the babies of the district into the world but also laying out the dead. When the war broke out, my father was forty-eight years old, too old to fight and so he was sent to work in a munitions factory just outside Berlin. I was eight when he left and he told me I must be a good boy, learn my lessons and look after my mother and sisters. Already I was showing proficiency in science and mathematics and, like you, would sit for hours reading my text books, trying to drown out the drone of the bombers by reciting quadratic equations.

The air raids were terrifying – I would curl up in a ball, hold my hands over my ears and recite my times table all the way to the hundreds. And there I would be safe, hidden among the numbers, far away from the sound of airborne giants hurling bombs onto the earth, the screeching and crashing of buildings as they fell onto burning streets; the smell of fire and rubber and fear. But the aftermath was worse. We would emerge from the shelters like wide-eyed rats scurrying up to the light, bracing ourselves for what we would see when we opened the front door. Rubble, bodies strewn along streets, empty spaces where houses and shops once stood. One morning as we walked along the street, stepping over shells of bombs and pieces of burned furniture, we saw Magda, the mother of my best friend Albert, running towards us holding a package in her arms. Her face was black with dirt and dust and she was screaming and sobbing, lifting her eyes to the sky like a woman possessed. As she came closer we saw what she was holding. We gasped as the woman thrust the lifeless body of her boy into my mother's arms. Little Albert with the red hair and cheeky grin who brought me packets of sweets from his father's shop and told anyone who would listen how he was to become a great doctor one day, how he was going to cure the world. My mother, the midwife, my mother who tended the sick and laid out the dead seemed, to this woman, a messiah, a Jesus Christ figure who could perform miracles in this desolate wasteland. 'Make him wake up,' the woman implored before dropping to her knees and grinding her fists into the battered cobbles. 'Please can you make him wake up!'

It seemed endless, the onslaught we lived through those years. And though inhuman atrocities were being committed by the Nazis in the name of our country at that very moment, we knew nothing about them; all that would come out later. All we knew was that we had to live minute by minute and concentrate on staying alive.

30 May 1942 started well: a beautiful spring day, though the sun's light only served to expose the decimation and ruin of our beloved city. My mother prepared lunch for us – a treat – she had been given half a pound of bratwurst by a neighbour whose baby she had safely delivered the day before. We sat, my sisters and I, eating the meaty dish, slowly, savouring every

mouthful. Later, while my mother sat in her battered leather chair mending our socks, we children played a game of dominoes on the floor. We didn't know what was happening as we sat listening to our mother singing as we laughed and giggled and rubbed our full bellies, we didn't know that a thousand airplanes were heading across the channel bound for Hamburg with enough bombs to smash the city into pieces.

As the bombers approached they saw that Hamburg was covered in thick cloud; Cologne's skies were clear. At the final moment they altered their target and our fate was sealed by a change in the weather.

When we heard the sirens, we ran, my mother, my sisters and I, to the shelter at the end of the street. With other raids we had some kind of warning; this one had taken the city by surprise and there was chaos and panic as people fled towards the shelter. I was up ahead and when I got there I threw myself into the mass of bodies that were already huddled inside, thinking that my mother and sisters were behind me. I spent that night with my face squashed up against the wall as one thousand bombers pounded our city and turned it into dust. When morning came, I followed my fellow inmates out of the shelter and as we emerged squinting into the light of the sun, I saw them: my mother, Julia and Hannalore lying on the street, just metres from the shelter. They must have stumbled and fallen as the first bombs dropped; as I ran on ahead to my salvation.

So you see, my dear one, when I heard the news last month, when I saw the faces of those people who had been killed, those innocent men and women, when I heard your frightened voice on the phone, I knew something of what you must be feeling, what the families of those people must be feeling, of how London must feel. If my thesis offers you any comfort, if the patterns and laws and theories it identifies helps you find some reason, some order to the random outrage that has befallen you, then that is good.

But I have lived a long life now, I have lived seven times as long as my sisters, I am older than my mother and my father, and I have spent that life trying to find answers, trying to make sense of it all. Have I found it? My answer can only be no. I will never find it. My thesis is but a drop in the ocean of infinite pools that exist in human history, the wars and disasters, the extinctions and diasporas, the revolutions and discoveries, the births and deaths and futile accidents. What I am trying to say is that I wish, more than anything my child, for you to be happy, for you to find peace because I spent my life running away from human touch, from love and family because I thought any kind of intimacy could only bring me pain. Your mother tried to break that down, she tried to warm up the ice in my veins and I loved her, I loved her very much. She has done the most remarkable job in raising you into a fine adult and though you may have inherited my scientific mind, I see so much of your mother's kindness, her wonder at life, her spirit in you and I would hate to see that extinguished through fear.

Do not fear life, Kerstin. Let it take you on its journey, let it surprise you and amaze you, for no matter how hard we try we can never know all its secrets.

With my love,

Papa

PS Will you be home for Christmas?

Kerstin folds the letter up once, twice, three times then returns it to the envelope. Seven Christmases have passed since she received the PhD and the letter. When she had received the package she had taken the letter out and skim-read it, her mind in too much of a frenzy to really focus on the words scattered across the page. She had been impatient to get started on the book, to immerse herself in the mathematical equations that had always brought her such peace as a young girl. But though the thesis was a work of genius, with ideas thirty years ahead of its time, there was nothing in there to persuade Kerstin to loosen her grip, nothing to convince her that the world was not a dangerous place. With its descriptions of bombs dropping onto her home city at a rate of 20 tonnes per minute, it simply reinforced the terror she had felt on 7/7 as she heard the train explode in the tunnel. When she had finished reading it, she felt that her anxiety had been validated, that all it made clear was that life is precarious and full of random acts of violence and destruction.

So as 2005 drew to a close she began battening down the hatches – putting a big cross through every potential source of danger – trains, tubes, aeroplanes. By the New Year, she had shut out the world, shut out every risk, every unknowable element. There had been no Christmas visit to Cologne that year.

She stands up and puts the book back onto the shelf; her father's words locked inside their envelope where they cannot be heard. She looks around the room and her eyes meet the Bruegel print. She walks towards it and presses her nose up against the glass frame. The tiny figures blur in front of her eyes until they disappear and all she can see in front of her is a great black shadow.

'You will never leave me, will you?' she mutters under her breath in German. 'You are everywhere, wherever I go you're there.'

She pulls her face away and, as her focus reshifts, sees that her breath has left a smudge on the glass. She rubs at it frantically with the back of her sleeve, until the glass is clear. As she steps away, she feels the familiar sensation of taintedness. She will have to wash her blouse immediately; she will have to remove the stain of that picture from her clothes and her face.

She walks to the bathroom and turns on the shower, making sure the water is hot, steaming hot. Then she steps out of her trousers and hangs them carefully on the square wicker laundry basket. The blouse must not touch the trousers, the blouse must go somewhere else. She shrugs herself out of the delicate fabric then wraps it in a large white bath towel. They can be washed together, the blouse must not touch anything else, it must not come into contact with the floor or any other item of clothing. She removes her underwear, steps into the hot shower and begins to scrub her face, every bit of it must be clean, the taint from the glass must be washed away, otherwise something truly terrible will happen. She reaches up to the shelf and takes an unopened box of soap. Sliding her finger along the seal she removes the white oval bar and continues to pummel at her face. Her skin feels sore and tight but she must carry on until there is no trace left, no residue of whatever darkness lies behind the glass.

13

Mark sits in a small café off Leicester Square, piling cubes of sugar into a pyramid. His large mug of tea sits by his elbow, steam seeps out of it into the air that is thick with the sound of plates clattering, orders being shouted, coffee machines whistling and the clunky footsteps of waitresses, diners and delivery men as they weave in and out of the tiny space.

He still can't quite believe that he has spoken to her, been near her, stood on the threshold of the restaurant. Standing next to her was the strangest experience, like being close to a famous landmark or statue. He knows almost everything there is to know about this woman and her life – her date of birth (10 October 1976), her Moroccan ancestry (father, Solly, born in Tangier, deceased), her career path (sous chef in Colette, Waterloo via The Green Room, Lavender Hill then Aquitane, Mayfair, before teaming up with Henry Walker to launch The Rose Garden), her wedding anniversary (21 December 2005), the birth date of her daughter, Cosima Rose Bailey (14 August

2006) . . . The data had flashed up before him like a great list as he stood there.

She was shorter than he imagined but prettier than in the photographs he had seen, and she smelled amazing – a musky, evening scent like violets. It reminded him of something he had liked as a child, powdery purple sweets his dad used to bring home from trips to Germany. Her voice was pure London, not plummy as he imagined Seb's to be, and it was husky and quiet, her words direct and clear. She had folded her arms across her chest as she spoke to him. Protectively? Defiantly? Mark wasn't sure but she was certainly confident despite her small stature.

He hadn't planned the encounter. He had actually seen today as a day of research, walking in and around Frith Street, finding his bearings, checking the back of the restaurant for fire exits, seeing what route he should take when he makes his entrance tomorrow night. But then curiosity had got the better of him when he saw her standing in the doorway taking delivery of some boxes of fruit. He watched her for a few moments from the other side of the street, watched as she signed the delivery note then bent down to lift up the large box. By the time she stood up he was there in front of her, a dark shadow in the glaring sunlight that shone so brightly in her eyes she had to squint.

She had gasped and almost dropped the boxes but Mark did nothing to reassure her, keeping his voice hard and direct as he enquired after her husband. But then, possibly without realising it, she had given him what he wanted – a piece of information that meant he had something solid to prepare for, could spend the next twenty-four hours making sure he got it just right.

'He'll be here tomorrow morning,' she had said. 'He's going to be hanging pictures from around ten so you'll probably catch him then. Can I pass on a message?'

Mark had smiled; ecstatic to finally have a time and a date for his confrontation with the man who had ruined his life, but he had managed to keep his excitement contained as he shook his head at the attractive woman in front of him and told her there was no message. He had left her then, left her dragging the box of fruit into the restaurant, the precious restaurant built on the wreckage of dreams and lives, in this shithole wasteland where young girls can disappear like stray dogs or discarded potato peelings thrown out to rot in the putrid air.

He drains his cup of tea and throws a handful of change onto the table. Picking up his heavy black bag, he pulls it onto his back like a piece of armour and heads for the door. There is one more place to visit before he returns to his room.

Stella and Paula walk out of the clinic in silence, neither knowing quite what to say. Eventually, after they have crossed three intersections, wordlessly navigating the late-afternoon shoppers, Stella breaks the impasse.

'Well, that seemed to go okay,' she says, her voice half-drowned out by the shrill beeping of a reversing delivery van.

Paula smiles but her shoulders are raised like a cat about to pounce and they carry on in a daze through the back streets, pretending to look in shop windows, going through the motions but something is wrong. Something is very wrong.

The scan had only taken a few minutes then she and Paula were led back to the consultancy room where Sarah discussed the results – 'all looks healthy and normal' – and they were told that the most appropriate treatment plan for them would be donor insemination or IUI: INTRAUTRINE INSEMINATION as it read on the front of the booklet she handed them.

After the consultation they were taken to yet another room to meet a specialist fertility nurse who talked them through their treatment plan. Yet through it all, Paula looked like she was only half-present, like she was floating above the scene looking down onto the square room; at Stella sitting in the chair nodding her head and asking intermittent questions; at the nurse gesticulating with her flabby white arm and ticking boxes on the sheet of paper in front of her. When they finally emerged into the cool air of the street, Stella had touched Paula's hand and it was like ice; it was as though the happy, excited woman who had entered the clinic had been left behind; sucked into a strange portal, a land of probes and forms and smiling babies.

They head onto Bond Street and a sleek black Bentley pulls up outside a gold shuttered store. Stella shakes her head as the black-hatted driver gets out and opens the back door of the car. Some things never change, she thinks, as they cross the road towards Green Park. Leaders come and go, fashions change, great people live and die, the world turns and still there are Bentleys on Bond Street. And very likely when the end comes, when these streets are swallowed up, release their secrets, their jewels and sparkle, and revert back to marshy bogland, there will still be Bentleys on Bond Street.

'Shall we go and get something to eat?' Stella's voice trails across the noise of the traffic as they stand on Piccadilly waiting to cross. 'It would just be nice to sit down and have a chat, go through all this.' She waves the thick wedge of forms and booklets in front of her.

Paula looks at her watch. 'It's almost three,' she says. 'I hadn't realised it was so late.'

'Almost rush hour,' says Stella, as a wave of people come towards them. 'So, where shall we go?'

'Anywhere,' says Paula, pulling her hands through her hair, as she always does when she is apprehensive.

Stella looks up the street: Hyde Park to the right, Soho to the left. She is not ready to go back to Soho, not yet, and not with Paula in this strange mood.

'I know,' she says, trying to sound bright and jolly. 'We'll go to the café in St James's Park. It will be nice, we can watch the herons.'

She takes Paula's arm and as they cross the road a great gust of wind whipped up by the traffic blows into their faces. It feels so good after the stale heat of the clinic and as Stella looks up the street she catches a glimpse of the neon lights of Piccadilly Circus flashing on and off and a flutter of excitement catches in her stomach as they reach the other side and head for St James's.

Mark clutches a limp bunch of lilies in his hand as he stands waiting to cross the northern end of Oxford Street. He clears his throat but his chest remains tight, the fumes from the traffic are making him wheeze but his inhaler is in the front of the rucksack and he can't get to it easily with his arms full of flowers and the dead weight of his black bag.

The lights change and he steps out into the road. It is all so ordinary, so blank, with its McDonalds over there on the corner, its Caffè Nero, its cheap sportswear shops, somehow he was imagining a much darker place but he knows there is still a little way to go. A few metres, one foot in front of the other and he will be there, he will see what she saw.

He turns onto Hanway Street, a narrow little lane that curves into a crescent as he walks along. It's little more than an alley-way, a short-cut, he thinks as he walks past a Spanish bar and a tatty-looking shop selling second-hand records. The street is claustrophobic and cramped and the crumbling Georgian buildings lean inwards, like they are bearing down on him, imploring him to listen to their secrets.

What was she doing here, he asks himself as he follows the road toward its final destination. His little sister, the baby of the family, the one he promised his dad he would look after, had spent her final moments in this rotten place, this forgotten sorry excuse for a street and he had not been there to save her. Why hadn't she phoned him, earlier in the night, after the party? If she had phoned him he would have helped, he would have told her what to do. His feet feel as heavy as his lungs as the street curves to the left; the air suddenly feels thin and icy cold despite the warmth of the day.

Hanway Place. Such a pretty name, it sounds like the home of an Edwardian novelist. He feels like there should be window boxes full of flowers and a horse-drawn carriage making its way down the road but instead there is just an empty side street dotted with black bollards and a glass-fronted restaurant whose name Mark can't read. He walks a couple of steps past the restaurant and there it is: a tiny deserted strip of concrete and brick, dark, airless and piled with boxes of food waste and bulging black bags.

He puts his own black bag down at his feet and takes the rucksack from his back, and as he does so his heart begins to pound inside his chest, the familiar pulse-like sensation rises in his throat as he tries to get his breath. He gulps at the stale air like a drowning man. The inhaler, he needs the inhaler, but the attack is so strong he can't bend down to retrieve it from his bag. His body feels like it's breaking down as he drops the lilies to the floor and clutches at his chest, trying to massage his lungs back to life. But inside his head, his voice is screaming out at him, trying to make itself heard above the desperate gasps for breath. The inhaler, get the inhaler. He falls to his knees and wrestles the bag with one arm, ripping through canvas and metal until he feels the reassuring hard plastic between his fingers. With shaking hands he brings the inhaler to his mouth. He sucks a huge mouthful but it's not enough, another, still no relief, a third and he feels his lungs loosen, a fourth and he slumps down onto the hard cobbled ground and feels himself coming back. In and out, in and out, his breathing slowly returns to normal.

After a couple of moments, he stands up and goes to pick up his bags, his eyes stinging with tears and grit, and he sees that his hands are stained with the pollen from the lilies that he had been clutching so tightly. He sees the discarded bunch of flowers lying among the bin bags and he lets out a howl, a cry so raw it seems to come from somewhere outside of his body.

'Zoe,' he screams, and his voice echoes against the grimy brick walls of the alley. The shout seems to open up his lungs and he launches himself at the bags and starts kicking them, smashing them open with his feet until there is just a mulch of tins and cardboard and rotten food spread out along the ground. He keeps kicking and kicking until every bag is split, until every ounce of anger and grief and bitterness oozes out from him like the slime seeping from the decaying rubbish.

Scraping his shoes against the ground, he picks up his bags and takes one last look at this bleak, filthy place. The rubbish is piled up against the wall and in the dim light it looks like a mound of earth atop a grave, with empty crisp packets and congealed Chinese spare-ribs in place of soil. As he turns to leave, he notices movement among the mess. A rat scurries across the top of it and begins to feast on a piece of food, pulling and pulling to release it from the sticky waste until it loosens and brings with it a sodden, grey lily petal.

14

Kerstin turns the dial on the washing machine to sixty and with a thud the machine stammers into life. She watches as the grey blouse spins round and round behind the thick clear glass.

This is the second wash. Five more to go. Seven washes will be enough to satisfy Kerstin that nothing of the picture will remain on the blouse; not a trace of its oily residue; not an atom or a speck. The washing powder will expunge the stains, the rank breath that has seeped from the print and worked its way into the fibres of her top.

The laundry room is silent but for the gentle clicking of the machine as it kneads the blouse into a sopping, soapy dough. There are three washing machines lined up in a row underneath a long, bare window. One of the machines is unused, the second, by the door, is Clarissa's. She has the machine open and Kerstin can see a flash of pink inside: a crumpled cotton handkerchief? A pair of old woman's knickers? Who knows, and Kerstin will not be investigating. On the shelf above the machine is a large oilcloth bag decorated in a red-and-gold print. Bottles of laundry detergent and fabric softener poke out of the top of the bag and Kerstin notices that the lid of one container is congealed with old crusted blue liquid. It makes her feel uneasy just looking at it, knowing it is there, so she turns away and starts preparing a batch of detergent for the third wash.

Kerstin's washing paraphernalia is lined up in a neat row on the shelf above her washing machine – hers is by the wall, far enough away from Clarissa's to remain untainted by the forgotten pink underwear and the congealed blue liquid.

She leans across the machine and picks up a large metal measuring jug from the shelf. Then, opening up the industrial-size box, she dips the jug into the snowy white powder. As she does so she thinks of the experiment that had ignited global interest in her father's thesis: the Avalanche game. Back in the eighties, a group of theoretical physicists had conducted an experiment – or played a game, as they liked to describe it – where they sprinkled grains of sand onto a table one at a time and monitored how the grains piled up. As the pile grew it became steeper and the sand started to slide downwards, sparking little avalanches. As more sand was added the pile rose and fell; instead of growing in a linear movement, it fluctuated. She had read about this experiment during her time at the University of Cologne where she was studying for a degree in Pure Mathematics and was about to embark on a career in finance. It fascinated her, the avalanche; the grains of sand seemed to represent the fluctuations of the money market, rising and falling, plateauing and collapsing, with more money being added somewhere in the world every second of the day, piling up and falling down.

Into this maelstrom her mathematical reason would introduce some element, no matter how small, of order, she had told herself as she sat outside the Cologne office of Sircher Capital waiting to go in to be interviewed for a job as a junior research analyst. She would highlight patterns, rip through financial forecasts, compute profits and losses, reconcile and assimilate until out of a chaotic flurry of information, order and reason would emerge. It was what she had loved as a child, sitting on the floor separating her building blocks into neat piles in order of colour, size and shape; from building blocks to equations to numerical theory, all the way to the heady world of corporate finance where she would come into her own.

Detailed reports were presented each week; meetings were attended in New York and London, Tokyo and Paris. She was regarded as a high achiever, a financial whizz with a computer-fast brain , the perfect candidate to take on the role of Research Analyst at the newly opened London office of Sircher Capital and for a year she was just that.

She places the jug of powder onto the top of the machine and watches as the gentle vibrations cause the powder to ripple ever so slightly; the tiniest fraction of movement. Like the grain of sand, it takes just one tiny, microscopic element to be added to an unsteady structure and the whole thing will come tumbling down.

The machine builds to its frenetic spin cycle and Kerstin crouches poised by the machine door, ready to open it at the first click, to grab the blouse and start all over again. She starts to count: one, two, three, four . . . the machine whines agonisingly as though pushing itself to its limits . . . five, six, seven, eight . . . Kerstin hears a creak, a tapping from behind, it might be rain, who knows, she carries on counting . . . nine, ten, elev—

'Oh, it's you!'

The voice is unexpected, it slices through Kerstin's counting like a blade through skin and she loses her balance and tumbles backwards, landing with her arms stretched out behind her. The machine clatters to its climax with a whirr of grinding noise as she picks herself up and sees a familiar figure standing in the doorway.

'Clarissa,' she half-whispers. 'What are you doing here? You gave me a shock.'

'I could ask you the same question, my dear,' says the old lady, edging further into the strip-lit gloom. 'I heard noises down here. Thought it was an intruder. Why are you washing at this time of day? Shouldn't you be at work?'

'I came home early,' says Kerstin, picking herself up. 'Thought I'd get some washing done.' She counts to seven and back in her head; warding off whatever dirt may have contaminated her hands from the floor.

'It's a travesty, a cultured, clever girl like you having to do her own washing as well as a job.'

Clarissa leans across the machines and her arm touches the edge of Kerstin's metal jug.

'Of course, in my day we had servants to attend to that sort of thing, laundry maids we called them. Red-faced creatures sent down from the North or the West Country, oh they were ghastly. We had a particularly rough one, Hattie they called her, well us children had lots of fun with that name . . . Fatty Hattie we called her. "Has Fatty Hattie ironed the sheets yet?" Mother would scold us but she must have had a quiet giggle to herself all the same. My mother never washed a sheet in her life – she had the most beautiful hands, pale and soft as butter. You see back then the world knew where it was, people knew their place, people like Fatty Hattie and Edie the cook, Bruton the butler, they knew what they were sent to this earth to do and they didn't question it. They wouldn't have dreamed of questioning it. Now you see, it all started with the unions, that's when this country started on the path to destruction, giving the labouring classes a voice, a vote, preposterous. And now you have these dark-skinned thugs rioting, I saw it on the television, great mobs of them smashing windows and grabbing clothes and shoes. Monstrous, but that's where the unions have got us to . . . in my mother's day it was simple.

She campaigned for votes for women, ladies, daughters of educated men. Labour tried to convince the suffs that they should support them in their crazy bill for Universal Suffrage and I remember Mummy and Daddy saying – down that road is the way to ruination, giving the great unwashed the vote is tantamount to legislating anarchy. That's why you have these coloured chaps rampaging down the street and why clever young ladies like you have been reduced to blistering their hands with soap suds . . . it's all down to the unions, Daddy was right. It was the road to ruination.'

Kerstin bends down and opens the machine door, trying to ignore the tirade that is emanating from Clarissa's mouth. She must have been in the flat by herself all day, thinking, reminiscing about the good old days of bullied servants and mothers with butter-soft hands, and now out it all comes, like a torrent pouring into the room, washing away Kerstin's counting, crashing over the walls, sending everything into disarray. If I don't say anything, thinks Kerstin, then maybe she will go. She pulls out the blouse, but aware of Clarissa above her, she only half inspects it before putting it back into the drum and closing the door.

'What are you putting it back in for?' Clarissa's voice drills into the side of her head as she pours the jug of powder into the drawer. 'You'll find, dear, that it's perfectly clean. You'll wear out the fabric with over-washing, you know. See I do know a little about washing. Once I got married, a wife was expected to do her bit, what with the war and what have you. And unfortunately, my husband was rather a tight-fisted old so-and-so and wouldn't shell out for staff. Said I'd been a pampered brat and I'd have to learn to cook and clean with the rest of them. Can you imagine? Still, in the end I got rather good at it, particularly after the baby was born, all those nappies, yes, got rather good at it. . .'

Kerstin can feel herself getting hotter, her face burning with rage. She turns the machine on again and stands staring at the clear glass-fronted drum. She will not respond, she will not engage, she will just stand here like a statue until the old biddy gives up and goes back to her flat.

But as the cycle starts up, Clarissa leaps across and bangs her fist on the top of the machine. 'Trust me, my dear, that blouse was clean. You're going to ruin a perfectly good garment with all this washing. Now let me switch this thing off for you and we'll recover it.'

'No!' The word screams out of Kerstin's mouth almost of its own volition. She has to get this woman out of here, she is obstructing her on this, one of the most serious of procedures. Her father is dying, her blouse has been tainted and this bigoted old wretch is going to make everything worse, she will bring the bad thing down upon her, she will make death triumph, make the darkness claim her father and Kerstin has to stop her.

She grabs the old woman's shoulder, it feels as hard and brittle as a branch of a tree.

'Clarissa, you must stop. I know what I am doing. Please will you leave me to attend to my washing in peace.' Kerstin hollers the last of this sentence in German and Clarissa freezes then turns gingerly.

'I know that language,' she hisses. 'Hun language. My brother-in-law, God rest his sainted bones, was in the RAF. He fought for this country against the purveyors of that devil language. They burned babies in ovens . . . the Nazis . . . they killed millions of innocent Jews. I will not listen to that language in my home. This is my home, no matter what they say, and I will be wherever I want to be. I will walk these corridors, I will do as I please. I am Clarissa Burton-Lane. You are a German! A Hun in our midst and I never realised it. You talk like an English woman but your anger has let it slip. Ha, they will let anybody in here now . . . a German . . . a madwoman washing her clothes to smithereens. My brother-in-law was in the RAF you know . . . dropped the bombs on Dresden . . .'

For a second, as Kerstin stands watching this onslaught unfold, she feels weightless, as though she is floating on the ceiling looking down on this emaciated old lady, her face contorted with hatred shaking her fists at a pale haired young woman with blistered hands. Then suddenly she is back in her body, her heart pulsating against her chest, aware that if she leaves now, if she does not complete the task then God help her, she will be ruined, darkness will claim her. There is one obstacle between her and the machine and as she reaches out and smashes it with the metal jug, time seems to slow down, like the waning spin cycle on the machine. There is a crack as metal meets skull and the old lady flies in a blur across the room, her head scraping against the edge of the skirting board, her body rolling and twisting until it stops and lands in a crumpled heap by the door.

Silence. A deep, empty silence fills the room and it is thick, like gloopy liquid has been poured in from the ceiling. The silence fills Kerstin's lungs, choking her from within. She goes to speak but no words come; her brain and body are frozen to the small patch of linoleum where she stands staring at a lifeless body.

She should go to her; check her pulse, call an ambulance, do the things that any fully functioning human being would do. It was an accident, nobody would suspect her, they would think the old woman had tumbled, like she had on the way to the post office.

Kerstin looks at the washing machine. She has to finish the wash, she has to ward off the darkness, otherwise her father will die. She goes to move but then she sees it; deep red blood stuck to the floor in patches. It is seeping from Clarissa's head, leaking out like a thin river coursing through a map. She cannot step across the blood; she cannot get to her clothes. Soon the blood will have reached the machine and that will be it. She has to get out of here.

She places the metal jug on the top of Clarissa's washing machine; still reticent, even amid this mayhem, to taint her washing with blood. Then she tiptoes towards the door, counting to seven and back before opening. Taking one last look at the room, she sees the silver machines neatly lined up; the packets of washing powder stacked onto the shelf and the pale, white lump lying in the middle, eyes open as if asking 'why?'

Closing the door behind her, she makes her way to the narrow lift and presses the silver button. No one will know, she tells herself as she steps inside. She will go back to the flat, and work out what to do. She has an overwhelming compulsion to clean, to scrub and rinse from top to bottom, to remove the stain of death from her. She can smell it now, a clammy, sweaty smell clinging to her nostrils. She must wash it away immediately.

The lift reaches the ground floor and Kerstin waits for the jolt; the rackety noise before the doors open. It seems to take longer than usual, and Kerstin starts to panic. Please do not stick, not this lift, this narrow airless space. She has to get out. She closes her eyes and starts to count but before she gets to three, the doors slide open and a man and woman stand in front of her.

It feels like her heart is going to explode and for a moment she thinks about standing her ground, not letting them into the lift. Then the man smiles at her, he is holding a clipboard.

'Oh, hi,' he says brightly. 'I didn't think anyone would be at home. I'm from Elizabeth Charles Estate Agency. You must be the lady from Flat 2?'

He holds out his hand but Kerstin doesn't respond. Instead, she steps out of the lift. The man looks at her quizzically and Kerstin looks down at her white top and black skirt, fearing for a moment that she has blood on her. There is nothing.

'Well,' says the man. 'Nice to meet you.' He turns to the woman by his side. 'Now, if you want to come this way, Mrs Farthing, I'll show you the laundry room.' She is in her mid-forties by the look of it and she smells of lemons. The scent sticks in Kerstin's throat as she squeezes past her.

She watches as they get into the lift; the man smiles, the woman stares straight ahead. As the doors close Kerstin starts to run, she has no idea where she is going and there is no time to return to the flat and collect her things. She must go now, this minute, before they find her.

Seb stands in his studio adding the final touches to The Lake: his gift to Yasmine, an oil painting of the lake in Battersea Park that they sat beside after getting married almost seven years ago. Tomorrow he will hang it in the restaurant and maybe it will be a lucky charm, who knows. Not that he believes in all that. Someone once told him that there was no such thing as luck and he agrees to a certain extent; you make your own luck in this life, by working hard and being kind, by opening your heart and loving.

The light in the studio is starting to fade; in the mornings it is filled with bright sunshine, it is one of the reasons he took it, that and the fact that it is pretty much equidistant between home, Maggie's flat and the gallery.

He dabs a silvery dot of paint along the outline of the lake, then stands back and puts his head to one side, squints his eyes and walks towards it again, checking to see if the ripple effect he was aiming for has worked. As he walks back and forth, the painting stands on the easel like a child waiting to be dressed. To anybody else, it would look complete but Seb is exacting when it comes to his work and nothing less than the best is allowed to leave the studio.

Almost six months of work has gone into this piece; snatched moments here and there between his paid commissioned work and the day-to-day demands of the gallery. He hopes she likes it. He thinks she will but he can never be sure. He knows when she really loves something and when she's just pretending, something about the tone of her voice and the presence of a gleam in her eye tells him when it is right. He and Yasmine, though deeply in love, have very different tastes. There are films he adores that she doesn't just 'not like' but downright despises, same with music – he loves Primal Scream, she says they make her cringe, and writers – she loves Isabella Allende, he can't get past the first page of her novels.

Yet they come together for the important things, the funda-mental beliefs that need to be in sync for any partnership to survive – they have the same values, the same moral compass and they have Cosima, the little ball of flesh and giggles that binds them for ever. Oh, and then there is the physical side: Seb has never felt as connected to someone as he is to Yasmine and, even after all these years, he is still drawn to her body like a thirst that can never be fully quenched. The air in the room changes when she walks into it, becomes fuller and more vital, he can tell she is there without looking up. And despite their punishing work schedules, the exhaustion of parenthood and the pressures of London life, he still has to start and end each day holding her in his arms, he can't ever imagine not being with her, can't imagine a world without her in it.

The music changes as he dabs the paint with the lightest of touches, he's not aware that Rachmaninov has seagued into David Bowie's Heroes, but then he is not really aware of any-thing but the picture. When he is painting he forgets himself; his body is just a vessel, a machine, his arm an extension of the paintbrush. He feels in perfect sync with the work of art unfolding before him, and yet despite his success, the hours he can dedicate to painting are few and far between; which is why these two hours, from three to five on a late August afternoon as the sun begins to wane in the grey London sky, are so precious.

He is getting better; he can see his line get stronger, more confident as each year passes, he can see maturity seeping into the spaces between canvas and oil. Seven years ago he painted a huge piece that went on to sell to an anonymous US dealer for the astonishing sum of £100,000. It depicted him and Sophie, the married woman, his long-dead love, on the beach at Rotherhithe; he curled up on the sand holding a gas mask to his face; she standing above him draped in a long scarlet dress and carrying a bundle of rags in her arms. He finished it in the early hours of what would go on to be referred to as 7/7, that strange moonless night when he left Zoe standing in Soho Square and ran like a madman to his office on Shaftesbury Avenue to say goodbye to his dead lover. For months after her death, he had tried to paint her face but it would not come, it was like there was a great blockage standing between him and his memory. Every attempt he made looked wrong. That night as he stood in the office, he had felt a burning sensation, felt her spirit leave him as he painted each delicate feature onto the canvas. By morning she was complete and Zoe was gone.

When he met Yasmine, he didn't want to have the painting around the flat. It seemed wrong, inappropriate somehow, to hold on to it so he let Henry sell it to a business contact in the States and, as always, Henry got the best price. The money allowed him to put down a deposit on the flat in Battersea and gave a significant boost to the fledgling gallery that he had named Asphodel, after the flowers that grow in the Ancient Greek resting place that lies between heaven and earth. That's where he imagined Sophie had gone, and now he could get on with his life, unencumbered by the past while the painting hangs in a mock-Venetian chapel high in the Hollywood Hills, on the grounds of the vast estate owned by the multi-millionaire record producer who bought it.

Seb knows that if he saw that painting again he would cringe, he would pick it apart and find fault everywhere. He would wince at the clumsy use of colour, the position of the figures, the shading of the sea. He will never be satisfied with his work and that is how it should be. He wants to go on perfecting it until he is so old he can no longer hold the paintbrush. Wasn't it Matisse who said, propped up in his bed as he neared the end of his life, that rather than reaching the end of his painting career, he was only just beginning to see.

Seb stands back and looks at the finished painting. It's okay, he thinks. Everything is as it should be: the evening light glimmers across the water like a swarm of muted fireflies, like it did on the night of their wedding. Seb liked that, it felt like affirmation, as though nature had somehow acknowledged the two of them standing entwined by the lake, it felt like they had become part of the landscape and when they walked away they would leave a part of themselves embedded in the scene. That's what it's all about, thinks Seb, as he runs his hands along the outline of the painted sky, we all hope to leave something behind, some evidence that we were here, that we made an impact. Will his paintings endure after his death? Will they hang alongside his heroes in the great galleries of the world or will they be bundled up and left to gather dust in some forgotten, airless attic? Is it arrogant, this quest for immortality or is it just human nature? Paintings, books, music, children, ideas, pockets full of lucky charms and rusty trinkets scattered across the earth as you swallow dust and dream of soft meadows.

His phone beeps on the desk. He picks it up and switches off the alarm. It's five p.m.: time to go and collect Cosima from her guinea pig-fest at Gracie Marshall's. Time to step out of this portal and return to real time, to people and cars and food and sugary kisses.

He takes his jacket from the back of the chair and takes one last look at the painting. 'Yes,' he thinks. 'It will do.'

15

'Are we going to talk about it?'

Stella stands in the doorway of the tiny bathroom in the apartment as Paula lies back in a very hot, bubbly bath. They had eaten ham sandwiches and crisps in the little café in St James's; sitting side by side they had talked about Paula's brother's wife's broken ankle, about whether Carole at the Chelsea Physic Garden had received Paula's email asking if they could visit tomorrow, about the restaurant launch tomorrow night and whether or not the woman sitting three tables along was the one who had married Noel Gallagher. They talked about everything except what they had just experienced in the clinic. After months of incessant baby talk, Paula had suddenly gone quiet.

'Talk about what?' Paula sits up and turns on the hot tap, adding more scalding water to the already full bath.

'Come on, Paula,' says Stella, stepping into the room. 'What's the matter?' She moves Paula's clothes from the lid of the toilet seat and sits down, folding her arms across her chest.

Paula lies down in the steaming water and sighs deeply.

'It's nothing,' she says, her voice a near whisper. 'It was just a bit of a shock, I guess.'

Stella nods her head, though there is something about the way Paula is staring into space that makes her think there is more to it than she is letting on.

'It's a big step,' says Stella. 'We've always known that and it's your body that has to go through the pregnancy, having people poking and prodding you. It can feel like your body's not your own anymore. I love you. You know that don't you?'

Paula doesn't answer, she just keeps staring straight ahead as though trying to find the answer to whatever is worrying her in the blue flowery pattern on the tiles.

After a couple of minutes of silence, Stella stands up.

'I know,' she says. 'Let's have a drink eh? You've been abstaining for months, your body should be in peak condition by now. How about I pop downstairs and get a bottle of champagne, we can toast the baby, the soon-to-be conceived baby. What do you say?'

Paula looks up at her. Her face is red with the heat of the bath and she looks tired.

'If you want a drink, you have one. I don't feel like champagne,' she says.

Stella walks towards the bath and kneels down on the floor by Paula's face. She runs her fingers through Paula's wet hair and gently kisses her mouth.

'Come on, angel,' she says. 'Let's have a night off, eh? A night off worrying about the baby and about work and stuff. We deserve a break, it's been so long since we just relaxed together.'

She kisses Paula again, on her forehead, her nose, the crook of her soft, damp neck and she hears Paula sigh with what sounds like pleasure. 'It's a beautiful evening out there. I'm going to book us a table in the garden and we can have a long, leisurely dinner. Come on; for old times?'

Paula smiles the ghost of a smile. 'Okay,' she says. 'Book it for seven though, won't you? I'll have to dry my hair and get ready and I've got to send a couple of emails first.'

'Excellent,' says Stella. 'I'll go and do it now and I'll pick up a bottle of champagne and two glasses, okay?'

Paula rolls her eyes at her playfully. 'Okay, but get me a packet of Twiglets as well will you? I can't drink on an empty stomach.'

'Twiglets and champagne,' laughs Stella. 'You've always been a classy girl.'

She ducks as Paula throws a damp towel at her.

'Ha,' she cries. 'Bad shot. Right, I won't be long. And you should get out of that bath now, you're in danger of turning into a prune and that is not a good look.'

She hears Paula snort as she walks across the living room towards the door. If only they could always be as light as that. It seems like happiness and frivolity only come to them in snatched moments.

Why isn't this enough?

Stella turns the question over in her head as she walks down the stairs to the restaurant. She thinks of Dylan O'Brien and all the questions she wants to ask him when they meet. In the car on the way down those questions had been clear and concise; now her brain is fuddled with images of babies and nervous receptionists and at the heart of it all, the feeling deep in her stomach. The guilt that she is deceiving Paula; that she has come here for her own selfish reasons.

Is it wrong to want to be a person in her own right; not simpy an appendage to Paula's world? And if she is capable of deceiving Paula like this, of going behind her back and taking steps to create a whole new future then what hope do they have?

She tries to push her worries to the back of her mind as she opens the door to the tiny, darkened restaurant and heads towards the bar, hoping with all her heart that tonight will be different.

Mark sits on the bed holding the black bag on his lap. He had staggered back to the hostel like a drunken man and lain on the bed for half an hour until he got his breath back. He had felt her presence in that alley way, she was there, she was all around him. As he kicked that rubbish he thought he could smell her perfume wafting on the air – Calvin Klein's CK One – the sharp citrusy scent mingling with the rotten eggs and decaying vegetable peelings. It was there for a split second hovering above the mound of rubbish like a mirage. She was still there, he thought as he navigated the back streets of Soho, sweating in his thick sweatshirt. She was trapped in that manky alley way. His father used to talk about the dead soldiers, the ones who had been killed in battle and how you could feel their presence, their energy all around you. Restless spirits he used to call them, unable to find peace, trapped in the places where they had died. His father said that because they had been struck down in the height of battle, all that energy, all that adrenalin just got sucked into the ether and remained in the atmosphere like some opaque gas. Zoe is a restless spirit, he knows it, she's trying to tell him something. All those weird dreams he's been having lately, it's a sign, a message from her. It's not about that druggie bastard, he's dead now, no, it's a sign that he has to act, act now.

He slowly unzips the bag and takes out the long, thin canvas package. Putting the black bag to one side, he carefully removes the shotgun from its slip and holds it in his hands. He strokes the cool metal tip, runs his fingers along the wooden stock and smiles to himself as he thinks about the first time he held a gun in his hands.

It was his granddad, Ernie Bradshaw, who taught him how to shoot. When Mark's dad died Ernie had moved in with them, thinking that the children would benefit from having a man around. His wife Sadie had died when Mark's mother was a little girl and Ernie had brought his daughter up single-handedly in their tiny terrace house in Redcar. He was still a relatively young man when he moved in, fifty-five and as lithe and fit as he had been in his twenties. He soon settled into the ground floor flat with its tiny patch of garden and neat, pretty hanging baskets, lovingly tended to by Mark's mother.

Mark was twelve years old when his grandfather took him out to the moors to watch his first grouse shoot. In the three years since his father's death, Mark had grown inward; barely speaking, communicating only in grunts and shrugs of his shoulders, emerging from his bedroom to go to school and eat his meals then retreating when both were finished. Ernie thought the lad could do with some fresh air, or at least that was what he told his daughter when she waved them off.

They drove in Ernie's ancient Ford Escort up to the Cleveland Hills and the wild expanse of the Ferensby Estate. Ernie's father had been a gamekeeper on the estate in the thirties right up until the outbreak of the Second World War and he used to take his young son out with him, pointing out the pheasants and the partridge, the kestrels and woodcocks. But it was in the cloying heat of August that the estate really came into its own, when car loads of titled gents in tweed jackets strode across the moors in search of grouse.

The Glorious Twelfth, Ernie told Mark, was as big a deal as Christmas Day to him as a child. Young Ernie used to walk behind the men and play paper, scissors, stone with Lord

Ferensby's son, a skinny red-head they called Harry, though he had been christened Henry Edmund De Vere Ferensby, the future sixteenth Lord Ferensby. A bond formed between the two boys that was to endure over the years, it survived the War when the estate workers marched off to fight Hitler and didn't return; it survived Harry's time at Oxford and Ernie's apprenticeship at the steel works, and when the old Lord Ferensby died and Harry took on the title he let Ernie come and join in the shoots on the estate. Ernie's father had suffered a stroke in the early sixties and spent the rest of his days in a nursing home. He never saw his beloved moors again and Ernie wanted to keep the tradition going, wanted to keep his father's spirit alive by trekking up to the top of those moors each weekend, swapping the thick sulphurous heat of the steel works for clean northern air.

Mark had come out of himself after that first shoot and though he had not been allowed to use a gun that day, he had watched the men take aim and fire at the birds, watched the way they treated their shotguns with reverence, drying and cleaning them after a shot, keeping them safe in the crooks of their arms like sleeping babies. The next time they went Mark had been allowed to be a beater, alongside Ernie, and he felt his weak lungs expand as he beat the heather with a stick and watched the grouse rise into the air as though they had been hypnotised. The noise of the gun as it released a cartridge was like a great clap of thunder and Mark watched as it scattered into the air like a fan, hitting its target with one clear shot.

After that Mark would bombard Ernie with questions. When would he be allowed to use a gun? Would he teach him? What type of gun did his dad use? Ernie had smiled at the lad's interest though his mother had been concerned and asked Ernie not to wave his guns around in front of little Zoe. She was only six then and a curious little thing. So Mark and Ernie would retreat to Ernie's room with its gun cabinet and pictures of grouse and pheasant hanging on the walls. Ernie dressed for the countryside at all times – green wax jacket, wellies, his tweed cap – and he subscribed to *The Field* magazine which he would read out loud to Mark's mother as she sat trying to watch *Coronation Street*. 'Oh Dad, will you be quiet,' she would say, straining her neck to hear the television. 'I'm not interested in bloody gundogs.' His mates in the pub called him The Squire; he liked that, he liked the fact it set him apart from the dead-eyed men he had worked with. He had the countryside in his bones and it had saved him from the despair a lot of his co-workers had fallen into when the steelworks closed down. He would throw test questions at Mark over the dinner table. 'Right lad, at what point do you release the safety catch?' 'You release it at the moment you fire,' Mark would answer, his voice deadly serious. 'That's right lad, not a moment before. Safety is the first rule of a civilised shoot, remember that and you'll not come a cropper.' Ernie had been strict about obeying the country code – after all he was a friend of Lord Ferensby, not some scally up from the smog for a jolly. 'Respect earns respect, son,' he used to say. 'Close the gate, stick your litter in your pocket till you get home, keep your dog under control . . .'

Ernie had taken Zoe's death badly. He had sat in the armchair in front of the window, looking at the thick net curtain, not moving, not speaking. If he hadn't blinked every so often you'd be forgiven for thinking he had stopped breathing. When Mark popped round to see his mam and Ernie on a Saturday morning, he would find the old man in the same position. 'Tell you what, Grandad, shall we have a drive up to Ferensby today, see if there's owt going on?' But the old man would shake his head and carry on staring at the curtain with the same intensity as he had once lined up a shot. Almost a year later he was dead. Heart attack was what was written on his death certificate but they all knew his heart had given up long before his death, it had stopped the day he was told his granddaughter had been murdered and though he had lived for a year after that, his spirit had left his body and he had sat by that window waiting for oblivion.

They scattered his ashes on the Ferensby Estate on a crisp June morning while kestrels circled overhead and a line of tweed-clad gentleman bowed their heads in respect for the passing of The Squire. Lord Ferensby had organised tea and cakes in the Hall and Mark had stood and looked around at the assembled men and women – workers from the estate mixed with peers and real-life squires. Lady Ferensby was deep in conversation with Frank Ludlow, Ernie's best friend from school who was battling emphysema and could only speak in a near whisper. Ernie would have liked it, he would have thought it a fitting send off, a respectful one. When his will was read, Mark discovered he had left him his shotgun. He had taken out the yellowing papers that stated that the gun was licensed to one Ernest George Bradshaw of 24a Mackenzie House, Eston, Middlesbrough. He had left strict instructions for Mark to look after the gun, to remember the safety advice he had instilled and to enjoy the moorland as he had enjoyed it. 'Return to it when you can, son' he had written on a little piece of notepaper. 'And think of me every Glorious Twelfth.'

Every year on the anniversary of his death Mark would visit the estate, breathe the cool air and say a little prayer for Ernie. He thinks of his granddad's ashes circling the air like a grouse in flight, an eternity flying across the place he loved. Ernie's soul will be at peace, Mark is certain of that. Now it is up to him to let Zoe rest in peace, he can feel Ernie's voice in his ears as he holds the gun in his hands, telling him about respect and decency and doing the right thing. 'Don't take the safety catch off until the moment you want to shoot; not a moment before.'

The words reverberate around Mark's head as he returns the gun to its slip and places it carefully back into the bag. Not a moment before.

As he slides the bag back underneath the bed he hears a loud thudding on the door. Who the fuck is that, he thinks as he rearranges the covers and walks across the room. Before he gets to the door whoever is out there bangs it again, harder this time. Mark's mouth goes dry. Have they sussed him? He looks up at the ceiling, looking for a hidden CCTV camera. Of course this place will have security cameras, Fuck, fuck, fuck, he thinks. The door thuds again, but this time a woman's voice calls out.

'I know you're in there, cause I saw you come home.' It's an American voice, vaguely familiar. 'I just wondered if you fancied a beer.'

He opens the door tentatively and sees her standing there – the girl from this morning. Liv. She is holding a carrier bag in her arms. It looks heavy. She smiles at him and he notices that she has applied some make-up, her eyes look darker, more defined and her lips have been painted a deep red. She holds the carrier bag towards him. 'Beer and potato chips, I'm such a Canadian! Wanna join me?'

Mark hesitates. He really should tell her to go away, but then he thinks about Zoe, about those lonely final hours, the smell of that alley way. If he is honest, he really doesn't want to be by himself right now and he would love a beer.

'Okay,' he says. 'But it better be decent beer, none of your Canadian rubbish,' he laughs. The girl smiles as she edges past him into the room and empties the bag out onto the chair. 'You will be pleased to know that I have six cans of Boddingtons, is that British enough for you? When I heard your accent I thought you might be a draught bitter man. My dad was from Manchester and it was the only beer he would drink.' She takes a can and hands it to Mark then picks out one for herself. 'Cheers,' she says, raising the can in the air. 'Happy Tuesday!' She opens her beer and sits down on the floor, crossing her legs like a yogi.

Mark smiles as he cracks open his can and takes a deep swig of the thick brown liquid, feeling the alcohol seep into his veins. Then he wipes his mouth and sits down on the floor next to Liv. 'Happy Tuesday,' he says.

16

Kerstin's feet feel raw with pain as she walks up the familiar street. She had fled wearing her worn out pumps, her 'house' shoes, little more than slippers really; certainly not the best foot-wear for speed-walking the two miles from Chelsea to St James's.

She had run towards the Embankment after fleeing the estate agent; running in no particular direction just on and away from the man and his clipboard and the thin trickle of blood on the laundry floor. But she had fled empty-handed; her bag and money, her phone and all her cards were back at the flat and she couldn't go back there now, the body will have been found, the place will be swarming with paramedics and police. Panic had driven her on, like some kind of weird drug pushing her towards an invisible finishing line and then she had remembered the money. She always kept cash in her drawer at work, for emergencies she had told herself, but she had been thinking of lost wallets, leaving present collections, trifles, not real emergencies; not this.

She stops outside the elegant, stone and glass building and waits before stepping into the revolving doors. She can see Roy, the security guard through the window. There is a man with him; he looks official – police? Her heart feels as though it has dropped like a stone to the bottom of her stomach. The evening light is shining into the window, obscuring the man's face from view, she can only see the dark outline of his body, bending over the desk looking at Roy's screen – the CCTV monitor.

They are looking for me, she thinks, as she steps away from the doors. But what choice does she have; without money what can she do?

She approaches the door and sees her reflection in the glass. Her hair is still damp from the shower and she has no make-up on. She has never been to work with a bare face and wet hair, and the damp under her fingers makes her feel dirty. She pulls her hand through her hair, trying to pull it straight then counts to seven before pushing the revolving door.

As she walks in the two men look up. Roy, the security guard, recognises her and smiles.

'Late start?' he chuckles.

'No,' she says, trying not to meet the eyes of the man in the dark suit. 'I've just forgotten something. I don't suppose you have a spare entry fob, do you? I've left mine at home.' She wonders if Roy notices the fear in her voice, her shaking hands, as she holds them out to receive the fob.

But Roy looks nonchalant and barely looks up as he gives her the fob. As she walks towards the stairs, she hears the other man say something about Biata and her shoulders relax. They are talking about the cleaner, the Polish woman who is supposed to arrive at 5 a.m. each morning. Kerstin remembers there had been talk that she was arriving late, that the meeting rooms were still full of discarded papers cups and trays when clients arrived at eight-thirty. The man is looking at the CCTV to implicate the cleaner not Kerstin. Thank God, she thinks as she climbs the stairs.

When she reaches the door to reception, she peeks through the glass to check that the receptionist has gone for the evening. There is nobody there; the high sided pine desk is empty and the pile of post that sits on top of it at the end of each day is gone. Kerstin holds the small fob up to the grey panel and as the light turns from red to green she counts to seven and back before pushing the door open.

Silence. They must have all gone home, she thinks as she walks towards the office. But as she reaches the open door her heart sinks as she sees a familiar figure hunched over her desk.

'What are you doing?' Her voice quivers as she walks towards him.

'Shit, Kerstin,' says Cal, leaping back from the desk. 'You almost gave me heart failure. What are you doing here?'

What is she doing here? Suddenly her mind is blank and all she can think of is the sound Clarissa's skull made when the metal jug smashed down onto it. She closes her eyes and taps her fingers against her thigh ten times each side.

'Kerstin? Are you all right?'

When she opens her eyes, Cal is back at his desk, looking up at her with his large brown eyes, like a sad puppy dog waiting to be patted.

'I'm fine,' she replies tersely. 'I've just come to pick up a few things.'

'What things?'

Kerstin glares at him. Does he realise she is his superior? How does he think he can get away with this endless back-chat. But she hasn't the energy to spar with him; she just wants to take the money and get out of here.

'Cal, why were you at my desk?'

'What?'

'Just now when I came in, you were leaning across my desk.'

'Oh,' he says, with a tone of voice that sounds like he is addressing a small child. 'I was just stealing your identity.' He lets out a fake cackle, then slams his hand on the desk.

Kerstin stops and looks at him. Why is he here; him of all people, the office joker? Does he ever stop fooling around? She pulls out the top drawer and finds two crisp twenty pound notes in a little plastic wallet. Thank God, she thinks as she puts them into her pocket and shuts the drawer.

'Ooh, last of the big spenders,' says Cal, nodding.

'I lost my wallet,' says Kerstin. She wishes he would leave. If only she could sit here for a few moments in peace, she might be able to think straight; might be able to work out what to do next.

'Lost your wallet? How did you manage that?'

'I don't know,' she says. 'I must have dropped it, while I was at the dentist.'

'What are you like Kerst, always losing something. What was it last week, your keys? You need to be more careful.'

There is something about Cal that unsettles her. Despite being his senior, Kerstin always feels the need to defend herself; to assure him that she is not some flake. He had been there when she lost her keys three weeks ago; he even gave her the name of a locksmith to replace them.

'I might have dropped it or it might have been stolen,' she says. 'I don't know.'

'Well if it's been stolen you should go to the police. Let's trace your steps. When was the last time you saw it?

Kerstin's brain feels sticky, as though her capacity for thought is submerging in a deep vat of molten lava.

'I don't know, Cal.' As she speaks the room starts to spin and it feels like she is going to fall. She holds out her arms to steady herself and grabs clumsily to the back of her chair.

'Steady,' Cal's loud voice cuts through her consciousness and she feels his arms wrap around her back like a snake as she slumps into the familiar softness of her chair.

'Kerst, you don't look too good,' says Cal. 'Do you want a glass of water?'

She shakes her head. It is throbbing, but the last thing she needs is water. She never drinks water from the office cooler; even the thought of it makes her gag; drinking from a plastic cup that has been touched by the clammy, sweaty hands of twelve people. Never; she would rather die of thirst.

'Why don't you get off home, have a lie down,' says Cal, who is balanced on the edge of the desk, so close Kerstin can smell him: a mix of sweat and peppermint chewing gum. 'Shall I call you a cab?'

'I can't go home,' Kerstin mutters.

'What's that?' asks Cal.

'I can't go home,' she repeats. 'I've got . . . there's work being done in my flat and it's upside down. I was going to book into a hotel for the night but then my wallet got . . .'

'Well you're not going to get far on forty squids,' says Cal. He drums his fingers on her desk nonchalantly. The noise goes right through Kerstin and if she had a knife right now she would cut those fingers off, one by one.

'Tell you what,' says Cal, jumping off the desk. 'Why don't you come to mine. There's a spare bed – my flatmate John's in New York this week – and I was going to cook chilli, be nice to have a bit of company.'

Kerstin puts her head in her hands and lets out a small wail.

'Shit Kerst, don't get the wrong end of the stick. I'm not trying to sleaze on you or anything. I'm being a mate, yeah?'

From the darkness of her closed hands, Kerstin knows that she is running out of time. She needs to rest, needs to eat and sleep and work out her next move. Cal may be a pain in the backside but he is her only option right now.

'I'm sorry Cal,' she says, as she lifts her head from the desk. 'I just feel a bit dizzy that's all. I know your intentions were well meant.'

'So you'll come?' Cal stands up and takes his coat from the back of the chair.

Kerstin nods her head.

'Well come on then,' says Cal, holding out his hand. 'I don't know about you, but I'm starving.'

Seb switches off Cosima's nightlight and tiptoes down the corridor to the kitchen. He looks at the digitalised time on the oven: 8 p.m. Yasmine will be home soon and he's decided to cook dinner for them both, something simple and hearty, something to make her feel relaxed and calm before the madness of tomorrow.

He goes to the fridge and takes out two chicken breasts wrapped in paper, a stick of chorizo and a box of cherry tomatoes. Yasmine will giggle when she sees he has made his 'Sebastian Special' again, one of the very few dishes – apart from beans on toast and egg sandwiches – he can make with any degree of proficiency.

Cosima was worn out when he collected her from Gracie's house. As well as the guinea pigs, there had been trampolining, cake baking and a dress-up competition. She managed to tell him snippets of information as they walked home, but she was so tired he had to carry her for the last leg of the journey. When they got home he had ordered take-out pizza, as promised, then told her about Mummy's special painting.

'But you mustn't tell her,' he said, putting his finger to his lips. 'It's going to be a big surprise.'

Cosima had grinned excitedly. 'What does it look like?' she asked, between mouthfuls of hot pizza.

'Well,' began Seb. 'You know the lake in the park?' Cosima nodded. 'Mummy and Daddy got married right next to that lake; it was early evening in mid-winter on the shortest day of the year and the stars came out just as we were leaving the party and Mummy and I watched them twinkling on the surface of the water.'

Cosima put her pizza back onto the plate and wiped her hands on her skirt. 'I know this story. Mummy told me that when you got married all the fairies came out on the lake and Mummy asked them to send me down from heaven and they did.'

Seb smiled. Yasmine had been brought up to believe in fairies, her mother Maggie came from Irish stock and she would tell her young daughter about the power of the fairies. 'Ask them a question and they'll answer you,' she would say. 'It might take minutes, it might take years, but they'll answer you.' It had baffled Seb when they first met as it was so unlike his own upbringing with his military father and a mother whose idea of magic was the first day of the Harrods Sale.

Like with so many other areas of his life, Yasmine had taught him how to see things clearly, to believe in the fantastical but also in the beauty of real life. Until he met her his life had been one long escape, running from his childhood, from his cold, unfeeling family, from his dreams and ambition. And then one day there she was and he could stop running. She is the strongest person he has ever known and though she may believe in fairies and magic, she also believes in forgiveness and redemption, no matter how hard you fall there is always a second chance, and it was that belief that brought him back to life all those years ago.

'That's right,' he said. 'There were hundreds of them all gathered on the lake like fireflies, it was very beautiful. And that's Mummy's surprise – a big painting of the lake that's going to hang on the wall of the restaurant . . .'

'And remind her of the fairies,' said Cosima, taking another bite of pizza.

'. . . remind her of the fairies,' his daughter's words dance in his ears as he assembles the ingredients onto the granite work surface.

17

Paula leans back in her chair and breathes a contented sigh as she looks around the idyllic garden. It is still light and a cool breeze ruffles the flame of the tea lights making them shudder in their glass holders.

'This is beautiful, Stella. Who would have thought this place even existed? It really is exquisite.'

She picks up her glass of wine and takes a long sip. Stella smiles. It is wonderful to see Paula so relaxed, so at ease with herself.

'I knew you would like it,' she says, looking around at the beautiful walled garden with its wild tangle of fruit trees and plants, its white-washed brick wall and higgledy-piggledy tables and chairs hidden among the foliage. They managed to get a table for two tucked away at the back of the garden and Stella had giggled when she saw the red-and-white gingham table cloths, and red roses in thin glass vases, a little bit of fifties Paris in the middle of Earl's Court.

'I do. It's wonderful,' says Paula. She puts her glass down and rubs the petals of the rose in between her finger and thumb. 'It reminds me of home. I've missed the garden, missed the earthy smells and . . . anyway, I won't go on about gardening.'

The waiter arrives with their main courses and Paula orders another bottle of wine.

'It will do me good,' she says, a touch of cynicism in her voice. 'After months of caffeine-free teas and water and juice and looking after my body like some glass sculpture that's going to break into pieces, I think I deserve a night off.'

Stella watches her as she slips her cutlery out of the red paper napkin and places the knife and fork onto her plate. Will Paula mention the baby? Should she raise the subject herself, get it all out into the open? She can't read Paula at the moment, it's like she's hiding behind some clear glass door and Stella can't reach her. She was so excited yesterday when she left in the taxi, now it's like the light has been extinguished. Something irreparable has taken place, though Stella is not quite sure what.

'The restaurant was beautiful,' says Paula, slicing through her steak with the precision of a Samurai.

'Which restaurant?' asks Stella, holding out her glass to the waiter who has returned with the bottle of wine. She holds her palm up as the ruby-coloured liquid reaches the half-way mark. 'Thanks,' she nods.

Once Paula's glass is filled, she holds it aloft and clinks Stella's.

An old ritual, thinks Stella. An automated response; what does it mean? She has raised her glass hundreds of times over the years and still she isn't quite sure why she does it. She has raised it at weddings, at funerals, at dinner parties and book readings; she has raised it as a child, her glass filled with watered-down champagne, and as an adult; she has raised it with smiles, with frowns, with indifference; she has lifted the glass as high as it would go, she has barely raised it from the table; she has spilled droplets of wine onto the floor, she has been drunk and sober, elated and desolate; it feels like she has toasted the world and all who live in it over the course of her life and still she has no idea what it means.

The glasses meet for a split second, sending little crystalline droplets of sound out into the cool evening air, before parting. The ritual has been adhered to, now they can carry on.

'I was talking about The Rose Garden,' says, Paula, taking another bite of steak.

'Oh, yes,' says Stella. She hopes this isn't going to end up being a paranoid discussion of Seb and her long-dead association with him. 'Did she like the jasmine?'

Paula nods her head as she chews a mouthful of food. She swallows and takes another sip of wine. 'She loved it. I think she'll be a regular client, finger's crossed. It could really open up London to us.'

Stella raises her eyebrow. 'You mean . . .?'

'I mean in a business sense, Stella,' says Paula, wearily. 'I love London just as much as you, but we could never live here again and certainly not with a ch . . .' She stops and blinks away the word like it's a bad taste in her mouth.

Stella starts to eat her risotto. She won't press the 'living in London' thing any more than she will raise the subject of the baby. Let tonight be easy, let it be about nothing much; flowers and the lifting of glasses, anything but another bloody argument.

'So what was it like then? The restaurant?' She keeps her voice light, in case Paula suspects she is asking the question as some ruse to bring the subject round to Seb. But Paula seems keen to talk about it, her manner is warm and open.

'Oh, it was gorgeous,' she says, laying her knife and fork down. 'Very Moorish. The jasmine plants are going to be the focal point of the roof garden they've built out on the terrace. Yasmine showed me it and it's breathtaking. It reminded me of some of the little places we went to in Vejer. Do you remember the one in the town square? I think it was a hotel as well and it had that amazing garden with fig trees and jasmine . . . The Rose Garden's a lot like that. I was expecting typical Soho bravado and bling but it's different and Yasmine was lovely, she knows her stuff. Anyway, you'll see for yourself tomorrow night, she's invited us to the launch.'

Stella isn't sure what to say, remembering Paula's outburst

233

last night. She doesn't know whether Paula is actually sug-
gesting they go to the launch or is asking it as a trick question
to see how Stella responds. If she says she wants to, will Paula
get upset? The effort of avoiding confrontations and argu-
ments is starting to take its toll on Stella. She has forgotten
what an easy conversation feels like.

'And?' She manages to come up with one word.

'And what?' Paula seems okay, though Stella notices that she
has worked her way through the wine pretty rapidly.

'And do you want to go?' Stella says the words slowly, holding
them in her mouth for as long as she can.

Paula shrugs. 'Well, it might be nice. We're going home on
Thursday and business-wise it's probably a good idea. Actually,
yes of course we should go. Absolutely.' She sits up in her chair
as though suddenly remembering who she is, why she is here.

'Excellent,' says Stella, finishing a last mouthful of food.
'What time will we have to be there?'

'I don't know, says Paula. She leans down and picks up
her bag. 'I've got the invite in here, that should tell us. Here,'
she says, pulling out a wedge of cards. 'It says from 6 p.m.
You better hang onto these, you know me I'll probably forget
them.'

She hands Stella a wedge of cards; black with gold lettering
and red roses snaking across.

Stella looks at the cards. 'That should be okay.'

'I daresay we can get there around six,' says Paula, taking

another sip of wine. 'Anyway, you'll have bags of time. You'll only be at the London Library for a few hours won't you? Any more and you'll be goggle eyed,' she laughs.

Stella smiles; hating Paula for being glib and hating herself for lying to her partner. But of all the places to say she would be for the afternoon, the London Library was the only one that Paula wouldn't question; the only place where it would be plausible to be 'uncontactable' for a few hours, away from Paula's steady stream of text messages demanding to be answered immediately.

'Why have we got so many?' asks Stella.

'Oh, she gave me a few extra,' says Paula. 'Asked if we knew of anyone who might want to come. I said we don't know a soul in London any more, pair of country bumpkins that we are,' she laughs. 'Although, I might give one to Carole at the garden tomorrow, she's a real foodie.'

'They're lovely,' says Stella, as she puts them in the front of her bag. 'They must have spent a fortune on them.'

'Well apparently, they've got a wealthy backer,' says Paula, taking a sip of wine. 'I mean, you'd have to have money behind you to afford the lease on that property; it's prime West End real estate.'

Stella nods, remembering Seb's crumpled suits and his messy hair. He certainly didn't have money when she knew him, but good on him, she thinks, good on him for making something of his life.

'She's very beautiful.'

Paula's voice interrupts Stella's thoughts and she looks up. Paula is running her finger round the rim of her empty wine glass. She looks at Stella with a penetrating stare, like she is trying to read whatever response Stella's face gives up, whatever it betrays. But Stella keeps a smile fixed to her face, an anaemic, half-smile, a one-size-fits-all seal across which anything may glide.

'She's very dark, very Moroccan,' continues Paula. 'Beautiful face, hardly any make-up. And they have a child.' This time she manages to get that word out and it sounds like a bullet, as though she intended it to hurt, to cause maximum damage and pain.

She stares at Stella as though goading her. The word hangs invisibly over them, little wisps of it hover atop the creeping wisteria, it weaves around the fruit trees like little ghostly fingers trying to loosen the pregnant buds from their branches. The air has turned toxic, the sweet jasmine scent that just moments ago wafted across the table like freshly laundered linen now seems cloying and rancid. Paula's eyes are red and dazed; she is getting tipsy.

Stella once again searches for the right response, then something within her disconnects. It feels like the power has been switched off. Can she ever make this right? She looks at the garden and realises she has been seeing it through Paula's eyes; the trees and flowers, the herbs and hanging baskets, that's not what had drawn her to this place all those years ago. She had sat in this garden with her ex-boyfriend Ade and the band while they smoked cigarettes and dissected their performance. She had looked up into the sky, looked above the white-washed wall and the tables and candles and flowers up into the London night and felt that somewhere out there, out in that great, monstrous city, her life lay waiting for her. Men and women, books and songs, experiences, words and laughter and music – they were all out there hanging in the air like apples waiting to be picked from the tree.

'. . . tapas dishes and fresh fish . . . the most incredible spices . . . sumac and a gorgeous grain called freekeh . . .' Paula is talking about the restaurant again now. Her face is back to normal, she is animated and alive, the edge has gone from her voice. It is like the whole exchange never happened, as though Stella imagined it all.

The waiter comes to take their dishes away and asks if they want dessert.

'No, thank you,' says Stella. She needs to get out of here; to be among crowds. It feels like sitting here in this too-perfect garden is almost tempting an argument. As the waiter leaves she leans over to Paula and smiles.

'What do you say we go into town?' she says, squeezing Paula's arm lightly.

Paula looks shocked then a smile creeps across her face. 'No, we can't,' she says, unconvincingly. 'I mean it's almost . . .'

'Eight-thirty,' says Stella and they both burst into giggles. 'Christ. We're like a pair of exhausted parents already.'

Paula leans across the table and kisses her; it's a warm lingering kiss of a kind they haven't shared for a long time. Stella feels a tingle of excitement trickle through her body; a mixture of the kiss and the promise of a London evening spread out in front of them.

'Come on then,' she says, standing up. 'Let's go. And we'll get a cab, might as well travel in style.'

Paula giggles and they link arms as they weave their way through the glinting tangle of tables.

Mark feels lighter than he has in years as he stretches across the floor and drains the last can of beer. He looks at the woman who has kept him company for the past hour or so. It might be tiredness or the blur of the beer but she seems to have grown more and more radiant as the minutes have gone by. He is noticing things that had escaped him this morning. The piercing blue of her eyes, the contours of her cheekbones, the long, toned legs encased in cotton and denim, the hair, wild and messy like she has just woken up, the smooth pale chest peeking through the sheer cotton of her shirt. He can feel the blood building up in his groin and he shifts position, hoping she can't see the lump in his jeans.

'Think that's the last of them,' she says, holding up an empty can, and giving it a little shake for good measure.

'It's given me a thirst,' he says, squelching his can into a compact square.

'And an appetite,' she says. She looks at him for a moment; it's a quizzical look, as though she is weighing up whether or not to ask him a question.

He notices her looking and puts his hand to his hair. 'What? Have I got something on me head?'

She starts to giggle, light at first then great snorts of laughter.

'What?' He is laughing too now. 'You're making me paranoid.'

'It's nothing,' she says, regaining her composure. 'It's just you looked so funny just then, so . . . cute.'

The word hangs in the space between them like a diver perched on the edge of the board, wondering whether to walk back down the steps or throw himself into the depths of the water.

Mark smiles. The beer has taken the edge from him. When he thinks of why he is here, of Zoe and Seb and that filthy street, it seems like they are outside of him, outside of his head, connected to him by the thinnest of strings. He feels like the man he once was; confident and relaxed, working out his next move on this sexy young woman sitting opposite him. He had been a good-looking lad back in the day, he had worn his dark hair longer than it is now and girls would comment on his big blue eyes and long eyelashes: 'Our Mark's got eyelashes like spiders webs,' his mam would say.

Sex was fun back then, it was a laugh, a distraction from work and real life. He thought about it a lot, it was what got him through most of his days, and he had amassed quite a collection of lads mags in his room, though he lost interest once Zoe got it into her head that she wanted to be a glamour model. He couldn't open up one of those magazines without picturing her face in place of the model's face. It made him feel sick; his kid sister spreading her body out for all to see. He was a lad, and he knew how other lad's minds worked, he knew what they talked about when girls weren't around. It appalled him to think that he might overhear the men at the factory talking about Zoe that way, poring over her photographs in a magazine.

A couple of months before Zoe left to go to London he met Lisa and by then his laddish days were well and truly over. They moved in together, got engaged and when she fell pregnant he took his pile of lads mags, dated all the way back to the late nineties, and burned them on a bonfire in the back garden. He was glad to put that part of his life behind him, he was going to be a father, he had met the woman he wanted to spend the rest of his life with, everything was going to be perfect. And then they got the call.

He claps his hands together, dispelling the memory from his head. He is enjoying this moment, he wants it to go on for ever, wants to touch the woman in front of him, feel something resembling warmth and intimacy for the first time in so many years.

'Cute,' he says. 'I suppose that's a compliment?'

She giggles and puts her head to one side. She's young, he thinks. Younger than him, but that's good, he wants to be young tonight, he wants to do stupid, mindless things and stop the incessant noise in his head, he wants to have one night where he can forget everything that has happened and just be in the moment, the moment that seems to be passing in front of his eyes in a blur.

'Come on,' he says, pulling himself up of the floor. 'Let's go out.'

'Out where?' She looks rather confused as though she was expecting him to kiss her.

'Out there,' he says, pointing out of the window. 'What do they call it? Twenty-four-hour party land? And we're here in the middle of it. At the very least, we can nip out and have a beer can't we?'

'Okay,' she says. 'We can have a walk, it will be nice. But let's go to a pub, yeah? I hate clubs, I'm telling you this now, I am not going to any clubs.'

'I never mentioned clubs,' he laughs as he reaches across to the bed and picks up his wallet. 'And I don't think I'd be let in to any of the clubs round here, I'm too old.'

'You're not old,' she says. 'You're mature.'

'Ha,' Mark snorts. 'That, m'dear, is just a polite way of saying old.'

He ushers her towards the door with the crook of his arm and feels the warmth of her breath on his skin. He wants her, he wants her badly but he is going to savour the feeling, draw it out for as long as he can and then lose himself within her.

As they open the door, he remembers the bag. He is not sure if he zipped it up when he shoved it under the bed earlier.

'I tell you what,' he says to Liv as she steps out into the corridor. 'You go on ahead and I'll meet you in the corridor. I just want to charge my phone while we're out.'

She nods her head and smiles and as he watches her walk away down the corridor he thinks she could be a hologram, a vision that only he can see. The bright light makes his eyes sore and he blinks the harsh colour away as he steps back into the room and kneels down by the side of the bed. The sudden movement makes silver stars flicker in front of his eyes and the black bag looks like a cowering animal hunched up beneath the metal hinges of the bed. He reaches his arm towards it and, finding the zipper, seals it shut in one swift movement.

As he goes to stand up he stumbles slightly, the beer on an empty stomach has gone straight to his head. He sees himself in the small smudged mirror above the sink; his cheeks are flushed and the hood of his sweatshirt has got tangled up; he looks like a cartoon character. Then he does something he hasn't done for a long time; he starts to laugh. A grinning red-faced fool looks back at him from the mirror but he doesn't care. Tonight he will let himself laugh, he will let himself drink and fuck and forget; forget about the ghosts that cry out in his head night after night – his dad, his granddad, Zoe – they can be all silent for one night, and then tomorrow he will let them in again.

18

Kerstin follows the stream of bodies as they file down the stairs,
desperately trying to bat away the urge to run, to squeeze
through their bulk and escape. But she knows that she can
only move in a forward direction now; she must stay close to
Cal.

She feels Cal's hand holding her arm, pulling her down. It is
the heat that hits her first: thick stale air that sticks to her face,
her arms, her legs as she pushes her way down the steps. After
the heat come the smells: a thousand smells swirling under
her nose, coagulating and merging into one another: BO; damp
fibres; sickly-sweet perfume that lodges its odour deep in her
throat and makes her want to gag; greasy fried chicken; soil;
petrol fumes, the smells unfurl like noxious gases as the bodies
carry her down, down into the depths of the earth.

At the bottom of the steps she feels the weight of the crowd
dissipate and she is released into the artificial light of Green
Park Station ticket hall.

'Come on,' shouts Cal, as he runs towards the turn-styles. But Kerstin is unable to move; her brain has turned to mush and a familiar panic rises from her chest. She has no idea what she is supposed to do next, no idea how this all works.

'What's the matter?' Cal is walking towards her. He looks irritated; tired.

She looks around and her eyes alight on the small ticket booth and the line of people snaking its way from it. She sees a fluorescent jacket and her heart leaps; she looks again but the station guard is busy helping someone retrieve a ticket that has got stuck in the machine. He is not on his way to arrest her. But the police will be on alert; they will have her description; will be looking for her right now. It feels like a thousand eyes are upon her as she stands in the middle of the hall like a drowning woman.

'I . . . I don't have a ticket,' she says to Cal; his face looks hard. Exhaustion, maybe. Perhaps this is the last thing he wants; having to babysit his nutty colleague for the night.

But Cal puts his hand onto her arm gently. 'Oh, shit I forgot . . . you lost your purse. Hang on a sec.' He leaves her and walks towards the ticket machines. Kerstin watches as he inserts his card then leans down to retrieve the ticket from the bottom of the machine. 'Hurry up,' she whispers. 'Please hurry up.' Any minute now she will get a tap on her shoulder, she just knows it.

'Here.' Cal holds out the ticket. 'Come on, let's go.'

Kerstin looks down at the ticket. She has no idea what to do with it. She feels like a child learning to walk and she winces as a sharp stiletto heel catches her foot. More people are coming from behind; she cannot turn and run, even if she wanted to; the crowd would crush her; and if she did escape, then what? She has closed every door now; Matthew, Cologne, Chelsea . . . All she can do is keep moving.

She grabs Cal's arm and grips onto it as they approach the turnstyles, then watches intently as he removes his arm from her grasp, flicks his wrist and walks through. Easy. But as she tries to replicate, something is wrong. She flicks the card against the panel, just like he did, but nothing happens; she feels the weight of people behind her, hears her blood thudding inside her head.

'You got to insert it.' A voice from behind; a woman's voice, kind, without a hint of irritation. Kerstin inserts the card and the gates spring open.

Cal is waiting by the top of the escalator and as he sees her approach he steps onto it. She watches his dark head slowly descend as she waves her foot above the moving steps, like a child dipping its toe into a rushing stream.

Someone shoves her in the back and she grips the side of the escalator as the steps move beneath her feet. She is on and as she regains her balance she looks behind her and sees a young boy in a baseball cap grinning at her. 'Don't look down,' he mouths and his face holds such menace in it, she turns round and does precisely that. She looks down at the vertical drop; the demonic metal monster that, in moments, will deposit her at the gates of hell.

Images streak past her as she descends: a green-faced witch with bright red lips; a silver neck tie that looks like a noose. She tries to catch the words on the posters but just catches parts of them: Wick . . . Fifty sha . . . Shaftesb . . . bestsel . . . Then the witch's face again, and again and again and again, those red lips and the screams, incessant screams that are getting louder and louder as Kerstin reaches the final step and stumbles into Cal. .

'Whoah there, steady,' he says, as though calming a nervy colt. 'You almost knocked me flying. Come on, let's get the train.'

Kerstin holds out her hand and Cal takes it. She notices his look, the smile; he thinks she is flirting with him when actually she is holding onto him out of fear; holding onto him because he is the only tangible, solid thing left.

She holds his arm tightly as they reach the platform. It is packed and they have to squeeze their way through. Kerstin's mouth is dry; she tries to concentrate on her breathing but no air seems to be able to reach her lungs; her head feels light as though only connected to her body by the thinnest of threads. And then it comes:

Sssssssssssseeeeeeeeeeekkkkkkkk . . .

A scream so loud, it cuts through the platform like a molatov cocktail, turning the ground beneath Kerstin's feet to liquid. Her legs buckle, she can feel herself going. She hits the filthy ground with a thud, shielding her head with her hands, as though waiting for a blow; waiting for the bang.

'Kerstin,' She hears Cal's voice, feels his hands around her back, pulling her but she mustn't look up, she daren't look up. She knows she has been caught; if she opens her eyes she will see the uniform; the hard face; the handcuffs. This is it.

As she gets to her feet, she covers her face with her hands which are shaking uncontrollably. She feels Cal's arms around her waist, hears him saying something but she cannot hear what; her ears feel like they are full of sand. She feels movement, feels the familiar weight of people pressing down on her back. She takes her hands from her face and sees the thick metal bulk of the Piccadilly Line train. It was just the train coming into the station. She had forgotten what it sounds like; the screech of brakes; the air rushing onto the platform; the bullet-like speed.

Cal guides her to the open doors and they stand wedged up against each other, so close she can feel his heart pumping against her cheek. His chest is warm and his heartbeat so steady she almost starts counting. If she stays like this she will be okay, she can close her eyes for the six minutes it will take to get to Leicester Square tube. Two minutes per stop; funny what facts the mind retains.

Inside her closed eyes, she sees speckles of white light, flashing on and off, on and off. Then the lights expand, and seem to dance round her consciousness to a strange melody that fills her head.

'Oh, here we go,' says Cal, stepping back, and Kerstin opens her eyes to a brightly lit carriage. The music grows louder and louder until it feels like it is crawling up her spine.

'Don't catch his eye,' says Cal, gesturing with his head.

'What?'

Kerstin turns round and sees a young boy making his way up the quieter part of the carriage. He is playing an accordion, so big it almost obliterates his tiny frame. It is a slow, hypnotic gypsy melody, the kind used by snake charmers in old black and white films. The boy's face is half-hidden in the hood of his sweatshirt.

'Don't look at him,' says Cal, but Kerstin cannot take her eyes off the boy. She watches as he walks towards them, his music momentarily drowned out by the announcement for the next station.

Cal gently guides her to the doors, but she wants to wait, she has to see the boy's face before they get off. She twists out of Cal's grip as the train pulls into Leicester Square station, and cranes her neck towards the boy, but he is staring down at the accordion. Look up, she wills him, as the train doors open. Why won't you look up?

And then, in the pause between the train stopping and the doors opening, he looks up and the blood in her body evaporates. Clarissa's face, dappled in liver spots and rouge, stares back at her from beneath the boy's hood. Kerstin pushes past Cal and out of the doors, she darts between the commuters, cutting through them like a blade. She leaps onto the escalator, taking two steps at a time, she runs and runs, up the steps, through the turnstiles, thrusting her ticket into the slot, one, two, three times, until the gates part and release her into the damp air of Charing Cross Road where she stumbles into a side street and vomits so violently she almost passes out. When she is done, she stands up and wipes her mouth with the back of her sleeve, then presses her body against the rough stone wall.

'Kerstin.'

She looks up and sees Cal.

'Listen, you're not well,' he says, gently. 'Come on, let's get to the flat. It's just a couple of minutes away. We'll get you cleaned up and you can have a rest, yeah?' He holds out his hand to her.

'I'm fine,' she says. 'Honestly, I'll be fine'

'Well, you don't look fine to me,' says Cal, as they start to walk up Charing Cross Road.

As she walks, she realises she hasn't asked Cal where he lives; she has no idea where he is taking her.

'Where are we going? Where's your flat?'

'Haven't I told you before,' says Cal, as they dip down a

narrow side street. 'I live in Soho. Bit mad, eh? But it's well cool and saves me a fortune on cab fares.'

Kerstin nods her head as she follows Cal to the traffic lights on Shaftesbury Avenue. As they cross the road he squeezes her hand gently.

'Nearly there,' he says. 'Just a few more blocks and you'll be fine.'

Seb is just taking the food out of the oven when he hears a key in the lock. The noise makes him feel secure; his family is back together, all safe under one roof. He reaches up to the cabinet and takes out two glasses. He fills one with a glug of ginger cordial and a splash of sparkling water; the other with pomegranate juice – Yasmine's favourite. He takes one in each hand and walks out into the hallway.

Yasmine is sitting on the little wooden stool by the door fiddling with the laces of her shoes. She looks up at him as he approaches; her face looks drained and tired.

'Everything okay?' His voice echoes against the narrow walls.

When she finally gets the laces undone, she pulls off the shoes and flings them onto the floor.

'Why did I ever think this would be a good idea, Seb?' she says, taking the glass of juice and walking ahead of him towards the kitchen.

She gives a little shrug as she enters the room, then plonks herself down heavily onto the soft velvet sofa by the window and looks up at him. It looks like the filling has been pulled out of her, leaving just an empty wisp of body.

'You're exhausted,' says Seb, taking the glass from her hands and putting it onto the table. 'Why don't you have a nice bath? I can keep the food warming in the oven until you're ready to eat.'

'Eat,' she repeats, her voice a glum monotone. 'I don't think I can face food tonight. I just want to curl up and sleep and wake up next week when all this is over.'

'I'll go and run you a bath,' says Seb. 'It'll do you good.'

He walks to the bathroom and turns on the taps, then opens the large wooden cabinet and rummages through Yasmine's various lotions and oils, looking for something suitable. He picks up a handful and scans the labels: Ylang Ylang body scrub, peppermint foot balm, lemon and ginger exfoliator. No good. He replaces them and pulls out a long glass bottle with a silver lid: Soothing Lavender Bath Essence. That should do, he thinks, as he unscrews the lid and pours a generous glug under the running water.

Leaving the bath to fill, he returns to the kitchen and sees Yasmine sitting where he left her. Her feet are spread out at a strange angle and her arms are folded across her chest. She is sound asleep. Sleep will be better than a bath, he thinks, as he takes the thick woollen eiderdown from the end of the sofa and spreads it across her body.

He walks back to the kitchen and looks at the mangle of chicken, tomatoes and herbs sitting impotently on the work surface. He didn't have much of an appetite anyway, after munching half of Cosima's ham and pineapple pizza. The food was going to be a diversion, an aside to the conversation he and Yasmine were going to have. There were things he wanted to say to her over dinner. He wanted to tell her how proud he was, that he will be there with her tomorrow, he will be her eyes and ears, making sure everything runs smoothly. He wanted to tell her that all she has to do is focus on her work; he and Henry will sort out the rest. He wanted to commemorate the evening, raise a glass of ginger sparkle to this, the eve of her great venture; he wanted, more than anything, to tell her he loved her. To have an hour or so, just the two of them to take on board all that has happened these last few years. To talk.

He looks over at her sleeping form as he covers the food with foil. There will be plenty of time to talk, they have years of talk ahead of them, he thinks as he goes into the bathroom and turns off the taps. Then he steps quietly across the room and eases himself onto the sofa next to her. Taking her hand, he gently kisses it then holds it in his. Yes there were things he wanted to tell her tonight, things that would have made him feel better to have expressed and he feels the words pressing against his tongue as he sits looking at her, but something stronger than words exists between them, some unfathomable bond that has linked them from the start. She knows I love her, he thinks, as he strokes the rough skin on her fingertips, and watches her chest rise up against the thick green eiderdown, she has always known. He cuddles up next to her and as he closes his eyes, he sees clusters of silver and blue lights dart across his consciousness like moonlight streaks the surface of a lake.

19

Paula looks at Stella incredulously as they step out of the cab.

'Old Compton Street,' she giggles. 'Stella, you're turning us into a walking cliché. Next thing you'll be standing on the bar giving it the whole Gloria Gaynor.'

'Oh, come on grumpy,' says Stella, as they make their way into the Admiral Duncan. 'It'll be fun. We haven't had a night like this for ages.'

'I thought you'd want to go to The Dog and Duck,' says Paula, as they step into the packed pub. 'For old time's sake,' she shouts above the noise of the bar.

'No, I thought I'd save the whole prodigal daughter bit till tomorrow night,' says Stella, as they make their way to an empty table. 'Frith Street can wait; for now let's just have fun.'

'Okay,' says Paula, taking off her coat. 'So let's kick off our fun night with some champagne. Who's buying?'

'Tonight is on me, my love' says Stella, leaning across to kiss

Paula on the nose. 'After all you've been through today you deserve to be pampered tonight.'

'Hah,' says Paula, raising her eyebrow. 'I'll keep you to that when we get back to the hotel.'

Stella smiles as she makes her way to the bar. If she can keep smiling; keep pretending all is fine then maybe it will be.

Jesus Christ, thinks Mark as he follows Liv into the pub.

He looks uneasy as they elbow their way past a group of men. One of them, a tall, thin Japanese guy in skinny jeans and a close-fitting striped top, steps out from his companions and stands in front of Mark.

'Ooh, look. A real man,' he purrs, his voice light and slurry with drink. His friends gather behind him and nod their heads while the Japanese guy slowly licks his top lip with his tongue then kisses his hand and blows it towards Mark. 'We like,' he giggles. Then he pats Liv on the arm and winks. 'Lucky girl,' he says as he and the group make their way out of the door.

'What the fuck was that?' Mark looks at Liv and she is laughing. He can't understand why she would be laughing.

'Oh, come on, loosen up,' she says. 'This is Old Compton Street; it's full of gay men. Anyway, you should be flattered, you nearly pulled there,' she says, putting her hand into his pocket. She tries to kiss his cheek but Mark is uncomfortable now and he pushes her away. Fucking shirt lifter, he should have smacked him in the mouth.

As they approach the bar, Liv turns to him and smiles.

'Will you get the drinks? I just need to nip to the loo.'

'What,' says Mark. 'You're not leaving me here?'

'I'll only be a minute,' says Liv. 'I'm desperate. Anyway, you'll be fine, there's just a nice woman waiting to be served. No scary men,' she laughs, as she walks away.

Mark stands at the bar and sees the woman Liv had pointed out. Slim, dark hair, attractive face; she is just the kind of woman Mark would normally go for. She looks sophisticated; certainly not the type of woman who would wear cut off shorts and show off her knickers. He watches Liv as she disappears into the crowd and wonders if he should just leave now and get back to the hostel. Then he hears something that makes him want to stick around.

'The Rose Garden, that's right.'

It's the woman. She's talking to the barman. Mark moves towards her so he can hear better.

'It's been seven years, Frank. Can you believe it? And I haven't been back once,' the woman says.

'Well, it's lovely to see you,' says the barman. 'You haven't aged a day.'

'Oh you're very generous, Frank,' she says.

'So do you know Yasmine, then?' asks the barman, and Mark's heart leaps at the sound of the name.

'No,' says the woman. 'My partner knows her. Paula's a herb gardener. She supplied some rare plants for the restaurant roof

garden. I've never met Yasmine before, but I know her husband
Seb. Do you remember him?'

The barman shakes his head.

'No you probably wouldn't,' says the woman. 'The Dog and
Duck was his local. I don't think he'd ever step foot in here,
no offence, Frank.'

'Is he a dish?' asks Frank

'Well he was a good-looking chap when I knew him,' says the
woman. 'Bit of the young Robert Redford about him.'

'Sounds lush,' says Frank. 'Here let me get that champagne
for you.'

Mark watches as the barman walks towards the fridge at the
far side of the bar. He can't quite believe what he has just heard.
A roof terrace. He didn't know the Rose Garden had a roof terrace. He thinks about the proximity of the hotel he's booked
into tomorrow. It will be a waste of time if they're all up on the
roof terrace. How the hell would he get to Bailey from there?

He looks at the woman. She is playing with her phone. He
has to say something now, before Liv and the barman come
back.

'Er, excuse me,' he says, moving a fraction towards her. He
can smell her perfume. Chanel No 5. Lisa used to wear it but it
was too heavy a smell for his liking. He preferred it when she
smelled of skin and baby powder. He blinks away the memory
of his estranged wife and looks right into the woman's face.
She's lovely and suddenly he starts to feel tongue-tied.

'Yes,' she says. Her face is warm and friendly and Mark relaxes.

'Sorry to bother you,' he says. 'But I just heard you mention The Rose Garden. Is that Seb Bailey's place?'

'Yes it is,' she says. 'Well it's actually his wife's. Do you know Seb?'

'I do, yeah,' says Mark, thinking fast. 'My dad and his dad were in the army together. We used to play when we were little. God I haven't seen him for years. It would be lovely to catch up with him again.'

'Wow, what a bizarre coincidence,' says the woman, as the barman comes back with a bottle of champagne. She opens her handbag and pulls a couple of twenty-pound notes out of her purse. 'Thanks Frank,' she says. 'What's your name?' she asks, turning to Mark. 'I'll tell Seb you were asking about him when I see him tomorrow. I could pass on your number if you like.'

'It's Denny,' says Mark, blurting out the first name that comes into his head, a familiar name stained with sadness. 'Denny Lowe.'

'Okay, Denny,' says the woman. 'I'll tell him. Oh, hang on a sec.' She reaches into her bag and pulls out a piece of paper. It looks like a flyer. 'Why don't you come to the launch tomorrow? Give him a surprise. Here, you can have this.'

Mark cannot believe what is happening. He holds out his hand and takes the invitation, recognising the black-and-pink branding from the restaurant website. 'Are you sure?' He looks at the woman quizzically.

'Yeah, we've got loads,' she says, as she picks up the champagne bottle and tucks the two glasses under her arm. 'Anyway, it was nice to meet you, Denny,' she says, as she walks away. 'Might see you tomorrow.'

'Yes,' says Mark, tucking the invitation into his pocket as Liv comes back from the loo. 'Yeah you might.'

'Here we are,' says Stella, as she places the bottle of champagne onto the table. 'Is this sparkly enough for you?'

Paula laughs as Stella pours her a glass.

'It's a bit flat actually,' says Paula, as she takes a sip. 'Just joking. Oh, dear we forgot to make a toast.'

Stella winces. Please, not another toast. She pretends not to hear and instead takes a long sip of the ice-cold drink. She looks at Paula; she looks so much more relaxed now than she did earlier. Perhaps she can risk broaching the subject. She puts her glass down and leans forward.

'Paula,'

Stella has to shout to make herself heard above the noise of the bar, even though Paula is sitting right beside her.

'Are we going to talk about today?'

Paula folds her hands and looks up at the pearly fairy lights that are strung around the walls. Her eyes glisten and she lifts her head skywards and blinks into the light.

'I'll be thirty-nine this year, Stella,' she says, her eyes still on the lights. 'Almost middle-aged,' she murmurs. 'And one of the things I have always wanted to have by the age of forty was ...'

'A baby,' says Stella, holding her hand out to touch Paula's arm.

Paula turns and looks at Stella, her face half-lit by red light.

'No, not a baby, though that has always been up there on the list of priorities. No, what I always wanted to have found by the age of forty was happiness, pure, uncomplicated happiness.'

Stella nods her head as Paula continues.

'When we were in the clinic today, and we were listening to the consultant I felt you draw further and further away from me until it seemed like I was quite alone, all alone with some mad woman's desire to have a baby.'

'No, Paula that's ...' Stella begins but Paula interrupts her.

'Please Stella,' she says, gently. 'Let me say this, I need to say this.' She takes a deep breath, steeling herself to go on. 'When I was lying on the examining table, looking at my empty womb on the screen, the room seemed to shrink around me, it got smaller and smaller until all that was there, all I was conscious of, was the image on the screen and the rhythm of my heart. I stared and stared at that screen, waiting to hear your voice, to feel your touch but it never came. It was as though you had left the room, you were nowhere, I couldn't find you. And I realised, there in that moment, that I was asking too much of you. I have always asked too much of you. I have given you this impossible task of being my happy ending and that is a heavy weight for anyone to carry.'

Stella shifts in her seat, leaning forward to listen.

'When I'm with you,' Paula continues, 'I feel elated, turned-on, unsure, worried, paranoid . . . but do I feel happy? I was happy tonight. When we walked into that garden, I looked at you with your beautiful face reflected against the lights and my heart hurt. It made me think of the day I first met you, that hot afternoon when you were sitting in your parents' garden reading *Mrs Dalloway* and you looked up at me and asked: "Are you the writer?"'

'And you said, "Something like that",' Stella replies. 'I was wearing a big white sunhat and I thought you were the most amazing thing I had ever seen.'

'But *you* were the writer Stella, not me,' says Paula, placing her hand on Stella's. 'I remember you shouting at me in The Dog and Duck, the night we got back together . . .'

'The night before 7/7,' says Stella, her mind suddenly full of old faces: Ade; Seb; the red-haired barmaid from the pub – what was her name again? Val. That was it, a real old Soho-ite.

Paula nods her head. 'You told me I was a fuck up, that I had sold out, that I lacked the guts to be a writer. And all the time you were saying those things I was looking at you and thinking: "This is *your* dream not mine". I never had plans to be some big-shot writer. I just wanted to find peace and I thought I had found it in you.'

Stella takes Paula's hands and turns them over, stroking the smooth skin as though making sure she is real. The rose petals she was rubbing in the garden have left pale pink stains on her fingertips and Stella threads her own fingers around them, a sensuous movement that seems out of place now, in the light of what Paula has just said.

'Do you still love me?' Stella whispers, not looking up.

'I will always love you,' says Paula, her voice cracking 'You are my one true love, the dark lady of my dreams. I love you so much it hurts me . . . and I think my love is hurting you, it's holding you back. I heard what you said last night about not letting you recover, I know I'm controlling and overbearing and I hate myself for being like that. I feel like you're a butterfly and I'm this great big net always poised above you, waiting to swoop down and smother you.'

The words march up and down Stella's head like a thousand footsteps getting louder and louder. Happiness; love; happiness; love. Are the two interchangeable? Can you have one without the other? Would she be happy without Paula? She tries to imagine her life without Paula in it; she sees a university, a building peeking out of a London street, she sees the books on her shelf at home, the spider's web . . . she sees her happiness flutter down from the sky like thousands of petals, light and delicate and each with their own unique imprint. What does happiness look like? She sees the faces of her parents, her sister, her grandparents, her bedroom in her childhood home on the moors; she sees the white stubbly town in Southern Spain; the old man with the kind eyes; she sees Frith Street in the early morning light, bleary eyed and virginal; she sees the flashing lights of Piccadilly and Dylan O'Brien's email; she sees a lifetime's worth of thinking and writing and discussing and learning. But though she tries, really tries to, she cannot see Paula.

20

Kerstin stands at the window looking out onto Dean Street. It is heaving with people; bodies stream down the centre of the street like a wave gathering more and more momentum.

'Nice view isn't it?'

She nods as Cal comes towards her holding a glass of white wine.

'I've fixed you a drink.'

'No, really I shouldn't,' she says.

'Go on,' he says, 'One won't hurt you. Might calm your nerves. You seem on edge today, Kerst. Are you sure there's nothing wrong?'

'I'm fine,' she says, taking the glass. 'Just tired that's all.'

'You work too hard, that's your problem.' Cal has returned to the kitchen and busies himself grabbing plates out of the cupboards and clattering them onto the wooden bench that serves as a table. 'First one in, last one out. You're like a machine; and you know what happens to machines when they get overloaded with data. They freeze.'

Kerstin doesn't reply. She is mesmerised by the view of the street; of the expressions of the people passing by below, they look so carefree and relaxed. It's like looking at visitors in a zoo; and she is the caged animal.

'Grubs up.'

She turns from the window and sees that Cal has placed two plates of food on the table. He has also placed tea lights in the centre and Kerstin suddenly feels uneasy.

'Where is your bathroom?'

'Oh,' says Cal. He has already sat down at the table and jumps up immediately to direct Kerstin to the bathroom.

He takes her wine and puts it next to her plate then puts his hand on her lower back and guides her out of the open plan room into a dark, narrow hallway.

'First on the left,' he says. 'You might need to give the door a shove, it's a bit stiff.'

Kerstin stares at the wooden door. It is the same as the one at her flat and her skin starts to prickle as she remembers the series of rituals she has to undertake before she can even enter her home. She reaches out to turn the handle but some invisible force holds her back. She cannot touch it. So, instead she places her elbow on the top of the handle and pushes it until the door yields.

She feels Cal's presence behind her. He is watching her; probably wondering what the hell she is doing. Her neck prickles as she enters the bathroom and closes the door with her foot.

She hears Cal's footsteps disappearing down the hall as she approaches the sink. She counts to seven then runs the tap until the water is steaming hot, then plunges her hand under the water, scrubbing and scrubbing until her fingers resemble swollen pink sausages. Once satisfied that her hands are completely clean, she looks up and sees her reflection in the huge oval mirror. Her face is pale and her eyes look dark and hollow.

'What have I done?' she whimpers. And suddenly she doesn't want to be alone; she needs to be near another human being, even if he is the most annoying man in the world. At least the noise of Cal's incessant chatter will drown out the white noise inside her head.

When she comes back into the kitchen, Cal has already started eating his meal.

'Sorry Kerst,' he says, talking with his mouth full. 'I was so hungry I couldn't wait. Don't mind me, I've got the manners of an alley cat, I have. Do sit down, won't you. And tell me if you need me to warm yours up.'

Kerstin stands by the chair and counts to seven and back before sitting down. Cal looks up and goes to say something but then seems to change his mind.

Kerstin sits down and looks at the gloopy red mass on her plate.

'What is it?' She looks up at Cal, his plate is almost clean.

'Chilli con carne,' he says. 'I got the recipe off the Jamie Oliver app. Tuck in.'

She picks up her fork and tries to scoop some of the food onto it but there is no way she can put it into her mouth.

'I'm really sorry, Cal, but I'm just not hungry.'

'That's my cooking for you,' says Cal. He laughs as he picks up his empty plate and Kerstin's untouched one and takes them over to the work surface. 'Can I get you anything else? Cheese on toast? Ham sandwich?'

'No thanks, Cal,' says Kerstin. 'I'm fine, just really tired that's all.'

'That's cool,' says Cal, as he scrapes Kerstin's chilli into a metal pedal bin. 'Have a drink of your wine and I'll show you to your room.'

Kerstin picks up the wine glass by the stem. She is thirsty and the wine is dry and cold and though she means to just take a sip, she ends up drinking half the glass.

'Woah, steady,' says Cal, as he sits down at the table. 'It'll go straight to your head if you haven't lined your stomach.'

But the wine has made Kerstin feel better. It has been a long time since she drank alcohol and it feels good; her mind relaxes and the sharpness of the day, though still there, is blunted. She takes another long sip and drains the glass.

'So, then,' says Cal, folding his arms. 'What do you fancy doing? We could watch a DVD or go and have another drink

– on me of course. You can pay me back when you find your wallet.' He laughs and the noise makes Kerstin jump. Of course she can't go out. The police are out there, right now looking for her. She just needs to lie down; she needs to sleep.

'I think it might be best if I go to bed, Cal,' she says.

'No worries,' says Cal, standing up quickly. 'I'll show you to the room. I thought you could take my bed tonight –it's nice and clean, I just changed the sheets – and I'll take John's room.'

Kerstin nods. Clean sheets. There is no such thing anymore. As she follows Cal down the hallway, the image of Clarissa flashes in front of her: the thin papery skin, the hands dotted with brown liver spots and bulging blue veins; the blood smearing the floor.

'Here you go,' says Cal as they reach the small bedroom. 'There's a bedside lamp if you need it. I'll shut the curtains too, it gets really bright with all the neon from the street. But it shouldn't be too noisy. It's double glazed and we're on the top floor, so you should manage to get some kip. Right then it's all yours.'

Kerstin stands at the door, looking at the bed: someone else's bed, with someone else's germs saturating it. There are a hundred rituals she would need to attend to just to touch that bed let alone climb into it. She counts to seven and steps into the room.

'Kerstin, you know there are people you can go to who can help.'

Cal's face is suddenly serious and he sits down on the bed and looks up at her.

What is he talking about? He knows; he has figured it out or else he has heard something on the news. Kerstin turns to run, but he stands up and touches her arm gently.

'It's okay, Kerst,' he says. 'It's a very common condition, OCD. My cousin had it. She couldn't stop cleaning, morning till night, you should have seen her hands, they were like sandpaper. But she got help. CBT, they call it: Cognitive Behavioral Therapy. I can ask her to talk to you about it if you like, give you some phone numbers.'

He's talking about the counting. Thank God, she thinks, yet still she feels exposed; as though he has seen her naked. She didn't think people noticed the counting; in the office she always did it under her breath.

'Honestly, Cal, I'm fine,' she says. 'Just tired and I get more uptight when I'm tired. Thank you again for letting me stay. You've been a great help.'

He lets go of her arm and smiles. 'Okay, Kerst, I'll leave you to it.'

He walks to the door then turns.

'Night night. Sleep well, yeah? Oh, and if you get cold, there's some extra blankets on the top shelf of the cupboard there.'

'Thanks, Cal,' she says and she watches him close the door.

She hears him cough as he walks away. With tentative steps

she goes towards the bed. She holds out her hand, but it's impossible; she cannot touch it, let alone sleep in it. But her body feels like it is closing down; her eyes are heavier than she can ever remember. It feels like she hasn't slept for days though it has only been a few hours since she fled Old Church Street. She looks at the floor; it is wooden. She could sleep on that; hadn't Cal said there was a blanket in the cupboard; a washed blanket, she can lay it over her feet so it doesn't touch her face; so she can't smell it.

She pulls her sleeve over her hand and turns the metal handle of the cupboard. Inside it is half wardrobe/half shelves. Cal's suits are lined up neatly on the right hand side; on the left are various sweaters and tops, again neatly folded. Kerstin is surprised at the order; Cal is always so chaotic at work. Maybe he has a cleaner. She reaches up to the top shelf and feels thick wool under her fingertips. This must be it, she thinks as she pulls it down. But something else comes with it, clattering to the floor with a loud smash. Kerstin looks down at the heavy wooden box, lying at her feet and the scattered objects it has released and she can't believe her eyes.

Her things.

She looks at her possessions and can't work out what they are doing in Cal's cupboard: her memory stick, she knows it is hers because she had written her initials on it in black permanent marker; a bottle of Aveda shampoo for dry hair – the one that had gone missing from her bathroom cabinet; and a set of keys attached to a square, white key-ring with the words 'Elizabeth Lord Estate Agent' printed in red lettering. Her keys.

He has been in the flat; her flat. He has taken her things, moved them around. She thinks about her ripped purse; the unsaved reports. She has to get out of here now. But before she can move, she hears his footsteps outside the door; her head starts to pound and it feels like she is going to be sick. She hears the click of the door opening but it is a fuzzy shape that enters the room and before she can work out who or what it is, everything goes black.

As they step out onto Old Compton Street, Mark puts his hand in his pocket, making sure, for the fifth time that the invitation is still there. As his fingers touch the embossed lettering, he smiles. It couldn't have been easier.

The air is warm and sticky and as he and Liv make their way through the crowded street Mark feels a dull pain in his chest. Crowded places always make his asthma worse; he just wants to get out of here, get back to the room and lie on the bed. He breathes out slowly as they continue up the street. He can't sense Zoe in this place, she won't have been here, he can tell. The alley way was full of her, he could hear her voice, smell her perfume, she had permeated that space. Don't think, don't think, his sober voice intercepts his thoughts. Just one night without thinking about it, one night in seven years is allowed.

He can hear Liv chattering beside him, pointing out various

bars and landmarks she thinks he should be aware of, and he nods his head, makes encouraging noises, but really he just wants to get out of here. He wants to be alone; to scrutinise the invitation and plan his next move in peace. But he can't get rid of Liv yet, he will just have to go along with it for another hour or so, then turf her out.

They turn right at the top of the street, Liv leading the way, and then take a left onto a wider road. Mark reads the names of the neon-lit shop fronts: Soho Original Bookstore; Madame JoJo's; Soho DVD. It's a worn, shabby street, he thinks, dated and decaying. It smells like rotten eggs, like sour breath and old food. His army mate, Tony, had told him about the deserted villages in Afghanistan; the army would come in and check for signs of life, a flutter of curtain, smoke from a fire, cooking smells. They would step across the remnants of a community, a place where life once flourished, where bonds were made and broken, children were born and raised, marriages were sanctified, funerals conducted, the whole spectrum of a life. And when you went to these places, Tony said, it was like stepping into a graveyard; everything that made it vital, that gave it purpose and energy had been eliminated, its inhabitants had gone, dispersed like migrating birds, and only the husk, the discarded shell remained. This is what this street feels like to Mark; like the end of the line, the end of the world.

They stop at a side street and as they go to cross, he feels Liv's arm tighten.

'I hate that place,' she whispers.

Mark looks at her and she nods her head towards the street they are about to cross. He turns his head and sees a dark, narrow lane, lit with muted neon signs: Floor Show; XXX; Models.

'Really, it's more like a pantomime now,' says Liv, her voice low and serious. 'There's even a nightclub down there that celebrities go to – play-acting prostitution, what fun! It's out there on the street for all to see but what about the ones you can't see, the ones outside of Soho, across London, the trafficked girls who get picked up at Victoria Station with the promise of work. I wonder if the celebs would still see it all as a big laugh if they saw where those girls ended up.'

Mark stares down the street. The red neon 'Model' sign is flashing on and off; there are a couple of women standing underneath the sign. They are smoking and the smoke rises above their heads like a ghostly veil. One of them is wearing a hood pulled up over her head, hiding her face and in the half-light she looks like some medieval monk. Mark shivers. The place is giving him the creeps but he can't draw himself away from it; its revoltingness seems to be enticing him, pulling him into its folds.

'Over the border,' he mutters as they stand rigid at the edge of the kerb.

'What's that?' asks Liv. He feels her hands wrap around his arm. They are cold.

'It's the place where the prozzies stand in Middlesbrough,' he replies. 'When me and my mates first learned to drive, we'd pile into a car and drive past them for a laugh. They were a right bunch of skanks; crack whores the lot of them. You'd have to be desperate to want to shag one of them.'

'Drug addiction leaves a lot of women vulnerable to prostitution,' says Liv. 'That, and abuse in childhood . . .'

Mark isn't really listening to her; he is staring at the back of the hooded woman, willing her to turn around. The red light blinks on and off, on and off, casting a sickly red halo about her head. Model; hooker; model; hooker, it seems to say.

'We should go,' says Liv, taking his arm.

He nods but still he can't take his eyes off the shrouded figure and he continues to look as they cross the road. When they reach the other side he turns round and sees that the girl has gone, leaving in her wake a blurry flash of neon and a cloud of smoke.

'Girls disappear all the time,' says Liv, as they quicken their pace up the street. 'When I get back to Canada I'm going to train as a counsellor. It's something I've always wanted to do, but even more so after travelling, after hearing so many stories. Big cities swallow people up, vulnerable people, and unless you have family or money or support you're easy prey.'

Mark nods. He is thinking of the girl in the hood, a faceless girl, nameless, no past, no future. A few streets away from here is Sebastian Bailey's restaurant with its pretty lights, its potted plants and candles. It's all bullshit, thinks Mark, as they reach the end of Brewer Street and cross the road towards Piccadilly. The Rose Garden – they should have called it The Sewer because that's what it is; a rancid, putrefying cesspit built on the bones and dreams of dead girls; dying girls; girls with death in their eyes and a pock-marked client between their legs. You can scatter rose petals over it; you can spray expensive perfume into the air; come up with swanky menus and poncey food and fragrant herbs and spices but nothing can mask the stench that permeates this place; nothing can stop the decay.

As they approach Piccadilly Circus, Mark's chest feels tight, he puts one foot in front of the other but some invisible hand seems to be pressing down on him, blocking his way. The garish advertising boards that make this place such a landmark shine their spotlight on him as he passes, illuminating his face, picking him out of the crowd like some contestant on a daytime quiz show. He feels conspicuous, as though his face is up there on the hoardings on some great big 'wanted' poster, flashing on and off amid the Coca Cola signs.

'Come on, let's get back,' he says to Liv, as they turn into the little side street and walk towards the hostel. He feels the beer rising through his bloodstream like a mist as he follows Liv up the steps, watching the curve of her behind press against the thin fabric of her shorts. He wants to get back to the quiet of the room and bury himself deep inside this girl, so deep that he can pretend, for one night, he does not exist.

WEDNESDAY, 29 AUGUST

21

Seb is dreaming of sunshine; thick, hazy sun, like honey dripping down from the skies, smothering his skin in its thick opacity. It is a sepia-tinted world; like the summers of the past, an endless road movie with cheap motels, palm trees and filmy pools, mirages, white skies, RayBans, polka-dot bikinis, tanned limbs, languid moves and a Neil Young soundtrack. He stands by the edge of the pool and its colour makes him shade his eyes, it is the brightest blue, cyan blue with ripples of silver and gold, like Hockney's 'A Bigger Splash', and he holds his breath as he jumps into it, puncturing the milky surface, ripping the canvas, diving down, down to the bottom where the blue begins to fade and white light as dazzling as the moon on a clear night fills the empty space, illuminating the way to the deepest part. He feels leathery hands touch his feet, soft fingertips caress his arms as he floats down with the current. Then a voice, a familiar voice, calls his name:

'Seb!'

He opens his eyes to a fractured world; the room dances in front of him as though split into atoms, like an abstract picture, its disjointed parts hang in the air, random and scattered like pieces of broken glass.

'Seb!'

As he comes to he realises that it is Yasmine's voice calling him. He feels a dull ache rising up his spine and he sits up, trying to stretch the pain away. He must have fallen asleep on the sofa last night with Yasmine. Yasmine . . . The restaurant launch . . . His mind comes back into consciousness with a jolt and he pulls himself off the sofa and walks in the direction of his wife's voice.

She is in the hallway bent over her bag. As he approaches she straightens up and turns round. Her face is hard and serious.

'Seb. Why the hell did you let me go to sleep on the sofa? My back is killing me . . . and I've overslept.'

Seb rubs his eyes and supresses a yawn. 'I'm sorry, Yas. I fell asleep. If it's any consolation, my back's killing me too.'

She shakes her head. 'Look, I've got to go, it's almost seven and the first of the deliveries will be arriving at eight.'

'Are you okay?' Seb puts his hands onto her shoulders. It's supposed to be a reassuring gesture but his arms are heavy and it ends up feeling like an aggressive one.

'I'm fine,' she says, brusquely. 'I just didn't want to start today feeling like this. Honestly I . . .' She stops and shakes her head as though shaking away whatever she was about to say.

'What?' Seb takes his hands from her shoulders. He isn't really awake yet and he desperately needs to use the bathroom.

'It's nothing,' says Yasmine. 'Nothing at all. I better go.'

'What time should I get there?' asks Seb.

She looks at him blankly.

'To put the painting up,' he says.

Yasmine sighs heavily. 'Oh, I don't know, Seb, why don't you just text me when you're on your way.'

'You said around ten when we talked about it yesterday,' he says. 'After I've dropped Cosi off at your mother's?'

'Okay, ten,' she snaps. 'Look Seb, I've got so much going on in my head with the really important stuff, I haven't got the room or the time to think about your bloody drawings. I just haven't.' She picks up her bags and lifts the latch on the door. 'I've got to go. I'll see you at ten.'

Seb stands in the hallway, shivering in his thin T-shirt and boxer shorts. He watches the door close, hears Yasmine's footsteps clicking down the corridor, getting fainter and fainter as she departs. Her voice hammers into his head, like a car alarm, shrill and unwanted.

Your bloody drawings. The months he has put into The Lake, the surprise gift he thought would take her breath away, a commemoration not just of the restaurant but of their love, the place where they began. That's not like Yas, that sharpness. He knows this is a huge day for her, of course it is, but he feels himself stepping back into the shadows, taking his place in the wings with his frivolous 'drawings' while Yasmine steps out onto the stage.

He tries to shake off the feeling as he walks into the bathroom and takes a pee. He flushes the chain then turns on the tap and splashes cold water on his face. As he lifts his head from the sink he sees his reflection beam back at him from the mirrored cabinet on the wall. Droplets of water cling to his face. He looks at the man staring back at him.

His eyes look tired, with grey circles that have grown darker and deeper over the years, his stubble is flecked with white and his forehead is creased into a permanent frown. Thirty-seven. Not old, not by anyone's standards, but not young. He peels off his T-shirt and steps out of his boxer shorts, running his hands across the contours of his body, this body that has served him these thirty-seven years, and despite all the abuse he has thrown at it, it has never given up. All those years of binge drinking, he should have the liver of an old man, but his doctor says he is in the best of health with a long and hearty life ahead of him, all being well. This body created a new life, that wild and bright girl sleeping in her bed along the hallway came from his flesh and bones, his blood runs in her veins, the history of his family is embedded in her DNA.

Emotional pain, grief, is just like physical pain – while it is hurting there is no end to it, and when Sophie died, oh how he grieved, how he ranted and raved and drank and railed at the world, and while he was trapped inside that grief he couldn't remember how it felt to not be in pain. But then one morning without noticing, it was gone, it had taken flight and he felt different, more alert, more alive. Yet the pain has left little reminders of its force, a scar upon the skin, a bruise upon the heart . . . His body has loved and hurt, mourned and celebrated, travelled through time zones, gone without sleep, starved and feasted, held and been held, and still here it is, here he is, standing on the threshold of another day of being him. The artist, the man who paints pictures, 'bloody pictures' that fade into insignificance beside his wife's demanding world of staff rotas, time schedules, employee forms, pomegranate molasses and honey-roast almond pilaff.

She didn't mean it, he tells himself as he steps into the steaming fog of the shower, she was in a rush . . . big day ahead . . . big day for all of us. The hot water loosens his muscles and he slowly starts to wake up, his brain clicks back into life, reason and understanding return, bringing clarity to his muddled head. He will be there beside Yasmine today, as he always has been, as he always will be.

It is the heat that wakes her; claggy, dead heat that clings to her skin like a layer of film. Her head feels wet and as she opens her eyes and lifts her head the dampness spreads across the back of her neck, down her back, her legs, her feet.

'Where am I?' she whispers through thick, jagged pain that slices through her temples. The pain is so intense it takes her breath away and she lies back down onto the damp pillow and closes her eyes in an attempt to blink it away.

And in the darkness of her closed eyes an image forms, pearlised and wavering like a reflection on the water: a pale wooden box falling from the sky, upsetting its contents into a scattered mess on the floor. And in that moment, she remembers, though at first it is more of a sensation than a memory; a feeling of deep unease.

Slowly, she begins to piece together the events of the previous evening. She remembers drinking a glass of wine; she remembers Cal showing her to the room and she remembers standing in front of the cupboard and seeing a box and a cascade of items pouring from it onto her feet: her things. She remembers footsteps, then nothing.

Using every ounce of energy she can summon, she pulls herself from the bed, the pain in her head almost knocking her back. She looks around the room; at the crumpled bed, Cal's bed, the one she said she wouldn't sleep in. She had said she would sleep on the floor; use the blanket from the cupboard, she can remember that. She looks down; there is no blanket and the cupboard door is closed.

She steps towards it; holding out her hand towards the metal handle and as her skin brushes it, she tries to count but the pulverising pain will not let the numbers in. She closes her eyes as the cupboard door releases with a creak. Her belongings have to be there; otherwise she really is going mad, but as she opens her eyes and looks inside the cupboard, she gasps. It is completely empty.

The pounding in her head intensifies and she feels like she is going to faint again. She needs air, but as she walks towards the window a shrill, piercing noise fills the room. It sounds like an alarm, but she can't get her bearings and has no idea where the noise is coming from; it seems to be emanating from every corner of the room. And then she recognises what the noise is and what its persistence means. It is a phone ringing and the fact that it hasn't been answered means that he is not here; she is alone.

She walks to the bedroom door and opens it carefully, listening for any movements. The hallway is dark and silent as she walks towards the living room and as she reaches it, the ringing stops and suddenly Cal's voice fills the empty room.

She jumps as she hears the crackly message. He has a landline phone. It seems archaic to her that anybody would want or need such a thing. Yet nothing about this man and his life makes sense to her.

'Hey there. Cal and John ain't here right now but please leave a message and we'll get back to you ASAP, cheers.'

With a crackle, a different voice begins to speak; an agitated, breathless voice, speaking in bursts:

'Kerst, it's me. Pick up.'

She shivers at the sound of Cal's voice; it feels so close, like he is standing right behind her.

'Kerst, pick the phone up' . . . pause . . . 'The police have been to the office, they're up there now talking to Stratton. Said something about a body, an old lady. Kerstin what have you done, darling? You gotta come and sort this out, yeah? If it was an accident – and it must have been – then you have got to come clean. They said they've got your passport and it's out of date. Come on Kerst, pick up. The police just want to talk to you, okay? They just want to ask some questions, it'll be fine I'm sure.'

Kerstin stands in the middle of the room listening to Cal's breathing. It feels like he can see her from wherever he is. As soon as he ends the call she will go, she will get out of here as fast as she can. Finally, after an endless pause he speaks.

'Oh and Kerst, they called your mother in Germany and she told them about your dad . . . I'm so sorry, Kerstin . . . he passed away last night.'

She is vaguely aware of other words coming out of the machine; of her name being repeated like a mantra as she staggers out of the room. She manages to get to the bathroom in time and she flops over the toilet and vomits clear, acidic bile into the bowl. And as she throws up, the pain in her head seems to subside as though giving way to the other pain; the piercing grief that judders through her body like a bullet. When there is nothing more to come up, she slumps onto the floor and grips the base of the toilet with both arms, not even registering the germs that she is letting through. Nothing matters any more, she thinks as she stands up and cleans her mouth with a piece of tissue. The bad thing has happened; the worst possible thing has happened.

She looks in the mirror and realises, for the first time, that she is fully dressed. Her white top is creased and her trousers feel damp and sticky. One glass of wine; how can she have been knocked out by one glass of wine, unless . . . She remembers his hand holding out the glass, his insistence she drink it. Had he drugged her? What had he done to her when she had collapsed? Is that what all this is about? Her head throbs with the weight of the unanswered questions as she walks out of the bathroom and goes back into the bedroom to find her shoes. She can't remember taking them off, but as she reaches the bedroom, she sees them by the side of the bed. Someone has placed them there; neatly. And then another memory comes back: the shirts and suits hanging in a neat row in the cupboard, now gone. She has to get out of here before the police arrive, and they will, she has no doubt of that. Cal has been her enemy all this time and she was so busy counting she couldn't see what was right there next to her.

She slips her shoes on and hurries along the hallway to the door. She has no idea where she will go but she needs air, she needs to get out of this oppressive, cloying flat. She turns the metal handle and waits for it to give, but if feels wrong and heavy in her hand. Panicking she tries it again and again, but it is no use. The door is locked.

22

Mark wakes up to a weight pressing down on his ribs. His mouth feels dry and he has a raging thirst. He stretches his arms out and hears a faint moan. He looks down and sees Liv's naked form spread across his lower body.

Fuck, he thinks, as he slowly comes to. He lifts her arm from his hip and climbs out of the bed, but as his feet hit the floor the dull thudding in his head becomes a sharp stabbing pain. The room fills with floating silver dots as he sits down on the side of the bed putting his head in his hands as he tries to piece together the last few hours.

He remembers getting back to the room; Liv put some music on – Paul Weller –and they sat listening to it and drinking beer. He vaguely remembers taking his clothes off, he sees them scattered across the floor: his black boxer shorts, Liv's white lace underwear, her denim shorts and vest, dotted around the room like bits of rag.

He rubs his neck. It is aching and stiff. He must have slept in one position all night. His skin feels sticky and hot; he puts his hand between his legs, his penis is damp and flaccid. Did they use protection? He can't remember. He scans the floor for traces of a condom wrapper but there is nothing, just a pile of scrunched up beer cans and an empty packet of crisps. He remembers Liv's mouth; she was kissing him down there. Had he fallen asleep – is that why he can't remember finishing? Had he fallen asleep with his cock inside her mouth? Jesus. His brain feels soggy and lumpen as he tries to make sense of it all.

He pulls himself up from the side of the bed and walks towards the sink. Turning on the cold tap, he cups his hands and scoops the water into his mouth. It tastes revolting – luke-warm and mossy – but it is liquid and his dry mouth greedily soaks up every drop. He swills it around his tongue, gurgles it in the back of his throat, feels it trickle down his grainy, sore gullet.

He switches off the taps and sees that Liv has shifted position. She is lying on her front now with one arm dangling down the side of the bed. Mark follows the direction of her arm and sees that it is almost touching the top of the black bag. Why the fuck did he leave the bag poking out like that, she could have seen it, could have woken in the night and gone looking about, opened it up and found him out. He berates himself as he stumbles over the detritus of clothes and rubbish and pushes the bag further under the bed.

This is madness, he tells himself. This was not meant to

have happened. He has to get her out of here right now, this minute. Seb will be at The Rose Garden at 10 a.m. and he has to be there to greet him.

He picks up his phone from the floor and looks at the time: nine-thirty. Shit. He pulls on his jeans and sweater and goes over to the bed. Kneeling by her face, he gently shakes Liv by the arm.

'Liv,' he whispers. She stirs and holds his hand up to her face.

'Come on,' he says, slipping his hand away, his voice firmer this time. 'You gotta wake up. I've got to go.'

She groans and pulls the duvet up to her face.

'Please, Liv,' he shouts. 'You've got to go.'

She opens her eyes and smiles.

'Hello you,' she says. Her voice is sleepy but dripping with languid sensuality.

Mark nods his head sharply then starts picking up her clothes, one by one, from the floor.

'Listen, I don't mean to be a bastard,' he says. 'But you have to go . . . now.'

She sits up in the bed, her face creased with the imprint of the pillow. She looks confused and young. Very young. He thinks of Zoe and shudders. He is no better than those men at the party, lusting after some young girl, getting her drunk, leading her on . . .What the fuck had he done it for? Why had he lost control like that? All he had to do yesterday was lie low, get an early night and be clear-headed for today, for the incredibly important fucking day that he has spent the last seven years planning.

'Please,' he says, holding the clothes out in front of him.

'Don't I even get a kiss goodbye,' she says, pulling the duvet around her chest.

'Look, I think we both know what last night was all about,' says Mark, impatience rising in his voice. 'It was just a shag, love. A bit of a laugh. Now please could you just . . . leave?'

He throws the clothes down onto the bed then walks to the window and opens the thin curtain. The noise of the traffic vibrates under his feet, people in gym-wear speed-walk along the pavement clutching bottles of water; he hears the screeching of brakes, the whine of a siren and a robotic voice warning of a vehicle about to reverse. Soho is open for business and he is stuck in this clammy room, a whole twelve hours behind. He needs to have a wash, get his brain in order, plan every sentence of what he wants to say to Bailey. He needs to be out of here.

He hears a shuffling noise behind him and he turns to see Liv pulling on her shoes. She has thrown her clothes on quickly – her vest is inside out, her shorts unbuttoned and her face is matted with spots of black mascara while her top lip looks pink and sore. She bends down to pick up her bag and iPod, then she turns and looks at him. He has no idea what state he must be in; if his appearance is anything like the inside of his mouth feels then he can't be looking good.

She stands like that for a minute, not moving just staring until Mark walks towards her and puts his hand on her shoulder.

'Come on,' he says, opening the door and gently guiding her out. 'You're a lovely lass,' he says, the words rushing out so fast they are barely discernible. 'Take care, yeah?'

She stops in the doorway and looks up at him. 'You were lovely last night,' she says, her voice shaking. 'Now it's morning and you're like a different person. I do understand you know . . . about Zoe.'

Mark freezes. What is she talking about? What had he told her when he was drunk?

'Your sister,' she continues. 'I understand how you're feeling. I lost my Mum to cancer last year . . . that's why I'm travelling, I'm running away from all the well-wishers, the anniversaries, the empty chairs.'

Mark taps his fingers along the door frame. He cannot be having this conversation. He has no idea how much she knows and he has to get away from her. Jesus, how could he have been so stupid?

'Look, love,' he says. 'As I said, I'm fine, but I've got to get on.'

She opens her mouth to speak but before she can he presses his finger to her mouth and shakes his head.

'Bye, Liv.'

He closes the door and stands with his back pressed against it. His neck feels like it is snapping in two and his head is jumbled and throbbing but he is alone and he can turn this around. He puts his hand into his pocket and feels the now familiar velvety paper. Pulling the invitation out, he presses it to his face and takes a deep breath. He is almost there.

Stella rubs her head as Paula directs the cab driver along Royal Hospital Road.

'I feel like death,' she mutters. 'Honestly Paula, you must never ever let me get that drunk again.'

Paula laughs as the cab pulls up outside the Physic Garden. 'Just here would be great, thanks,' she says, breezily. 'And may I have a receipt?'

As Paula pays the driver, Stella eases herself out of the cab, her head throbbing as it hits the warm air. Looking up at the high entrance gates of the garden she feels something akin to vertigo. She was supposed to be spending the morning preparing for her meeting. She had wanted to start the day with a clear head not this groggy fug that envelopes her now as she waits by the gate. She winces as Paula comes bounding towards her; eyes bright, face beaming. Stella frowns as she approaches.

'How come you look so sprightly? I swear you drank just as much as me.'

Paula shakes her head playfully as she guides Stella gently towards the entrance of the garden.

'You definitely had the lion's share of the champagne, Stel,' she laughs. 'But strangely enough, I do feel better today. I think the night out did me good. I really do appreciate you coming here first though, before you go off to the library. Carole will be thrilled to see you.'

Stella goes to speak but is overcome by a wave of nausea. If she can get through the morning without throwing up it will be a miracle, she thinks, as a large blonde woman, dressed in a green padded gilet and navy trousers, runs towards them, her arms outstretched.

'Darlings, you made it. It's marvellous to see you. And you've brought the sunshine with you too.'

Stella watches as Paula embraces Carole, expert herbalist and Chelsea stalwart.

'Come on,' says Carole, leading them up a broad narrow path that is dotted with blue wildflowers. 'I bet you're both gasping for a cup of tea. If we're lucky there might still be some breakfast buns left at the café.'

Stella's heart sinks. A cup of tea. Paula said it would be a quick hello. Yet the guilt of what she is about to do makes her follow Paula along the path, her head thudding with each step.

'Oh, goodness Carole, look at the rosemary,' gasps Paula, as they walk through a knotted herb garden. 'I've never seen rosemary that colour before. It's almost blue.'

'Amazing isn't it,' says Carole, as the two women stop to admire the plant. 'It's a Spanish variety, very rare. Our curator brought a cutting back with him from Grenada.'

'Oh you must tell me the name, Carole,' says Paula as she

bends her head to smell the prickly stem. 'You know all the time I worked in the herb gardens in Andalucia, I never saw rosemary this colour. And the smell is sharper than ordinary rosemary.'

'Saltier, isn't it,' says Carole, joining Paula in sniffing the plant.

Stella stands behind them, swaying slightly in the heat of the morning sun, willing them to carry on to the café. If she can just sit down, she will feel better. She coughs, but Paula and Carole carry on oblivious. She looks around and sees a wooden bench by the side of the gravel path.

'I'm just going to sit down,' she calls to Paula.

Paula looks up and smiles. 'We won't be long, Stel. Just going to have a closer look at this rosemary.'

Stella walks to the bench and sits down. It is shaded by a mulberry tree and the cool is a welcome respite for her burning head. She stretches her legs out in front of her and watches the two women disappear into the tangle of plants.

As she sits she tries to trace her restlessness, the uneasiness that has sprung up between her and Paula, when had it started? When they returned to England? When they moved to Exeter? No, in fact Stella had loved the city when they first arrived. She loved the people, the warm West Country accents, loved the Regency houses that seemed to curve around her, holding her in an invisible embrace as she walked by; the elegant expanse of Rougemont Gardens. She and Paula had spent their first summer there lying in the park on thick woollen rugs; eating in restaurants with pretty walled gardens; strolling hand in hand through the deserted early evening streets, luxuriating in their new-found home, and each other. Stella had enrolled on an MA course at the university, found a part-time job in a bookshop and immersed herself in both. The house was paid for outright from the sale of Paula's London home, the herb business was thriving . . . .

Still, though she cannot pinpoint when this feeling began, she knows that it has probably always been there, lying dormant, waiting to spring forth, Was it last Christmas, that disastrous dinner with Paula's family, her brother telling lame jokes, the children fighting, everyone bickering, Paula snapping at her about a dish of overcooked Brussels sprouts or had it started earlier? Were the seeds sown the previous October when Paula had insisted they attend the wedding of her school friend, Tina, at Babington House in Somerset and Paula had told everyone who would listen that Stella was a recovering bulimic and Stella had had to endure the glare of a dozen pairs of eyes following her every time she got up to go to the loo.

Or was the turning point far more recent? Was it last Sunday when she had taken her work out into the garden to make the most of the glorious late August sun? She had sat at the table, her books spread out before her but had found herself unable to concentrate through the fug of hedge strimmers whirring, ice cream vans blasting out tinny fairground tunes, dogs barking, children screaming. Paula had come out and asked her what she fancied for dinner at the exact moment that the man next door decided to charge up his lawn mower. Stella had slammed her books shut and tramped back upstairs to her overheated attic room, leaving Paula alone with the sounds of the suburbs ringing in her ears.

She looks across at Paula, lost among the herbs, revelling in row upon row of rosemary and dill; borage and pennyroyal. Carole is snipping cuttings for her and Stella can see Paula's dark head bent over the proffered hand, taking in the woody scent of the herbs, making notes in her ancient green book. She can see Paula holding a sprig of rosemary in between her finger and thumb, rubbing it gently to release its sweet fragrance.

Rosemary for remembrance. Paula had told her once that the Elizabethans used to place the herb into the coffins of the dead and Stella had shivered, for even as a child she had a strong aversion to that spiky herb and when her mother had asked why, she had told her it was because it tasted of sorrow.

She sees Paula's lean body weaving in and out of the herb beds, lifting her head to the sun every now and then, pausing to take in its warmth like she had that day in Andalucia when she had invited Stella to come and see the amazing herbs that grew in the scorched earth behind the farmhouse.

'Borage, basil, chervil, coriander and dill,' she had pointed out as they stepped carefully between the rows of green spikes.

'These are annual herbs; they flower, set seed and die all in one growing year. They're the flighty ones, the one night stands of the herb world if you will.' And as she spoke, Stella thought of a poem that had always scared her as a child: 'Gather ye rosebuds while ye may; Old time is still a-flying; And this same flower that smiles today; Tomorrow will be dying.' While Stella blinked away the doom-laden words, Paula had stopped at a patch that was set back away from the others. 'I would say we're more like these ones,' she said, pointing to the herbs that poked out like thin, wizened fingers.

'Rosemary for remembrance,' whispers Stella as she looks up into the sun. And in the piercing white light she sees an image of Paula lying on the grass, her hands shading her eyes from the glare of the sun, her feet scattered with sprigs of rosemary, sharp and spiky and digging into her skin like so many thorns.

It's a horrifying image and she blinks it away as she stands up and walks towards the exit. At the gate she looks back to see if Paula has noticed her departure but all she can see is a mass of tangled herbs.

23

Kerstin stands on Cal's bed frantically trying to prise the window open, but it is no use, it is double-glazed and double-locked. Like the door; like the windows in the living room; like every other possible exit in this flat. She is trapped and all she can do is wait here until the police arrive.

She climbs down from the bed and slumps onto the floor by the cupboard, the empty cupboard that just a few hours ago was filled with Cal's suits and her belongings. She is going mad, she knows it. She can feel her brain slowly disintegrating.

'You have a fine brain, Kerstin. Make sure you use it well.'

Her father's voice trickles through her harried mind, like water dousing dry land; her brilliant father who only wanted her to be happy.

She thinks about praying. She could pray and ask God to get her out of here. Ask for a miracle. Her mother will be praying, she knows she will. She may even be at the Cathedral, offering up her grief to God, reciting her lines to the stones

Kerstin's grandfather laid, those familiar prayers Kerstin grew up repeating like an automaton though she had no idea what they meant. If only she could summon them now, but her mind is empty.

She once knew every prayer by heart though they troubled and confused her in equal measure. At school, she would ask the priest 'why' but he just gave bluffs, half- answers, all delivered with a knowing nod and a pat on the head and Kerstin would try to grab hold of the answers, feel solidity in her hands but they would just fall through her fingers like water.

Now it is the only thing she has left; the only possible hope.

'Our Father,' she sobs into the folds of her creased top, twisting the material into soggy damp snakes. 'Who art in Heaven. Hallowed be thy name . . .'

Seb holds his breath as he hammers in the final nail, hoping against all hope that he has aligned them right, that he will not have to start again and leave a trail of nasty nail-sized gashes on the perfectly painted blood-red wall. He is glad, at least, to be out of sight, hidden in this alcove, resting his knees on the deep-cushioned banquette that surrounds this, the most exclusive part of the restaurant, the most private corner, home to the lover's table, a mistily romantic cavern surrounded by velvet cushions lined with golden thread, honeycomb lanterns and candles scented with jasmine and rose petal.

Seb stands back and looks at the painting; it looks fine to

him, but he is not going to take a chance. He reaches down to the large metal toolbox that is resting against the table leg and takes out his spirit level. His mouth feels dry as he holds it up against the wall, watching the fluid tilt back and forth like an unsteady sea until, at last, it aligns itself between the black bars and hangs weightlessly there.

'Good,' mutters Seb. He couldn't bear to let anything upset Yasmine who, thankfully, is in a much brighter mood than when he said goodbye to her at the flat.

He was surprised when she bounded over to him, when he arrived at ten on the dot, all smiles and hugs and bright eyes. The angry, waspishness of the morning had slipped from her and she looked like Yasmine again, fresh and happy in her gleaming chef's whites. As the morning progressed potential sources of worry were ticked off the list: deliveries arrived without incident; the staff were prompt and well-prepared; Henry called in with the RSVPs for his newly adapted guestlist and, though still dotted with Honey Vision contacts, it was looking far more Yasmine-friendly. Henry had also brought in a copy of last night's *Evening Standard* featuring an interview with Yasmine, conducted last week. Seb, Yasmine and the staff had gathered round Henry who held the newspaper open. The photograph was beautiful, from what Seb could see as he craned his neck to read the interview. She was wearing a deep scarlet dress, sitting at the lover's table with a rose in her hair. 'Christ, Yas,' exclaimed Henry, as he closed the magazine and the staff returned to the kitchen. 'You scrub up well, my darling. Will we see rose petals in your hair tonight, I wonder?' Henry had left soon after, his phone beeping in his wake.

From his hiding place, Seb can hear the soft sound of the radio trickling out of the kitchen, providing a staccato, dance-beat to the clinking of glasses, the slamming of fridges and sharpening of knives. It is very warm and Seb removes his sweatshirt and unbuttons the top two buttons of his shirt. The music stops and a slow, sticky summer beat strikes up, then a husky female voice begins to sing.

'I know this song,' says Albert, the bear-like commis. 'My mum used to play this song over and over when I was a kid. It was a geezer sang it, big fella with dreads, oh what was his name again?'

'Eddie Grant,' says Kia, the tall, boyish maître d', her voice deadpan and toneless.

'Eddie bloody Grant,' shrieks Albert. 'That was him. He was cool, he was.' He starts to sing along. 'Good version this one, she's got a well sexy voice.'

'Al, how are we getting on with the harissa?' Yasmine's voice cuts through the music like a teacher gathering up a group of rowdy students. 'Not too much mint remember, it needs to be a suggestion, a smattering, like I showed you.'

'It's going good, Chef,' says Albert. 'Here, have a try . . .'

The voices and music disappear as an electric whisk screeches into life and Seb stands back to take a last look at the picture. The spotlights above it pick out the blue and white and silver of the lake. It looks like a hologram floating over the burnished table and warm golden cushions. She will like it, he tells himself as he steps closer and squints, trying to imagine he is seeing the painting for the first time. In the darkness of his semi-closed eyes, the room seems to shrink, letting in only pinpricks of light, the silvery sheen of the lake bleeds into the russet, the wine and gold of the restaurant like an opalescent globe warding off a ball of fire.

It is only when he opens his eyes that he becomes aware of the presence; the laboured breathing, the sharp citrus deodorant scent mixed with the earthy smell of sweat. Seb pauses for a second before turning. In the kitchen, a multi-tude of voices shout instructions and demands, the extractor fan whooshes, fat spits, someone drops a knife onto the floor, water gushes out from the taps and a male voice hisses an expletive. But there in the hidden corner, there is unbroken silence and in the seconds it takes Seb to turn around, there is peace, and he will remember those seconds because they will be the last moments of calm, the last moments of clarity he will ever have.

'Sebastian Bailey.'

The voice is raw, familiar somehow, a particular strain of Northern-ness, a cold male voice, deep and resonating with a malice that seems so out of place in this romantic corner.

Seb turns and his stomach flips. He knows this man. He has put on weight since the trial, he looks unkempt, out of condition. His thin navy T-shirt sticks to his body, emphasising a rounded belly and his skin has an unhealthy greenish tinge. But there is a striking resemblance all the same, the slightly bulbous blue eyes, the thin sliver of a mouth, the straight nose; she is everywhere about him. The girl, the poor lost girl he had befriended on a bench. He gathers himself, drawing his arms across his chest, trying to regain some sense of composure. He can deal with this, as long as he keeps the man contained here in this corner, away from Yasmine, he can deal with it and send him on his way.

'Can I help you?' It sounds ridiculous and he knows it, but the words pour out of his mouth seemingly of their own will.

The man stands motionless, his fingers looping around a black bag that he holds in his left hand. He stares at Seb, but his expression is one of curiosity, wonder even. His eyes widen and he opens his mouth. Seb has no idea what he is going to do next. He sees that the man's hands are shaking and suddenly he starts to cough, a hacking violent cough that causes him to pound his chest with his free hand.

'Do you want to sit down?' Seb tries to direct the man towards the banquette but he shakes his head and starts to rummage in his coat pocket. For a moment Seb is unsure of the man's intention and he takes a step back; then he sees the inhaler. He watches as the man brings the tiny plastic tube to his mouth and takes three sharp sucks. The coughing subsides and the man's breathing slows down as he shoves the inhaler back into his pocket and stares at Seb.

'I'm Mark Davis,' he says, spittle falling in droplets from his mouth.

Seb nods. There is a lull in the kitchen noises and he prays that it will resume. He has told Kia what he is doing and asked her to keep Yasmine out of the alcove until he has covered the painting with a blanket, but if Yas hears raised voices, she will come to investigate, he knows her.

Mark puts the bag down by his feet and walks towards Seb.

'How's your little girl?'

Seb's brain freezes and for a moment he can't think properly. Where is Cosima? Has this man been near her?

'What do you want?' he whispers.

'What do I want?' Mark shakes his head and as he does so his gaze is averted to the painting. He walks towards it, Seb watching every move he makes. He stands in front of it and grimaces.

'I want you to pay,' he says, his voice so calm, he could be a supplier asking for a cheque. 'I want you to pay for my sister's life. Simple really.' He turns and looks at Seb as though waiting for an answer. Seb goes to speak but no words will come. He feels breathless himself, it is clammy and hot in the alcove but though he would love to sit down he knows he has to remain standing, remain at eye level with this man.

'Mark,' he begins tentatively. 'What happened to Zoe was horrific, it was appalling, beyond words . . . but the man who did that to her was caught, he was tried and he is in prison . . .'

'No, he isn't,' yells Mark, slamming his fist down onto the table. 'He's dead, isn't he? Hanged himself in his cell.'

Seb tries to take this in, tries to imagine that evil, dead-eyed creature hanging on the end of a makeshift rope. He shudders.

'But he was just the endgame,' says Mark, rubbing the edge of the table with his fingers. 'There is a long line of people who contributed to Zoe's death and you're at the front of it. Look at you, with your fancy restaurant and your flash clothes, your perfect family. It knocks me sick, all of it.' He looks up at Seb, his face is contorted and ugly, his top lip sticks to his teeth as he spits out the words. 'What happened in Soho Square, eh? What did you do to her? Why was she running away?'

Albert's voice cuts across the silence like some sort of demonic troubadour. He has switched the radio channels and is hollering a dance tune. Seb tries to think amid the noise, tries to remember something that happened seven years ago, to reason it, explain its nuances to a man who looks like he might explode at any moment.

'She wasn't running away, Mark,' he says, firmly. 'She was going to King's Cross. She was going home. She told me all about your mother and your granddad, she was excited about going home and having Sunday lunch, seeing you all again. And that pub, she told me about the pub where your father used to go, and how everyone knew her as Charlie Davis's daughter.'

'Shut up,' says Mark, his eyes bulging, fighting against the tears that are clouding his eyes. 'Just shut up. Don't you dare say my father's name, you arrogant prick. My father is dead, my sister is dead, we don't eat Sunday lunches anymore, we are not a family anymore. My wife was beautiful, just like yours, and my daughter too, but they have fucked off, haven't they, fucked off and left me. I don't have a family – it's been ripped apart.'

Seb hears something rustle; he looks up and sees Kia standing in the entrance of the alcove. She is holding a piece of paper in her hand.

'Hi Kia,' says Seb, trying to keep his voice light. 'What is it?'

'Er, Yas just wondered how long you're going to be. She wants to start getting the tables ready,' she says, looking at Mark quizzically. He has started to wheeze again and he is holding his hands flat in front of him as if trying to steady himself.

'Not too long now,' says Seb, he looks at his watch. 'Shall we say ten minutes?'

Kia nods her head. 'Okay, I'll go and tell her.'

She walks back to the kitchen and Seb can hear her telling Yasmine that he will be ready in ten minutes. Yasmine claps her hands. 'Come on guys, it's ten-thirty now, let's get cracking, yeah.'

'Let's get cracking,' repeats Mark, with a sneer. He picks up his bag and stands in front of Seb, his voice raspy and thin. 'As I was saying before we were rudely interrupted, I don't have a family any more, I don't have anything, so in a way, Sebastian, I don't have anything to lose, do you understand what I'm saying? Whereas you, you have everything to lose don't you. Life's like that you know, one minute you're on top of the world, the next . . .' He clicks his fingers in front of Seb's face. '. . . it all disappears just like that. Fathers, sisters, wives, daughters, they can be taken from you, just like that.'

Seb's mouth feels dry. He sees Cosima's face in front of him, smiling her gappy smile, asking him questions, dancing round the kitchen.

'She's a pretty girl, your little'un.'

Seb scratches the side of his head, little beads of sweat have formed at his temples and his heart is pounding so hard it feels like he is going to collapse. He hears Yasmine shout something to one of the chefs and he wants to call out to her but he can't speak, the words won't form. Instead, he stands there like a frozen statue unable to move, watching impotently as Mark walks out of the alcove and disappears into the dark folds of the restaurant. He hears soft footsteps then a click as the door closes. His head feels as though it is on fire and he clutches his hand to his temples as he flops down onto the velvet cushions and tries to absorb what just happened.

The noise of the key being turned in the lock doesn't register at first but then footsteps, heavy footsteps, thud across the living room floor and Kerstin jumps to her feet.

She tiptoes to the door and stands in the darkness of the hallway, listening. Someone is whistling; a man. She hears the creak of a window being opened, then the tap in the kitchen running and the clattering of crockery. This is not the police, she thinks, as she walks slowly towards the living room. Could it be him? Has he come to find her, to trick her? Has he got the police outside waiting for her?

When she reaches the living room she stands in the doorway and sees a figure standing by the kettle in the kitchen; a tall young man with blond hair wearing dark trousers and a blue shirt. He whistles to himself as he pours the boiling water into a mug. Then he turns and looks up.

'Jesus Christ,' he yells, dropping the cup and its boiling contents onto the tiled floor with a smash.

He stands holding his hands in the air. He looks scared. Kerstin has never seen that look on a person's face before.

'Who the fuck are you?'

She steps into the room and stands by the sofa.

'I'm sorry I shocked you. I'm . . . I'm a friend of Cal's,' she says, her voice sounds low and laboured. There is something seriously wrong with her brain, she thinks, as even the act of talking is making her feel dizzy. 'I stayed here last night, but when I woke up this morning the door was locked and I couldn't get out.'

The man holds his hand against his chest as if to steady himself then he looks up and smiles.

'That's my flatmate for you. I don't know, he's not that great at holding onto women but surely locking them in is taking things a bit far.'

He walks towards her and Kerstin flinches as though she has been hit. He stops and stands by the table, looking at her.

'Listen, the door's unlocked now, you are free to go,' he says as he picks up a clump of kitchen towel. 'And I'll have words with Cal when he gets home.' He walks back to the kitchen and starts cleaning up the spilled tea.

At first Kerstin doesn't move though she knows she has to. She looks at the hunched figure mopping the floor and she wants to scream, to cry out: 'Help me!' But instead, she walks out of the room towards the door, and as she touches the handle and feels it yield, she realises that nobody can help her now. She has to keep moving.

24

Stella looks at her watch as she crosses Gower Street and approaches the university: it is five to two. Now, if she can remember Dylan's directions to Foster Court then she should be right on time.

She walks towards the grand porticoed building and thinks of the National Gallery, designed by the same man, and of the July morning seven years previously when she had sat on the gallery steps and looked out across Trafalgar Square as thousands of people cheered and celebrated London's bid to host the 2012 Olympic Games.

It seems as though everything London was that day; everything *she* was, has been transmogrified; thrown inside some great petrie dish and emerged as something else; as the London she walks through now; a battered but strong city that has suffered horrors and bears its scars stoically like some ancient soldier. And Stella's scars, the deep hurt she felt when she lived here, when she almost killed herself with bulimia: an enemy she thought she could never defeat, are fading too though they will always be there as a reminder of how far she has come.

Hearing Dylan's words in her head she turns right at the edge of the great building and crosses an equally impressive quad and as she does the pounding in her head starts to ease as she remembers all the questions she wants to ask him. She reminds herself that she is a confident, professional woman, no matter what Paula says. She is strong now, stronger than she has ever been. Seven years ago she had been working in a dead-end job, throwing up her potential each night in a poky Soho flat; her self-esteem zero, her prospects nil and here she is weeks away from getting her doctorate.

Yet, still this guilt; she has never been good at deceit and she has felt terrible hiding it from Paula all these weeks and lying about being at the London Library. She has never lied to Paula before but how could she ever try to tell her; how could she broach the subject of Paula leaving her beloved Exeter to join her in London; the city that almost broke her. How could she convince Paula that this is for the best?

But now as she walks towards a modest brick building and sees the sign Dylan has directed her to: a small stone plaque with the words Foster Court written in gold lettering, the voices of the past are silenced; she can do this, she is more than capable of teaching. Her PhD is due to be handed in at the end of September and then she is free to do what she likes and with the academic record she has established at Exeter University, surely this is the next step?

Pulling her bag close she walks up to the entrance, through the glass doors and up the stairs to the second floor. The building is warm and smells of new carpet and as it is still the summer holiday there are no students about. She reaches the second floor and steps into a narrow corridor lined with posters and notices. One catches her eye: 'Woolf and the City: A series of lectures looking at Virginia Woolf's London, commencing 7 October 2012 at the London Library.' Stella smiles as she walks on to the end of the corridor towards Room 220. And there it is, the third door on the right: the office of Dr Dylan O'Brien, Head of Literature Studies, University College London; the tutor who guided her through her MA; who encouraged her to undertake a PhD and who now has the power to change her life.

Taking a deep breath she knocks gently on the door.

She hears movement from inside the room then the door opens and there he is; dressed in a beige shirt and creased navy trousers; a pen in his hand and long, greying hair flopping over his eyes like a messy puppy.

'Stella,' he cries as he approaches and kisses her on the cheek. 'It is great to see you.'

'Likewise,' she says, and for the first time since she has been back in London she means what she says.

'Do come in,' he says, ushering her into the tiny study. 'And please excuse the mess; my room at Exeter was a lot bigger. I'm swamped in paperwork for the new term and I still have that lot to get through.' He points to a pile of bound manuscripts. 'PhDs,' he says, raising an eyebrow. 'God help me if I can get them all marked by mid-September.'

'Good luck,' says Stella, sitting down onto a squishy moss-green armchair.

'Can I get you a coffee?' asks Dylan. He walks across the room to where a plastic kettle and a couple of chipped mugs sit on a shelf surrounded by box files and books.

'Yes, please,' replies Stella. 'White, no sugar.'

'So how's the PhD coming on?' asks Dylan as he spoons instant coffee into each mug.

'I'm almost there,' replies Stella. 'It's due to be handed in on 24 September so the pressure's on.'

'I can imagine,' says Dylan, handing her a mug of hot coffee. 'And I really appreciate you taking the time to come down here to meet. It's a bit of a trek from Exeter isn't it?'

'Yes it is but I was so excited by what I read in your email,' she says. 'I had to come and find out more.'

'Well, let me tell you all about it,' says Dylan, taking a sip of coffee. 'When the idea for this new module was mooted a few months ago, I felt you would be the ideal person to take it on. Your PhD is one of the most exciting I've read on Woolf for a long time. Thanks, by the way, for sending me little snippets. I can't wait to see the finished, published piece.'

Stella nods. It *is* exciting, yet she has never allowed herself to be excited about it. 'Leaden Circles: Virginia Woolf and the Deconstruction of Time.' A thesis that has been three years in the making; hours of research and time and late nights and now it is going to be published. She should be beyond excited but then her work has always taken a back seat to Paula's priorities: the herbs and the baby and Paula's ever-increasing business demands. 'That little college course' is how she described it, as though it were a hobby or an evening origami class at the local community centre. Even when Stella got the funding to undertake the PhD, Paula had told her to take it slowly; that any undue stress could cause a relapse.

'Anyway,' says Dylan, as he stands up and takes a large green box file down from the shelf above his desk. 'I'll tell you a bit about the new module and then outline the role. Remember this isn't a formal interview – that will take place in a couple of weeks – I just wanted to talk it over with you first before the post is advertised.'

'Okay,' says Stella. She watches as he takes a sheet of paper out of the box file then sits back down in his chair.

'So then,' he says, taking another sip of coffee 'We're setting up a new module and as head of programme I've been assigned the task of taking on a new full-time lecturer. It's an undergrad course but as lecturer you'd also be involved in some postgrad classes too.'

Stella nods and he continues.

'The module is called Introduction to Modern Literature and in it we will cover the work of three major modernist writers: Woolf, Joyce and Richardson. Within this we'll look at the concept of the writer's voice and then explore this further in a sub-module called "Writing the City" where the students will look at the writers in their own contexts: Joyce's Dublin; Woolf's London and see how far they created not just their own voice but the voice of their respective cities.'

'So it will be *Dubliners*, *Ulysses*, *Mrs Dalloway*, *Pilgrimage*,' says Stella. 'And you mentioned *The Years* in your email too which was music to my ears. That is the core text of my thesis.'

Dylan smiles. 'Yeah. There is so much you can take from your thesis when it comes to planning tutorials on this. We'll also be cross-referencing texts so after introducing the students to Joyce, Woolf and Richardson over a series of weeks we'll then start to compare the texts and engage the students in a wider-reaching debate on modernism. We'll also look at the wider society, what was happening in the world during those years; how it influenced visual arts, music . . .'

'Excellent,' says Stella.

'The role itself is a full-time one,' continues Dylan. 'Starting salary of £35,000 with London weighting. And it will commence in January 2013'

Stella goes to speak but she feels overwhelmed. The idea, the hypothetical question she has churned over and over in her head for three weeks since she received Dylan's email, has just taken shape in front of her eyes. This is all real; living and working in London again could actually be a possibility. And Paula has no idea of any of this.

'There's a lot to take in I know,' says Dylan, leaning back in his chair. 'And I imagine a lot to talk over with your partner.'

'Yes,' says Stella. 'And that's where the difficulty lies, you see my partner, Paula, well she would never move to London. She has a successful herb business in Exeter that she runs from home and she loves it where we are, she's close to her family and they live nearby.'

'Oh,' says Dylan, looking serious all of a sudden. 'I'd say commute but that's one hell of a journey each day and most of the lectures start at nine. You would have to live either in London or just outside if you were to take this on, Stella.'

'Where do you live, Dylan?' Stella tries to bat away the feeling of hopelessness that is welling up inside her. How could she ever convince Paula to move to London; it just wouldn't happen. Why has she been trying to kid herself all these weeks?

'I live in Angel,' says Dylan, 'it's great for work. I walk to the campus every morning, really clears the head.'

Stella smiles. 'There's nothing like London mornings,' she says. 'I miss that.'

'You used to live here didn't you?' asks Dylan, draining his cup of coffee.

'Yes I did, many moons ago,' says Stella. 'In Soho of all places.'

'That must have been interesting,' says Dylan. 'In a cool sort of way.'

'Yes it was,' says Stella.

She looks out of the window behind Dylan's head and imagines herself working here in Bloomsbury each day; teaching young people, sharing their ideas and dreams. If someone had said to her seven years ago when she was working as a receptionist in a dreary asset management company, that one day she would be working in this magnificent university, talking about Woolf and Joyce with her own messy office and box files full of work to be marked, she would have called them crazy. Back then she was a lost soul in need of rescuing then Paula came along and whisked her away and made her better. But she is not ill anymore; she is healed. And what she needed then is not what she needs right now. She looks up and meets Dylan's eye.

'There's a lot to take in, I realise that,' he says, stirring his coffee. 'If I were you I'd take your time over this. Give it some thought this week and how about we speak on the phone next week? You can let me know then if you'd like to come for the formal interview.'

'I'll do that, Dylan,' says Stella. 'But I think I already know what the answer will be. This is an amazing opportunity for me; yes, I would like to have the interview.'

'That's wonderful news Stella,' says Dylan. He reaches down into his bag and takes out a small desk diary. 'Now, how about we set a date for that?'

Mark stands looking at himself in the long oval mirror weighing up the steel grey suit and white shirt he has spent the last ten minutes squeezing into and the hundred-pound price tag that comes with it. He had hoped to find a cheap option but Topman was as cheap as he could find and it was still expensive. But he has no choice, if he is to blend in with the clientele at the posh hotel he's booked into for the night.

He had checked out of the hostel as soon as he was sure Liv had gone and he was grateful that it was a bored-looking young woman called Sal on the reception desk rather than the over-zealous Stuart. There were no questions, no offers of advice, just a swift handover of his room card and he was out of there, released into the back streets of Soho, to Frith Street and his confrontation with Bailey.

Mark had noted that Seb's hands were shaking as he left him, he had scared him, just as he intended, taken the sheen off his perfect world; though Mark was angry with himself for coughing, having to use his inhaler, that bloody inhaler. All his life his weak lungs have let him down, stopped him living the life he wanted.

He had wanted to join the army but his asthma was deemed too acute; that rejection had almost killed him. There he was, sixteen years old with no qualifications, he had pissed his way through school because he knew that as soon as he left he was going straight to the army recruitment office, he was going to follow in his father's footsteps and be a soldier. There was no other life for him, no other choice. But then his lungs let him down, his wheezing, his breathlessness, his sodding blue inhaler.

Nothing much mattered after that, he trained as a welder and got a job in Guisborough with a mate of his granddad, and he sleepwalked through the weeks, living for the weekend when he could go out into Middlesbrough town centre and get shitfaced with the lads. Lisa had stopped all that and when Rachel came along, he lived for the evenings when he could come home and give her a cuddle, tuck her up in bed, sing her the songs his mam had sung to him and Zoe when they were kids. Weekends were spent at soft-play centres and country pubs, DIY outlets and the Riverside Stadium watching their beloved 'Boro FC, the three of them, him, Lisa and little Rachel; that was all he needed. And then one Sunday, when they were all in the car coming back from a walk in the Cleveland Hills, his phone had rang and his mother, barely coherent, told him the news that his sister had been found dead.

And after that there were no more trips out, no football matches, no laughing, no talking, no cuddles. The man Mark had been died that day and would never return; he became haunted by horrific dreams of his father and Zoe, her eyes wide open, staring lifelessly out at him, his father screaming at him to do something; just do something.

But six months ago, Lisa had left him, taken Rachel with her and moved to Gran Canaria, where her mother lived. She told him he had become an obsessive, told him she couldn't put up with his mood swings, with his lack of conversation and his hours sitting on the computer. She had found the press cuttings, said he was in danger of becoming a stalker; of getting himself locked up. It was the week they found out that the man who murdered Zoe had killed himself in his cell. Mark was working nights in a meat-packing warehouse in Redcar. He had just come home after a nine-hour shift; his hair and body stinking of dried blood and cow shit when Lisa told him. She said that was the end of it all; he was dead, now they could truly get on with their lives. But it was just the beginning for Mark; the catalyst for a burning rage that will not cease. It cannot end like this, he had told himself, it's too simple – the bastard hangs himself and we all go on as normal.

And so Mark had taken his anger and poured it into Bailey, he had held onto it, obsessed over it until it was all he had left, he clung onto it as his wife and child packed their suitcases and left him; as he was handed his redundancy cheque and sold his car, it was all he had left, all that connected him to Zoe. Even as he found himself back at his mother's house, he still knew that this plan he had put in place was right, that it was what his father would want, that, despite all that had gone terribly wrong, he could make it all better if he just did something.

He takes his T-shirt, and jeans and stuffs them into his rucksack, then picking up his black bag, he walks out of the changing room still wearing the suit and goes across to the counter where he asks the baffled young assistant if he wouldn't mind scanning the price label of the suit with him in it. Then he hands over his card, types in his pin, grabs the receipt which he crumples up in the palm of his hand and makes his way out of the shop.

KARIN ALEX

25

Kerstin holds her breath as she walks up the narrow staircase, praying that she hasn't been followed. She steps into a wide, wood-panelled room and looks around for somewhere to hide, but the room is full of wooden dining tables. She can't stay here without being seen. There is another set of stairs in front of her and she tiptoes towards them.

She walks up the steps in the darkness, like a hypnotised person following instructions. When she reaches the top she sees a curved bar with bottles and glasses lined up behind it. She walks on and the room opens out into a vast, warehouse-style space filled with leather bean bags and round tables. Then she sees it, a narrow door on the far side of the room. An exit.

She pushes the door open and steps into a small room. There are a set of lockers, metal ones like she used to have at school, running along the length of one wall. On the other side of the room, there is another door, a wider door than before, with wooden slats on it. She walks over to the door and opens it. It looks like some kind of pantry, though there are no packets and tins here, just rubbish by the look of it. Old paint pots; a plastic bucket; assorted brushes and mops with rigid bristles and a pile of papers. This is a forgotten place, she thinks as she steps inside and closes the door behind her, a place she can hide.

When she fled the flat she had run like a flailing child in no particular direction; pushing through the bustle of Dean Street at midday. Then she had seen them; police officers, a man and a woman, coming towards her, so close she could hear the crackle of their radios. So she had darted down a side street, a half street really, and as she ran she saw a little wooden gate leading to a yard. She didn't have time to think about what she was running into, she just had to get away from the police.

Once in the yard, she realised what it was; the back of a restaurant. She could hear someone singing in the kitchen and the smell of garlic mixed with discarded vegetables wafted out of the open door. She could see the chefs inside the kitchen, the backs of their heads moving in time to the music. Any second one could turn around and see her. Then she saw the door; a fire exit by the look of it, to the side of the kitchen window and she had darted into it just as a woman's voice called out into the yard.

She squeezes herself into the cupboard, moving the pots of

paint and the brushes to the far end then sits on the floor to catch her breath.

This can't go on much longer, she thinks, as she stretches her legs out in front of her. She can't keep on running. She has no money, no phone, no passport and the pain in her head feels like it could kill her any minute. But she cannot give herself up and spend the rest of her life in prison.

Just then she hears something. Someone is out there. She hears breathing; and a voice, a male voice speaking.

'This effing suit.'

The voice is agitated and Kerstin holds her breath as she peeks through the wooden slats of the door.

She sees a man. Tall with longish curly hair. He is standing by the lockers, taking off his clothes. She watches as he throws his jeans and T-shirt onto the floor, then takes a heavy-looking suit from a hanger and slowly puts it on.

Then he stands motionless for a few moments before stepping across to the other side of the room. Kerstin cannot see that part of the room but she knows he is still there; she can hear him sighing and muttering.

After a few minutes she sees his shadow flash across the room, then hears his footsteps depart down the stairs.

Kerstin exhales and she feels her heart pounding. All her life she has been scared of enclosed spaces, of germs and dirt and here she is cowering in a cupboard on the top floor of God knows where. She thinks of Clarissa but the image is blunted now; the thought of the incident no longer makes her wince. She thinks of Clarissa's words 'You're nothing but a Hun', and they merge with her father's voice:

'Civilians will always be caught in the crossfire, Kirsten.'

Did he know? Did her father have some second sense of what was to come? She imagines the rueful look on his scientist's face – second sense, pah! But maybe he *had* known, maybe her mother too, and Matthew – is that why they had all kept away, because they knew that she was dangerous, that bad things happened when she was around, that she was an unlucky soul, born under a dark star. Her mother had told her that as a baby she had never smiled, never laughed. Life was too much, even then, even as a small child she knew that there was too much darkness in the world to allow herself to live.

Seb sits in lover's corner, hunched rigidly amid the cushions like a statue frozen in time. Above his head a sheet hangs over the painting and without the silvery sheen of the oil paint, the wall suddenly seems dark and insipid.

As he sits, he plays over Mark's fragmented words in his head. Had it been a threat? He is not sure though it had certainly seemed as much. Mark's eyes were the coldest he had ever seen, devoid of any feeling, any compassion. When he had coughed Seb had expected some kind of vulnerability to emerge, a sense of hopelessness but there was nothing; just hatred and malice. He had stood there inches from Seb's face

and warned him. He had referred to Cosima, he had specifically asked if she was going to be at the launch. And how did
he know about the launch?

Seb's heart sinks as he thinks of the mountain of publicity
that has been generated around the restaurant and his arts
projects, the interviews with Yasmine, the 'Life in a Day' piece
he did for the *Sunday Times* last month, the Vogue interview; the
grand unveiling of the Olympic portraits at Leicester Square
Tube and his accompanying commentary on ITV news. When
he was doing all this, he didn't realise just how many people it
would reach, well he did, but he just thought of those people
as abstract, sales figures, potential clients, invisible, a line on a
chart; then there are the Twitter and Facebook pages for both
Asphodel and The Rose Garden, his Wikipedia page, all with
references to his life, his time schedule . . . his daughter. He
is a prime candidate for being stalked – his whole life is out
there for all to see. Mark could track him minute by minute if
he wanted to, he might be tracking him right now, watching,
waiting for his next move.

When Mark had left him he had stumbled to the kitchen in
a daze wanting desperately to see Yasmine, to talk to her but
he knew that would be impossible. He had stood at the pass
like a rookie waiter looking for the next dish to be delivered
while Yasmine flitted across the floor, shouting instructions to
the team, stirring sauces, tasting morsels of food and shaking
her head, gesturing the sous-chef to add more salt, her face

growing redder and sweatier as steam rose in a thick haze around her, almost obliterating her. At one point, she looked up and saw him standing there.

'Seb, what is it? Why are you standing there like that? I thought you were helping Kia with the list.'

He had opened his mouth to speak but no words would come. What would he say? How could he begin to describe what had happened, what could happen?

There was an almighty bang and Yasmine turned from him to berate the young kitchen porter who had dropped the large, copper pan, the contents of which were now seeping across the floor in a thick, red sludge.

Seb had left the pass then and gone upstairs to the tiny area off the bar on the second floor that Henry had converted into a sleek changing room for the staff. Its tiny window looked out onto the street and he had stood there for a few moments, watching tiny ant-like creatures as they scurried below. It felt like he was waiting for someone, something, though he wasn't quite sure what: a face? a mob? A gang of masked men armed with baseball bats? But there was nothing, just the familiar movement of post-lunch Frith Street on a late summer day, with the same figures taking the same routes they always did: Syed from the doctor's surgery across the road walking up to Bar Italia for his afternoon take-out cappuccino and sticky bun; Anya, the Polish waitress from the deli opposite sitting on the step having a cigarette; a group of tourists in big hats and backpacks huddled round a tour guide, following the trail of his pointed finger as it picked out the rickety, Georgian façade of Hazlitt's Hotel, 'dating back to 1718 . . .' Just a normal afternoon in Frith Street, nothing out of the ordinary, nothing to be concerned about.

Still, Seb had felt uneasy as he slipped out of his T-shirt and jeans and took his tweed Vivienne Westwood suit from its hanger. Yasmine had chosen it specifically for tonight, said it made him look like a Soho dandy and though he wasn't sure that it was quite his style, he had laughed and said 'whatever makes you happy'. And she is happy, he had thought, as he buttoned up the cream shirt and felt the cold, ripple of cotton next to his skin. She is happy and excited and about to launch the biggest project of her career. The air up there felt heavy then and, with only half of the trousers on, he had to sit down and catch his breath.

And now he sits hidden in lover's corner, like an overdressed mannequin, willing his hands to stop shaking. He has to stay calm, for Yasmine's sake. He can watch her all night if need be; he can stand by the pass, make sure no one but the waiters and the kitchen staff gets near to her. He can do that, he can watch his wife but there is someone else he can't watch, his slippery, boisterous, curious daughter, who will certainly not stay still, not for one minute. How can he do it? How can he watch them both in a darkened restaurant packed with people?

'Oh there you are, I've been looking for you.'

He lifts his head and sees Yasmine standing under the arch. Her hair has flattened to her head, her face is moist with sweat and her white chef's jacket is splattered with faint red stains. She looks like she has just come out of an operating theatre, thinks Seb, as he rises to his feet and goes towards her.

'Two hours. Can you believe it?' She raises her eyebrows inquisitively at the white sheet above Seb's head. 'I must say, darling husband, that suit looks veery sexy.'

'Thanks,' says Seb, leaning over to kiss her cheek. She tastes of fried onions and salt water. 'It's a bit hot though; definitely more of a winter suit.' He loosens the top button and wriggles his neck. It feels like a strait jacket but he tries not to show Yasmine his pained expression.

'Well, the kitchen's good to go . . . just,' she says, tapping a dishcloth against her leg. 'Mum's just texted and she's going to aim to get here for six-thirty. Cosima's got her gladrags on already, Mum said she's really excited. Little angel, I've missed her so much this last week. I can't wait to see her.'

Seb closes his eyes, the suit's fibres digging into every pore. He feels like he is about to pass out and he puts his hand to his forehead which is damp and clammy. He can see Cosima in her green silk dress, the eye-wateringly expensive treat they bought her in Paris last Christmas. 'She's a pretty girl, your little 'un'. He tries to shake the words and their loaded connotations out of his head but they remain as he opens his eyes, they are all around him as he slips out of the alcove and into the twinkly lights of the fully made up restaurant.

He turns to Yasmine and smiles. 'Wow,' he mouths. 'It looks amazing, truly amazing.'

This should be one of the greatest moments of his life; standing here with the woman he adores, about to launch a restaurant in the middle of Soho, about to watch her life's dream be realised. Instead, it feels like he is suffocating with fear and panic, made all the worse by his desperate attempts to hide his concern from Yasmine.

'You think it looks okay?'

'I do,' he says, putting his arm around her waist and pulling her towards him, feeling her heat burning through the itchy fabric of his suit. He has to say it, he cannot risk anything happening to their child, he can't.

'Listen,' he says, gently releasing himself from the embrace. 'I've been thinking . . . about Cosima, and, er, maybe it's not such a good idea that she comes tonight.' He can see Yasmine's mouth drop open in an expression of shock but he continues; he has to say it. 'I mean, there's going to be all sorts of people here tonight, some drunk, some leery, she might be a bit daunted by it all.' Even he doesn't believe this, both he and Yasmine know that Cosima will talk to anyone, and the odder the better, so he changes tack. 'Also, you'll be run off your feet in the kitchen, I'll be needed front of house, we won't get a chance to see her, and she'll be wanting to talk to us, it'll be awkward . . . So I thought, maybe it might be for the best if she and Maggie stay in Battersea, have a little "at home" celebration. What do you think?'

Yasmine's eyes have grown so wide they are in danger of bursting forth from their sockets. She holds the dishcloth in the air and for a moment he thinks she might hit him.

'What the fuck are you talking about, Seb? You want me to tell our beautiful, excited little girl, who is all dressed up and ready to come and celebrate, that she can't come to Mummy's launch after all? Have you completely lost your mind? Cosi comes everywhere with us, always has and always will. I'm not leaving her out of one of the biggest nights of my life . . . and Mum as well, you want my poor Mum to stay at home after everything she has done for us? What do you think she is, some sort of hired help?'

'It was just an idea . . .' He wants to rip this bastard suit off; the heat is creeping up his neck like burning lava.

'Well, it was a crap idea, a preposterous idea,' she yells, still glaring at him with bulging eyes. 'All of this is for her,' she says, waving the cloth at the room. 'The eighteen hour days, the sweat and turmoil, the sleeplessness . . . Christ Seb, Cosima named this restaurant, she planned the colour scheme, the flowers, the pictures, everything. She would be devastated if we said she couldn't come, and so would I.'

'I just don't want her to get lost in the crowd,' Seb replies, his voice sharp with panic and irritation. 'You know how she likes to wander off . . . and I won't be able to watch her all night, there's the front of house and the VIPs to talk to and then I'll have to sort out the p—'

'Your painting.' Yasmine spits the words out. 'The bloody painting. You always have to be centre of attention. God forbid we can have one day, just one day, that's not about you and your sodding paintings.'

He shakes his head, feels a rage stirring inside his gut but he has to contain it, if he retaliates then the whole night will be shot to pieces.

'You're just like your bloody mother,' Yasmine snaps as he walks back to the kitchen where the team are standing by the pass watching the show. 'Next thing you'll be packing Cosi off to boarding school. Well that's not my world, Seb. You don't mess with my child, nobody does.'

Seb is so angry, he almost rips the suit from his body. He could throw it at her right now, smack her on the back of her sweaty head. How fucking dare she say that about boarding school, after he had told her what happened to him as a child, after he had opened his heart to her, sobbed in her arms. He needs to get out, have a walk, get some air.

'Fuck you,' he shouts as he storms out, pulling the door so hard it almost comes off its hinges. 'Fuck it all.'

26

Mark follows the dark-suited man up the narrow staircase, crouching to avoid banging his head on the low wooden beams. Unlike the hostel, the check-in procedure here had been seamless; a quick glance at the reservation book, a swift handover of a wedge of twenty pound notes, and an offer to be shown to the room; painless, but at two hundred pounds a night, it had almost cleaned him out. Still, thinks Mark as they reach the first floor, he doesn't need money anymore.

The building is old and rickety with uneven floorboards and Mark trips over twice as he follows the concierge along the corridor. It is shabby opulence, the kind that some people would savour, but not Mark. For him it is simply a watchtower, a base to conduct his covert observation. It could be a Travelodge, it could be the Ritz, it makes no difference, it is the position of the hotel that matters. A month ago, when he started to formulate his plan, with the name, address and launch date of the restaurant firmly imprinted in his mind, he had typed the postcode into Google Maps to see what was near, whether there was a hiding place he could occupy, one where he could make himself invisible and watch the comings and goings of the occupants of The Rose Garden. When he saw there was a hotel directly opposite he could not believe his luck, but then he saw the prices and his heart sank. There was no way he could conduct a three-day reconnaissance at that cost. But one night could be possible; one night was all he needed, to watch and wait for the right moment to strike.

The concierge stops at a low, wooden door.

'This is your room, Mr Lowe.'

He unlocks the door and pushes its heavy weight with the flat of his hand, holding it open to let Mark enter.

'If you need anything, please do say.'

He gives a slight nod of the head, a gesture barely perceptible, then lingers, his face expectant. Mark wonders why the man is looking at him like that; then it dawns on him; he rummages in his pocket and hands the man a five-pound note. The man takes it between his thumb and forefinger; nods again, then turns and leaves; his footsteps echoing down the ancient, dark corridor as he goes.

The room looks like a museum display and Mark laughs in bewilderment as he steps inside and closes the door. The walls are painted gold and are covered in oil paintings in dark wooden frames. The bed is draped in a dark-green coverlet edged in silver thread and is framed by a giant mahogany headboard. Mark shudders. He has never liked old furniture, it gives him the creeps, and the bed looming out of the centre of the room makes him think of those vampire films he used to watch as a kid, where the undead spring out of the shadows, draped in red velvet cloaks. There is a table by the bed with a lamp, a plain, wooden chair and a bookshelf dotted with slim, ancient-looking volumes.

Still, it's good enough for Mr Lowe, Mr Dennis Lowe, the name he booked the room under and as he stands in the doorway, he thinks of the man whose identity he has taken: Denny, a wheeler dealer of the old school, his father's best mate from childhood, he had been like some mythical hero to Mark and his mates when they were growing up. They would see him driving round in his sleek, burgundy Jaguar, a heavy gold Rolex hanging from his wrist, a ruby sovereign ring squeezed onto a chubby little finger, the sun bouncing off his bald head, shiny and tanned from the Marbella sun. Mark and his mates would follow the car on their BMXs, watching as it crawled up the hill and turned right towards upmarket Nunthorpe and Denny's mock Tudor detached house with its white leather sofas and faux Canaletto prints. Sometimes he would see them gathered at the electric gates, peering at him as he stepped out of the car and crunched his Italian loafers across the gravel, and he would beckon to them.

'Come on lads. Who fancies cleaning the Jag?'

And they would throw their bikes onto the ground and set

to scrubbing and polishing the car until it gleamed like some exotic jewel. Then Denny would reach into his pocket and pull out a wad of tenners. 'Good work, lads, nice job.' Denny had been part of the furniture when Mark was little; he would come downstairs and see him sitting at the table, the *Evening Gazette* spread out in front of him, cup of tea in one hand, cigarette in the other, charming Mark's mother and regaling Ernie with his latest deal.

Yes, Denny would have suited this place, thinks Mark as he looks around the room, he would have patted Mark on the back and said 'classy' in his soft, slightly effete Middlesbrough twang. Mark can see him now, standing in the middle of the room, nodding his head and smiling at the opulence oozing from every corner, 'You've done well, son.'

Denny died of a heart attack in the late nineties, the same week Princess Diana was killed, and while the country mourned, Mark said goodbye to another hero; another man he had looked up to and loved; the Jag was sold, and the fancy house was stripped of its furnishings by Denny's sister and her husband. Over time, he slipped from being a man to being a local legend, Mark had lost count of the number of times he'd heard someone in the pub begin a sentence with some reference to the great Denny Lowe.

So, tonight as far as anybody here is concerned, he is Denny. A nice tribute, thinks Mark as he puts his bags onto the bed and goes across to the window, drawing back the gold damask curtains that hang heavily down to the floor, a good luck charm, even though he doesn't believe in such things. There is a soft armchair by the window and he sits down and looks out onto the street. He shakes his head and smiles. It couldn't be more perfect: he has a direct view of the restaurant; he can see the waiters milling about in the doorway and a young woman in a black suit stringing red-and-green bunting above the door. He opens the window a fraction and the noise of the street seeps through the tiny space. He slides his hand through the crack in the window and feels the cool afternoon air ripple through his skin like a caress. This is better than he could ever have hoped for. He had asked specifically for a street-facing bedroom when he rang to make the booking, and the woman on the other end of the line asked if he was sure, as it gets very noisy in the evening. But this was what Mark wanted, a view of the restaurant and enough noise to mask the screams. Perfect.

He unfastens the top button of his shirt, takes off his jacket and drapes it across the bed. Then he goes over to the wooden chair that is wedged up by the far wall. He picks it up and takes it to the window, pushing the soft armchair back into the room. He puts the wooden chair by the corner of the window and sits down. It is just the right height for him to get a clear view of the street, but the heavy curtain hangs at such an angle that he can hide behind it and still see out. The chair is hard underneath him, but the discomfort is good, it will keep him alert, keep him sharp, for now he is ready, now he is in position; now all he has to do is sit tight and wait for the enemy to emerge.

Stella's phone vibrates in her coat pocket as she comes through the ticket turnstyles at Leicester Square tube station.

She stops to answer the call as irate commuters rush past her, elbowing her in the ribs and expressing their displeasure in loud tuts. Squeezing herself into the far corner near the ticket machines, she holds the phone to her ear and waits for Paula to answer:

'Stella, is that you?'

'Yes. I've just got to Leicester Square. Are you all right?'

'I'm fine but poor Carole's had the most awful shock.'

'What's happened?' Stella holds her finger against her ear as she tries to hear Paula's voice above the noise of a train announcement.

'Well we were just by the borage beds when two police officers arrived. They said they wanted to ask Carole some questions. Anyway, they told her that Clarissa Burton-Lane, one of the patrons of the garden and a dear friend of Carole's has been found dead in her flat, just round the corner from here.'

'Oh, that's awful,' says Stella. 'Was she very old?'

'Yes, in her late eighties I think. But it's worse; according to the police she was murdered. Hit over the head. Poor Carole, I thought she was going to collapse when they told her.'

'It was probably a break-in,' says Stella. 'Properties in Chelsea are a prime target and if she's elderly and lives on her own, she was even more vulnerable, poor lady.'

'Talking of death. How's your hangover? Did the library help?'

But before Stella can reply she hears another voice in the background.

'Hang on, Stella, Carole's back . . . two tics . . . Carole what did they say?'

'Paula, should I call you back,' says Stella, as more people push past.

'No darling, stay on the line . . . two secs.'

'She was such a great supporter of the garden.' Carole's voice crackles down the line.

'I know, Carole.' Paula's voice soft and soothing.

Stella coughs. This is insane, having a three-way conversation with a grief stricken stranger.

'She even had her own little seat by the . . . Oh, that wicked, wicked girl.'

'Girl? Which girl?'

'. . . no sign of a forced entry,' Carole's voice fades in and out. '. . . killed by someone who lived in the top floor flat.'

'My God, Carole.'

'. . . young woman . . . it was the estate agent who found Clarissa in the basement . . . this woman comes up from the lift just moments before. And now she's gone missing.'

'But why would she want to kill an old lady?'

'That's what we shall find out when they catch her. And they *will* catch her . . . oh this is too much . . .'

Carole's sobs splutter into Stella's ear.

'Oh Carole, that's terrible. Hold on I'm just going to speak to Stella then we'll get you home. Stella, darling are you still there?'

'Paula, what should I do?' asks Stella. 'Shall I go on ahead and meet you there?'

'Yes, I think that would be best,' whispers Paula. 'Carole's in a bad way. I should get her back to her flat, make sure she's okay.'

'We don't have to go to this launch,' says Stella. Right now the idea of returning to Earls Court and having a good sleep is so appealing. 'I can head back to the room and we can just have a quiet night if you like?'

'No,' says Paula. 'I have to show my face; the jasmine's going to be such a talking point I might get a few orders. And I told Yasmine we'd be there. You just go on ahead and I'll meet you there. I won't be long . . . an hour max.'

'Okay,' says Stella, her eyes stinging with fatigue. 'Text me when you're on your way.'

'Will do darling. Love you. Bye.'

Stella takes the phone from her ear and looks at the time on the screen: 4:30 p.m. After saying goodbye to Dylan she had gone for a walk through the streets of Bloomsbury; trying to take in the new options that had opened up: a generous salary;

an amazing role with a wish-list syllabus and London opening its arms to her once more. 'We're going to make this work,' she told herself as she sat on a bench in the British Museum and looked up at the great cranial ceiling. 'I *am* better now; this just proves it. I'm ready for this.'

She will make Paula listen, she tells herself as she walks towards the exit, she will make her see that they both deserve happiness and if that means returning to London then so be it. She cannot hide away for ever; she can't keep running away from a past that is long dead. She shivers as she thinks of the old lady and the strange girl on the run.

As she walks up the stairs she sees tell-tale signs of the recent Olympics: the iconic posters with their pink and blue neon lettering flutter above the square, faces of athletes bear down from almost every corner and on the hoardings outside the station, an eight-foot painting depicting the stars from the 1908 Olympics competing in a ghostly run-off with the athletes of 2012. Stella walks over to take a closer look at the imposing piece, there is something about it, something about the squiggly line, the hazy colours that resonates with her, it looks like the inside of her head. Up close she can see the lines clearer, they tail off as if unfinished, some of the athletes are only half-complete; the edges of the running track are blurred and sepia-tinted, locked into a freeze-frame that has lasted over a hundred years. She smiles and goes to walk away when she sees a small plaque just to the right of the painting: 'Running Out of Time' by Sebastian Bailey, 2012.

She looks again at the name: Sebastian Bailey: then up at the picture. Wow, she whispers, as she looks beyond the picture to the great sprawl of Charing Cross Road. What an achievement. She thinks about the Seb she knew, the slightly dishevelled handsome man, who always shook her hand when they met. It's funny the things one remembers, the silly, incidental things amid all the important, life-changing ones. Wow, she repeats as she turns from the painting and makes her way towards Soho.

She puts her phone back into her pocket and as she turns from the heat and noise of the tube station she steps back; back through time and space. She remembers without even thinking, the little side street on her left, that links Charing Cross Road to Chinatown. She can smell it as she threads her way through the early evening crowds, that unmistakable smell of rotten vegetables, prawn shells and incense; smells that she has never experienced anywhere else. As she walks along the street, past the wok shop and the T-shirt shop, the Chinese medicine store and the window with red, headless ducks, she feels like she is walking against the tide, walking back through time, to a place she has only ever returned to in her dreams, a strange, twilit place where time stops and the air is thinner.

Her head feels empty, her body numb as she follows a route

so familiar she could walk it with her eyes closed. On she goes, past the gold pagoda and the blank, sixties building where Seb used to work. She tries to remember the name of the modelling agency: Honey something or other. As she exits the side street and emerges onto the vast swoop of Shaftesbury Avenue, a chill ripples up her spine. There it is, right in front of her: her old home, the place she had lived and almost died. She waits for a lull in the traffic then half-runs, half-walks until she reaches the other side and stands looking up towards the dirty neon sprawl of Frith Street.

It hasn't changed, yes there are a few new bits – a deli has sprung up in place of the twenty-four hour hair salon – but fundamentally it remains the same.

Thank God Paula isn't here, she thinks as she steps off the pavement and walks down the centre of the street. This was always going to be something she had to do alone. She knows she will have to look up soon, as she walks past Ronnie Scott's on her left and Bar Italia on her right, just a few more steps along and she will be there. She counts it: one, two, three, four, five, and there it is. The flat. The exterior is cleaner than it was; someone has given it a lick of paint and the whiteness of it looks odd somehow; the rickety door that would never close properly has been replaced with a thick, steel one and the railings leading down to the karaoke bar in the basement have also been painted a glossy black. She looks up at the second floor; the new occupants have put blinds up, smart white ones, and the window is closed. It looks like an office, a shell; any life that had gone on there is just a memory now, a whisper floating off into the air.

They say that after a while the body stops registering shock; that sometimes a thing is so huge, its impact is impossible to be felt. What's the term again, she thinks, as she sees another familiar landmark, The Dog and Duck, looming up ahead – sensory overload, that's it, that is exactly what is going on here, that is why she feels numb, why her body feels weightless and ethereal, so much so that when she sees him, she doesn't flinch, though she can see the surprise in his face as she walks towards one more familiar sight.

'Seb.' Her voice doesn't sound like her own as she watches him approach, his hands outstretched, his big smile lighting up his face.

'Oh. My. God. What are you doing here?' He pauses before hugging her, as though weighing up whether he should or not.

'I'm here for your restaurant launch,' she says, as he kisses her lightly on the cheek. 'I mean, your wife's restaurant of course. My partner, Paula, supplied the jasmine. I've come with her . . .' Her voice trails off as she looks at his face and years suddenly become minutes.

'Christ, this is insane,' he laughs. 'I've got so much to ask you, when, where, who, what . . . Oh it's lovely, truly lovely to see you, it really is.'

'It would be nice to have a catch up,' she says, 'A drink or something but I guess you'll be run off your feet right now.'

'Yeah, I am, I mean, we are,' he says, briskly. 'In approximately thirty minutes, the great and the good of London society will be crammed inside that little building. It's crazy, fucking crazy, believe me.'

'Paula's running a bit late, she's going to meet me here,' says Stella, stepping onto the pavement outside The Dog and Duck, to let a delivery van get by.

'And Paula's your business partner, yeah?' asks Seb, looking distractedly at the van as it pulls up outside the restaurant.

'She's my civil partner,' says Stella, watching his face as the words come out. 'We've been together seven years now.'

She can see him mentally putting the pieces together, his mouth fixed in a slightly uneasy smile.

'Oh wow,' he says, with unconvincing brightness. 'That's . . . that's great. Good for you.'

'You've met Paula, actually,' says Stella. 'I introduced her to you in here, do you remember? It was the last time I saw you . . . the night before the tube bombings.'

'Oh yeah, of course,' he says, and Stella can see that he too looks like he is battling sensory overload.

They stand in the doorway of The Dog and Duck, not moving, though both fully aware that one of them will have to soon.

'Listen, Stella, do you fancy a drink?' he says. 'A quick one before doors open next door.'

'Are you sure,' she says, noticing his shaking hands, the beads of sweat on his forehead. 'Won't you be needed?'

'Not right now, no,' he says. 'Anyway, it will be good to clear my head first, and I'd love to hear all your news, though I warn you I may just expire from heat exhaustion in this bloody suit.'

He laughs a strange, nervous laugh as he pushes the pub door open with one hand and beckons Stella to go ahead.

'Christ,' he says as they enter. 'The last time I was here was with Ade . . . whatever happened to him?'

Mark watches as the two figures disappear through the frosted glass doors. He didn't see her face, just the back of her head, but it was enough to startle him: dark, glossy hair pulled back into a loose ponytail, a simple white dress falling just below her bare knees, navy blue converse trainers – all very measured, very faux casual but it was the look on Bailey's face that said it all. An indifferent look that turned to shock in a matter of moments, nobody else could have seen the change, not even the woman, but Mark, from his vantage point high above the street, saw that expression play itself out second by second: and as the woman walked towards him, in the moments before he put his arms out, Sebastian Bailey wore the look of a man who has just seen a ghost.

Mark had watched as they embraced, noted how Bailey's hand had touched the small of the woman's back; again a discreet gesture that was over in seconds, but it was enough for Mark; enough to validate his opinion of Bailey and of what went on in Soho Square in the final hours of Zoe's life.

How many other women are there? How many young girls has he sweet-talked, put his arm around and led off into pubs and gardens and back streets? There is more to it; more to all of it than what was described in court; it was too obvious: young girl lost in London gets killed by mad junkie. No, there was a reason she was wandering like that on Oxford Street, she was a sensible girl, twenty-four years of age, not a kid, and if she wanted to get to King's Cross, she would have been on the tube hours before that. She had left the junkie's house at nine in the evening; why the hell would she have wandered round Soho until three in the morning? It just doesn't make sense; and Bailey's line about her climbing into the garden square to check if he was all right, well that's just bonkers. She barely knew him.

No, it is clear what happened, and after seeing Bailey with that woman just now, Mark is even more sure that something much darker went on in that garden square: he can see it now, see Bailey's face, those cowardly eyes, he sees his hands grasping Zoe, forcing himself on her, scaring her so much that she went running off into the night, towards her death. Zoe didn't climb into that square, he enticed her into it. He wasn't her friend, he was just another chancer, another Martin Harris albeit in a more expensive suit. Mark knew the moment he walked into the courtroom; he couldn't look at him and his mother, he just stared straight ahead, smiling at the judge, reciting his lines like a good little public schoolboy.

He looks down onto the street; it's getting busier now. Groups of drinkers have congregated outside the pub and he can hear a faint drumming noise coming from the restaurant, a hypnotic sound that carries up the street, bringing a stream of people in its wake. He watches as the large group of men and women stop outside the restaurant, waiting to be admitted. The men wear well-cut suits with pastel-coloured shirts and soft, pale loafers; the women, trouser suits with kitten-heeled shoes, exposing a sliver of tanned flesh; all eyes hidden by aviator sunglasses that glitter like tiny space probes when the light hits them. They look out of place, wrong somehow, their sleek, sharp angles at odds with the rickety curves and decaying decadence of the building.

He tries to imagine Zoe walking down this street, late at night, towards Soho Square. His sensible sister, who used to take her car everywhere, who used to ring her mother if she was going to be late home from work; who shaded her eyes if a scary scene came on the television. He tries to imagine her now, weaving her way through this crowd of bankers, conspicuous in her skimpy, clubbing clothes, avoiding eye contact, trying to block out their disapproving stares, the whispers, the nudges. Zoe was not part of this world, she was not part of Bailey's world, and yet he claimed she had helped him see sense, she had sat and talked him through the death of his girlfriend.

How can that be when they spoke a different language, and Middlesbrough *is* a different language to the one spoken by Seb and his posh mates down there on the street; they are as alien to each other as German and Inuit. There is more chance of him breaking bread with the jabbering freaks at the Waterloo Road Mosque than there would be of Zoe pouring her heart out to someone like Seb.

And yet, what does he know about her? What did he ever know apart from some vague, abstract notion, what did he really know of her beyond the familial role of 'little sister'? They had never really been close, though he would always leap to her defence if he saw anyone bothering her when they were out clubbing with their respective mates. He knew men looked at her, knew that she was considered an attractive girl, but as to her personality, well he had never really got much further than surface talk. When Zoe opened up, it was to their mam, they were as close as sisters, sharing their worries and dreams and secrets, while Mark had his mates, the pub, the Ferensby Estate and then later, Lisa and Rachel. The only time they had really disagreed was when that Asian lad got stabbed outside the club and Zoe had challenged him; asked him outright if he and his mates had anything to do with it. And when he had told her his opinion of that lad and his ilk, that they should all be shipped back off to Fuckistan or wherever they came from; that they were the kind of people his father would be fighting had he been a soldier today; that they were terrorists and haters who wouldn't think twice about planting a bomb next to a baby's buggy; she had gone ballistic, called him a small-minded sod, a racist. Two days later she left for London and when he had joined Lisa and his mother to wave her off as she left for the bus station, Zoe still wouldn't look him in the eye.

Well now he can make up for that, he can be the person his father wanted him to be and if he has to go down fighting then so be it. As more people gather on the street below, Mark reaches across to the bed, picks up his rucksack and takes out a small pad of paper and a pen. He flips the pad open but before he has a chance to write, there is a knock on the door.

He closes the pad and gets up. He isn't worried. This is not the hostel; you get a better standard of service in hotels like this. It's probably the concierge with a tray of tea. But as he opens the door and sees a flash of bare skin, his mouth goes dry.

'What the hell do you want?'

27

Seb turns from the bar, a glass in each hand, and makes his way to the small table where Stella is sitting, her face half in shadow. The pub is filling up, as it always does at this time of day, as it did the evening he last saw Stella; the last time he set foot in this place.

He puts a glass of sparkling water in front of Stella then sits down on the low stool opposite her and takes a sip of his pint of orange squash, but his mouth feels as dry as sandpaper and the juice tastes like metal. Panic and fear always make things taste like that, he thinks, as he puts the glass down on the table.

'Keeping a clear head for tonight?' asks Stella, nodding towards his glass.

'No,' he says, realising that there is so much she doesn't know, a whole lifetime, it seems, to catch up on. But there is no time for that, not now, not with what is happening. 'I don't drink anymore. Haven't touched a drop in seven years,' he says.

He scratches his neck and sees Stella looking. He can imagine what he must look like, trussed up in this itchy suit; the skin round his shirt collar all pink and rashy. Yet he doesn't care about that, he just needs to be around someone calm, someone who will tell him everything is going to be okay. When he saw Stella on the street, it was like she had been sent for precisely that reason; a constant in a day of flux.

'Oh, right,' she says, and Seb remembers the last time they met. He had swayed on his chair, raised his glass to her and Ade, her boyfriend, had thought he was . . . well did it really matter what Ade thought? The name sounds like a relic now, a whisper from another age. He would not recognise his old self now; that troubled young man sitting by the bar, drinking himself to death alongside a man named Ade.

'Still, I don't blame you,' says Stella, taking a sip of her water. 'I've had the monster of all hangovers today. I drank way too much champagne last night and . . . oh I'm sorry I shouldn't say that.'

'Oh, please, don't be silly,' says Seb. 'If I was that sensitive around booze, I couldn't function next door.' He lifts his glass but his hands are shaking so violently he has to put it down.

'Seb, are you okay?'

He looks at her and smiles, his eyes meet hers for a microsecond then he looks away. He can feel an old sorrow rising up from his gut; it's like the last seven years haven't happened and he is here with this girl-woman, the one who always made him feel sad, sitting in the pub falling to pieces. He can feel the liquid bubbling to the surface and he tries to blink it away but as he does, a tear escapes and runs down his cheek in a thin rivulet.

'Seb, what is it?' She shifts her stool towards him and puts her hand on his.

He looks at her and closes his eyes, wanting to pause the moment; to stop whatever he is about to say before it can come out of his mouth. The inertia seems to last an age but can only be a couple of seconds, then he opens his eyes and looks straight ahead as he talks. Stella's hand remains tightly clasped on his.

'That night, the last time we met, I was drunk, I was so drunk I could barely see, barely speak. I don't think I ever told you, but there was a woman, a woman I loved, had been with for two years and . . . and she died.'

'When was this?' Stella looks at him and her gaze is so intense he doesn't think he can go on so he directs his words to the grimy table top. An inanimate object cannot judge.

'December 2004. A couple of months before I met you, before I started working at Honey Vision. Anyway, this woman, Sophie her name was, well she looked very much like you, so much so that when I first met you I thought I was going mad, thought I was seeing things.'

He looks up and Stella nods, and he notices the shadow of a frown pass across her face. Had she thought something could have happened between them? No, of course not. She is with a woman; she had been with a woman, the same woman, that night. Yet he can't help feel that she seems disappointed somehow. He looks at her now: she is still beautiful, but it is a borrowed beauty. To him she will always be a mirror image of his dead love, and though he may have entertained amorous thoughts back then, they were just that, thoughts, abstract 'what ifs'. And even though she is sitting here in front of him, flesh and blood, talking and listening, it still feels like she is a figment of his imagination. And when she touched him to offer comfort, her hands were cold.

'It was the best and the worst year of my life, 2005,' he continues. He looks up at her and smiles and suddenly it feels like they are looking at each other for the first time, without barriers. 'That night, when I saw you in here, I just wanted to end it. I went from bar to bar, drinking myself into oblivion, then I stumbled into Soho Square Gardens and collapsed on a bench.'

Stella nods her head but she doesn't look up at him.

'When I woke up, there was this girl,' he says.

Stella raises her eyebrow. It's a momentary reflex but it seems like a private thought, a judgement has been allowed to slip through her composure and Seb sees it.

'No, no, it wasn't like that. It was a girl from the office, poor thing, she'd been messed about by Becky and she was trying to get home to Middlesbrough —'

'Zoe,' says Stella, so softly, Seb has to bend his head to hear.

'Yes,' he says. 'How did you. . .?'

'I bumped into her that night as well,' she says, twisting the damp cardboard coaster between her finger and thumb. 'In here, in the ladies loos upstairs. I've never forgotten it. Paula and I had argued, she had stormed off and I had locked myself away in the loo. I was scared I'd bump into Ade and have to explain why I hadn't gone to that party.'

Seb nods, remembering Ade's fury as he marched into the pub that night, blustering about lost record deals and Stella messing up his chances of stardom. Christ it seems like a lifetime ago now, all that upset over someone not going to a party. It seems crazy now in the light of what he is facing.

'I was standing by the sink when she came in,' Stella continues. 'She'd been crying and her face was covered in snot and mascara. I lent her my wet wipes and we got talking. She had grown up a few miles from me. If I'm honest she unsettled me; reminded me of the girls I used to avoid at school.'

He sees Zoe; her face lit by the streetlights of Soho Square; her northern voice soft and comforting as he sat offloading his sorrow onto her.

'She sat with me on the bench and she listened to me talk about Sophie,' he says, choosing not to acknowledge Stella's comment about the girls at school. 'I talked and I talked and she made me feel better then I said goodbye and I headed back to the office to finish a painting of Sophie that I had started the day of her funeral. Zoe gave me the strength to finish it; I worked through the night and I got it done . . .'

'So it all turned out well in the end,' says Stella.

Seb looks up at her. She has no idea. How can she not know about all this; this huge thing that has dominated his life; those horrific details that haunt his dreams and make him triple lock his door at night.

'She was murdered that night, Stella.'

The sentence hangs in the air like cigarette smoke, waiting for someone to speak and blow it away with the weight of their words.

But Stella cannot speak, he can see that. Her eyes glaze and he recognises the confusion. He can see her mind rushing images through like an express train, so fast, it is impossible to settle on any one scene. Like him, she will try to grab hold of one of them but they will fall away like the images on a shaken kaleidoscope.

'And I was the last person to see her alive.' Seb's voice finally cuts into the silence and he looks up, letting the tears fall, allowing his hands to shake, showing her that this is not about grief, this is fear, raw, unbridled fear. He sees it register in her eyes as he leans forward in his chair and grabs her hands.

'Stella, you have to help me,' he says, his voice suddenly louder. 'Christ, there's so little time. I have to be at the restaurant, I should be there now, Yas will be going ballistic, we had a big fight and I'm telling you all this back to front. You look confused . . . I'd be confused . . .'

'Seb, slow down,' she says loosening the tight grip of his hands. 'Tell me what you're scared of. What's happened?'

'Zoe was murdered by a junkie . . . it's a long story . . . I haven't got time to tell you the ins and outs of it all. But anyway, as I was the last person to see her alive, I was called to give evidence at the trial.'

Stella nods her head slowly, like she is trying to pace him, to calm him with her body language.

'The courtroom was packed, the details of her murder were horrific, her mother and brother were there . . . they watched me as I gave my account. Well, her mother didn't, it was the brother, he wouldn't take his eyes off me. It was like he didn't believe me, as though it was me in the dock, standing accused of her murder.' He stops and takes a long glug of his drink and he feels the muscles in his neck contract as the liquid goes down his throat. When he finishes he goes to put the glass down, but his hands are shaking so badly, Stella has to grab it before it falls to the floor.

'He is here,' says Seb, as Stella moves the glass from his reach. 'He came to the restaurant this morning and said, more or less, that he thought I was responsible for Zoe's death and that he was going to get his revenge.'

'What? That's crazy . . .'

'He knows everything about me Stella. It's like he's been following me, all these years since the trial, like he's been biding his time, waiting for the right moment to pounce.'

'Seb, are you sure about this? I mean, maybe what with the stress of the opening night and everything, maybe you're reading too much into it.'

'He mentioned my daughter, Cosima,' says Seb, as another tear escapes and drops onto the table spreading across the surface like a stain 'He said he had nothing to lose, but that I had a beautiful daughter. It was his tone, Stella, he was definitely implying something . . . though he may not have come right out and said it.'

'Well then you should call the police,' says Stella, firmly. 'If you think this man is threatening your daughter then you have to report it – immediately.'

'And what if I'm wrong? What if I'm just being paranoid, then I end up ruining Yasmine's big night, the biggest of her life, the thing she has worked towards for twenty years.'

He wants her to tell him to err on the side of caution, to tell him what he already knows; that his child's life is immeasurably more important than a restaurant; that he should be telling all this to his wife, not to her, but he knows that all of that is too little, too late. It is six now, the doors will be opening, the guests will be on their way and Yasmine will be elbow deep in harissa sauce and adrenalin.

'Where is Cosima now?'

The name feels strange coming from her mouth. He imagines her referring to her own little girl, taking her hand and leading her away from danger. He feels secure, for just a moment.

'She's getting here for six-thirty,' he says, wiping at his eyes with the back of his hand. 'Her granny, Yasmine's mother, is bringing her. But that's what I'm worried about – Maggie will have a drink, and she's lovely and everything, but she lets Cosima do what she likes, she won't have her eye on her all the time. And I'll be running round like a blue-arsed fly dealing with the press and what have you . . .'

'What does she look like?' asks Stella.

'Who, Cosima?'

Stella nods her head and smiles.

'She's absolutely beautiful,' says Seb, as tears fill his eyes once more. 'She's got dark-blonde curly hair and deep-brown eyes and she knows everything there is to know about animals . . .' His face collapses then and he puts his hands over his eyes and starts to sob.

Stella puts her hand on his and takes it from his face so she can see his eyes. 'Seb, listen to me. I will look after Cosima. Now I know what she looks like. I will stand by the door and look out for her arriving and then, I promise you, I will look after her. After all, you always looked out for me.'

'Stella,' he begins, then stops, the words too heavy to come out. 'Thank you,' he whispers. 'Thank you for doing this.'

'It will be a pleasure,' says Stella, standing up from the table. 'Come on, we'd better get there, eh?'

Seb nods as he stands up. 'Oh, and . . . she's wearing a green dress, you won't miss her,' he says, as he picks up his jacket from the back of the chair. 'Stella, you will make sure you're with her . . . all the time won't you?'

'Don't worry, Seb,' says Stella as they walk towards the door. 'I won't let her out of my sight.'

Mark stands in the centre of the room, his arms folded across his chest.

'Liv, you're going to have to get out of here. Now.'

'I'm not going anywhere until you listen to me,' says Liv. She walks over to him and puts her hand on his arm.

'Don't threaten me, you stupid little girl,' says Mark as he yanks her hand away and walks towards the window. 'Now I'm going to count to three and if you're still here when I turn round, you'll be sorry. One . . .'

'Mark, I want to help you,' says Liv. 'All those things you told me last night, after we made love, all the stuff about this Seb guy and getting revenge, it's wrong.'

'Two . . .'

'Count all you like, Mark, I'm not going to stop. If you carry out what you told me last night then you are going to jail. For a very long time. Is that what you want? What about your daughter?'

'Three,' Mark screams. 'Don't you dare mention my daughter, you stupid little slag. You know nothing about me or my past; you were a quick shag and a crap one at that. Now get the fuck out of here.'

'You'll regret it, Mark,' says Liv, standing her ground. 'You'll regret this for the rest of your life.'

'Jesus Christ, I haven't got the time for this,' says Mark as he walks across to the en-suite bathroom and opens the door. 'I need a piss. Now take your concern and your slutty clothes and fuck off.'

He slams the door behind him; unzips his fly and takes a long piss into the immaculate china lavatory. He hears the muffled sound of the room door closing.

He pulls up his zip then washes his hands slowly in the sink. Then he opens the bathroom door and calls out:

'Oy! You better not still be there, you hear me?'

There is no noise; just the muted sounds from the street.

He steps into the room and smiles with relief to find it empty. Then he crosses to the bed and takes the notepad and pen; he must try to find the words again. But as he flips the pad open he is suddenly aware of an absence. The black bag that had been sitting on the bed isn't where he left it. He flings the covers back; yanks the heavy damask blanket off but there is nothing. Panicking he looks behind the curtains, under the bed, he goes back in the bathroom.

Nothing.

'Fuck,' he screams and he pounds his fists against the bath-room mirror shattering it into spiky shards as a new reality dawns on him.

The gun has gone.

28

Stella and Seb walk into a wall of noise and colour and smells;
so potent Stella feels drunk again. Moroccan music threads
through the air, a repetitive, hypnotic melody being played
on a guitar; live music, though she cannot see the musician
as the place is already packed with people.

As they make their way through the restaurant she sees
snippets of detail: red roses strewn across tables, terracotta
bowls edged in blue painted flowers; warm flickering lights;
velvet cushions. She sees the open kitchen up ahead just
beyond Seb; hears the clatter of plates and the unmistakable
smell of cumin – the earthy scent that transports her back
to Andalucia. She remembers taking a boat with Paula from
Tarifa where Southern Spain and Morocco almost touch and
spending a morning wandering round the markets of Tangier,
the smell of cumin and garlic hanging in the air, like it is now.
It is a summer smell; a reassuring smell. She cranes her neck
to see further into the kitchen, to see the person behind this;

the chef, the beautiful woman Paula had told her about, the goddess who had mended Seb's broken heart and given birth to a glorious girl.

A cloud of steam hangs in the air blocking the kitchen from view, but as they walk towards it, the steam dissipates and Stella sees her. She is small, definitely shorter than Stella, and her face, though contorted in concentration as she leans over the pass reassembling a dish of roasted aubergine, is certainly an attractive one. Yet she is not the great beauty Stella had been expecting, the Amazonian princess Paula had alluded to. She watches Yasmine clean the edges of the plate before clapping her hands at the waiters and disappearing back into the mist.

Stella feels Seb's body next to her as they squeeze further into the crowded room; he is still shaking. She takes his hand and holds it tightly, forcing him to look at her.

'It's going to be all right,' she says, releasing his hand, but her voice evaporates into the steamy fug of the room.

'There are too many people,' he hisses. 'I told Henry but he wouldn't listen.'

'Seb, what time did you say Cosima was getting here?' He has his back to her, and she can see his head darting from one corner of the room to the other; searching. She taps his back gently and he jumps.

'What?'

'I just asked what time Cosima is coming.' Her face is so close to his she can smell the orange squash on his breath.

'Six-thirty,' he shouts, like a sergeant major issuing an order over a chaotic scene of battle.

Stella looks at her watch. 'Well it's twenty past now.' He is not listening; he is scanning every table, every face. 'Seb, I'm going to go and stand outside and wait for her, okay?'

He nods his head.

'It's going to be fine, Seb. Just you go and concentrate on this fantastic evening, okay. I'll be with Cosima, I promise you.'

'I haven't checked upstairs,' he says, and before Stella can speak he is gone, off towards the stairs, his tweed suit conspicuous among the muted navies and greys of the business suits that seem to make up the bulk of the guests.

Finally alone, she tries to recall the events of the night before. The man at the bar; the one who said he knew Seb, what was his name? She racks her brain but she can't remember. She hadn't told Seb; thought it was the last thing he needed, the state he was in. But it had to be him, Zoe's brother, it had to be, and she had given him the invitation, she had told him to come.

Her heart pounds as she makes her way to the door where two black-clad waitresses stand holding a tray full of drinks. As she passes one of them holds out a champagne glass.

'No thank you,' she says, waving the glass away as she steps through the open door out onto the street.

The evening sun is warm on her back as she stands waiting for Cosima, though the pavement is glossy with shallow puddles. There must have been a shower of rain while she and

Seb were in the pub. Strange how the weather does that in late summer: volleys back and forth between elements, never settling on any one in particular.

She looks up the street, trying to spot a little girl in a green dress amid the crowds of early evening drinkers. She is glad to have the diversion of Cosima, glad not to be dwelling on thoughts of Mark. She takes her phone out to see if there are any messages from Paula; but there is nothing. She has probably been held up in the rush hour commute.

A few hours ago everything had seemed new and wonderful: she had felt excited about the future for the first time in years, about her new job and all the promise it held. Now, back in this street where she had felt such sorrow all those years ago, she feels her throat tighten and a familiar anxiety creeping up her chest. Seb and his family could be in serious trouble and it is all her fault. She wishes she had stuck to her guns and gone back to Earls Court then she would have avoided all this drama; all she wants is peace.

She looks at the people standing outside the restaurant, young women with back-combed hair, skinny jeans and tight-fitting tops; men in open-necked shirts and loafers – most of them puffing on illicit cigarettes – and she feels invisible. This street had once been her home; it was once impossible to walk its length without saying hello to someone she knew, now people look through her, beyond her. Seb had done the same thing, in the pub.

Everything about this impromtu reunion with Seb is making her uneasy, not just the thought of some deranged man issuing threats. Though it has been years since they last met, she can still remember the way he used to look at her, like she was the only woman, not just in the room, but on the planet. Someone once said that the act of writing is like being alive twice, but for Stella the same could have been said for being under Seb's gaze. It was like being projected onto a vast screen surrounded by a million twinkling lights. Ade used to notice it and say that if Seb wasn't such a nice guy he would have got a smack in the face for the way he looked at her. To be honest, it was Ade's reaction that first made her notice; she had been so mired in her own world she hadn't been aware of it. When they had met in the street earlier, when he stood back to say hello, when he walked back from the bar; it was no longer there, that look. She could be anybody; it was as though whoever he saw in her all those years ago, whatever light poured out of her to make him react the way he did, must have departed. It shouldn't bother her, but it does. All this time she had thought he was wildly in love with her. Now it all makes sense; he hadn't been looking at her, he had been looking through her, to someone else.

The girls throw their cigarette butts onto the ground and head inside, leaving a thin wisp of smoke in their wake. *Do you miss Middlesbrough, Zoe?* The words come into her head unbidden but she is suddenly back there, back seven years to that night, to a row of sinks and a girl's bewildered expression. At the same time as Seb was folded up on that bench, she had been making love to Paula for the first time; and as she had curled up to sleep in Paula's arms, Zoe –a girl whose path she had crossed momentarily – had been fighting for her life in a dingy back street. It feels odd to think of all those lives, all those stories being played out at the same time because, for her, time had stopped for those few hours, real life had hung above the bed like a fly caught in a spider's web, dazed and immobile, while she and Paula had become one. Suddenly she feels Paula's absence, like a great hole has appeared in the ground beneath her and she is hanging over it, with nothing to hold onto.

She looks up and sees a red-faced man in a navy blazer standing in front of her. He is smiling and for a moment she thinks she knows him, but then everything about this evening is tinged with familiarity; everything seems the same though so much has changed.

'Henry,' he says, extending his hand. 'Henry Walker. Co-founder of the restaurant.'

She smiles and shakes his hand. 'Stella.'

'How do you do, Stella,' he says, removing his hand and taking a long swig of champagne. 'So, what do you think of The Rose Garden, then?'

'It's beautiful, though I haven't had a chance to have a proper look round yet. I'm waiting for someone.'

'Well, when you go back in, make sure you take a look at the roof terrace. It's our recreation of a Moroccan rose garden – hence the name. It is absolutely stunning; there's nothing else like it in Soho. A first.'

He sounds like he is reciting a script, thinks Stella.

'Which paper are you from?' he asks, narrowing his eyes. 'I don't think I've seen you before.'

'Oh, I'm not a reporter. My partner, Paula, supplied the jasmine for the restaurant. But I'm actually a friend of Seb's too . . .'

'Friend of Seb's,' he repeats, but he is not looking at her, his attention has been diverted up the street. 'It's not,' he mutters as he watches a figure come towards them. 'It bloody is! Adrian Gill, how the hell are you?'

He strides towards the food critic, leaving Stella standing impotently. She watches them shake hands, watches as Henry steers Gill towards the restaurant and as she stands back to let them pass, Henry doesn't even look at her. She feels lonely, out of place and scared. All the bravado and confidence of the afternoon bleeds out of her and suddenly she wants to be back there; sitting in the little room with Dylan talking about Joyce and Woolf and Richardson; she wants to feel strong again. She closes her eyes and imagines life in a few months time: working in Bloomsbury every day. She wants to be a million miles away from Seb and whatever twisted plot this Mark guy is hell-bent on carrying out. This is not her world; this is simply a fragmented collage of memories and hurt; of people that no longer exist; of dead girls and love that never was.

And then she sees it; a flash of green at the far end of the street. As it draws closer she sees the little girl inside the dress, the long dark-blonde curls bouncing as she skips alongside the small, red-haired woman who is holding her hand.

Cosima.

She is beautiful, thinks Stella, and now she can understand Seb's concern, she can understand Paula's need; the fertility clinic, Paula's disappointment when Stella didn't hold her hand during the scan. She had only ever imagined an abstract; an idea called 'baby'; she had never imagined how it would feel to have a living child, to watch it grow, to look out for danger, to nurture and support it. As the little girl reaches her, she realises that now, in this moment, she can understand what it means to be a parent. She steps forward and puts out her hand.

'Hello, Cosima,' she says. 'I'm Stella.'

Kerstin opens her eyes. She feels groggy and her muscles have tensed up from lying in one position. She can hear music, faint strings, somewhere in the distance. It is pure and hypnotic, like church music.

She hears voices above the music and she stands up shakily and opens the door. The room is empty but she can hear her mother calling to her:

'*Kerstin, come on we'll be late.*'

'Okay, Mama,' she replies as she follows the voice out of the room.

Within moments she is in a crowded bar, but she sees nothing, her eyes seem to be shrouded in mist and the people she pushes past are a colourful blur; a series of waves parting to let her through. So as she follows her mother's voice out into the night air she doesn't see a suited figure step out from the crowd of drinkers and slowly follow her out onto the terrace.

The air feels magnificent on her face as she approaches, clean air, filled with a familiar smell that she can't quite place. It feels like she has woken from a deep sleep; like she is seeing things for the very first time. The cloud lifts from her head and she blinks into the light; she can see everything now.

Soft lights twinkle along the fig trees and rose bushes and as she walks towards the railings the familiar smell grows stronger. She looks down and sees two large terracotta pots standing on either side of the railings. She bends down to smell the plants and she is back in Cologne, sitting with her mother in their back yard eating marzipan sweets and drinking in the intoxicating scent of jasmine; the night plant, whose smell becomes more potent as darkness closes in. The scent is so heady Kirsten feels dizzy, but it is a good feeling.

She thinks of the dusty flowers in the office; the cardboard lilies and paper-thin tulips that smell of nothing; this is paradise, she thinks.

29

Mark seals the last envelope and puts it into the large jiffy bag that he bought at WHSmith at Darlington Station. He knew then that this was going to be a one way journey; that after the battle has been fought, the soldier must do what is noble. There is nothing left of his life now; the people who matter have left him – his father, Zoe, Ernie, Lisa and Rachel; even his mother, who, though physically present is but a shadow, an empty shell, rattling around the flat; her life frozen in another age.

He knows that a good soldier will sacrifice his life for the greater good; will go down fighting for what is right. As he places the envelope onto the bed and retakes his position at the window, he knows that it all ends here; that the ghosts of his dead family are too much for him to bear; their voices too loud to live with. He knows that when this task has been carried out; when the promise he made to his father has been fulfilled, he will join them, wherever they are; and they will be at peace.

But there is one more thing to do.

He walks to the bathroom and picks up the shards of shattered glass. He puts four of the longest, sharpest pieces into the inner pocket of his suit. A soldier must think on his feet; he must use his initiative and not give up even when it seems that the battle has been lost. Liv taking the gun will not stop him; nobody can stop him now.

Stella stands with Maggie and Cosima in the only available bit of empty space left: a small alcove underneath the stairs.

'So it's your partner we have to thank for those amazing jasmine plants,' says Maggie, raising her voice over the band that has just struck up a faster number.

'That's right,' says Stella, casting another nervous glance at the door. Would she even remember what he looked like? It was so dark in the pub last night; all she can remember is his voice: soft and northern, and the dark outline of his body. She wishes Paula were here; Paula would know what to do.

She looks at her phone again, but it is remarkably silent. On any other day it would be full of new messages from Paula. She tries not to worry; rush hour in London can add a good hour to a journey. She puts the phone into her pocket and smiles at Maggie. She looks rather awkward and Stella feels for her, it can't be much fun spending your daughter's opening night, wedged up in an alcove, and unlike the other guests neither she nor Maggie have had a drink yet. Stella tries to think of something to say but there is only so much polite chat you can have with a person you barely know. As if reading her thoughts, Maggie rummages in her handbag and brings out a packet of cigarettes.

'I don't suppose I could ask you to keep an eye on the little one while I just pop out for some fresh air,' she says, not even trying to hide the cigarettes.

'Sure,' says Stella, wondering how much fresh air will actually reach Maggie's lungs when it is mired in cigarette smoke.

'Aw thanks, love,' says Maggie. 'You'll be okay with Stella for five minutes while Granny has a ciggie won't you?' Cosima nods her head then looks up at Stella and smiles. She has exactly the same smile as Seb, thinks Stella; wide and benevolent.

'Good girl,' says Maggie. 'I'll grab you a lemonade when I get back. Ooh look there's a couple of free chairs.'

She grabs two low stools from behind a pair of departing guests and plonks them down next to Stella and Cosima. 'Here you go, girls, that'll save your legs.' She smiles and Stella watches her walk towards the door, stopping to take a glass of champagne from Kia's tray as she goes.

'I can't see Daddy anywhere,' says Cosima, as she wriggles onto the stool.

'Oh, he'll be about,' says Stella. 'He'll have a lot to do tonight I expect.'

'They're always busy,' says Cosima. Her smile has faded and Stella recognises something in her; a faint memory from childhood of sitting all dressed up at her parent's annual New Year's Eve party, watching as the adults danced and laughed and drank champagne while she sat there like a spare part.

'I hear you like animals,' says Stella. 'Your Daddy told me you're something of an expert.'

Cosima nods her head. 'How do you know Daddy?'

Stella pauses. How do you tell a child that you met her father while he was drinking himself into a stupor.

'Well I used to know him a long time ago, when I lived just across the street from here. Your Daddy used to work nearby and I used to see him . . . around.'

'Did you know that in South America, crocodiles are called caimans,' says Cosima, utterly unimpressed by the half-hearted account of Stella and Seb's meeting.

'Wow, no I didn't know that,' says Stella. 'Have you ever been to South America?'

'No,' says Cosima. 'But I'm going to go there when I'm older. I'm going to be a zoologist you know?'

'Really? That would be a fun job.'

'Yes,' says Cosima. 'But I would have to pass lots of exams first and that would be a bit boring so I might actually become a vet instead.'

'But wouldn't you have to pass lots of exams to be a vet too?'

Cosima shrugs. 'I suppose so. But did I tell you that my friend Gracie Marshall has not one but five guinea pigs. I'd really like a pet but we're not allowed to have any in our flat and Mummy says it's okay because we've got the zoo at Battersea Park to go to, but it's not the same.'

'Well, maybe one day,' says Stella. 'When I was a little girl I had a pink horse, can you imagine that?'

Cosima's eyes widen. 'A pink horse,' she gasps. 'Was it a unicorn?'

Stella giggles, remembering how as a child she had always wanted a pet unicorn. 'No, it was just a horse, a strawberry roan. She had a blonde mane as well. Still, it would have been very cool to have a unicorn.'

Cosima nods. 'I have a toy unicorn,' she says. 'She's called Ursula and she comes from the land of spells. You know the only people who can see unicorns are the fairies. Granny Maggie told me that.'

'Yes, that's probably right,' says Stella. 'My granddad came from Ireland and he used to tell me stories about the fairies; about the forts where they would hide their gold. And they play tricks on people too. Grandad once had his bicycle stolen by the fairies when he was on his way to a dance; he had to walk two miles to the next town and when he got to the place where the dance was being held, there was his bicycle parked up outside the door. He always insisted it was the work of the fairies.'

'But not all fairies are naughty like that,' says Cosima. 'My mummy told me that when she and Daddy got married, the fairies sent me down to them. That was a very kind thing to do wasn't it?'

'Yes, it was,' says Stella, smiling. Talk of fairies is taking her mind off Mark. Just then her phone beeps in her pocket. She takes it out and reads the message:

Still at Carole's – she's in a really bad way so am staying a little longer. Will get there as soon as I can x

Stella closes the message and sighs. Paula to the rescue again.

'I know a poem about the fairies,' she says, turning to Cosima as she puts the phone back into her pocket.

'Do you? Is it the one about the fairy and the porridge pot? Daddy tells me that before I go to sleep.'

'No, it's not that one – though that does sound like a good one,' says Stella. 'I didn't know fairies ate porridge. Do you want to tell me about it?'

'No,' says Cosima, matter-of-factly. 'I'd rather hear yours first.'

'Okay,' says Stella, pushing her seat back to let a group of people get by. 'Gosh, I hope I can remember it. My daddy used to tell this to me before I went to bed.'

'Like mine,' says Cosima, and she looks up at Stella with such an innocent look of expectation, Stella's heart hurts.

'Here goes,' says Stella, and as she starts to recite, she hopes that by concentrating on the poem she can block out thoughts of Mark:

Where dips the rocky highland
Of Sleuth Wood in the lake,
There lies a leafy island
Where flapping herons wake
The drowsy water rats;
There we've hid our faery vats,
Full of berries
And of reddest stolen cherries . . .

Mark takes one last look in the wardrobe mirror before he leaves the room. He sees a man in a suit: Denny Lowe off to seal a deal.

'Win big, Denny, eh.'

His father's voice fills the room and he smiles as he steps out into the silent, wood-panelled corridor. He looks back at the jiffy bag lying on the bed; waiting for some nameless chambermaid to come and find it. As he closes the door he takes a deep breath and for once there is no crackle, no wheezing, no blockage at the base of his lungs. He feels more alive than he has ever felt before; his mind is clear, his body feels light and weightless; it's like he's on some wonderful drug, one that he will never come down from. As he walks down the stairs and into the grand entrance hall, he wonders if this is how his father felt the moment he went into battle; this surge of energy, this feeling of invincibility. He opens the door and steps out into the crisp evening air for what will be the last time. The hour has arrived; not a moment too soon.

30

Seb smiles half-heartedly at the woman standing next to him. He can hear snippets of what she is saying but nothing that could constitute a sentence. Henry is with them, regaling the woman who, Seb has gathered, is a journalist from the *Evening Standard*.

'Yeah, it's been about three years in the planning, if truth be told. I've always wanted to open a restaurant in Soho, and had come very close over the years, but for one reason or another it had never come to anything. But when I met Yasmine, and heard her plans, I knew that this was going to be pretty special . . .'

Seb nods in agreement as the woman listens intently to Henry. He hears someone call his name and looks up to see Liam Kerr and his wife waving at him from the door.

'Will you excuse me,' says Seb to the journalist.

'The kids had a better offer, I'm afraid,' says Liam, as Seb approaches. 'It was a toss-up between this and a Disney

DVD marathon with their Aunt Bella. This is my wife Kate, by the way, I don't think you two have been properly introduced.'

He holds out his hand to the tall, attractive blonde woman but as he does so he feels a shiver course through his spine. He looks around the room but he can't see her; he can't see Cosima or Stella. It's useless, he can't do this, he can't stand and talk while this threat hangs over his family and now he has lost sight of Cosima.

'I'm sorry,' he says to the woman whose hand is still outstretched. 'You must excuse me.'

'Seb, what is it?' Liam's voice disappears behind Seb as he runs through the crowd like a drowning man.

'Cosima,' he shouts as he pushes people aside. 'Cosima, where are you?'

But his voice is lost inside the music that seems to be growing louder and louder as he frantically calls out for his child.

> *Where the wandering water gushes,*
> *In the hills above Glen-Car,*
> *In pools among the rushes*
> *That scarce could bathe a star . . .*

Stella pauses as a familiar face appears in the alcove.

'Don't stop, it's lovely.'

She continues reciting as Maggie squeezes into the space between her and Cosima.

Kerstin stands looking out onto the streets of Soho. Down below everything is alive and thriving. She sees the lights of the BT tower twinkling on and off like a space ship waiting to take off into the starless night sky; she sees a million lives beginning and ending; souls rising and falling; happiness and sorrow being cast out into the night from a thousand different directions.

Amid the lights and neon she can make out a church steeple, pointing up into the grey sky like a witch's hat. But it offers no comfort. The time for praying is over, for what does it achieve? All those incantations, meaningless mantras, empty recitations that keep the world turning, keep secrets buried, the economy on its feet and people in their place. She remembers the statue of the Madonna in her room, maybe it was best that Cal had turned it to face the wall; at least that way it would be spared the sight of all those penitents on their knees and the noise of prayer; prayers in every language from the mouths of children and world leaders, beggars and nuns, murderers and priests, the voices rising in a great cacophony of sound; like birds twittering in the dawn their interchangeable anthems to faceless deities and invisible currencies.

She hears something move behind her and for a moment she thinks she is at home, back in Cologne, where she was happy and safe, and her mother is calling her to come and have dinner.

'Mama?' she whispers but her mother's voice has fallen silent and another takes its place.

'Hello, Kerstin.'

She turns and sees him, his face glowing in the light of a hundred candles.

Cal.

She turns her back on him; willing him to leave but he comes up behind her, so close she can feel his breath on her neck.

'Nice view,' he whispers. His breath smells of wine and cigarettes and as he speaks drops of spittle land on Kerstin's face.

'Get away from me,' she says, gripping hold of the wooden frame that stands between her and the street below. 'I know it was you who took my things; all this time it was you trying to drive me mad.'

'I have no idea what you're talking about, Kerstin,' he says, his voice measured and calm. 'All I know is that you are in serious trouble. An old lady has been murdered and you are the main suspect.'

Kerstin's head feels heavy like all the oxygen is being sucked out of it. He is lying. She saw her things in his wardrobe; a whole box of them.

'Why are you lying?' she yells. 'Why are you trying to make out I'm mad? I saw my things in your wardrobe; I wrote everything down; all the times you'd been in my flat; the things you'd taken, the things you'd moved about . . .'

The roof terrace is filling up and a band is setting up in the far corner. Kerstin feels her chest contract. She has to get out of here but the entrance is blocked by people; hundreds of people so it seems to her.

'I tried to help you,' says Cal, standing aside to let a group of women past. 'I told you about my cousin suffering from OCD, advised you to get help. Jesus Christ, I offered you my bed for the night. If I'd known you had just murdered someone I wouldn't have come near.'

'You are evil,' shouts Kerstin, her voice almost drowned out by the opening bars of Van Morrison's 'Brown Eyed Girl' that the band have just struck up. 'You drugged me then you locked me up.'

'Kerstin,' says Cal, putting his hands on her shoulders. 'You need help, serious help. Maybe you will get it in prison.'

'Get your hands off me and let me get out,' she yells, grabbing at Cal's hands but he pulls her tighter, squeezing her towards him until she can't breathe.

'You're sick, Kerstin,' says Cal, his grip tightening. 'You're not safe to be left alone.'

Kerstin grapples to disentangle herself from his arms but he is too strong. The music is growing louder and louder until it feels as though it is cutting into her skin. She has to get away from here and if she can't use her arms there is only one weapon left. With the last ounce of strength she sinks her teeth into Cal's arm.

He shrieks and jumps back.

'You fucking psycho,' he screams. 'I'm bleeding.'

There is only one way out now and Kerstin sees it.

'What are you doing?' shouts Cal, as Kerstin climbs onto the railings.

'Get away from me now or I'll jump,' she shouts as a hush descends across the terrace. 'I swear I will jump.'

> *And whispering in their ears*
> *Give them unquiet dreams;*
> *Leaning softly out.*
> *From ferns that drop their tears*
> *Over the young streams . . .*

Seb clambers up two flights of stairs, taking them three at a time. He tries to hear her voice; he knows that if she is there he will be able to hear, despite the noise of the crowd. He has always been able to hear her voice. When he goes to collect her from school, the shouts and screams of the children playing in the yard ring out in a cacophonous wall of sound; but he can always hear Cosima's voice in the midst of the din, as clear as day; he can pick out her voice because she is his child; his blood. He cranes his ears to listen but there is nothing.

'Cosima,' he yells. He feels someone touch his arm.

'Seb, mate, what is it?' says Liam. But he shakes his friend off and pushes his way through the tables and chairs that seem to be deliberately blocking his way.

'Cosima!'

He calls out her name, her blessed name, as he makes his way out of the open doors and into the intoxicating air of the terrace. A crowd of people are standing huddled at the far side; he tries to see what is going on but his vision is obscured by two giant pots of herbs. Then he hears something; a gasp, a scrape of metal against stone. He runs towards the noise, calling out into the cool air but no sound will come.

31

'That was lovely,' says Cosima, as Stella finishes the poem. 'I'd like to go and live with the fairies. They eat blueberry stew you know?'

'That sounds delicious,'says Stella.

'Oh, I hear Mummy,' says Cosima, leaping off the stool.

'She's making her speech,' says Maggie. 'Come on, Cossy, let's go and hear.' The older woman hauls herself from the cushion and takes her granddaughter's hand.

Stella goes to follow but she feels awkward as though she is intruding on a special family moment. Still, she promised Seb she would look after Cosima so she walks at a distance behind Maggie and the girl.

After the dimness of the alcove the restaurant seems bright even though it is bathed in soft candlelight. Yasmine stands on a chair, her face beaming as she welcomes the guests to the restaurant. Stella notices Henry standing at the front of the crowd, clapping his hands and nodding to his celebrity guests.

'Hi everyone and welcome to . . . The Rose Garden.'

A cheer rings out across the room led by Henry who whistles with two fingers. Cosima and Maggie stand by a pillar; Stella stands on the oppsosite side, not too close but near enough to keep an eye on Cosima.

'This restaurant has been years in the making,' continues Yasmine. 'And it would never have got off the ground if it hadn't been for the love and support of my lovely husband.'

She stops and scans the room, her eyes expectant.

'Where is he?'

'He's camera shy,' laughs Henry, looking around at the sea of smartphones recording and photographing the moment.

'Seb,' shouts Yasmine, playfully. 'Darling husband, where are you? Honestly, men,' she says, shrugging her shoulders. 'You can never rely on them.'

The crowd laughs but Stella feels uneasy. She thinks about going to look for Seb but she can't leave Cosima. She feels her phone vibrate in her hand and she grabs it, hoping that Paula has arrived.

'Hi Paula, where are you?' she shouts to make herself heard over the crowd.

'Oh, darling, I'm sorry, I'm so sorry but I'm still at Carole's. She's in such a bad way I feel bad leaving her. Are you having fun?'

'No, I'm not having fun, Paula. I'm tired and I'm only here because you wanted to come and now . . . now I've got myself into something that I can't get out of and I really could do with you being here.'

'Stella, I can't hear you, it's so loud in there. I'll call you back in ten minutes and give you an update. Sorry darling. Love you.'

The line goes dead but Stella holds it to her ear for a moment as though Paula is still there; as though somehow beneath all the noise and shouts and music she might still be able to hear her voice.

Seb strides across the terrace, his heart pounding as he pushes his way past the crowd of people. He hears someone call his name but he can't stop, he has to get to her; he has to find his daughter.

'Seb, quick I think she's going to jump.' It is Kia running towards him; her face ghostly white.

'Cosima,' screams Seb as he elbows his way through and then he sees it; not his daughter but a young woman standing with her back to him; standing with arms outstretched on the edge of the railings.

'Jesus Christ,' whispers Seb. 'Is she drunk? How the hell did she get up there?'

'I don't know,' says Kia. 'I came up a couple of minutes ago with the champagne and she was already on the ledge.'

'Kia, go and call the police,' says Seb as he inches towards the woman; holding his breath lest the slightest noise sends her falling.

'No need,' says a voice and Seb turns to see a young man. 'I've already called them. They're on their way. I'm Cal Simpson. I work with Kerstin. She's not well . . . she's seriously not well.'

'Get him away from me or I will jump, I tell you I will jump,' shouts Kerstin.

'What does she mean?' asks Seb, keeping his voice low.

'I told you,' says Cal. 'She's sick; she needs help.'

'I said get him away from me,' screams Kerstin, her body leaning forwards.

There are gasps and screams from the crowd and a flash from someone's smartphone.

'I'm going to go and see if the police are here,' whispers Cal. 'Stay with her; make sure she doesn't do anything stupid.'

'No,' says Seb. 'I need to find my daughter; she's . . . she's in trouble.'

'What?' says Cal, pointing to the shadowy figure standing on the railings. 'More trouble than that?'

Seb goes to speak but Cal has gone.

Taking a deep breath he walks slowly towards the girl; telling himself with every step that Cosima is fine, she is with Stella and no harm will come to her.

'Come down, you silly cow,' shouts a drunken woman in a pink dress.

'Ssh,' says her friend. 'You'll scare her.'

Seb tries to clear his head; tries to channel his father the army officer. If he were here he would know what to do. He

391

used to tell Seb about the terrified soldiers; the ones who would rather put a gun to their heads than face another moment of war. 'Keep them talking,' his father would say. 'No shouts, no sudden movements, just keep talking.'

'Could I ask you all to move aside, please,' he says to the baffled onlookers. 'Just go and stand over there, please, and let me deal with this.'

Kia shepherds them towards the doors of the terrace where they stand open-mouthed, watching as Seb starts to talk to the woman.

Mark hears her voice as he enters the restaurant; the low, sensuous voice he last heard as he stood on the street and enquired after her husband.

Straightening his suit he walks slowly towards the voice; past dull men holding champagne glasses and overly made-up women adjusting their hair; all standing around like lemmings; waiting on the words of the small dark woman who stands perched on her chair talking enthusiastically about a restaurant as though it is something important, as though these people really care; as though they don't spend their futile lives going from one opening night to another; chitchatting with strangers with rictus grins on their faces as they approach the host and tell him or her that their restaurant/painting/album/book is the best thing they have ever encountered.

It's all bollocks, thinks Mark as he elbows a skinny blonde

in the ribs and walks towards the curtained booth where he had spoken to Bailey yesterday.

'... sure he's here somewhere,' continues Yasmine, as Mark pulls back the curtain and enters the deserted lover's corner. 'But I know that he would join me in saying how delighted we both are to declare The Rose Garden well and truly open.'

A cheer rings out across the room and Mark flinches as he stands looking at a white mound on the wall. The painting Bailey was hanging yesterday is now covered in a sheet, waiting for the grand unveiling, no doubt.

Arrogant bastard, thinks Mark. He can't be left out can he? Even at his wife's opening night he has to be the centre of attention. Wanker.

He leans across the table and tugs at the sheet. It billows slightly like a feather caught in the breeze before dropping to the floor.

And there it is: an oil painting depicting a vast lake at twilight with shafts of light rippling across the surface.

Mark stands staring at the painting; he looks at the moon glowing in the right hand corner; the dark trees dipping their heads into the water; the sparks of light bouncing off the surface like bullets and an old rage stirs up inside him.

This man has it all; a beautiful family, talent, love. Everything Mark has lost flashes in front of him as he stands looking at the painting. He sees his dad lying in a bed with manky hospital sheets clinging to his emaciated frame; he sees his mother sobbing in her tiny kitchen with its cheap ornaments and own-brand tinned goods; he sees Ernie's face on the top of the moor, happy to be away from Middlesbrough, happy to be play-acting at being a toff. He sees a lifetime of making do and wrecked dreams and shattered lives. No wonder Zoe wanted to get away, wanted to create something better for herself and she almost got there didn't she, he thinks, as tears well up in his eyes, she almost made it. But he got in the way, Bailey and his sob story; he got in her way that night and he sent her to her death.

'All this is bullshit,' he yells as he pulls a shard of glass out of his pocket and lunges at the painting.

As the shard strikes the canvas, tears blur the image and as one strike becomes another and another; as each shaft of light is extinguished Mark feels the room slip away; voices merge into one loud voice, telling him to carry on, not to stop until he has done his father proud.

As he slumps on the velvet banquette, his energy spent, his lungs dry and tight he looks up and sees her, standing by the curtain like a gift from God.

'Has he gone?' asks Kerstin, looking down at the man who has appeared next to her. He has a kind face, she thinks.

'Yes, he's gone,' replies Seb, remembering, as his father once told him, to keep his voice bright.

'What's your name?' he asks, trying not to think about the fifty foot drop below.

'Kerstin,' she whimpers.

She is young, thinks Seb, too young to feel that this is her only option.

'I'm in big trouble,' says Kerstin. 'There's nowhere left to go.'

'There is always somewhere,' says Seb. 'I've often felt like it was all too much; years ago I even tried to. . .' He stops, reminding himself to keep it light. 'But it got better and it will for you.'

'It won't,' says Kerstin. 'It can only get worse.'

'Where are you from, Kerstin?' asks Seb, trying to reel her back word by word. 'Which part of Germany?'

'Cologne,' she replies, though her voice is barely audible above the roar of traffic below and Seb has to lean in to hear.

'Cologne,' he repeats, again trying to keep his voice bright. 'A beautiful city, famous for its cathedral I understand.'

Kerstin nods her head but the movement seems to unbalance her and she sways slightly. Seb instinctively goes to steady her; his heart in his mouth.

'You don't have to do this, Kerstin,' he says, his diplomacy skills deserting him with the shock of her near-miss. 'There is always a way out; always. No matter what happens we can all start again.'

'I can't,' she screams, this time her voice wins the battle against the noises of Soho. 'I can't start again; I am over, finished. You don't understand, I'm not a good person. I killed someone.'

*

Stella slips her phone into her bag and watches as Yasmine climbs down from the stool.

'Your mum did really well,' she says turning to Cosima but she is not there.

'Cosima,' she shouts.

She sees Maggie hugging Yasmine and she goes towards them, praying that the child is with them but there is no sign.

'Maggie, have you seen Cosima?' she asks as the older woman disentangles herself from her daughter's arms.

'No, I thought she was with you.'

The smile fades from Yasmine's face as she weighs up Stella.

'Sorry, who are you and why would my daughter be with you?'

Stella goes to speak but before she can someone screams. She turns and sees him; the man from last night.

He is holding Cosima to his chest. It's a pose that could almost be protective though Stella can see that it is not, she can see what he is holding in his hand; broken glass. A flash of silver glints in the candlelight as he presses it to the back of Cosima's head.

Mark's face is red and twisted but Stella carries on walking towards him, her arms outstretched.

'Don't come near or I'll cut her,' he shouts. 'I swear I will.'

The music stops and two security guards rush towards him.

'I'm warning you, you bastards,' he yells to the guards. 'I'll slit her fucking throat.'

There is a piercing scream and Stella turns to see Yasmine running towards them.

'My baby! Get your hands off my baby. Somebody do something.'

Henry grabs her arm to hold her back.

'Where is he?' yells Mark and he directs the question to Stella rather than Yasmine.

'Where's Bailey?'

'He's not here.'

Stella's voice, so calm in the midst of this terror, sounds wrong.

'Ah, we meet again,' says Mark, waving his free arm at Stella. 'Thanks for the invite.'

'What?' shrieks Yasmine as she lurches forwards but Henry stops her.

'Yasmine, no,' he whispers. 'The police are on their way. Don't do anything.'

'Seb's not here,' says Stella. 'Let her go. Whatever grudge you hold against her father, you can sort out between the two of you, as men. She's a child. Now let her go.'

She looks so vulnerable standing there; so delicate and slight; how could someone so refined, so unassuming, be a killer?

Seb tries not to dwell on this; it could be part of what her colleague had referred to as her 'sickness'; it might all be in her mind.

'We all make mistakes, Kerstin,' he says gently, and as he speaks he sees her face twitch slightly; she is listening.

'None of us are perfect,' he continues. 'And sometimes we do things that don't make sense; or we think we have done things that have caused others pain and hurt when really we have only hurt ourselves.'

She shakes her head.

'I need to be punished; I will be punished for what I did,' she says, her voice riven with fear.

Seb wonders how old she is; she can't be more than thirty. He thinks of her parents; all the expectations you have for your children; the daily fight for their happiness; their safety, and he knows he has to keep trying to get her down.

'You have people who love you, Kerstin,' he says. 'People who want you to get better.'

She lets out a sob and he feels he is getting somewhere.

'You are not going to die here, Kerstin,' he says. 'Your life is not going to end like this. You are going to have a long, wonderful life with people who love you. Whatever you have done; there is always a way out; a way to happiness.'

She turns to look at him and in that moment he sees she is ready to come down. Her eyes are full of trust; like Cosima's when he taught her how to ride a bike and she kept looking up at him, to see if he was still holding on to her; to see if he was still there.

She is shivering badly now and Seb is concerned that any sudden movement could send her falling. He extends his arms out to her; locks his eyes onto hers and smiles.

'Come on Kerstin, take my hand,' he says.

He feels her hand brush his and he grasps it tightly.

'Good girl,' he whispers. 'Now the other hand. I'm here, I won't let go. It's going to be all right.'

But as she turns and holds out her hand a voice cuts through the silence.

'The police are here, Kerstin.'

She shakes her head as Cal approaches and she looks at Seb pleadingly.

'Kerstin, the police are here,' repeats Cal, lunging forward to grab her shoulder.

'No,' yells Seb.

And with that word Kerstin closes her eyes, tightens her grip on Seb's hand, and begins to count.

'Do you know what? You're starting to annoy me, love.'

Mark glares at Stella as they stand in the middle of the room, face to face.

'Do you know he's been fucking her,' he yells to Yasmine, whose face is smeared with tears. She shakes her head at him.'Oh yeah, big time. I saw them with my own eyes; all over each other in the street. The man can't help himself; he fucked her like he fucked over my sister; my sister Zoe Davis, who he threw out on the street to be butchered, like a piece of meat. Here have your kid.'

He throws Cosima across the room; and she screams hysterically as she falls into Yasmine's arms.

'The police are here,' whispers Henry but Yasmine doesn't hear; she is enveloped in her daughter, holding her face to her chest.

But Mark hears him and looks up to see two police officers heading towards him. He has to end this properly; he has to go down fighting and as the first of the officers approaches he grabs Stella and plunges the shard of glass into her stomach.

'That's for Zoe. See how it feels, you snooty bitch,' he yells as he pulls out the glass and watches as Stella falls in a heap by his feet.

'No!' shouts Stella, her cry drowned out by the police radios and the mass of uniformed bodies bearing down on Mark.

She lies on the floor and looks down at the red patch of blood that is seeping through her white dress, her head feels woozy, but she knows she has to cling onto consciousness; she must not close her eyes. She feels someone hold her arms; hears people scream but she is above it all; she feels herself slip away; the room begins to fragment and she knows that she has to keep her eyes open if she is to stay alive. She stares at the faces bearing down on her; willing one of them to be

Paula but as a dark screen comes down over her eyes she knows that this time she is on her own.

In the seconds it takes to fall through the air, hand in hand with a stranger, Seb sees it, as clear and bright as the red lights glistening on the BT Tower. He sees a beach covered in drift-wood; an empty bed in a cold dorm in a wretched boarding school; he sees fireflies dancing on the surface of a lake and a little girl sobbing in a beautiful green dress. He sees his life; all thirty-seven years of his time on this earth, spread out before him as he tumbles down into the darkness.

EPILOGUE

March, 2013

'I should go,' says Stella. 'I have a lecture to give this afternoon.'

'Yes,' replies Henry 'Even in death life must go on.'

Stella smiles at him as they make their way across Battersea Park.

'It was a beautiful memorial service,' says Stella, tucking her freezing hands into the warm folds of her coat. 'Spine tingling to see all his paintings up there, what a collection; it's so sad.'

'Yes,' says Henry. 'What a legacy he left to us all. And the Sebastian Bailey Arts Scholarship will launch this month in a blaze of publicity. He would have liked that.'

Stella flinches; though she only knew Seb through fleeting encounters she knows that parties and publicity and launches were not what he was about. His legacy was greater than that; it was flesh and blood.

They reach the deserted North Carriageway and as Stella bids Henry goodbye and watches as he disappears through the park gates she hears a shout; a child's voice floating across the parkland like a wind chime.

'Stella,'

She turns and watches as Cosima comes towards her, flanked by her mother and grandmother. She is holding something in her hand; a thin parcel wrapped in gold tissue.

'I want you to have this,' she says, her childish voice, lowered with pain. 'It's a present for you.'

Stella takes the parcel and gently unwraps it and as the gift falls out into her hands, her eyes fill with tears. It's a tiny fairy, dressed in a green silk dress; the blonde curls of its hair cascading in loose coils down its back.

'Oh, Cosima,' says Stella, taking the doll and holding it to her cheek. 'It's beautiful, thank you. I love it.'

She tries to hold back her tears for the sake of Yasmine who had stayed so composed for the duration of Seb's memorial service, but it's no use and as she crouches down to hug Cosima, she starts to sob.

'Thank you, Cosima,' she says, wiping her eyes with the sleeve of her winter coat.

'This is the fairy that helped you,' says the little girl, returning to the arms of her mother and grandmother. 'The one who made you better.'

*

The crypt inside Cologne Cathedral is cool and dark and Eva Engel pulls her shawl tightly round her shoulders as she shakily lights the white candle and places it onto the metal shelf.

She closes her eyes and begins to recite the Lord's Prayer but the words will not come; instead she stares at the candle, watches as the pale yellow flame grows stronger and stronger until it is a vibrant orange glow.

She hopes her daughter is at peace now; hopes that what-ever demons disturbed her in life have fallen silent in death. And she wasn't alone; thank God she wasn't alone. In the months following her daughter's death she was comforted by several letters from that nice young man who was with her in her final hours. She has a lot to be thankful to Cal Simpson for; if it wasn't for him she would have never been able to piece together the last few moments of Kerstin's life. She would have been happy, Eva thinks, that he was given her role at Sircher Capital. As he said in his letter, it was a beautiful legacy.

She turns and walks away, leaving the candle to burn itself out, until all that is left is a thin, black wisp of smoke.

Stella stands watching the three figures depart; their shoulders hunched; their bodies riven with grief. Mother, daughter and granddaughter; a family, joined forever by their DNA; by their memories. Could there have been a happy ending for her and Paula? Could they have created a family together; been happy?

Stella had asked herself this question a hundred times in the months following the break-up but she knew that it could never be. Paula had come running into the hospital talking about rehabilitation and getting home and making healing herbal tea but Stella knew; she knew as she lay in the bed listening to Paula's chatter; she knew it as she had lain on the floor of the restaurant covered in blood and clinging onto life, that the only person who could save her was herself.

She shivers as she thinks how the sharp glass penetrated her skin. And Mark's eyes as he pushed the shard further into her stomach, holding the small of her back with his hand like an embrace. She will never forget the look he gave her as he pulled the glass out: it was almost like he was saying sorry. Despite everything she cannot hate him. It was grief that had made him do it. All the details came out in court: Zoe's death; the breakdown of his marriage; the loss of his grandfather. After all that, his obsession with Seb was the only thing he had to hold onto. She hopes he gets better; hopes he can get the help he needs to build his life again.

She looks at her watch; it's time to go. In just over an hour, twenty-five eager undergraduates will be waiting for her to deliver a lecture on Virginia Woolf's *The Years*; and she will stand at the front of the lecture theatre and tell them about the transcience of life; of five stories interwoven; five destinies playing themselves out against the tumult and precariousness of time.

But before she leaves she takes one last look at the park and the forlorn trio walking back towards the gallery. She watches as the figures get smaller and smaller; as they dissolve into the rain; tiny specks against the wide expanse of green; twinkling like dots of moonlight across the surface of a lake.

ACKNOWLEDGEMENTS

I would like to thank the following people for their support and encouragement in writing this novel:

My agent Madeleine Milburn at Madeleine Milburn Literary, TV & Film Agency the best agent a writer could have; Jo Dickinson for her vision and enthusiasm for this book; Stefanie Bierwerth, Kathryn Taussig and the excellent team at Quercus; Mike I'Anson at Helmsley Walled Garden for sharing his knowledge of horticultural therapy; Jessica Jones for her meticulous Spanish translation; Kevin Hanley for his masterly instruction in Chaos Theory and Power Laws; my parents Luke and Mavis Casey for their love, support and faith in me; Nick Ellwood, whose beautiful drawings inspired The Lake, for sharing his artistic expertise and that wonderful quote from Matisse. Finally, my beautiful little boy Luke for reminding me on a daily basis to never, ever, doubt the fairies.

MORE ABOUT NUALA CASEY

WHAT INSPIRES YOU TO WRITE?

People first and foremost. I am a great people watcher, something that stems, I think, from being the youngest of five children. I spent most of my childhood listening in to conversations and trying to build up stories and characters around the snippets of gossip I overheard. I love developing a character, fleshing it out and working out how they will react to a set of circumstances. I am also fascinated by the past; how people deal with their own personal history and how certain decisions can change the course of your life.

WHO IS YOUR LITERARY HERO?

Virginia Woolf for her use of language and her boldness in creating a whole new literary form. I love the sombre beauty of her sentences and the way she uses words like scattered petals, throwing them up into the air and seeing where they will land. Whenever I read Woolf it feels like coming home. Like me, she liked to walk across London and once dedicated an entire essay, 'Street Haunting: A London Adventure', to her journey across town in search of a pencil. Woolf captures both the beauty and the brutality of life; moment by moment, breath by breath.

HAVE YOU ALWAYS WANTED TO BE A WRITER?

Yes. When I was a little girl I spent all my spare time writing plays and stories and ploughing my way through the books in my dad's study. My parents introduced me to literature and the power of the written word at an early age. Dad was a journalist and I grew up listening to the sound of the typewriter bashing out scripts to deadline. The house was full of singing and storytelling and music too, and being the youngest of five I had a wealth of material to draw on from the comings and goings and dramas of my elder siblings. To me writing is as normal and necessary as breathing.

DO YOU HAVE A WRITING ROUTINE?

Yes, and I have to stick to it as I write when my little boy is at school. I am usually at my desk by 9 a.m., coffee in one hand, pen in the other. If I'm writing something from scratch I like to write in longhand first. There's something about the hand-to-brain connection that gets the words flowing. If I'm editing, I will be typing away furiously to a soundtrack that differs depending on what kind of scene I'm writing. Death scenes are usually accompanied by Mozart's 'Requiem'; psychological scenes by Einaudi. I also try to read before I start writing each morning; something to get me into the mood of the piece, usually a poem or a short story. A particular favourite is Alice Oswald's *Dart* for her hauntingly precise interweaving of voice and landscape.

WHAT INSPIRED YOU TO WRITE THIS BOOK?

The idea for *Summer Lies Bleeding* came after reading of the death of an overworked young city trader and the comments of her colleague who remarked that 'this city sucks the life out of you'. Through this novel, I wanted to look at the coping mechanisms many of us employ to survive the pressure of city living and how, if left unchecked, these survival tactics can turn into dangerous obsessions. I also wanted to explore the effects of the economic crisis and the isolation and loneliness of urban living; how seemingly unrelated lives can impinge on each other and how, in a city of eight million souls, a stranger can dictate your fate.

DEAN

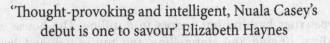

'Thought-provoking and intelligent, Nuala Casey's debut is one to savour' Elizabeth Haynes

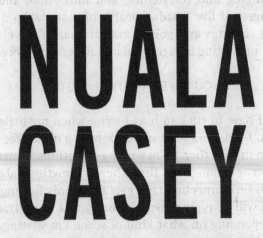

NUALA CASEY

'Quite the page-turner – an enthralling read'
Londoneer

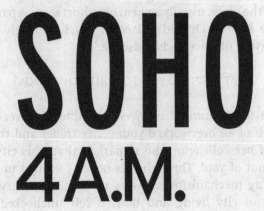

SOHO
4 A.M.

'Casey is the latest and no less valid a chronicler than Colin MacInnes, Jake Arnott or Zadie Smith' *Huffington Post*